M000311057

THE
STARS TURNED
INSIDE OUT

ALSO BY NOVA JACOBS

The Last Equation of Isaac Severy: A Novel in Clues

THE
STARS TURNED
INSIDE OUT

— A Novel —

Nova Jacobs

ATRIA BOOKS
New York   London   Toronto   Sydney   New Delhi

An Imprint of Simon & Schuster, LLC
1230 Avenue of the Americas
New York, NY 10020

First Atria Books hardcover edition March 2024

ATRIA B O O K S and colophon are trademarks of Simon & Schuster, LLC

Simon & Schuster: Celebrating 100 Years of Publishing in 2024

For information about special discounts for bulk purchases, please contact Simon & Schuster Special Sales at 1-866-506-1949 or business@simonandschuster.com.

The Simon & Schuster Speakers Bureau can bring authors to your live event. For more information or to book an event, contact the Simon & Schuster Speakers Bureau at 1-866-248-3049 or visit our website at www.simonspeakers.com.

Interior design by Jill Putorti

Manufactured in the United States of America

1 3 5 7 9 10 8 6 4 2

Library of Congress Cataloging-in-Publication Data
Names: Jacobs, Nova, author. | Olson, Kaitlin, editor.
Title: The stars turned inside out : a novel / Nova Jacobs ; Kaitlin Olson.
Description: First Atria Books hardcover edition. | New York : Atria Books, 2024.
Identifiers: LCCN 2023032969 (print) | LCCN 2023032970 (ebook) |
ISBN 9781668018545 (hardcover) | ISBN 9781668018552 (paperback) |
ISBN 9781668018569 (ebook)
Subjects: LCGFT: Novels.
Classification: LCC PS3610.A356483 S73 2024 (print) | LCC PS3610.A356483 (ebook)
| DDC 813/.6—dc23/eng/2023721
LC record available at https://lccn.loc.gov/2023032969
LC ebook record available at https://lccn.loc.gov/2023032970

ISBN 978-1-6680-1854-5
ISBN 978-1-6680-1856-9 (ebook)

For the scientists

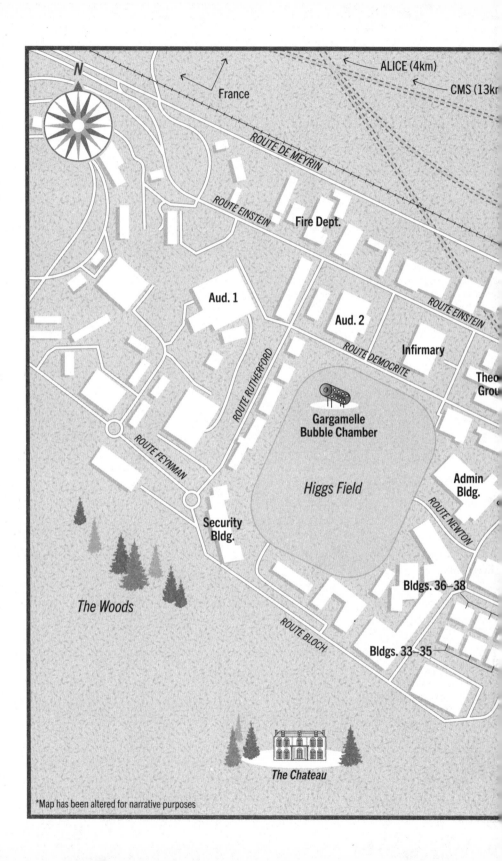

*Map has been altered for narrative purposes

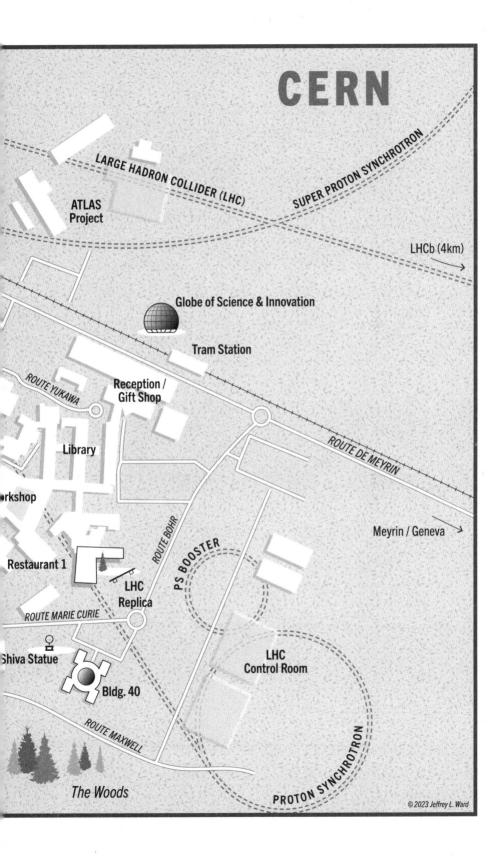

Time I am, the great destroyer of the worlds, and I have come here to destroy all people.

—Bhagavad Gita

Truth is no harlot who throws her arms round the neck of him who does not desire her; on the contrary, she is so coy a beauty that even the man who sacrifices everything to her can still not be certain of her favours.

—Arthur Schopenhauer,
The World as Will and Representation

PROLOGUE

O ne late-autumn morning, just before dawn, an electrical engineer pedaled his bicycle at a good clip through a subterranean tunnel, the stagnant air transformed into a breeze by force of his speed. In his daydreams, the engineer often imagined this circular tunnel would be the last thing to flash before him upon his death. He thought of this cold, gray passage so compulsively, in fact, it might well have been a person with whom he was having an intimate relationship. At other times, he supposed it would be the space through which he would move at the very instant of his passing, that proverbial tunnel of light one hears stories about. In such moments, he fantasized about his spirit traveling this powerful circuit while the people important to him floated into view. Then, much like the subatomic particles that circumnavigated this corridor every day, his ghost would near the speed of light to collide, in one fantastic blast, with the hereafter.

He picked up his pace, continuing his counterclockwise journey toward an eternal vanishing point of concrete and pipes. The powerful magnets that steered the particles through the largest of these pipes were in need of adjusting—as part of one of the collider's periodic recalibrations—and he had barely three hours to perform a final correction before the "Machine," as it was affectionately called, would go back online to hit its required number of collisions that day. At seven-billion-odd euros and counting, the Machine was the most extravagant of its kind—and the laboratory that built it couldn't exactly afford to have one of its employees taking a leisurely morning ride just because he entertained fanciful thoughts of his own death.

Don't make a picnic of it, his supervisor had said yesterday, knowing full well that the engineer was the dreamy sort, who could disappear for hours and had needed to be fetched from belowground more than once. *We all love those vintage bicycles, but in and out, Claude.*

Claude had nodded in agreement, but that morning he had packed a ham-and-Camembert sandwich and a single-serving bottle of Chablis, slipping them into an inner pocket of his green coveralls. His boss should have known that the mere mention of the word *picnic* would send Claude into visions of romancing himself a hundred meters beneath the Franco-Swiss border.

His colleagues often became claustrophobic down here; there were limits to how long some could spend encircled by concrete before premonitions of their own entombment crept in. But Claude could easily have spent entire days within the collider tunnel, cut off from the rest of the world, the only means of outside communication the call boxes installed every fifty meters. His happiest times were when the Machine was down for maintenance over extended periods, as it had been several years ago when a revamp shut everything down for fifteen months. He remembered the days he had spent cycling this twenty-seven-kilometer stretch, thankful that it was a circle and thus, by its very nature, infinite.

Claude was fast approaching his destination, and he slowed a bit, savoring the comforting hum of the tires hewing to the white ribbon of the bike path. To his immediate left, at shoulder height, ran the royal-blue steel collider pipe, a meter across, through which high-energy proton beams traveled in opposite directions around the tunnel to collide at one of four primary points. He sometimes wondered what it would be like to be down here when the thing was on. It would have killed him or anyone who dared attempt it, of course. But the sheer energy that traveled through this pipe was thrilling to contemplate. What a machine! How fortunate he felt to be servicing this beauty of science! No one could say Claude didn't appreciate his job.

He looked away from the hypnotic blur of the pipe and was startled to see someone coming into view around the bend, a few dozen meters off. A man, sitting against the tunnel wall. Claude didn't think anyone else was scheduled to be down in this particular sector. Had someone mentioned this yesterday and he'd forgotten? There were two more engineers working this morning at the opposite side of the tunnel, across the French border—and for a second Claude wondered if he hadn't accidentally biked too far—but, no, that was ten kilometers away at least. Besides, the man wasn't wearing the required safety helmet or emergency gas mask around his waist. In fact, he wasn't wearing a uniform at all, just shirtsleeves and jeans, a dark coat discarded at his side. The only thing to separate this person from somebody who had wandered in off the street was the small blue device hanging from a lanyard around his neck: a personal dosimeter for monitoring radiation levels. But most strange was the way the man sat slouched against the curve of the concrete wall, as though he had nodded off. In the cold light of the fluorescents, he looked very red in the face.

"Allo . . . ? Who is that there?" Claude called out in the charming accented English that one might have called the unofficial language of the laboratory.

When the man didn't respond, a tingling sensation zipped up Claude's spine. He pumped the hand brake, dismounted, and began to walk the remaining gap between himself and the motionless figure. The man looked young. His complexion was not just ruddy but appeared severely sunburnt. Closer still, and Claude saw that there were shiny lesions on the man's cheeks and neck. And, oh god, *his hands*. Claude stopped and began to back away. He had seen pictures of such lesions in the lab's safety training classes.

Feeling quite dizzy, Claude fumbled for his own dosimeter and peered at the screen. He blinked at it through his dated lens prescription, forcing his eyes to rack focus on the radiation readout: 0.5 millisievert. He exhaled and uttered an exclamation to God. The number was not ideal, but was still within the region of safety. Even so, he continued to back away. The man might still be contaminated.

Right before Claude turned to make for the nearest call box, he noticed something about the scene that made him take a cautious step forward. A collection of objects lay on the ground on the far side of the man: a stainless-steel thermos next to a leather book. There was also a phone, its screen blank, with a pair of in-ear headphones snaking out of it, the ends lying on the man's lap, as if they'd fallen out of his ears.

Claude lingered at the scene for a moment, aware of a familiar sensation of wanting to take something. A clue. A souvenir. It was a childish impulse, and he mentally scolded himself for it. A minute later, his dosimeter clacking against the zipper of his coveralls, and the bottle of wine slamming against his ribs, he sprinted to the last call box he had seen along the route. When he picked up the receiver, he panted at the woman on the other end that there was a man in the tunnel who looked practically incinerated, and very likely dead.

PART 1

CHAPTER 1

October 20

Before

O
n a breezy afternoon in mid-October, Dr. Eve Marsh claimed a seat at one of the bistro tables fronting the cafeteria known as Restaurant 1. Her colleague and lunch companion, Dr. Arnav Bose, followed, pausing to sweep away a dusting of needles that had rained down from the patio's resident fir tree. Eve guessed that he was low on sleep, as he sat down languidly and began to arrange his napkin and cutlery with an almost deranged slowness. Cloaked in dark aviators and an old army jacket, Arnav was the only physicist Eve knew who could make the day after a lab all-nighter look like the chic comedown of a party she hadn't been invited to.

"You never made it home?"

Arnav lowered his aviators, revealing wasted eyes on an otherwise boyish face. "The Machine wouldn't let me," he said. "It was like, *Come on, Arn, I smashed some protons together just for you. This might be* the one."

"Was it?"

He shook his head and picked up his fork and knife as if it pained him. The two tucked into their daily specials—an excellent whitefish pulled from the lake, sautéed in butter—but paused midbite when they sensed the surrounding diners turning toward the lawn. A large tour group had appeared on the grass between the cafeteria and the nearest road, Route Niels Bohr, named for the famed Danish physicist and cofounder of quantum mechanics. The Organisation européenne pour la recherche nucléaire, or European Organization for Nuclear Research, a laboratory known as CERN, had many such roads. These were part of the bittersweet charm of the place for Eve. She couldn't go for a stroll around the small city-state of her workplace without being reminded of how brilliant she was never going to be: Route Albert Einstein, Route Marie Curie, Route James Clerk Maxwell, Route Isaac Newton.

Members of the tour group were busy examining a large pipe of painted blue steel displayed along the grass, a replica of the real collider pipe that lay deep underground. "As far below our feet as Lake Geneva's Jet d'Eau is tall," their guide explained, "and spanning twenty-seven kilometers—or seventeen miles—in circumference." The pipe boasted the serifed motto *Accelerating Science*, and though the default language of CERN was English, the French was included: *Accélérateur de science.*

"Accelerating science, *ha-ha,*" the guide shouted with a self-aware grin, eliciting some polite laughter from the group.

This towering man was not an actual tour guide but a Canadian physicist named Niels Thorne. In his finely cut houndstooth blazer and fringed scarf fluttering dramatically behind him, Niels was at any given time the most well-dressed person at CERN—not a particularly remarkable distinction, given that denim and athleisure wear were the lab's reigning fashions. Still, Niels's immaculate threads led colleagues to wonder if he came from money, while others speculated his dress was merely overcompensation for a shabby childhood. Whatever the reason, Niels seemed to prefer swanning around their one-square-kilometer campus with guests to doing any real physics.

Arnav contemplated Niels Thorne with growing distaste. The more

4

animated Niels became, the more Arnav scowled. "He should just change his name to Niels *Bohr*," he said, letting his fork fall to his plate. "*Niels Total Fucking Bohr.*"

Eve tried to keep a straight face. Trading groan-worthy physics puns and riddles was a little game of theirs, but the true goal of the game was to receive each one with the utmost seriousness. No eye-rolling, no giggling. "Bohr . . . Bohr . . . Didn't he invent atoms or something?"

Arnav adopted his best tone of condescension: "Well, Ms. Marsh, it's complicated. Niels Bohr created a model of the atom, wherein the center nucleus is . . ." At this, he pretended to nod off at his own explanation, head lolling over his plate.

While Arnav's ongoing contempt for Niels Thorne amused Eve, she couldn't exactly fault the smartly dressed Canadian for preferring a job as esteemed CERN host to one as CERN physicist. Physics was an angst-making profession these days. Apart from the constant jockeying for positions and funding, there were the various existential crises of the moment. Not that she was going to let herself dwell on these right now; barely out of her twenties, she had nabbed a postdoctoral position here at the most illustrious physics laboratory in the world. She had the greatest job she could imagine, hardly something worth moaning about. Once, as a child growing up in the Arizona desert, staring out at those crisp, impossibly perforated night skies, she had thought being an astronaut would be the greatest job in the world. But when a high school science teacher had said one day in passing that "particle physicists are the astronauts of the small," she hadn't been able to shake the idea of high-energy physics as a grand exploration on par with the Apollo missions.

Still, Eve sometimes wondered what it was like for these tour groups to witness *serious scientists* on the Restaurant 1 patio with their plastic meal trays, chattering in lunchroom cliques or absently forking salad bar into their mouths. She and her colleagues were adventurers of a kind, it was true, drilling down to subatomic levels as if they were space walkers in miniature. But couldn't every job, no matter how exalted, ultimately be reduced to something that appeared drab? Isn't most work essentially the same? Whether you're a film composer or airline pilot or assembly-line worker, aren't we all just hunched over some piece of equipment, only to hunch at yet another surface to feed ourselves? Sometimes, when she was sitting at her office desk typing a string of code on her buggy computer, she would think: *This is particle physics.*

The difference, of course, between her job and any other was what happened in the space between the ears: inside one's "meat computer," as her dad had liked to call it. (As in, *How's the old meat computer, kid?*) Of course, there was also the most complicated piece of machinery human-kind had ever built—the Large Hadron Collider, or LHC—whirring away far beneath their feet. These were no small distinctions.

The breeze had shifted and Niels was now out of earshot, but judging from his flailing arms, Eve guessed he was reenacting the pipe explosion of 2008, the result of a helium leak just nine days after the LHC's maiden run. The visitors all frowned with great concern as Niels no doubt ex-plained how costly this accident had been. That's when she noticed that the visitors were all astonishingly tall (Swedes? Dutchmen?), taller than Niels, and she idly wondered who these giants might be. They were not ordinary tourists, she knew that much, as most sightseers were relegated to watching the documentary at the entrance's Globe of Science & Innova-tion, or to exploring the self-guided museum off the lobby. Niels Thorne, by contrast, catered only to visiting celebrities, journalists, and politicians.

"To my left is the cafeteria known, in CERN's tradition of numbering everything, as Restaurant 1, or R1," Niels was saying, his voice audible again as he neared the tables, "which is where we turn simple and com-plex carbohydrates into the energy that drives the brain of a physicist. You might even say that the Higgs boson particle of 2012 was discovered on the power of our spaghetti Bolognese." He cackled at his own joke.

"Doesn't Niels go boating on weekends?" Arnav wondered aloud. "It'd be a shame if he were to be caught in a freak storm, never to be heard from again." Though Arnav came from a Bengali Indian family, he'd grown up in London and had developed an Englishman's bone-dry humor.

"I kind of like the Bolognese bit," said Eve. "There's an equation in there." And she began to idly fashion mathematics in her head whereby thousands of plates of pasta were equal to the energy it took physicists to locate a new elementary particle.

Arnav interrupted her calculations. "When was the last time he did any work, you think?"

"Niels works harder than any of us. Have you ever seen him exit the premises?"

He stared at her. She imagined that behind his dark lenses, he was rolling his eyes. Arnav did have a point about the murkiness of Niels's job. His role at CERN had always been nebulous, made more so by his multipart response whenever anyone asked him what he did. Niels sometimes joked that he was like one of those students who piles on extracurriculars but rarely goes to class, which Eve thought a testament at least to his self-awareness. It had been long assumed that Niels simply lacked the talent to land a serious position on one of the LHC's four main detectors—like ATLAS or CMS—which were stationed at intervals along the tunnel. Yet to the surprise of everyone, he had very recently nabbed a coveted spot on an entirely new project devoted to hunting down dark matter.

"He is on the xenon tank now," she reminded him. "That's not nothing."

Arnav let his fork hover in the air. "Yes, funny how Niels glommed on to that project at the last possible moment. With pretty scant qualifications in dark matter science, I might add, other than boring everyone within earshot about it."

She searched his face for signs of professional bitterness. "You can't be jealous."

"Don't be thick, Eve. You couldn't pay me to go near that xenon monstrosity. Besides, we'll see how long he lasts."

Eve looked back across the grass, where Niels continued to shape wide arcs in the air with his beautifully articulated arms. He was mesmerizing to watch. It was no wonder he also headed up the lab's resident theater group.

"We should stop making fun of him," she said seriously. "It's because of people like Niels that we get funding. He also brings culture to this place, or at least makes the effort no one else does."

Arnav shook his head. "Do you know he actually asked me to join his drama troupe once? Said they needed someone with a convincing English accent."

She laughed, trying to picture Arnav pacing the grounds muttering Shakespearean verse. "I'd have paid good money to see you in that *Much Ado* they did in the spring."

"Oh, is that the play they thought they were doing?" Arnav turned to scan the patio. "And where's Howard today? Not like him to miss the seafood plate."

"Maybe he's finally discarded us."

Eve was trying to sound like she didn't care, although she knew Arnav saw right through this. They had known Howard Anderby for two months now, and at the mere mention of his name, Eve still got a little giddy. Her physical reaction to those five syllables, *How-ard An-der-by*, was completely involuntary, like a playful slap in the face or a one-two kick to the back of the knees. Yes, she had an intellectual crush on him, fueled in part by the fact that she found him mentally inscrutable. Not that she didn't have a perfectly healthy dose of self-regard on the intelligence front; people had been telling Eve how smart she was since she could talk, and by now the compliment almost bored her. Almost. But she wasn't the only person who found Howard more than a bit intimidating. Part of this may have been due to the air of mystery that had followed him from his previous position: consultant to a rival collider project that promised to be twice the size and power of the LHC.

Arnav began to laugh.

"What?"

"Look who's having a tour."

She followed his gaze across the lawn, where the visitors were now tailing the billowing scarf of their leader toward the road. But one man—who had evidently been hidden at the center of the group this entire time—stood quite still. To her surprise, it was Howard, in his usual jeans and half-tucked button-down, looking after the retreating group with interest.

Without a word, Arnav stood and headed toward him. Eve followed, her heart predictably quickening the nearer they drew to Howard.

"Hey," Arnav said.

Howard turned, frowning, as if trying to place them, or as if he'd just emerged from an immersive video game and was now adjusting to real life. As his gaze landed on Eve, she saw that his eyes, intense and lovely as they were, were bloodshot. This was hardly uncommon among overextended postdocs, but he appeared stunningly fatigued.

"Did you see him?" he asked.

"Him who?"

Howard nodded toward the departing visitors. "That man. The small one."

Eve saw that there was, indeed, a little man trailing the otherwise towering group, his legs working extra hard to keep up. He was partly bald, and his clothes looked worn or secondhand. In front of him, a taller man, walking backwards, had a video camera trained on him.

"You know who that is?" Howard asked.

Eve took a second look. She flipped quickly through her mental roster of various physicists of the moment but drew a blank.

"He's vaguely familiar, I guess."

"It's Wolfgang Shreft."

"Really?"

9

Arnav snorted in disbelief. "The German guy who's friends with Oprah?"

"Well," Howard replied, "it's hardly his defining characteristic."

Eve was amazed that he knew who Wolfgang Shreft was, despite the man's worldwide fame. Howard, who had always shown indifference to anything in the wider popular culture, never seemed to trouble himself with the things most people liked, let alone bother to keep track of celebrities. Wolfgang Shreft was a self-defined "explorer of consciousness," but the larger public would more likely have called him a bestselling author or guru. He titled his wildly successful books, which were translated into numerous languages, things like *Open Your Eyes to Now* and *Did You Know That You Are God?*. He was also the kind of spiritual figurehead who tended to cite bits of theoretical physics to bolster his own ideas, resulting in a kind of pseudoscientific mysticism that drove practicing physicists— the ones paying attention, anyway—slightly batty.

"Did you speak to him?" Arnav asked.

Howard continued to stare off. "Not as long as I would have liked. I'd been hoping to catch him without his attendant flock this time."

Eve studied what she now realized was either Shreft's entourage or film crew, or both. "Wait, you've talked to him before?"

"Several times," he said, still gazing after the group.

Was Howard Anderby starstruck?

Arnav scrutinized his face. "Are you okay?"

Howard looked down sharply, as if newly surprised to find Arnav standing there. "Why are you asking me that?"

"You look a bit crazed, frankly. And we didn't see you at lunch."

Howard absently glanced at his watch. "Are we a lunch club now?"

"Well—" Arnav stuttered. "If you put it like that—"

"Coffee later?" Eve broke in, growing increasingly uneasy with this exchange.

At the mention of coffee, Howard seemed momentarily returned to his normal self. "Yes. Coffee. Maybe tomorrow?"

His expression then lapsed into one of singular fixation, and without another word he strode off in the direction of the tour group, leaving his friends staring after him. The entire scene left Eve feeling off-balance. She wasn't sure if it was Howard's aloofness, his obvious exhaustion, or his evident enthusiasm for a celebrity guru. But whatever the cause, it had triggered in her a small, growing alarm.

CHAPTER 2

November 28

Now

The joint conference for the ATLAS and CMS particle detectors, held semiannually in Auditorium 1, arrived at a strange time, when the Large Hadron Collider was undergoing essential recalibrations, and with engineers disappearing belowground to adjust the powerful magnets. Just that weekend, there had been a series of these adjustments, but for some reason, much to the annoyance of the entire lab, the collider was still offline by Monday morning.

As Eve and Arnav took their seats near the center of the auditorium, their colleagues chattered and gossiped in search of answers. Someone wondered aloud if there had been an incident in the tunnel on par with the 2008 helium leak. Or could it be that animal mischief was to blame, someone else asked, as had happened more than once? Most famously, there was the Pigeon Disaster of 2009, when a common rock dove had strayed underground to drop a crusty piece of baguette into a crucial part of the apparatus, causing the entire collider to overheat. The story by this point had entered the realm of myth, yet the word *pigeon* around these parts was an eerie reminder that the Machine was not invulnerable to garden-variety entropy.

As the auditorium settled, the collider shutdown was momentarily forgotten in favor of the presentations from various ATLAS and CMS research groups. If CERN had favorite children, they were easily the ATLAS and CMS detectors, the lab's most powerful nets for capturing the subatomic particles that whizzed around the tunnel daily. Both projects had shared the credit in 2012 for finding the Higgs boson, which the popular news media had dubbed, rather nauseatingly, "the God particle." The Higgs had zero to do with God, of course, and everything to do with how mass is generated—but *God* sounded jazzier than *mass*, and so the name stuck.

Late in the morning, after a coffee break, Dutch physicist and research director Simon De Vries began letting everyone in attendance know, very audibly, that he was in a foul mood. As his colleagues returned with hot drinks from the building's antiquated vending machines, he grumbled his disapproval.

"Never ceases to amaze," De Vries said, eyes flitting to Eve and Arnav, who settled in two rows behind him. "Do you ATLAS people need steady infusions of cocoa? Would anyone like a snuggly blanket for their legs?"

"Mean physicist at one o'clock," Arnav murmured into his coffee. "My god, you'd think he was the only one who actually uses the Machine."

"He's just sore he's been left out of the *loop*," Eve said.

"Where's a quantum *mechanic* when you need one?"

Simon De Vries carried on with his complaints, muttering at no one in particular. He was not an especially tall man, but he had a robust, physically intimidating presence that commanded attention in any room. As both CERN's research director and project head for CMS, he was, out of necessity, a workaholic. The CMS detector was not supposed to be in rivalry with ATLAS; in fact, the two detectors were designed as particle-hunting partners, each with distinct technical strengths intended to enhance and complement the other. But you wouldn't know this from the aggressive manner in which Simon ran his group. He famously hired only fellow workaholics, and mostly Americans, because "Yanks don't require siestas and high teas every half hour. They'll work like mules straight through bedtime and run efficiently on junk food."

A few of Simon's colleagues snickered at his running commentary, but Eve noted they were all CMSers, no doubt accustomed to laughing at their boss's cruel monologues. Either that, or everyone was desperately trying to defuse the palpable tension that morning, which gripped the crowd like an off-color joke.

The other thing everyone knew about Simon De Vries, apart from his unpredictable moods and hatred of leisure time, was that he lusted after prizes and badly wanted a Nobel. This ambition radiated from him like an embarrassing stench. Physics wasn't supposed to be a competitive sport; they were all ostensibly in this together, but one wouldn't think so knowing Simon. He behaved as though they were all still living in the 1920s, when the Bohrs and Schrödingers and Heisenbergs could hog all the attention and claim sole author credit on their papers. Perhaps no one had told the Dutchman that those days, along with those giants of science, were long dead.

Resuming his contemptuous comedy, Simon asked a grad student seated a few chairs down if those were "Schrödinger's kitties" on his shirt, and if they were supposed to be both alive and dead. When the student sheepishly explained that it had been a going-away present from his parents, Simon inquired if this was an appropriate gift for a grown man embarking on a career in science.

"Isn't Holland supposed to be a kind country?" Arnav whispered. Then suddenly, glancing around, he added, "And is Anderby late? Or did Chloé let him off the hook today?"

At that moment, the mic buzzed to life and a Frenchwoman in her fifties, raven hair chopped into a girlish bob, appeared at the head of the room: Chloé Grimaud, leader of the ATLAS New Particles Group. She ran her eyes over the seats, as if casting a spell of silence. Like Simon, Chloé had been at CERN for decades, and her desire to be at the forefront of discovery burned just as feverishly. Yet unlike Simon, Chloé couldn't care less about the shiny baubles that went along with such discoveries. When someone had once complimented her on winning a not-insignificant award for women in their field, she had uttered, *What, that piece of tat? With one possible exception, prizes are just vulgar.*

Chloé's gaze stopped on Simon. She softly cleared her throat into the mic until he reluctantly turned in his seat. When Chloé located Eve, she raised her hand and beckoned her to the stage. The thought of speaking coherently about her work—very much work in progress, not exactly new particle on a platter—suddenly hit Eve hard.

"I thought you were on after me," Arnav whispered.

She didn't have time to wonder why Chloé had switched things around, so she reached into her bag for her laptop and hurried down the aisle to set up her projection. After a few minutes of fussing with wires, Eve stepped to the podium and introduced herself as a member of the ATLAS New Particles Group.

"I won't leave you in suspense," Eve said, willing her vocal cords to cooperate. "As many of you know, our group is one of several focused on identifying new particles beyond the Higgs, and so far, there are no smoking guns. But I've recently isolated some key collisions whose plots suggest energies that can't immediately be explained by any known particle. I should stress it's exploratory at this point, and obviously, my group and I are looking into mundane reasons for these irregularities."

Eve motioned at the event display projected behind her: a digital representation of the moment when two individual protons met violently at one of the detectors—in this case ATLAS—and splintered open into smaller particles, allowing physicists to inspect the collision's components. Event displays were basically snapshots of a subatomic crash in the form of a 3D graph. But when Eve turned to look at the display, she saw it had vanished, and in its place was a completely incongruent image: a Mercator projection of Earth, awash in animated swirls, growing progressively redder in color.

She fumbled with her laptop. "My apologies," she said, laughing to mask her agitation. "Clearly, this is not the correct file."

When she had managed to get the event display on-screen, Eve noticed Simon's hand shoot up. She pretended not to see him as she clicked through a series of similar spidery images, culminating in a line graph with a small peak in the center.

"As you can see, in these comparable events, we've got an irregular bump in energy at around one hundred and twenty-seven gigaelectronvolts. I'm calling it X-127, though my group has nicknamed it Baby Bump 127. Which seems appropriate given the speculative nature surrounding its existence." She magnified the pregnant energy bump until it took up most of the screen. Following the curve with a laser pointer, she continued, "It's too early to say what's causing this handful of irregularities, but let's take a look at the exact energies."

Simon, thoroughly impatient now, opted for shouting: "Spit it out, Dr. Marsh. What is it? Could it be dark matter? Should we break out the Veuve Clicquot? Or should I just put it on ice?"

Eve looked up at the outburst, which, even for Simon, was on a profound level of unprofessional. "It's obviously speculative at this point," she responded, pulling from a reserve of patience she didn't know she had. "It remains to be seen if the LHC is even capable of revealing a new particle at its current energies. But it's important for our group to be transparent about these things in the event that CMS is seeing similar results."

"Well, we're not seeing similar results," he said. "So maybe you've got your plot upside down, which would turn that baby bump into missing energy. A miscarriage, as it were."

Seated at the end of the first row, Chloé turned in her chair to face Simon. If one didn't already know that the two were rivals going back as far as anyone could remember, it was now obvious in a single glance.

"Her plot is upside down?" asked Chloé. "Funny, one wonders if your famous IQ score of 190, plastered all over the internet, isn't backwards."

The tips of Simon's ears grew pink as the audience strived to contain its laughter.

"Energy doesn't just disappear," she continued. "You would know that if you'd ever bothered to learn the first law of thermodynamics."

Simon expelled an audible lungful of air. "Don't play dumb, Chloé. There are many reasons energy could be missing from that plot."

"What, like it slipping into an alternate dimension? Or parallel universe? Are you suggesting Eve has discovered an entirely new world? If so, I second the champagne."

Simon leaned forward, looking straight at Eve. "You know what I wonder? What that map image was earlier. Looked an awful lot like climate science to me. I hope you're not using precious lab resources to fund your own side projects."

Eve was so stunned by the accuracy of this statement, she found herself unable to respond. Her face grew hot.

Chloé deflected. "Can we let her continue? I think the room is eager to hear her findings."

"Of course," said Simon. "May I offer my advance congratulations, Dr. Marsh, on discovering an entirely new particle? Maybe it is dark matter after all, and that new xenon tank I've only spent an entire decade building is redundant. You'll want to pack a warm coat for Sweden. It's brutal in December."

If Simon weren't a brilliant physicist, Eve imagined he'd have been dragged out of his office ages ago by a nearsighted mob. In an attempt to distract from her current discomfort, she pictured him being marched out to the center of Higgs Field, CERN's largest expanse of grass, and the entire lab thrashing the smirk off his overgrown-schoolboy face. But it didn't matter what an unbearable prick he was; he was a very good scientist. In this room, that's all that mattered.

17

Chloé couldn't let his last remark go: "Are you suggesting because you spent millions on that tank, that dark matter belongs to you? The rest of us are meant to stop looking for it?"

Eve tried to suppress a smile from spreading across her face. It was true, Simon had been obsessed with dark matter for so long, one might think it was he, and not Lord Kelvin back in the nineteenth century, who had first attempted to measure the stuff. Without thinking, Eve glanced around for Howard, wondering what he was making of this interaction. But he wasn't to be seen. And suddenly, the humiliation of standing up there while Simon berated her disappeared, as did the pleasure of Chloé's ripostes. Instead, a scene from the night before tried to surface.

"Eve, please continue," said Chloé.

Needing a minute to order her thoughts, Eve consulted her laptop. But before she could resume, a side door opened and a woman entered the room. Judging from her heels and matching pantsuit, she worked in an administrative capacity at the lab. She clicked across the tile and stopped just short of the podium, clearly waiting for Eve to cede the floor. The urgency radiating from her made Eve move aside.

The woman stepped to the mic and in an Italian accent said, "Good morning. I am very sorry to interrupt. My name is Anna Segre and I am the new head of security here at CERN."

There were vague nods of recognition, as if everyone were just now remembering that the lab had its own security force.

Anna Segre continued, "I'm afraid there has been an incident, and our office is asking for everyone's immediate cooperation."

The euphemism *incident* was not lost on the room. It was then that the physicists began to connect the word with their inoperative Machine, and curiosity turned to restless alarm. A vision of Howard from the previous night swam before Eve.

"As you know, the collider remains offline today," Segre went on. "There has been a very unfortunate accident in the tunnel at Sector 11. The good news is that there does not appear to be damage to the collider pipe." A collective wave of relief washed over the raked seats. "However, there is very bad news. I'm afraid to report there has been . . ." Segre stopped, searching for the words. "I'm sorry to tell you there has been a death."

She paused to let her audience take this in. The theater's momentary hush was interrupted by a few curses in the vein of *oh my god* and *bloody hell* and *putain de merde*. By comparison, Chloé and Simon's bickering moments before seemed petty and embarrassing.

"What do you mean, a death?" someone in the back blurted.

"In the actual tunnel?" asked another.

"I can't get into details here," Segre answered. "It will require further investigation. Which is why we're requesting that everyone, directly after this meeting, sign up for a time with the security office to offer any information you may have as to their unfortunate—"

"*Their?*" Simon objected. "You can't even tell us if it's a man or woman?"

"Is it staff?" someone else asked.

Segre appeared uncomfortable with the question, as though there were a difference between *staff* and somebody important like, say, *a physicist?* To name the unspoken class system of CERN—the physicists up top, the commoners below—was bad form.

Chloé raised her hand. "Sorry, but how are we to offer information if we have no idea what's going on? Or who died, for that matter?"

"That will all become clear during the interviews," Segre responded evenly. "It's best that we tightly limit information at this point, to avoid undue alarm and unnecessary dissemination to the media. Naturally, we ask that you keep news of the shutdown and death to yourselves. Do not discuss this with anyone, even family. No social media of any kind, please. The integrity of our lab depends upon it." Before backing away, she added, "Again, I'm sorry to have to interrupt with this very sad news. There will be security officers at the doors to take everyone's names and assign times for interviews, which will begin as soon as possible."

Segre exited the stage. The room gradually began to stand in unspoken agreement that the conference was over. In a kind of fugue, Eve unplugged her laptop from the projector, gathered her things, and began to climb the steps to where Arnav was waiting.

Was it her imagination or was everyone discreetly glancing around the theater to determine who was absent? Process of elimination was what their lab did every day. They sifted through subatomic collisions to determine which particles, or energies, were present, and which were absent. What was apparently missing was just as important as what was visible.

Eve noticed Arnav's eyes dart around the auditorium, as if he, too, had the same thought. Where was Howard this morning?

She approached Arnav in what felt like agonizing slow motion. Just as his face came into focus, the background seemed to tilt, as did the floor. She felt herself grasping at the air for support, before colliding with Arnav, striking her forehead on an armrest, and landing in an undignified heap on the auditorium steps.

CHAPTER 3

November 30

Now

Sabine Leroux, one of Geneva's most sought-after private investigators, stood at the third-floor windows of CERN's security building, taking in the snow-patched countryside surrounding the lab. *Slush-patched* might be more accurate. Snowstorms in the low-lying areas of Lake Geneva—*Lac Léman*, as it was known to the locals—were increasingly rare this early in the season, and when it did snow, as it had the night before, it quickly turned to mush. In the distance, just across the French border, the swell of the Jura Mountains was made more beautiful by a hint of snowfall and a skirt of puffy white clouds. Not an image to put on a chocolate bar—it wasn't Mont Blanc, which on a clear day could be seen hovering behind Geneva—but a pretty view nonetheless. Sabine would have liked to do some skiing that weekend in the real mountains (because if it wasn't an Alp, was it even a mountain?). But recreation these days was proving hard to come by.

Her last job should not have mentally drained her as it had. It had been a fairly straightforward case of a disappeared Swiss banker whom Sabine had, after modest toil, tracked to an island off the coast of Belize. It wasn't the banker's digital footprints that had done it—Sabine had to hire out for that sort of work anyway—but a touching set of analog clues, the most conspicuous of which was a tropical-themed mood board Sabine had found stashed in his study closet. This, among other evidence, had led her to a hut in the jungle, where the banker's new life revolved around taking long naps and learning to surf. Upon her return to Switzerland, Sabine had informed the distraught wife of her husband's location. But Sabine knew that the banker would not be returning; she had seen his face, and it had been happy.

Naturally, the case had led Sabine to wonder where she herself would vanish to should the middle-aged impulse overtake her. She turned from the windows and stepped to an antique globe that stood in one corner of her assigned CERN office. After giving the globe a spin, Sabine stabbed her finger at random: Siberia.

She snorted. *"Mais non."*

On the other hand, Siberian winter sports would be something. Her brilliant escape would have to wait, however. With this new case suddenly dropped into her lap, even an afternoon off was unlikely.

The news had not yet hit the press, as CERN's director-general Yvonne Faye was hoping to keep the incident under wraps for as long as possible. Given that the Global Physics Conference—at which the lab basically went hat in hand to CERN member states asking for more money—was approaching in the new year, keeping the investigation covert was vital to the lab's solvency. Which was why the case required a "consulting detective," as Yvonne had so wryly put it. Sabine loved that sepia-tinted term, redolent of calling cards and fireside appointments. As anyone passingly familiar with the stories of Arthur Conan Doyle or Agatha Christie knows, consulting detectives are prized for their ingenuity, often surpassing the mental abilities of the local police. But the Swiss Police, Yvonne had made clear, needed to be kept far away from the lab for as long as was possible.

It went without saying, there was no homicide or investigative unit at

CERN. No one had ever died on the premises under suspicious or mysterious circumstances—and these were certainly both. Due to periodic recalibrations of its powerful magnets, the LHC had been officially nonoperational at the time of the victim's death. No one had been on duty in the control room for that entire weekend, as the collider had been in the hands of the engineering team for maintenance. And as Yvonne had made clear to Sabine when she hired her: *One does not simply waltz into an inactive particle accelerator, flip the On switch, and get blasted with a lethal dose of radiation without some help.*

Given that CERN was an international organization sitting on the border of two nations, it had been granted by its member states a certain degree of legal independence. While not operating outside the bounds of the law exactly, the laboratory was mostly left alone by both Swiss and French law enforcement. For that reason, CERN had installed its own security force decades ago, though it was not a proper investigatory unit. The lab also had its own fire department and hospital, but if the miniature fire trucks and ambulances, of which Sabine had caught a passing glimpse, were any indication, these vehicles were merely on hand for minor emergencies. In fact, extracting a body from the tunnel, storing it, and performing the ensuing autopsy—all on lab grounds—had taken everything in the way of CERN's medical and emergency resources.

It had been more than forty-eight hours since the body of a young man had been found in the LHC tunnel, and nearly thirty-six hours since the scientists at CERN had been officially informed of their dead colleague's identity. Was he a beloved colleague? Admired? Hated? Feared? Envied? She had yet to determine anyone's actual feelings about the man. There was no set scientific personality, of course—and yet, in her experience, scientists in their natural habitat tended to nibble around their emotions, suspicious of the more tender regions of the human experience. After all, one does not *feel* one's way to the next particle discovery.

Sabine returned to the desk and opened a file already thick with facts and images pulled from the lab's records and the internet. She still preferred to print paper copies, just as she preferred to read paper books. There was nothing like the sensation of skin on fiber to send neurons firing in the brain. Dr. Howard Anderby. Age thirty-one. Born to Boston academics. Professors David and Felicia Anderby had earned handsome salaries at their respective private colleges, and in addition, both appeared to have inherited substantial wealth. In short, Howard had been a smart, moneyed, privileged only child. He had no doubt been exposed to copious amounts of culture and art: the child-as-orchid school of parenting. But both parents had died when Howard was a sophomore in college. A car accident, just rotten luck. Howard's aunt, his closest living relative, had taken her nephew under her wing and nurtured his interest in the sciences. In fact, "Aunt Frances" herself had been a CERN engineer back in the salad days of collider construction and still served as a consultant to the LHC. She had even brought Howard over for tours of the lab on several occasions. *There was no nepotism involved,* Yvonne had assured a skeptical Sabine. *Howard earned his spot here without any string pulling from his aunt.*

Sabine believed it. Howard's academic career had been glorious: prep school, MIT undergrad, Princeton PhD, an education accompanied by an almost unseemly number of accolades. At the time of his death, he had been in year one of his postdoc at CERN, assigned to the ATLAS New Particles Group.

She riffled the pages to find Howard's previous residence: Qinhuangdao, China, of all places, a hop and a skip from the Great Wall. There wasn't much in the file about Howard's time there, apart from the fact that he had been a consultant to the Chinese on a planned rival to the LHC—a much larger and more costly accelerator, because that's where particle physics was headed. More circumference meant more power. From what Sabine had gathered from Yvonne, there was something of a geeky arms race going on. There were even rumors that in a fit of Cold War nostalgia, Russia was flirting with a multibillion-ruble collider of its very own. *And why not? Life on Earth is going to hell in a handcart, but by all means, particle colliders all round!* As she looked over the scant evidence of Howard's time in China, the sarcastic narration in her brain continued: *Who's going to build the bigger atom swirler? European nerds or Chinese nerds? The world is on tenterhooks!*

Sabine supposed the Chinese must have compensated Howard handsomely for his time there, because from what she could gather, most of the world's physicists found it odd, or an outright betrayal, to work on anything but the great international lovefest that was CERN. But given his family inheritance, Howard likely hadn't done it for the money. Maybe he had just needed a break from the West.

A hesitant knock at her office door brought her back to her surroundings.

"Come in, please."

The door opened, and a small, timid man in coveralls and a too-large coat entered. He glanced around the room as if fearing a tribunal.

"Mr. Touschard?"

He nodded, eyes wide.

Switching to French, she asked, "May I call you Claude?"

Another nod.

"Please, have a seat." She motioned toward a chair, in front of which sat a carafe of water and a set of tumblers of 1960s vintage glass that had come with the office. The entire CERN campus gave off that peculiar vibe of old and new, as though one had just emerged from a time machine in which someone had monkeyed with the controls.

Claude grasped the chair unsteadily and took a seat. From his file, she knew him to be in his late forties, though he moved like someone older.

"Water?" Sabine would have offered this poor man soup if she'd had it.

Claude reached for a glass with a quaking hand and, to her surprise, pulled a small bottle of white wine from his coat, unscrewed the cap, and

25

poured himself half of it. He held the rest out to her, but she shook her head.

"I had this bottle with me in the tunnel that day, if you can believe it," he said. "It's time I be rid of it."

Just as well that he drink. It looked as if the man could do with some psychological tenderizing. As he brought the glass to his mouth, she noticed on the inside of his wrist a small tattoo made up of four interlocking circles, each progressively larger in size. The smaller circles, she knew, represented the three injector tunnels that spun protons to increasing speeds before shooting the accelerated beams into the LHC. Evidently, Claude was sentimental about his job.

"Thank you for coming in, Claude," she began, closing the file on Anderby and opening her laptop. "I understand you've been unwell?"

He took a long swallow of wine. "I've been in hospital. Not due to radiation, thank god." He crossed himself. "Radiation levels in the tunnel drop rapidly once the Machine is off. The doctors say it's exhaustion."

"Perfectly understandable. It's not often that such things happen in the course of a day's work. Not even in my profession."

His eyelids fluttered. "Yes. It was a shock."

"I won't make you go into all of it again," she said gently. "Apart from your initial statement to the security office, we have surveillance stills from the tunnel itself. But if you'd indulge me with one thing . . ." She turned her screen around to face him and toggled between two still images of the tunnel. "I was hoping you'd be able to spot the difference between these two."

The images, which had been shot from a ceiling camera several meters away from the scene, were time-stamped two minutes apart. On the left ran the blue pipe of the collider, and on the right, at the bottom of the frame, sat the slumped figure of Howard Anderby. The frames were nearly identical.

Claude peered at the screen.

"I really don't know," he said. "They look the same to me."

"They do look similar, don't they?" She paused to let him consider the shots again. "You know what I find helpful? If you pretend it's one of those brainteasers. 'See if you can spot ten differences between these photos'? But I'm asking you to find just one."

Claude leaned in closer and squinted. "Well," he said after several seconds, "there's a sort of dark spot here, near the thermos." He pointed to the ground on the far side of Howard, near his hip. In the first photo, the dark spot was there, and in the next it had vanished.

"That's exactly right," Sabine said. "It's subtle, and unfortunately, the camera's resolution, combined with the lighting of the tunnel, doesn't allow for a clear view. But as you can see, in the second image, this rectangular shadow is very clearly gone. As you may know, the tunnel cameras snap an image every sixty seconds, right on the minute." What she didn't say was *How the hell a world-class lab doesn't have continuous video surveillance on its prized machine is beyond me.* It wasn't actually beyond her; being a Geneva native exposed to a fair amount of physics news, she knew that the bulk of CERN's funding went into the collider itself. Besides, all one had to do was take a look around the place, at the peeling paint and aesthetics dating to the midcentury, to know that anything outside the mission at hand was extraneous.

"Because these shots are two minutes apart," she continued, "it means there's another between the two." She hit a key and up popped a third shot, the back of Claude in coveralls, partially blocking the body.

"Those images were taken on either side of your discovery of the body," she continued, "which means that mysterious 'shadow' was present upon your arrival. My guess is the shadow was an object. Any idea what it might have been?"

Claude swallowed and shook his head. "I . . . I can't be sure. A phone?"

"His phone is here." She pointed to a smaller object, identifiable from the headphone wire leading to Howard's lap. "The phone was of no help, of course. Its contents were erased by the radiation blast."

Claude nodded before turning to the windows. "Maybe he was enjoying music, at least, when it happened?"

Sabine followed his mournful gaze, which appeared fixed on the mountains. Or perhaps he was contemplating the tunnel that circled out from the lab to the countryside of the French border, smashing protons far beneath the feet of the unwitting shepherds, farmers, and townspeople of the Pays de Gex region. Not today, of course. Today, the collider was still.

Claude pulled a sandwich bag from a paper sack. "Sorry, my blood sugar." He pushed the sandwich through the plastic, like a chef about to fill a pastry.

Sabine looked away, the smell of egg converging unpleasantly with the image of Howard's body. She slid her card across the desk.

"If it occurs to you what that object might have been, will you call me? There will be no judgment. Sometimes we forget."

Claude took the card and rose unsteadily.

"And please, get some rest."

"I don't want rest," he said. "The Machine may be down, but there is much to do."

He shuffled out of the room, leaving the door ajar. Looking back at the desk a moment later, she realized Claude had taken the vintage tumbler with him. A case of sticky fingers, it seemed. She might have called after him, but didn't have the heart to wrest his wine from his hands. Besides, her next guest was due any minute.

Sabine turned back to the image of Howard on her screen. Then, scrolling backwards through hours' worth of surveillance stills to the preceding night, she paused at the very first half-blurred shot of the physicist walking into frame. He was looking down, as if he knew precisely where he intended to go. Where he had walked *from* exactly was impossible to tell. Next came more than a dozen stills—representing nearly twenty minutes—of Howard sitting against the concrete wall, eyes closed. Most of these looked identical, until the one that wasn't: Howard crumpled, head bent forward, his skin darkened with burns. With that level of radiation, it had been a somewhat quick death, at least.

She scrolled forward again, through hours of apparently identical frames, to that morning, right before Claude arrived on the scene. Studying the mysterious dark shape on the ground next to Howard's body, she saw that it had a slight sheen to it, suggesting possibly vinyl or leather. The more she played around with the image contrast and sharpness, the more it appeared to be a book.

Yesterday she had done a cursory search of Howard's apartment just across the French border. Many lab employees preferred living in the quiet towns of the French countryside to the bustle and expense of renting in Geneva. Howard had lived in a spacious one-bedroom in Ferney-Voltaire, just down the road from the mansion of the writer-philosopher for whom the town had been named. Given Howard's interest in philosophy, Sabine wondered if his choice of lodging hadn't been intentional. But then, that was before Sabine discovered that his aunt had lent him the place.

Consulting the basic inventory of items from Howard's flat, she reviewed the accompanying photographs she'd taken. There were few sentimental belongings to be found, apart from two frayed snapshots of a middle-aged couple, presumably Howard's deceased parents, magnetized to his refrigerator. There had also been a spare toothbrush found in his bathroom. This, plus a second pillow on his bed, seemed to indicate he had someone spending the night. If he'd had a regular guest—and potentially on the night in question given the rumpled condition of both pillows—who was this person? And why wasn't there more evidence of them?

If Howard's personal life was murky, his intellectual one was amply reflected on his bookshelves. Most surprising perhaps were the Eastern philosophy texts, including Buddhist and Hindu scripture, filling an entire section of shelving. While she'd heard that early celebrities of quantum physics—Niels Bohr and Erwin Schrödinger among them—had found echoes of their discipline in the Hindu and Vedic texts, nowadays the

Bhagavad Gita and the Upanishads would hardly be considered a legitimate route to the next particle discovery. Yet it was Howard's interest in Western philosophy that dominated his collection—numerous volumes on and by Spinoza, Berkeley, Kant, Hume, Wittgenstein, Gödel, plus a healthy dose of the existentialists—and at the time of his death, he appeared to have been consumed with the nineteenth-century German philosopher Arthur Schopenhauer, whose books and essays in various translations sat in precarious stacks in the living room and at his bedside. *Obsessed* would have been one way of putting it.

Sabine had snapped up Howard's well-loved paperback of Schopenhauer's *The World as Will and Representation*, volume 1, and had brought it back to her office. As she flipped through its pages, margins graffitied with notes, she thought back to the single philosophy course she'd taken at school. But apart from a general flavor of pessimism, she recalled little about Schopenhauer other than his fondness for animals and music—something about dogs and sonatas possessing the singular ability to keep humans pinned to the present moment. But then, this was hardly a remarkable philosophy; who among us isn't a sucker for puppies and a good tune?

Without warning, the door to her office swung open. Setting down the Schopenhauer, she looked up to find a man stepping decisively into the room as if making a stage entrance. Like most everyone at CERN, he appeared to be roughly twenty years her junior, late twenties or early thirties. But as he stepped into the light, the lines around his eyes betrayed midthirties, at least. Sabine had the immediate impression from his style of dress—with its lack of synthetic sheen or athletic utility—that he was not a scientist, but a banker or businessman, though one with very good taste.

"You must be Detective Leroux," the man said in a very direct, American sort of way. It was the kind of manner meant to convey that the speaker intended to make things happen, shake things up. Sabine disliked him immediately.

Stepping around the desk for his outstretched hand, she glanced behind him into the corridor. Her next appointment was supposed to have been a woman from the ATLAS New Particles Group.

"Dr. Niels Thorne," he said.

Sabine knew the name. Yvonne had flagged him as someone useful to know. Having been brought to the lab years ago by Yvonne herself, Dr. Thorne's role over the course of his postdoc had morphed into one of education and media outreach, interspersed with only occasional research.

Niels's grip was so strong that Sabine had to tug her hand away.

"You'll be wondering about Dr. Eve Marsh," he said. "Unfortunately, she had to postpone, as she's resting."

Sabine frowned. *Wilting violets, this entire lab.*

"I took the liberty of calling off the rest of your afternoon. Slight change of plans." When he could see she was puzzled, he added, "We'll reschedule your interviews for another day. Did Yvonne not tell you?"

"She did not."

"Apologies," he said with a smile. "I understand you've been wanting to find out more about the control room on the night Dr. Anderby died?"

"I have." Sabine had been waiting to see the control room since her arrival at the lab, but had been put off due to workmen installing an upgraded security system. *A little late for that.*

"Well, good," Niels said. "Follow me."

CHAPTER 4

October 21

Before

The day after Eve and Arnav had caught Howard entranced by Wolfgang Shreft, the pair waited in the glass-enclosed patio of Restaurant 1 for their friend to show at the usual three o'clock coffee break. In European fashion, much of the lab took an afternoon recess of some sort, the traditions of their respective countries—siestas, afternoon teas, extended lunches, or, in the case of Americans, the watercooler break—merging into a catchall reprieve.

Neither Eve nor Arnav had acknowledged out loud that they were waiting for Howard, and by quarter past three, when he hadn't shown, neither made mention of it. It was as if both were shamed by his dismissal of them the previous day, a brush-off that seemed to call into question the friendship they had begun to take as a given. Howard had been similarly distant at their work group meeting that morning. When his gaze did land on Eve, he looked at her with something resembling concentration, as if she were a problem to be solved, before glancing away again. At the end of the meeting, he missed their habitual stroll back across the grass to their respective offices. That hadn't entirely been Howard's fault, as Chloé had whisked him off to speak with him privately.

"Maybe she's firing him," Arnav had speculated as they headed back to their shared office.

"For what? Failing to discover a new particle in eight weeks?"

"No, for being an opaque weirdo who has yet to discuss his research with the rest of us."

Eve wasn't worried about Howard being fired. But his evident enchantment with Wolfgang Shreft the previous day had begun to tug at her thoughts. The memory of Howard standing among Niels's tour group began to seem less an oddity and more a scientific emergency. Initially, it was just bafflement, the kind you'd feel if someone you respected suddenly confessed that they didn't think the Earth was spherical or that Joseph Stalin had been such a terrible person. The fact that Howard, who was ordinarily oblivious to popular culture, had been caught staring at Shreft like a Beatle-struck teen seemed impossible—like breaking-the-first-law-of-thermodynamics impossible. *Energy cannot be created or destroyed; ergo, Howard Anderby could not possibly admire a cheesy spiritual celebrity.*

As Eve now tried to put Howard out of her mind, she focused on dipping a stale croissant into a cappuccino while she and Arnav made conversation with Teo Rico, a bearded Argentinian blackboard physicist. Instead of grappling with the particles that raced around the tunnel, Teo, as part of CERN's Theory Group, wrestled entirely inside his own head with arcane mathematics. When anyone asked Teo why he'd become a theoretical physicist, he would explain with a twinkle that the Spanish word for "theoretical" was *teórico*, and that he simply enjoyed hearing his own name repeated back to him.

Sometimes there was friction between theorists, like Teo, and the experimentalists, which was pretty much everyone else at the lab. Theorists argued for their own pet theories that the experimentalists would either test or declare untestable—but any tensions were seen as part of the agreement between theory and experiment. On this particular afternoon, Eve couldn't seem to escape the topic of Wolfgang Shreft. Word of the guru's recent appearance on the grounds had evidently spread, causing Teo to bemoan what he called *occult science.*

"Do you know that Yvonne and Niels have been quietly allowing Shreft into the lab for weeks?" Teo asked. "*Weeks.*"

"He and his people are filming a documentary," Arnav explained. "Presumably, they need loads of B-roll of him wandering around, looking mystical."

Teo groaned. "Have you ever seen one of Shreft's documentaries? He actually uses Erwin Schrödinger's wave equation to bolster his arguments about the so-called law of attraction. You've heard of this nonsense, right? It's basically: *Um, think of something you want badly enough and it will appear like a miracle from Papa Christmas.* The fact that this charlatan's been allowed beyond our gift shop gives me full body hives." At this, Teo nervously scratched at his beard.

"We had the pope visit back in the eighties," said Arnav. "I don't really see the difference. If we keep the public happy, we get money."

The Argentinian stopped midway into his bite of Danish. "You're honestly comparing Pope John Paul II with a spiritual snake-oil salesman?"

Arnav shrugged. "Both men were apparently deferential, both asked intelligent questions, each is nutty in his own way."

Eve glanced up from her cappuccino. "How do you know Shreft asked intelligent questions?"

He looked suddenly sheepish. "Oh, I ran into Niels earlier. In the loo, actually. Not that I trust that guy's account by a mile, but he did go on and on about what a great guy 'Wolfgang' is: *He's not at all what you'd imagine, Arnav. He's very deep, actually. 'A profound little man'* is how he put it. Do you think anyone will ever say that about me when I'm dead? *He was a profound little man.*"

Teo gave a snort of amusement. "That guy."

"Which one?"

"Both. But I meant Niels."

Eve really wasn't in the mood for another round of Niels-bashing. "Don't get Arnav started, please . . . What's this?" She leaned over to inspect Teo's coffee-flecked notebook. Not being a strict mathematician herself, she had trouble deciphering what he had been scratching out with his No. 2 pencil. It might have been doodles, or it might have been brilliant string theory.

"Just a little supersymmetry," Teo replied.

Arnav broke into a grin. "Haven't given up on that, eh? How many decades has it been?"

Teo ignored the comment as he traced a Greek symbol with his pencil. Eve sometimes felt anxious for colleagues whose entire sense of self rested on an unproven, if beautiful, theory. Theorists like Teo posited that for every subatomic particle out there, there was a hidden double or "twin" particle, which, for a host of complex mathematical reasons, would go a long way to tidying up the Standard Model of elementary particles. Teo believed that the theory could not be proved at the LHC's current energy levels, that upgrades were needed. Physicists disdainful of supersymmetry—Arnav among them—claimed that theorists kept moving the energy goalposts, forever insisting that the discovery was just out of reach. In other words, someone like Teo could potentially spend his career obsessing over a theory that would never be confirmed in his lifetime, if ever.

Seeing that Teo had gotten sulky, Arnav changed the subject back to Shreft. "I'm not saying I'm a fan of the guy. Behind his raggedy-old-man routine is just a shrewd capitalist recycling Eastern philosophy for the West, mixed with a dash of science to make it go down easier. My god, his name alone, *Wolfgang Shreft*—it almost gives his hokum some ring of authority."

While Arnav and Teo continued on about the various spiritual kooks of their time, Eve glanced out the window to find Howard strolling across the lawn toward R1. At his side was Bella Yoshimura, a fellow American postdoc in the New Particles Group. No matter how intently Eve tried to focus on the content of Bella's work, she could not help but notice her radiance. She was angular and beautiful, and Eve sometimes imagined her being discovered one day on the sidewalks of Geneva, to be whisked to a catwalk somewhere, never to be heard from again. The feminist in Eve found these feelings unacceptable and would try to stifle the discomfort she sometimes felt when she caught other physicists enthralled by Bella's combined intelligence and beauty.

"Looks like Howard's ditched you," Teo said, catching sight of the pair as they passed the R1 entrance and continued across the lawn. Eve stared at the spot of leaf-strewn grass where Howard had been walking a moment earlier, wondering if there would ever be a time when the sound of his name would not do crazy things to her body chemistry.

"You've been quiet," Arnav said.

"What were we talking about?"

"Oh, just the lab being infiltrated by lunatics."

Eve searched for something to contribute. It wasn't as if she, too, weren't repulsed by the quasi-scientific pablum currently infecting the culture—it seemed everywhere you turned these days, some nut was misappropriating quantum mechanics for his own dubious ends—but she was suddenly weary of the topic. Not wishing to betray her true agitated thoughts, mostly about Howard, she said instead, "Yeah, well, criticize Shreft all you want, but it's not as if we've got it all figured out. State of our planet being what it is, we can hardly justify our wildly extravagant Machine anymore, or our own positions, for that matter." As the words came out of her mouth, Eve was surprised by how much she meant them—or at least, part of her meant them, the part that wasn't still very much entranced by her job.

Teo frowned, perplexed by the sudden shift in mood. Arnav stared at her as if witnessing her live mental disintegration.

She gestured toward the lab. "We can all go about our work this afternoon, picking through our proton collisions and pretending we're not living in a giant runaway greenhouse. But the truth is, when we're old—not even *that* old—we're all going to be living on wartime rations and reminiscing about migratory birds. The jig is up."

Arnav nodded in sudden understanding. "I see. You're having a mid-postdoc crisis."

Eve knocked back the rest of her cappuccino. "I'm having a what's-it-all-for moment. I mean, what are we doing apart from chopping matter into smaller and smaller crumbs? We find this particle and that particle, and it just goes on and on."

Arnav gave her a clap on the back. "You know what? You've just described our job."

She pulled away from him.

"It sounds like you've been talking to Howard again. You can't let the philosophy part of this trip you up."

"This has nothing to do with philosophy or Howard," she insisted.

"Listen," Teo cut in. "It's only projects like the LHC that will save us from ourselves. It's always the offshoot of what you're working on that becomes the bigger technology. Microwaves, satellites, cell phones—"

Eve interrupted, "Sure, we wouldn't have our smartphones if it weren't for Einstein and general relativity. But tell me, how the hell is smashing protons together day in and out going to save Venice, or stop the Atlantic from engulfing the Eastern Seaboard?"

"That's just it," said Teo. "We can't yet know."

"Comforting. I'll sleep easy tonight." Her own sarcasm made her cringe.

"We're all terrified," Arnav said. "If you really feel passionate about it, you could certainly switch disciplines."

Teo snapped his notebook shut. "A second PhD is not so crazy. I have two myself. I started off as an experimentalist, you know."

Eve laughed. "You don't need to remind us you're a genius, Teo."

Everyone knew that Teo was now on his second postdoc, having begun his physics career at the prestigious Gran Sasso laboratory in Italy.

"I'm only saying," he continued, "why not switch to one of the clean-energy projects here at the lab? But even if you stick to your field, it's not impossible. Didn't someone write about this in the new *Courier*?"

From his backpack, Teo produced the latest copy of CERN's official magazine and flipped to a page reading "Can Particle Physics Be Enlisted to Save Us from Climate Catastrophe?"

"The refreshing thing about the piece is that the focus isn't nuclear power. Instead, it explores atmospheric particle physics in a quite novel way."

Eve glanced at it. "Yeah, it's pretty speculative—and did you notice that the byline is anonymous? It's not even a safe topic around here." She stood. "I should get back."

Arnav finished chewing. "You want me to walk with you?"

But as he said it, Eve was already across the enclosed patio, sliding open one of the glass doors and exiting into the brisk air.

CHAPTER 5

November 30

Now

After Sabine was appropriately bundled, though not as comfortably as Niels Thorne in his layers of cashmere and finely tailored wool, the two made the ten-minute walk from the security building to the nerve center of the lab: the LHC control room.

As they leaned into a chilly wind, Sabine wound her scarf tighter. "Dr. Marsh is resting, you said? Is she ill?"

Niels nodded. "She took a nasty tumble in the auditorium after the announcement, poor thing. Eve and Howard were in the same work group, you know. She thought she'd be feeling better by now, but the news hit some of us hard."

Evidently not you, Sabine thought, struck by his almost breezy manner. As she studied him, she realized with something close to shock that Niels Thorne was quite handsome, with the kind of high-contrast bone structure that conjured up notions of eugenics labs or footage of the 1936 Olympics. It had long been a quirk of her imagination that she was incapable of regarding a good-looking person of Nordic or Germanic lineage without mentally casting them in a Riefenstahl film.

But the longer she looked at him, the more it seemed to her that his confident demeanor didn't quite match his eyes. In her nearly three decades of law enforcement, she'd had enough experience with people putting on a show for her benefit to recognize that this is what Niels Thorne was now doing. Of course, there were many reasons people did this, most completely innocent. Some lived their entire lives this way, not knowing any other way to be.

She tore her attention from Niels to take in their surroundings. Despite the lab's mostly utilitarian architecture, the autumn foliage and grassy expanses gave the place a distinctly university atmosphere. As if to emphasize the collegiate vibe, a small gathering of young people playing Frisbee came into view.

Spotting Niels, they began to call out with the unbridled enthusiasm of groupies. One of the women shouted in an affected British accent, "Scratching could not make it worse, an 'twere such a face as yours were!"

Niels responded in kind, "Well, you are a rare parrot-teacher."

A young man rejoined, "A bird of my tongue is better than a beast of yours," before tossing Niels the Frisbee.

When he gamely caught it and tossed it back, the group applauded and resumed their game.

"Grad student researchers," he explained. "For the majority, of course, CERN is merely a way station on the road to somewhere else. Then again, that applies to most of us here."

"They're fond of you," she observed.

He glanced back at them proudly. "Oh, a few belong to the Spooky Action Players, a theater troupe I run here at the lab, hence the little performance. We did *Much Ado About Nothing* in the spring, and they were quite good."

Sabine was not surprised to hear that Niels dabbled in theater. This seemed to fit his performative tic.

"Then, of course, there's the annual holiday roast," he went on, "where we have a bit of fun at the expense of our resident physics celebrities.

Keeps things light around here. Otherwise, there's the danger of taking all this particle stuff too seriously."

"But isn't it? Serious, I mean."

He smiled. "Of course. I can't think of anything more serious."

Sabine looked back at the group, remembering that Yvonne had promised to send a graduate student from Caltech her way to assist in analyzing the lab's security footage. *James Spencer is not just a promising physicist,* Yvonne had told her, *he's also a quite terrifying computer whiz.* Sabine didn't know that she needed a quite terrifying computer whiz at this stage; she would have been happy with merely a second pair of eyes.

To their right, an undeveloped patch of lab property appeared, thick with evergreens and darkly inviting. Sabine could already sense small creatures scuttling above, busy with their winter preparations. As the sharp scent of pine hit her nose, she suddenly wished she could ditch Niels and take a scenic detour.

"Does one always need a chaperone for the control room?" she asked.

"You think we'd just let you wander as you like?" He shot her a smile. "Yvonne mentioned you two are old friends, but given what's happened, security is more important than ever, wouldn't you say? This may be a publicly funded lab, but if we don't keep a tight lid on things, any country with physics ambitions can go make the next big discovery before we do—steal all our hard work and then top it. With China trying to surpass us with a bigger and better accelerator, you might say that secrets are back in vogue."

As they passed a nondescript one-story building, Sabine observed a conspicuous security camera mounted on one corner, pointed in their direction. It was a boxy, rusted thing that half a century ago might have been considered high-tech.

"Unfortunately," Niels added, noting her scrutiny of the camera, "as Howard's death has demonstrated, current lab safeguards leave something to be desired. So, yes, an escort is necessary."

Sabine didn't remind him that given her purpose in solving an unexplained death, and preventing possibly more fatalities, she *was* security. "I didn't notice your name on my interview list."

He nodded, clearly expecting this. "I do have my fingers in many pies across the lab, but Howard and I didn't work together. He was also relatively new, as he'd just come from a competitor lab in China. No doubt Yvonne filled you in on all that." Niels gave a thin, uncomfortable laugh. "In any event, I'm more than happy to escort you where you need to go."

Sabine chewed over the prospect of having this man tag along wherever she went.

"Yvonne mentioned that your role here is a bit unusual for a postdoc?"

He flashed a ready smile, evidently used to the question. "Since Yvonne brought me here years ago to fill a temporary position on one of the smaller research projects, I've been sort of a jack-of-all-trades. Mostly I work in education with our outreach programs or act as a kind of docent."

As if to illustrate this, he gestured toward a truncated replica of the LHC pipe in the distance and began in an official voice: "Beneath our feet, the twenty-seven-kilometer collider pipe steers each bunch of protons—billions in each bunch—in opposite directions around our tunnel to meet at one of the detectors, like CMS or ATLAS. We smash protons as opposed to, say, electrons, because the proton's mass gives us higher-energy collisions." He snuck her a sideways glance. "Stop me if this is redundant."

"No, no." Sabine nodded for him to continue, not letting on that she actually knew something about the topic. Better to let him talk as he liked. He went on to give a brief overview of CERN's history: After the Second World War, a team of visionary scientists conceived of a laboratory that would rival anything in America and keep Europe's brightest physicists close to home. And so CERN was founded in 1954 by twelve European member states, growing later to twenty-three member states, and ten associate members internationally, including India and Turkey.

"By the way, don't let the jumbles of letters throw you, because it's all acronyms here. ATLAS, for example, is *a toroidal LHC apparatus*. Ridiculous, right? Quite honestly, we could name the four detectors Bob, Carol, Ted, and Alice for all the sense the actual names make." He laughed heartily. "As it happens, one of our detectors *is* called ALICE—*a large ion collider experiment*—which aims to create matter similar to that of the early universe."

Sabine listened politely as though this were all new information. Of course, Niels couldn't know—or evidently, Yvonne hadn't told him—that thirty-five years ago, in an intermediate particle physics course at the University of Paris, Sabine had sat directly between Yvonne, eventual director of CERN, and Chloé Grimaud, future leader of the ATLAS New Particles Group. The three young women had been instantly drawn to each other that term, not least because the class had been made up almost entirely of men. Niels couldn't know the level of friendship and trust that would form during those years in Paris: a bond so strong, in fact, that decades later, a desperate Yvonne would ring up her friend for help—*A physicist is dead, Sabi, and you're the only investigator I dare call*—and Sabine would drop everything and come running.

"What really brought me here was the hunt for dark matter," Niels said, answering a question Sabine hadn't asked. "A boyhood fascination of mine growing up in Toronto, where I was spoiled with no shortage of observatory and planetarium field trips. The fact that dark matter and dark energy combined make up the vast majority of the known universe, yet still elude our most sophisticated instruments? Well, it's a mystery I've never been able to shake. Sooner than we imagine, of course, it may no longer be a mystery." He lifted a knowing brow.

Plucking a tidbit from one of her internet cram sessions, she asked, "You don't mean the underground xenon tank, do you? The one in the cave looking for dark matter?"

Niels clapped his heart. "I must say, always warms the cockles when members of the public are so informed. Of course, the live camera feed is available to anyone with access to the internet—which, by the way, CERN sort of invented." That hearty laugh again. "Sometimes I just go down into our cave and marvel at the xenon tank. Not that there's anything to see exactly. But I guess in many ways, I'm still a kid."

"How long is your fellowship?"

He sighed, as if not caring to be reminded. "I'm in year five."

This was old for a postdoc, Sabine knew. His university likely wouldn't allow an extension past his fifth year.

"Do you think you'll find dark matter before your time here ends?"

"It alone composes more than a quarter of the entire universe, so how hard can it be?" He grinned. "If we do find it, hopefully before the Chinese, I intend to be there."

Sabine found nothing particularly repellent about Niels Thorne, apart from the kind of pride that likely masked deep insecurities, but then, that was a common enough flaw. Yet there was something about him that made her skin prick. She was grateful when their destination appeared before them: a single-story windowless structure that might have been a movie soundstage as much as the aboveground nucleus of the LHC.

Niels swiped his badge at the entrance and, after ushering Sabine into the lobby, announced, "This is where the science happens."

CHAPTER 6

October 21

Before

Eve was relieved to be away from R1 and the uncomfortable feelings her coffee break had inspired. Besides, she needed to get back to her desk to prepare for the upcoming November conference—at which she was expected to present her progress on a certain group of ambiguous proton collisions—but even so, she opted for a lazy serpentine route back to her office. The days were getting shorter, and the sun had already dipped below the most conspicuous of the lab's buildings. Much of the campus, however, lay fairly low to the ground, as though adhering as close as possible to the beating heart of the tunnel below.

She turned in the direction she'd seen Howard and Bella go moments before, not exactly sure why she was heading this way, other than this was where her legs were carrying her. As she passed beneath the bronze Shiva statue—a flame-ringed ornament that stood like an oversized brooch on the grass near Route Marie Curie—she wondered why she insisted on being coy about her entirely reasonable interest in the *impending planetary cataclysm*, and how she felt called to puzzle through ways in which their esoteric discipline might be of some immediate use to humanity.

Most everything, after all, when you break it down, even the *weather*, is particle physics. Why, then, was she unable to admit, even to Arnav, her authorship of that *Courier* article now circulating the lab? Was the idea that physicists might actually do something beyond categorizing ever increasingly tiny bits of matter foolish? Naive? Quaint?

As Eve glanced up at the multi-limbed Hindu god, a gift to CERN from the Atomic Energy Commission of India, that haunted quote from the Bhagavad Gita seemed to issue from the sculpture: *Now I am become Death, the destroyer of worlds.* J. Robert Oppenheimer had aptly summoned the line from Hindu scripture upon the occasion of the first A-bomb test. But the true Shiva, the real dance of global destruction, would not be as spectacular as a nuclear fallout. It would instead be a slow and steady devastation that would take them all out as surely as a mushroom cloud, but with a far more agonizing timeline. *Would it were the bomb, Dr. Oppenheimer. One bright light and we're out.*

The truth was that owning up to the *Courier* piece would likely jeopardize her CERN fellowship. At best, she might push her career to a crisis point (*Where exactly are your priorities, Dr. Marsh?*) and be forced to make a choice. At worst, she would be shown the front gates. Then again, it was possible she'd be in this position whichever life path she had chosen. Doesn't everyone eventually come to the *what's it all mean, what are we even doing* fork in the road? Eve wondered if she should confide her current state of confusion to Howard, for she sensed that he, too, was encountering his own version of the same crisis. Eve and Arnav were often catching him at breaks or in his office devouring Schopenhauer or Spinoza, like a kid preferring comics to his homework. Despite Arnav's impatience with Howard's discursive thoughts on whatever he was reading, Eve had always listened with interest. But now, in light of Howard's evident fascination with Wolfgang Shreft, this fetish for metaphysical philosophy over real LHC-driven science seemed to her a kind of desperate flailing for the truth. Or was she, in fact, projecting her own

46

professional flailing onto him? Searching for a deeper connection, as one does when infatuated?

She veered away from Shiva toward Route Felix Bloch, named for the Jewish Nobel laureate who, during the rise of German fascism, had prudently fled his academic position in Leipzig to later become CERN's first director-general. One needn't go looking for history on the lab's byways: it leaped out at you at every turn. Upon getting her letter of acceptance two years ago, she had committed the CERN map to memory, pinpointing the discoveries behind each of the streets that carved up this peculiar isosceles triangle of Switzerfrance. As she turned onto Route Röntgen, a street honoring the German physicist whose name was also a unit for radiation, Eve paused at an outdoor readout station. Regular dosimeter checks were required of all employees, even those who worked aboveground. Radiation was a sneaky devil, and one couldn't be too careful.

Eve slipped her dosimeter inside the reader and reflected on the work awaiting her: the task of pulling apart her precious collisions to find where a bump in energy had come from. Energy, of course, cannot be created or destroyed in a closed system. If apparent excess energy had appeared in the dozen collisions assigned for her analysis, it was her job to find out what that meant. There were three possibilities: (A) the energy had snuck in from outside the detector, infecting the collisions through microscopic faults in the Machine; (B) her calculations were incorrect, and the misleading bump was simply a known particle she hadn't recognized; or (C) the thing every physicist dreamed of. She could hardly admit to herself what C could mean because it could mean a lot of things. The answer wasn't C, of course; she knew that. It was either A or B. Yet one could write entire papers on a hypothetical C; one could do a series of impressive presentations arguing for C, until one day a colleague came along and crapped all over it with a smile. It never paid to get sentimental about these things. She must do the math, write the code, Sherlock that shit up, and present it like a responsible member of the team.

When the light on the readout station blinked green, Eve replaced the dosimeter around her neck and walked on. The lab grounds were unusually quiet, with only a handful of grad students lingering from coffee break. She couldn't bring herself to return to her office just yet, as she found the stillness combined with the cool breeze soothing. Entering the dark chill of the forest at the edge of campus, she headed for a cloistered stone house known simply as the Chateau. The two-story building, with its slate mansard roof and arched windows, was an oddity from the eighteenth century, which the lab had inherited back in the '50s when it bought up the surrounding countryside. Stephen Hawking had stayed here decades ago with two acolytes to work on his black hole mathematics. The three were said to have sequestered themselves in the house for ten days, coming out only to take in the air before disappearing again to tussle with the black-hole information paradox. The house was now locked for much of the year, opened only for visiting luminaries.

Eve was just passing beneath a thicket of evergreens near the back of the house when she heard footsteps crunching a few meters ahead. This was not surprising. A little jaunt around the border woodlands was the preferred activity of physicists stuck on a particular problem. Two figures came into view within a copse of oaks. The first was Chloé, and for an instant, Eve thought the young man with her was a grad student, possibly a new hire.

But as Eve drew closer, she saw that the man was Niels Thorne, and that the two appeared to be in a serious discussion. His neck and cheeks were flushed, though whether it was due to the chill or to emotion, it was hard to say. The whole scene was odd, as Niels did not work—had never worked—in the New Particles Group. Then again, he did have a way of making everything at CERN his business. Eve had the sense she shouldn't come any closer, and after retreating behind a large tree, she changed course and traced her path back toward the lab.

She had nearly returned to the Shiva statue when Howard appeared across the grass. He was heading toward Building 40: six stories of concrete brick, split down the middle by a glass atrium and ground-level café. Though it dated to the '90s, it was one of the lab's newer constructions. Their work group held meetings on the third floor, and many of her colleagues had offices here, though Howard was not one of them. She thought of calling out but instead watched him continue toward the rear of the building. Curious, she followed at a distance. Rounding the corner, she spotted him kneeling, cursing beneath his breath. After picking up something from the ground and returning it to his bag, he hurried off in the direction of the woods. Eve wondered if there was a single physicist this afternoon, including herself, doing actual work.

At the spot where he had knelt, she paused and looked down at the scattered dirt mingled with sneaker prints, wondering if her crush on Howard was now veering into stalker territory. She noticed something at the tip of her shoe: a small round pill, bright white, as if it had not been lying there long. She crouched to inspect it, but the markings were too small to make out. Slipping it into her pocket, she stood and looked in the direction of Shiva, whose bronze was fading in the diminishing light. Dusk was approaching, and as she realized how long she must have been walking, she became aware of an encroaching sensation she couldn't quite identify. It felt like something close to dread, but with no discernible source.

———

At eleven o'clock that night, Eve was still at her desk typing out the code that humans used to communicate with the Machine. In the adjoining space, separated by a low partition, Arnav clicked away at his own keyboard, working to illuminate his chosen shadows of LHC physics.

It was sometimes tempting for Eve to think of the LHC as a kind of mechanical god, miraculously transforming the subatomic world while simultaneously answering coded prayers. Of course, the Machine's very power led some to believe that it was, in fact, the work of the devil. Back when the collider had first gone online in 2008, thousands of conspiracy-prone laypeople around the world feared that CERN would create a miniature black hole that might devour the planet. Even now, there were those who imagined the Large Hadron Collider to be an all-powerful nostril that would one day inhale everything they held dear.

Arnav left the room and returned with a steaming mug from the kitchen down the hall.

She glanced up. "Coffee or cocoa tonight?"

"What do you call it when two LHC protons fail to collide?"

"I don't know, what do you call it when two LHC protons fail to collide?"

"A Swiss Miss." He took a satisfied sip.

Eve received his joke with the requisite solemn nod, but she was secretly pleased that any tension from coffee break had since dissipated. "Find any new particles yet?"

He shook his head. "I've rediscovered quarks several times over. Is there a prize for that?"

"Why our obsession with prizes, I wonder?"

"Because they're spackling paste for low self-worth. Ask Simon."

She took a swallow of her now tepid coffee. "I don't know. Seems like a too obvious explanation for his behavior."

"Trust me, his self-regard is garbage. This is a guy who had his Physics Society medal made into a belt buckle just so he could gaze at Newton every time he takes a piss."

"That's a myth."

"Just think of the unspeakable things he'll do to Alfred."

Eve didn't want to think about it. "He's not going to win a Nobel, Arnav."

"You're wrong. Guys like that find a way."

"Not if we beat him to it." She was joking, but as she said it, she became aware of that very real flame of ambition within her, ignited years ago by a public school science teacher. Despite its quivering light from all her recent doubts, there it was, still burning.

Before Eve could turn back to her desk, Arnav had grabbed a stuffed toy weasel from the top of his monitor and was making it walk along the partition. This furry toy was Arnav's bit of scientific kitsch, a nod to a stone marten that several years ago had chewed through the wires of an LHC transformer, temporarily bringing their Machine to its knees. The marten was not as notorious as the pigeon of 2009, but was nonetheless a symbol of the collider's shocking vulnerability to outside infiltration.

Arnav made the weasel study her. "Are you sure it was Niels you saw with Chloé in the woods? I hope she's not thinking of hiring him. I swear I'll quit."

Eve wondered if she should have kept the sighting to herself.

"I'd almost rather they were having a tawdry affair," he continued.

She made a face. "Not sure that Niels likes women."

"Well, I'm not sure Chloé likes her husband, the way she talks about him."

Eve nodded toward his computer. "You know, if you're not careful, Kennet is going to hog all the muon glory at the next conference."

Both Arnav and their colleague Kennet Olstad were studying the same movement patterns of muons, a type of exotic particle similar to electrons. The muons themselves weren't the treasure, but were one of the clever tools in a physicist's particle-hunting arsenal. Her threat was evidently all Arnav needed, because he returned the weasel to its spot and resumed coding.

Eve did the same, but her stamina was flagging. When the figures of the algorithm she was tussling with began to blur and merge, she blinked and reached for another swallow of cold coffee. Maybe she needed something stronger, though she wasn't sure what. That's when she remembered the pill. She fished it out of her pocket and laid it on the table. Swinging her gooseneck lamp over, she squinted at the imprint but could only make out a faded *10*.

She snapped a picture with her phone, and after a reverse image search, up popped thumbnails of various generic drugs, most of them some kind of benzodiazepine for anxiety, though none a perfect match. If this was

Howard's pill, this was a violation of his privacy at best, obsessive behavior at worst. Howard would not have been the first physicist to require pharmaceutical help in the psychologically demanding practice of babysitting the collider. Adderall use, for instance, was rampant among overworked grad students and postdocs, though she'd never personally succumbed. Nature, she had always believed, gave with one hand and ransacked with the other. But then, so far, nature had been kind to her in the chemical balance department.

Eve tossed the pill into a trash bin and turned back to her algorithm, but she was unable to focus. Was she ashamed of having followed Howard, or was she simply worried for his mental well-being?

For comfort, she found herself staring at her miniature diorama of the 1927 Solvay Conference, a representation of the world's most esteemed physics gathering. It was her own bit of desk kitsch, a trinket her father had picked up years ago at, of all places, a Los Alamos gift shop. To be fair, *trinket* wasn't an accurate word for what was a meticulously colorized 3D replica of one of the most famous photographs in the history of physics. Rendered in painted plastic, ten inches long, sat twenty-nine of the greatest scientific minds of the twentieth century in their best attire, arranged on the steps of the Solvay Library in Brussels, as if for a school photograph. A miniaturized Max Planck, the father of quantum mechanics, looked out from his seat front-row left, a tawny fedora in his lap. To his left, Marie Curie gripped a scarf and black cloche. A middle-aged Albert Einstein sat front and center in his three-piece suit and brightly printed tie, looking almost bored—or, more likely, soured by the recent revelations from Niels Bohr and Werner Heisenberg, which insinuated that God played dice with the universe. Standing next to young Heisenberg in the back row, Wolfgang Pauli, ever the class deviant, turned to catch the eye of a natty Erwin Schrödinger a couple of spaces down. Schrödinger, meanwhile, stared off camera into the distance, as if contemplating the implications of his wave equation for which he would later win a Nobel. Eve still marveled at how her father had intuitively selected this gift for her, though at age eleven, her interest in physics had yet to fully blossom. Its spot on her desk never failed to warm her.

Beside the diorama sat a framed shot of her parents grinning in close-up. The casual snap had been taken the same summer as the Solvay Conference gift, which had been two years before her father, a field technician for Tucson's public power company, had been killed in a freak accident while laying cable underground. As it had been explained to her, no one was to blame; the earth and asphalt above him had simply given way. He had died instantly and had not suffered. Eve suspected this had been said to comfort, and to this day, she had nightmares about her father trying to claw his way out from under the street. After his funeral, a sizable payout from the power company had allowed teenaged Eve to abandon all worries about funding her education. Years later, while she was studying physics, first at the University of Arizona and later UT Austin, it occurred to her that the photons she was so entranced by, those irreducible specks of electromagnetic radiation—the same ones that circulated through the power company's cables—had been indirectly responsible for her father's death. The settlement money had also funded her mother's very early retirement from teaching middle school English so that she might follow her dream of watching BBC murder mysteries full-time while drinking cabernet sauvignon. Eve had never judged her mother's coping strategies. With the love of her life vanished from the Earth, why shouldn't she spend her remaining days on wine and whodunits? She suspected that, for her mother, raising a child was a poor replacement for the sort of love she had found with her husband. But, then, for Eve, an alcoholic mother was a wanting substitute for her favorite parent.

She turned to ask Arnav how late he was staying, but when she peered over the partition, she found his chair empty, his bag and jacket gone. Only the weasel remained, black eyes shining.

Realizing it was nearly midnight, Eve put her computer to sleep, gathered her things, and hurried to catch the next tram home.

CHAPTER 7

November 30

Now

Sabine followed Niels Thorne through building security—including an employee badge swipe and eye scan—after which she was ushered down a bland hallway toward the LHC Control Room.

"Those eye scanners were put in just yesterday," Niels explained. "As of two days ago, eye scanners were reserved for the lifts."

"The lifts to the tunnel and detectors, you mean?"

He nodded. "For obvious reasons, we need to monitor who's disappearing belowground."

"I understand there were no badge swipes for this building on the night of Howard's death?"

Niels slowed in front of a pair of opaque glass doors. "Right. Normally we'd have a couple of technicians on control room duty, but we were down for standard recalibrations that weekend. As I understand, the only eye scans for the tunnel were from three maintenance engineers the following morning—and out of those three, Claude Touschard was the only one on the Swiss side of the border."

As they passed through the automated doors into the startlingly frigid air of the control room, Sabine secured her scarf and buttoned up her coat. Her eyes adjusting to the dim, she was reminded of every mission control scene she'd ever seen in the movies. What was most notable about the room, apart from its expanse, was that it was empty of people. There were fifty computer stations at least, most lining the perimeter, with the rest arranged in clusters throughout the room. A few dozen oversized monitors ringed the walls, and on a ledge above them, a vast collection of empty champagne bottles and framed group photographs lent the otherwise sterile space the vibe of a bistro. Drawing closer, she saw that many of the bottles bore home-made labels, like "Higgs Brut 2012" and "In Case of Higgs, Pop Cork." Many of the labels were discolored and curling at the edges. It had, after all, been over a decade since this room's most glorious celebration; on the relatively brief timeline of particle physics, these bottles were nearly ancient artifacts.

"Must have been some party," she said, taking in a group photo of ecstatic faces, their bubbly held aloft.

Niels smiled wistfully. "Alas, I was born a few years too late."

Sabine noted that the room was not entirely empty; along one wall, there was a man awash in light from a computer monitor. As Niels ushered her over, the spectacled man swiveled to greet them. He had a wide face and deep-set eyes that squinted at his visitors in what looked like amusement.

"Welcome to mission control," he said in a thick Slavic accent.

She extended her hand. "Sabine Leroux."

"Nikolay Levkin. Chief operator."

"I've never met a chief operator of a particle accelerator before." Noticing a large candy jar at his station, she added, "Let alone a rabid licorice fan. A man after my own heart."

He offered her the jar, which featured Cyrillic lettering and an illustration of a goggle-eyed bear dumping candy down its throat.

"Russian licorice is strong, I warn you. Of course, it's not really Russian. We stole it from the Finns."

"Hey, you're looking at a salmiakki eater," she said, slipping a piece into her mouth. "This is nothing."

Levkin took one for himself. "For me, it reduces the stress of wrestling with our Machine day after day."

"Nikolay here basically has his finger on the switch of the entire operation," Niels explained. "Isn't that right, Nik?"

Levkin raised a hand in protest. "It's only partly true." Gesturing to the empty stations around them, he added, "I asked my team to go home for the day so that we can speak freely."

"Did you know Dr. Anderby?" Sabine began.

He shook his head. "CERN is like a very small country. And yet, not everyone in the Vatican knows each other, if that makes sense."

"Would that make Yvonne the pope?"

Levkin smiled. "Yes, and I an archbishop."

"Don't be modest, Nikolay," Niels said. "You're a cardinal at least."

Sabine continued, "I understand the control room was empty the night of November twenty-seventh? At least, that's what I've been told. Security has been slow in getting me surveillance footage."

The Russian spun back to his computer. "You can see for yourself."

He turned on a large overhead monitor, and a few clicks later, a wide-angle image of the control room appeared: empty, with a smattering of lights winking in the dark.

Sabine located the corresponding camera mounted in a far corner of the room, only slightly more updated than the one she'd seen outside. "This is the only view in the building?"

From over the rims of his glasses, Levkin gave her a pained look. "Do you think this is a London crime show? We cannot simply pull up CCTV and identify the killer, you know."

"I do know," she said. "The security office warned me that coverage is spotty."

"At CERN, we invest in what matters," Levkin went on, "which is the science. No one thinks, *Oh, but what if one physicist murders another physicist . . . ?*" He gave her a wry look. "Not that I'm suggesting this is what happened."

She nodded toward the screen. "This is continuous surveillance?"

"Yes, but there was no one here that night, so you're not going to get more than this. Except for a few blinking machines, most everything was shut down."

"Can you send this to me?"

Niels stepped forward. "The security office can see to that. But if you don't mind, Nikolay?" He grabbed the mouse and scrubbed ahead through the footage, revealing hours of an unchanged room. "We may as well be looking at a photograph."

The instant Niels stopped scrubbing and allowed the footage to play in real time, Sabine noticed something at the edge of the frame.

"Could you go back a few seconds, please?"

Niels obliged, and Sabine moved closer to the monitor. After a few seconds, two small dots appeared, traveling from left to right. She followed them with a finger.

"See that?"

Niels practically recoiled. "Vermin, I'd say."

He was likely right. The dots looked to be a small pair of eyes reflecting the surrounding computer lights.

"Can you play it back?"

They watched again as the rodent moved along a ridge of the wall and paused at a tangle of wires before disappearing.

Sabine stepped to the corresponding wires at one end of the room. She inspected the wall, running her hand along the ridge. "Where do you think he went?"

"Who knows?" Niels said. "We probably should be setting traps."

Levkin shot him a look of disapproval. "We get a curious mouse or two in the colder months. They do no harm. They're just searching for warmth."

She stepped back to the screen. "Don't tell me a mouse turned on the collider."

He smiled. "If it had the password, it's not impossible."

"Okay, mice aside, how did a man in the tunnel get blasted with radiation when there's no evidence of anyone being in the control room that night? And the collider was, by all appearances, off?"

Levkin wagged a finger. "Not entirely off, of course. Or we wouldn't have an irradiated corpse on our hands." He turned to his monitor and hit a few more keys, replacing the surveillance footage with what looked to be a graph. A flat line moved along the center before spiking drastically and returning again to normal.

Sabine studied the image. "This is an energy plot?"

Niels gave her an approving nod. "Yvonne said you'd catch on."

"A plot of the LHC's collisions," Levkin continued. "Time is along the bottom, with teraelectronvolts—that's the energy—on the y-axis. This is just a simulation to give you an idea. When the Machine is running properly, the graph tells us how many collisions are occurring per second. Now, if the motion sensors in the tunnel are triggered—by a mischievous pigeon, or God forbid, a human being—this is what is supposed to happen . . ." With that, he hit a few keys, and the line of the graph plummeted to zero.

"Auto shutdown?"

"Right."

"I take it that's not what happened that night?"

He shook his head, then produced another graph. "One of my team pulled this from the night of November twenty-seventh."

Sabine stepped back to take it in. This plot differed dramatically from the other in that the spikes rapidly followed one another. It may have been just a graph, but it told a gruesome story. The spikes struck her as almost violent. In the light of the monitor, she noticed that Niels had turned nearly white. He had momentarily dropped his casual demeanor and was now staring at the screen with barefaced nausea.

"Why does this plot look so different?" she asked.

Levkin considered. "My best guess is that it's some kind of system failure. Both my team and the engineering team are looking into the possibility of a serious mechanical or computer malfunction."

Sabine nodded but wasn't sure she found this entirely convincing. After all, complete LHC breakdowns were rare. "You think a system malfunction happened to occur the night a physicist strayed belowground?"

He hedged. "It would be bad luck, yes."

Having regained his composure, Niels broke in, "You know what it makes me think of? It's as if someone were in a hurry. It'd be like climbing into a rocket ship and flipping all the controls."

Sabine turned to him, intrigued. "You mean, someone not familiar with the control room coming in here and hastily turning everything on?"

"Plus somehow managing to disable the auto shutdown." When Nikolay cast him a dubious look, Niels held up his hands. "Not my purview, of course, just an impression."

Sabine moved closer to the screen. "So, despite the control room being empty, the Machine got turned on, and its safety features disabled, due to (A) a system malfunction or (B) human mischief? Does that sound about right?"

Levkin gave a noncommittal shrug. "As I say, we have some techs and engineers looking into it, but so far, apart from this strange plot, the computer data shows nothing unusual from that night. Not so much as a log-in."

"There must be a digital trail somewhere, no?"

"You would think," he said. "Which makes me lean toward the malfunction theory."

It was Sabine's job, of course, to consider less innocent explanations.

"You do have some of the smartest people in the world working here," she reasoned. "If a person familiar with the computer system wants to cover their tracks badly enough, is such a thing inconceivable?"

The two men looked at each other doubtfully, before Niels said, "Not totally inconceivable."

Levkin frowned. "I don't like to think that my control room could be that vulnerable. Of course, it would have to be someone very familiar with the equipment, despite any possible hastiness. Might that include the deceased himself? I don't know."

Sabine hesitated to respond either way, reluctant to fuel rumors. She'd also begun to feel rather protective of Howard over the past thirty-six hours.

"Whatever he was doing down there," Levkin continued, "he should have known the dangers of trespassing, even if the Machine was inactive. Do you know what happens to a body when it sustains that level of radiation?"

"I saw the postmortem," Sabine said grimly. "His face and hands—it reminded me of photos from Chernobyl." She frowned, willing away the ghastly images. "If he didn't gain access by way of the elevators, is there another way to breach security to the tunnel? Some kind of fire exit?"

"None that I'm aware of," Levkin said. "We can't have a porous particle collider, can we? Apart from designated elevators, there is no other way underground."

"So, he magicked himself down there?"

He made a face. "Scientists are not fans of this word *magic*."

She looked from the screen to the darkness surrounding them. "Would you be able to send me footage of the control room on a normal operating day?"

By way of a response, Levkin tapped a few keys until a brighter version of the room appeared on-screen, half its stations populated by what looked to be an international representation of physicists. He let the video run. Nothing much happened, other than the movement of twenty-odd scientists tending to their computers.

Niels smiled. "The exciting world of high-energy physics, eh, Nikolay?"

Sabine held up her hand. "What's that? That sound?" She cocked her head toward the speakers.

Levkin upped the volume until a pop song was just audible in the background.

"Oh, yes. We like to have a little fun," he explained. "Every action of the collider is associated with a piece of music. This one—'One Way or Another' by Blondie?—is a kind of catchall tune for when our Machine is up and running after a shutdown. We play Queen's 'Another One Bites the Dust' when an uncollided proton beam dies."

"Dies?"

"It's called a beam dump," Niels cut in. "An unused beam is routed to a massive hunk of cement, where the protons are safely absorbed."

Levkin pulled up a list of musical tracks, mostly '80s tunes, including Prince and the Smiths.

Sabine nodded appreciatively. "The soundtrack of my youth. What kind of media player is this?"

"Our own invention. Pretty bare-bones. You just type in a song and it crowdsources an audio file—not strictly legal, but don't tell anyone."

"You're not worried about malware?"

"We have safeguards."

Levkin called up a Smiths track while Sabine wondered at the priorities of a lab that allowed for the safe piracy of MP3s, yet didn't guard against one of its own getting blasted with a lethal dose of radiation.

As a mournful Morrissey began to ask what difference did it make, Niels clapped Levkin on the back. "Shall we leave you to it, Nikolay? I assume you still have plenty of work, despite everything."

That's when Sabine noticed something at the bottom of the playlist.

"Can you play that one? The Mozart?"

Levkin frowned. "Must be new."

He hit Play, and the unmistakable melancholy strains of Mozart's Requiem in D Minor, first movement, filled the room.

"It looks like someone cued it up for the first run of the day," Levkin said. "Doesn't really fit, it being a requiem mass. Should be for the last run, if anything."

Sabine noted the rest of the title as it scrolled across the screen: *Sir Colin Davis, London Symphony Orchestra.*

"How long has that track been there?"

He shrugged. "Hard to say. These get messed with from time to time."

"Can you find out who may have added it?"

"If you think it's significant, I'll ask around."

Sabine paused, momentarily hypnotized by the introduction of the baritones, followed by the tenors, in an entreaty for God to grant the deceased eternal rest.

"If it is significant," she said, "it's a bit on the nose, isn't it?"

Requiem aeternam dona eis, Domine . . .

She could sense Niels edging toward the doors, a sign the interview was now concluded. But this particular moment struck Sabine as pivotal somehow, one of those scenes she would look back on and think: *I stood in the control room of the LHC and listened to Mozart's Requiem.* As if in agreement, Nikolay Levkin increased the volume, allowing the movement to permeate the room. Sabine closed her eyes and let possibly the most beautiful music ever written fill her body.

CHAPTER 8

August 15

Before

It had still been summertime when Howard Anderby first arrived at CERN. One week he had been just another name attached to a university, and then one Monday morning, he appeared at the New Particles Group meeting. There had been a heat wave that weekend that had barely burned off, and despite intermittent wafts from a ceiling vent, the air in the small conference room felt pressurized.

Eve couldn't yet know the significance of this hour, of how many times she would mentally replay it. Still, she was aware of some obscure agitation within her. As the seven of them waited for their new eighth member to arrive, Eve saw her own unease reflected on her colleagues' faces. Was it that word of Dr. Anderby's previous employer had preceded him? Or was it that Chloé had fast-tracked his hiring? Their group leader had said little about the man, apart from an unceremonious announcement the previous month—*Dr. Howard Anderby of Princeton will be joining us in August. I think you'll find him a bright addition to the group.* After a brief rundown of his credentials, they had heard nothing more. Not that Chloé was required to get anyone's permission.

Chloé studied their faces from her seat at the head of the table. "Anyone do something fun this weekend?"

It was such a frivolous question coming from their group leader, no one was sure how to respond.

She widened her eyes. "I don't know, something human?"

"Human?" Arnav inquired from the other end of the table. "Is that code for dumb?"

Chloé laughed. "It's code for life. Art appreciation? Cinema? Dancing?"

"*Dancing*," Arnav repeated. "Well, why didn't you say so? Yeah, I went to the club. I go clubbing pretty hard most nights with the boys, not that it's anyone's business."

His characteristically arid delivery drew a round of laughter from the room.

"What?" he protested, with a sly glance across the table at Eve. "I don't see what's so funny."

Chloé drew her lips together in mock disapproval. "We'll put you down for your usual weekend muon investigations, then? Anyone do anything away from their office?"

Eve avoided Chloé's eyes. She preferred not to detail what had been a deeply unremarkable weekend of working at her office alongside Arnav, before both had grabbed takeout on their way back to their respective apartments. He was supposed to have come over to her place Saturday night to watch old BBC sitcoms on her laptop: classics from the 1980s and '90s he'd introduced her to. But he had backed out at the last minute—not for the first time—in favor of working from home late into the night. And so she'd been left to eat stir-fry alone while taking in that strangely pleasing combination of British one-liners delivered against a backdrop of atrocious production values.

Thankfully, Chloé's gaze landed one chair over. "Weiming?"

The Taiwanese postdoc Weiming Wu looked put out by the question. Sweating heavily, he plucked at his button-down in a vain attempt at air circulation.

"You okay, Weiming?"

"Not really," he answered. "A bit warm."

Eve wondered if it was really the room's stuffiness that was bothering him, or the fact that their new colleague was coming to them from a competitor particle accelerator in China. When Chloé had initially breezed through Howard's qualifications, Weiming had not hidden his displeasure at the mention of the Qinhuangdao lab. The Chinese had been boasting for some time that, allowing for the LHC's future upgrades, it would be their collider that would dominate the planet. Ever since China had broken ground on its accelerator tunnel a year ago, paranoia about spies infiltrating CERN had risen. In the past month alone, Eve had overheard more than one conversation about the possibility of China embedding a mole in Switzerland. This was just speculation, as far as she could tell, but the anxiety surrounding the topic was palpable. CERN had its own trade secrets, after all, and no one wanted a Chinese version of the Cambridge Five cropping up.

Weiming ran a hand across his brow.

Chloé stood. "It is slightly tropical in here, isn't it?" After crossing to the room's single window, she slid it open as far as it would go.

Bella offered Weiming some tissues from her bag, which he began to plaster across his forehead.

Pietro Moretti, an Italian postdoc from the University of Milan, leaned back in his seat and studied his overheated colleague with amusement. "These are the sacrifices we make to science, my friend." But Pietro himself showed zero signs of discomfort. Growing up in southern Italy had evidently made him indifferent to heat.

The opposite could be said for the Norwegian Kennet Olstad, who in sympathy with Weiming began to fan himself with a folder, his flaxen hair lifting with each puff. "My god, I'm all for sacrificing electricity at the altar of our Machine, but there are limits."

Arnav, who was looking a bit flushed himself, sighed wearily.

Chloé turned to him. "Something you'd like to say, Arnav?"

"Just that maybe instead of all this chitchat about our fun weekends and the scandalous lack of central air, we might learn a bit more about the new guy before he arrives. I mean, apart from his impressive schooling. What are we to expect from him exactly?"

"I think," Chloé answered, steepling her fingers, "I'll leave that to Dr. Anderby to elucidate. But point taken on the chat. Why don't you share your muon status update with us, Arnav? The one you've been beavering away at all weekend?"

Arnav shot a look at Kennet, as if expecting him to protest. Although they were ostensibly working together on muon research, an edge of competition had begun to creep in. When Kennet gave him a nod, Arnav plugged his laptop into the room's projector. Moments later, an energy plot appeared on the back wall.

Being closest to the switch, Eve stood to hit the lights. But just as she reached the panel, the door swung open and their group's newest member stood at the threshold. His slight huffing suggested he'd just run up two flights of stairs.

Eve had seen photos of Howard Anderby, of course. For lack of information from Chloé, their group had nosed around a bit online. But most available images of him had been pixelated or blurred, or had been just another face within a larger group. The man in front of her now bore only a passing resemblance to those digital ghosts. She scanned his frame, which was well over six feet. He wore a dark-blue button-down rolled up to the elbows, its tails spilling from his jeans, as if he'd been interrupted midtuck. His legs were so long, or perhaps his jeans too short, that his sockless ankles showed between hem and sneaker. His hair was the sort of vague color that had probably once been light and would be again if he ever spent any time in the sun, which clearly he didn't. In one gesture, he wiped his forehead with the back of his hand and pushed back a swoop of hair. Then, stepping farther into the room, he took in the faces staring back at him.

"Hello," he said.

He was not a bulky person exactly, yet there was something about his mass, as though the air pressure of the room had changed when he'd entered it. Or maybe it was Eve's spatial orientation that had changed, because she had the absurd impulse to steady herself against the wall.

"Dr. Anderby," Chloé said, extending an arm to the empty chair across from Eve's. "I hope you didn't have trouble finding our charming room?"

He glanced around the space, as if earnestly assessing its charm. "No, no. Got chatting with your director-general, I'm afraid. We lost track of time." He pulled out the chair and settled himself upon it.

"I'll have to scold her later," Chloé said with a smile. "Eve, why don't you have a seat?"

Realizing she was still standing awkwardly near the switch, she abandoned her task. She could sense Howard noticing her for the first time as she crossed to the table and sat down in the seat opposite his. She hoped she wasn't blushing, as was her tendency at the slightest provocation. But at least it might be written off to the heat.

When Howard looked toward Chloé, who had launched into a brief welcome speech, Eve turned to examine him again. His face was not extraordinary; at least, there was no single compelling feature. Later, she would find herself trying to summon its shapes: the large forehead, the hooded eyes, the fairly ordinary nose. What was it about a face? Why one face captivates a person while another doesn't—that was one of the world's great mysteries, wasn't it?

After Chloé finished speaking, Howard said he was happy to be among them and hoped they could find some exciting things together. It was the kind of unremarkable statement that seemed designed to give nothing away, not even a hint of personality. Afterward, they each introduced themselves starting clockwise as if it were the first day of class, each giving Howard a brief idea of his or her line of research. Eve remembered having spoken but could later barely recall what she'd said, except that it must have been *Hi, I'm Eve, postdoc at UT Austin,* something about her current analysis of energy surpluses, welcome to the group, excited to be working together, or something to that effect.

Arnav was the last to introduce himself, after which he added: "Just curious, Dr. Anderby, if you might *elucidate* your intended area of research for the rest us?"

The comment drew a warning glare from Chloé.

"I'd be delighted to," Howard responded, almost blandly. "But I wonder if it might not be better to get a general sense for the group's research before subjecting you to my own ideas."

His eyes traveled around the table.

"I think that's wise," Chloé agreed. "In fact, Dr. Bose was just about to show us some very interesting muon tracks. Should we dive in, Arnav?"

Swiftly hiding his discomfort, Arnav attended to his projection—and after Eve hit the lights, and someone lowered the blinds, they were left in semidarkness to follow the glowing paths of muons throughout the multiple layers of the ATLAS detector. But for the rest of the meeting, Eve could think only of the curious question mark that was Howard Anderby.

CHAPTER 9

December 1

Now

The only thing to distinguish the conference room on the fourth floor of the CERN administrative building from any other conference room on the planet were the shiny cylindrical scale models of the LHC's four detectors hanging suspended from the ceiling. From her place at one of the large windows, Sabine considered this intricate representation of billions of euros' worth of human ingenuity. The miniaturized ATLAS and CMS, known for their mutual discovery of the Higgs particle, were joined by their less famous siblings—ALICE and LHCb—which favored more arcane, or at least less headline-grabbing, physics. By force of the warm air jetting from a vent, the four miniatures spun on their mobile hangers like shrunken satellites.

Dead colleague or no, experimental physicists did not react well to their prized Machine being shut down pending an investigation. Around the table, the directors of various CERN projects, including those of the four detectors, were either scowling or staring into a bleak middle distance. At least Sabine was not tasked with delivering the bad news. That job fell to Yvonne Faye, who stood at the head of the room in front of a large whiteboard.

The low autumn light streaming in through the windows seemed to amplify her cheekbones and large eyes to dramatic effect. As she spoke, Yvonne's gaze briefly alighted on Sabine at the window before moving to Chloé seated below, both looking back at her, then at each other, in an unspoken exchange. Despite her friends' still-shell-shocked expressions at their colleague's death and the resulting tumult, Sabine could feel in that moment the force of their shared bond. For the past decade, Yvonne's and Chloé's lives had pulled ever further from her to the point where the monthly phone call or coffee date was all that remained. Even Chloé and Yvonne complained that they hardly saw each other outside of meetings and weary salutes from across the lab's expanses. This was far from their University of Paris days, when the three would attend parties and, drinks in hand, hold forth on the nature of spacetime to a small, rapt audience. Back then, had you asked Sabine which of her two friends would be the future head of the greatest physics laboratory in Europe, she would have said Chloé without hesitation. Chloé was the most unapologetically ambitious person Sabine had ever met, even to the point of an ethical misstep or two. When applying to grad school, for instance, Chloé had taken a few liberties with research credit and had reworked letters of recommendation to better flatter her application. *Women have to look twice as good on paper as men to get the same positions*, she explained. *Besides, don't think our male classmates aren't all doing the same thing.* And yet, it was not calculating Chloé, but scrupulous Yvonne, daughter of Senegalese immigrants, who had fought her way to the top of a predominantly white, male profession. To Chloé's credit, Sabine never sensed a moment's envy radiating in their friend's direction. Even now, as Yvonne paced in front of a timeline of the coming months, Chloé was regarding her with what could only be called admiration. Still, Sabine sometimes wondered what lay behind that exterior of unerring support—if there wasn't in fact some small cache of resentment.

By contrast, Simon De Vries wasn't one to temper his own problematic emotions. "So, what, we have to wait for it to fucking snow and then melt again before we resume work, is that what you're telling us?" he asked, red-faced, from the center of the table. "What am I supposed to tell my group?"

Sabine sensed that Simon's Novel Particles Group was the unofficial rival of Chloé's New Particles Group, even though both groups had the same aim, and rivalry purportedly did not exist at CERN. *What do you imagine we're all competing for, Ms. Leroux?* had been uttered more than once in the past few days, as had *We're not in this for the money, obviously,* which made Sabine wonder if these talking points hadn't been handed down on orientation day.

"I suggest you tell your group the truth, Simon," Yvonne responded coolly. "We're all going to have to put on our big boy pants and wait, okay?"

Yvonne's composure seemed to come from somewhere deep and self-possessed. When Sabine had once asked how she managed to remain so unfazed in her position, Yvonne had laughed wearily. *Smoke and mirrors? When you grow up in France looking like me, you learn to modulate your behavior in favor of "being French." I watched my country demand it of my parents. I suppose by now, it's automatic.* In a profession that dealt in probabilities—as in, the odds of how a particle would behave under given conditions—it seemed to Sabine that Yvonne had overcome the highly improbable, if not the impossible.

Simon was leaning forward now, speaking through gritted teeth. "I don't see how an unhinged, probably depressed physicist breaking into our tunnel just so he could irradiate himself should be allowed to put our research at risk."

"Howard Anderby is the man's name," Yvonne said.

"Yes, well, I'm not the one who hired him," Simon muttered, turning pointedly to Chloé.

"We don't know that it was suicide," Yvonne continued. "And before we can resume operations, we need to figure out how the Machine got activated in the first place when it was supposed to have been dormant.

And second, we need to isolate the breach to determine how Dr. Anderby gained access to the tunnel while evidently bypassing the eye scanners and lift cameras."

Simon leaned back in his chair, attempting a sudden breeziness. "That's easy. He used CERN's supersecret underground maze."

Yvonne shot him a look of dwindling patience.

"I'm serious," he insisted. "What if the labyrinth hiding beneath the lab is more than just a legend whispered among grad students? Maybe this Anderby was kidnapped by CERN's colony of trolls." At this, he widened his eyes and wiggled his fingers spookily.

For a moment, Sabine could see that when Simon wanted to, he could turn on a certain silly charm. Though she felt sorry for anyone who might fall for it.

Yvonne sighed. "We can't expect to run a world-class laboratory if, as you say, a depressed scientist can just wander down there and get blasted with radiation. Not that I believe that's what happened."

"Obviously that's what happened. Unless Dr. Anderby couldn't tell the LHC elevator from the door to the toilets?"

Nikolay Levkin, who had been sitting quietly at the far end of the table, groaned.

Chloé eyed Simon with patent disgust. "You mean to say he couldn't tell a wormhole from his own asshole? Is this the tasteless joke you're attempting to make?"

Her quip elicited laughter from the room, a welcome release of accumulated tension. But Sabine could see from Chloé's expression how much the comment had cost her. She took zero pleasure in it.

Threatened by even small moments of upstagery, Simon grew quiet.

"We're not ruling out suicide entirely," Sabine said, speaking up for the first time. "But I should add that it doesn't square with Anderby's profile and health records."

Simon turned to her. "Oh, you're a forensic psychologist, then?"

She ignored the question. "I had a conversation with Anderby's psychiatrist, whom he saw regularly. Of course, without a warrant—which is out of the question if we wish to avoid law enforcement—she refuses to reveal specifics. But she did make perfectly clear that if Howard Anderby was depressed, it was the kind of general depression modern life tends to inspire."

"That's not what I heard," Simon shot back. "I heard he was totally off his head, much like his aunt."

Yvonne raised her brows. "This based on what?"

"Oh, come on," he continued. "Everyone knows she's a complete loon, a shut-in down the lake with her cats. Can't imagine why she's still consulting for us. That kind of mental instability doesn't fall far from the tree."

Sabine could sense Simon awaiting her reaction. She couldn't speak to the mental health of the aunt, but it was true that Howard's psychiatrist had prescribed him not-insignificant doses of both a common antidepressant and anxiolytic—which had been found on his body and in the medicine cabinet of his bathroom. But so what? Sabine herself had been prescribed that exact antidepressant a few years ago after the death of her mother, when she'd needed something to get herself back to work. Even if Sabine could convince the therapist to hand over the session transcripts, would it really be as simple as *Gosh, Doc, I just can't take it anymore. Thinking of offing myself in the most impractical way I can think of . . . ?*

Yvonne echoed her thoughts: "There are easier ways to dispatch oneself, surely. Besides, Howard was wearing his dosimeter, per regulation. Doesn't exactly scream suicidal behavior."

"Don't we all wear them by force of habit?" Simon asked, gesturing to his own dosimeter. "My point is, this Anderby guy was clearly imbalanced. There's no need for us to make an Interpol case of it."

"An Interpol case is exactly what we're trying to avoid," said Yvonne. "Which is why we've hired Ms. Leroux. Obviously, keeping this out of the press is crucial. The lab's independence—and its funding going into the new year—is wholly dependent on international goodwill."

Sabine could feel the room examining her.

"And how long do we have to wait for Madame Trench Coat here to crack the case?"

Chloé spoke up in defense of her friend: "You may as well ask: How long will it take you to find a mote of dark matter? That's not how scientific inquiry works, Simon."

"Scientific inquiry?" he practically sputtered. "If this woman is a scientist, then everyone is."

As Simon and Chloé quarreled about what did and did not constitute scientific inquiry, Sabine gazed out of the window at the khaki-colored stubble of Higgs Field below. She had once seen a photograph of the grass in the warmer months, when it had been artfully mowed to create a kind of map of the interlocking collider system. In the dead grass, she could just make out the faded circles of the three feeder tunnels, which in the middle of the last century had been mighty accelerators in their own right. Now, they were used as mere injectors for the all-powerful LHC. The larger pattern was, Sabine realized, Claude Touschard's wrist tattoo magnified. At the thought of Claude and the object missing from the tunnel, she made a mental note to call on him later that day.

The bickering continued. Sabine didn't volunteer that before she had joined the Swiss Police decades ago, only later to turn private investigator, she had once aspired to be one of them. For all her left-brained talents, however, she didn't quite have the mind for particle physics. Still, there were many delightful parallels between science and criminal detection. She often wondered why there weren't more physicist-detectives in mystery novels. After all, she'd always found Albert Einstein and Hercule Poirot to be astonishingly similar. Hadn't both mustached men retreated to the laboratories in their own minds? Performing complex thought experiments of their own devising while their colleagues chased after scraps of external evidence? Maybe she would write that mystery series herself one day. Theoretical physicist by day, gumshoe by night? She'd call it *Crim-*

inal Entanglements, and the hero would wrestle with all the contradictions that interested her, both human and scientific, the ones she observed and lived with but didn't feel fully represented in art or fiction.

Simon's raised voice brought Sabine back to the room. "And what does the security footage show?" he demanded.

"I'm afraid we can't discuss that yet," Yvonne responded.

"Well, I'd like to see it. It affects my group."

Sabine stepped toward the table. "I assure you, Dr. De Vries, we will find out what happened, and when we do, you'll be among the first to know. Meanwhile, I'm hoping to secure interviews with each of you, regardless of your relationship with Howard." She looked at De Vries pointedly. "I believe we haven't yet spoken?"

From the way Simon stared at her, Sabine could see that he hated women. She almost never leaped to such conclusions, preferring to believe that men were complex; that they, too, suffered greatly; and that each end of the gender scale—and everywhere in between—was awful in its own peculiar way. But his contempt for half of humanity seemed almost carved into his features. She had done her research, of course: Simon De Vries was divorced, twice actually, and in the middle of a third from his French wife. Family across the border. She didn't judge him for the divorces; Chloé told her it was frightfully common at CERN, a side effect of working with a machine that demanded everything of its attendant clergy. For high-ranking physicists like De Vries, it must be like choosing between your spouse and the entire universe.

"Just maybe, Simon," Yvonne suggested, "you could give the detective a few minutes of your time? Join in the effort to keep the police out of our little scientific paradise?"

When he didn't respond, Sabine said, "While the security office arranges a time for us to speak, I'd like to ask that if anyone in this room remembers anything unusual about the night of November twenty-seventh, or events leading up to that night, to please contact me immediately."

With growing impatience, Simon watched her pass her cards around the table. "Wow, I didn't know detectives actually uttered lines like that. And what are we expected to do in the meantime, sit on our hands?"

"Well," said Yvonne, drawing from her wellspring of calm, "I imagine what you do is filter through the gobs of data the Machine has produced over the past year. I believe that's our actual job, no? Even Nikolay and his team in the control room have plenty to do, not to mention figuring out how an inactive collider got tripped."

Levkin shrugged. "It's true. There is always something."

"In your case, Simon," she concluded, "a brief shutdown is not such a tragedy."

"How would you know, Yvonne, when you haven't practiced real physics in years? When you're up here in the clouds, with your desk and your view?" He made a dismissive sweep toward the windows.

"Have you *seen* my office?" she asked in disbelief. "And if you're referring to my decision to accept a role that offers me a somewhat saner schedule in which to enjoy my life, sleep for longer than six hours, and occasionally see the people I care about, then yes, you are correct. We all choose our priorities. How's your choice going?"

Yvonne smiled sweetly.

Simon knocked back his chair and whacked the hanging models with a swift hand before exiting the room. The mobile swung back and forth for a few seconds before dislodging the CMS detector, which clattered to the table, leaving its delicate appendages mangled in the fall.

CHAPTER 10

August 20

Before

One clear Saturday in late summer, their friendship tentatively began. In the weeks following, Eve would run these scenes over in her mind, like some kind of giddy montage from a romantic film. Months later, after Howard was dead, she wouldn't be able to shake these cinematic moments from that day in August. Looking back, they seemed to be among the happiest of her life, though at the time she didn't imagine it to be anything other than an ordinary day off with Arnav.

Working weekends was standard practice at CERN, but much of the lab had taken advantage of that especially brilliant Technicolor Saturday to go biking in the countryside or kayaking on the local waterways. A few members of the New Particles Group had gone boating farther up the lake, but Eve and Arnav had begged off in favor of taking the tram into Geneva in an effort to be, as their group leader had suggested, *human*. After lunch at a brasserie on the Rhône's left bank in view of a windswept Jet d'Eau, the two wound their way on foot to the city center and to the grand Beaux-Arts structure of the Musée d'art et d'histoire.

Though the previous week's heat wave had subsided, the air was sultry, made blistering by the greenhouse effect of the museum. The building was not the most archival of containers for the precious canvases on display within, and by two o'clock, the pair were wilting in the heat. They confronted Raphaels, Lucas Cranachs, Félix Vallottons, and various Netherlandish painters with something more resembling forbearance than admiration. Wiping perspiration from his brow, Arnav said he doubted the National Gallery back home would let Giovanni Arnolfini and his delicate wife sweat it out under these conditions. Nor could he see the Prado leaving the family of Philip IV to suffer in their petticoats in those blazing Spanish summers.

Arizonan metropoles not being known for their stockpiles of Western art, Eve felt at a loss to offer equivalent masterpieces. Most of her museum memories revolved around school field trips to Native American collections: Hopi kachina dolls and Navajo hogans preserved coolly behind glass. The absurdity of taking these items from the reservations and locking them in airless conditions completely out of character and context only occurred to her years later. But even from a young age, she intuited that the Navajo were a mathematically inventive people. The fractal geometries spinning out of those showstopping rugs and blankets seemed laden with coded meaning; even the looms themselves might have been precursors to the Turing machine.

Yet one of the universal joys of museums, whatever its contents, was that cool, churchy cube of air that envelops you upon entering. The eco-conscious Genevans admirably shunned air-conditioning, but the odd sensation of stepping into a world-class collection, air thick with humidity, brought on a wave of panic in Eve, a *Hello, art police? I'm standing in front of a Rembrandt and it's a sticky ninety degrees* sort of panic.

In their heat-stricken daze, the two began to find every painting hysterical.

"Isn't the goddess of love supposed to be attractive?" Arnav asked as he inspected a somewhat alien-looking Venus by Lucas Cranach. "Look at her proportions. She's a mathematical disgrace."

Eve considered her. "She's not golden ratio maybe, but she's no slouch."

"Well, 1.618 is not some arbitrary number. There's a reason Michelangelo used it. If you want to say everyone is beautiful, you may as well say *everything* is beautiful, and then the word becomes meaningless."

Eve nudged him. "And I took you for a feminist."

"I am, but give me a Titian or Rubens over the Northern Renaissance any day. Those ladies were at least of human proportion. They also enjoyed the odd meal."

She gave him a sidelong glance. "I have to wonder what your fiancée looks like." As many times as she'd inquired, Eve had not gotten much of a visual on Arnav's existence outside of physics. It was true that neither of them indulged in social media, but he could be weirdly cagey about his personal life.

"Have you really not seen a picture?" he asked, as if it were the first time she'd mentioned it. He retrieved his phone and produced a wide-angle selfie of a petite Indian woman, skin shining with youth and happiness as she slid a tray of cookies into the oven. "My sweet Parvati. She sends me treats sometimes." He smiled at the screen with genuine affection.

"She's lovely, Arnav."

"I know."

"Like, golden-ratio lovely."

He gave her a skeptical look and they were soon caught up in another fit of heat-induced laughter.

As they made their way toward the exit, Eve noticed a man enter from another door. With obvious intention, he strode to within inches of a canvas by Juan de Flandes, an outdoor scene depicting the beheading of John the Baptist. Eve didn't see how anyone could get a good perspective on the piece from that close. That's when she noticed the man was very tall, and also that he was Howard Anderby. Friday's group meeting had been called off by Chloé—due to "an emergency meeting with the boss"—and they hadn't seen Howard since his Monday-morning introduction.

"Isn't that . . . ?" Arnav whispered.

Eve nodded.

"Do we have to say hello?"

"Why wouldn't we?"

"Because once we do, we won't be rid of him."

"I thought you wanted to know more about his work. Here's your chance."

"That doesn't mean I want to spend my Saturday with him."

As she started toward Howard, Arnav hissed after her, "What if he's awful?"

They had barely walked a few steps before Howard spotted them and smiled.

"There's two of everything," he said, turning back to the painting. "Did you notice that?"

Arnav widened his eyes at Eve.

Howard continued, "Doubles everywhere. Two identical heads, two identical women, twin peacocks on the wall. The discarded scabbard mimics the executioner's sword."

He blinked at them, waiting for an answer.

Eve stepped in for a closer look. "No, we hadn't noticed that." He was right: the slayer of John the Baptist and the severed head—which he placed on a platter as though it were a rack of beef—were identical. A woman, presumably Salome, held the platter as she stared at the head with cold appraisal. A nearly duplicate woman stood behind her, while the corpse of the slain Baptist lay in a doorway, its neck a faucet of blood.

"Like two worlds lying side by side," Howard mused. "I wonder what he meant by it."

The scene was hypnotic, yet from Eve's and Arnav's perspectives that day, its cumbersome staging was ripe for mockery. "To be honest," Arnav said, stepping to the wall, "we thought the whole scene looked like one of Niels's terrible plays."

When Howard appeared confused, Eve explained, "Niels Thorne, you probably haven't met him yet. He and his drama troupe stage the occasional production in Auditorium 2." She shot a look at Arnav. "They're actually not that terrible."

That's when she noticed Howard examining her face, as if seeing it for the first time. He held out his hand. "I'm Howard, by the way."

She hesitated. Had she really been so forgettable in the group meeting?

Arnav cut in. "Yeah, mate. Eve? We all met earlier this week. Tiny conference room, no air-con?"

Howard frowned. "Of course. Eve," he stammered. "The weather has made me completely deranged; forgive me. Arnav, right?" He clapped Arnav on the shoulder, which left Eve feeling slighted.

Howard looked back at the De Flandes painting, as if still trying to decipher it. "You ever get the feeling that you're seeing doppelgängers in everything?"

Arnav crossed his eyes at Eve—*Told you he's weird*—but promptly responded, "What, like in your work?"

"Maybe."

"Do you mean superpartners?" Eve asked, referencing the "twin particle" theory.

"Can we not?" Arnav objected. "I really don't think I can stomach a supersymmetry debate right now."

Howard grinned. "Sore subject?" He broke off to look at his watch. "Have you two had lunch?"

"Just ate, in fact," Arnav answered, a little too quickly.

"It's just that I'm dying for a sandwich and a beer, and I could use the company." He looked back and forth between them, as if unaccustomed to being refused.

"Something cool might be nice, actually," Eve said before Arnav could protest. "I'm roasting alive."

Howard beamed down at her, and for a moment his smile was so warm, she forgot about feeling entirely unmemorable.

"You in, Arn?"

Arnav gave a resigned nod, and the three made for the exit.

They were grateful for the slightly cooler air outside as they headed down the main steps and in the general direction of the water. A few blocks from the museum, the three paused for a moment as the lake shone between buildings, a small boat suspended on twinkling waves. The water had that effect of magnetizing one's gaze no matter where in the city you happened to find yourself.

"Geneva is awfully beautiful," Howard said.

"Isn't it?" Eve agreed meaningfully. Having never been outside the States—let alone the Southwest—before her early twenties, she found it continually astounding that she now lived in a part of the world with such spectacular color, richness, and varying altitude. Whenever she flew back home to the desert of southern Arizona, despite its stark beauty, the landscape felt depleted somehow by comparison.

"The problem, though," Howard continued, "is that Geneva is a city with all light and no shadow. I mean, we assume all sorts of shadowy things go on with the financial institutions, but it's essentially invisible to the eye. Same with the UN Headquarters. And what *is* visible—the trolleys, the parks, the families, that inescapable water—verges on boring. Which, for a continent haunted by a very unboring past, is strange, isn't it?"

Arnav rolled his eyes in her direction. She mouthed *What?* but he just looked away.

They continued down and back up increasingly narrow streets, shaded by some of the city's oldest architecture. Encountering multiple lively cafés and pubs along the way, Howard marched right past them. It was only when they came upon a pub at the top of a small hill, nearly deserted of patrons, that he gave a nod of approval. After claiming a table out front beneath a red awning, they began to peruse the menu. Eve observed that Howard took in the pub's offerings with the same intensity he had used to examine that painting, as though all things in life deserved equal scrutiny.

When a waiter appeared, they ordered in that tentative, overly polite way that people do when dining in an unfamiliar group. Then, turning toward the cobbled view of Old Town, and to a slice of lake visible between medieval stonework, they were quiet again. Howard adjusted himself in his seat, and Eve noted again his very long legs. When he crossed them, there was an equivalent gesture—a kind of defensive crossing—somewhere within her.

Howard peered skyward. As if continuing his earlier thought, he said, "But then there are the thunderstorms. Aren't those incredible? They seem to bring the city some much-needed drama."

Arnav leaned forward. "Did your city in China have drama?" It felt like a question one wasn't supposed to ask. Eve scrutinized Howard's face for a reaction.

"Oh, I don't know," he said impassively. "I didn't get out much."

"Weren't you there for, like, a year?"

Eve knew he was guessing. No one, except maybe Chloé, knew how long Howard's China stint had lasted.

Howard shrugged. "You'd think I'd have more to say about one of the largest countries on Earth, but I was indoors for most of it."

Eve could see Arnav clenching his jaw, clearly aching to press Howard on specifics.

"Any weekend visits to overheated museums?" Eve asked, trying for a gentler approach.

"Not nearly enough. Do you know I've been to the art museum here three times since I arrived? I'm realizing you can't spend every minute holed up at a lab—as unending as our work is—otherwise you go fucking crazy."

The swift topic change was not lost on Arnav. He opened his mouth, no doubt to utter something antagonistic, but they were saved by the waiter bearing a pitcher of beer and plenty of food. Despite their earlier meal, Eve tore into her fish sandwich and fries, washing it down with gulps of cool Feldschlösschen.

As Howard drank, he began to talk rapidly, though the beer couldn't have been more than 5 percent alcohol. Eve suspected he was not a chatty man by nature and that this patter of his was a kind of nervousness. She would later confirm that he was generally shy and introspective, with occasional bursts of ideas pouring forth without warning. Yet that day, his conversation veered toward the manic, as if he were suddenly relieved to have like-minded souls to talk to.

They had somehow circled back to the Northern Renaissance paintings of the museum.

"But isn't that half the charm of those Netherlandish artists?" Howard protested after Arnav had called Flemish painting bloodless.

"If you find waxworks charming, sure," Arnav answered, not bothering to hide his peevishness.

"Artifice can be beautiful," Howard countered. "It makes me wonder if those painters didn't see the deception in everything. This . . ." He waved at their surroundings. "This convincing window dressing we're all living in."

"Right," said Arnav. "Because we're all living in the Matrix."

Howard met his sarcasm with a patient smile. "Isn't that why we all became physicists? To discover what's behind the curtain of matter?"

Eve broke in, "Here I thought we were just slicing things into finer and finer bits."

Howard turned to her, his eyes shining in a way that sent a flutter through her chest. "Maybe we are. Don't we all have that memory of when we first asked our parents what something was made of? And then we asked what *that* was made of, and what *that* was made of, on and on until they just changed the subject. My incredibly smart mother got as far as *The world is made of tiny things we can't see, sweetheart* before returning to the novel she was reading."

Eve smiled back at him. "My father got as far as saying everything is made up of nothing—just empty space that appears solid. I thought he was being funny."

"Wise man."

Her throat constricted at the memory. "The day I learned about protons and electrons in school, I came home to show my dad how wrong he was. He listened as I lectured him on all the tiny particles that make up everything. He didn't contradict me. Much later, of course, I learned how right he had been." *After he was already gone*, she didn't say.

Howard blinked at her, as if waiting for more.

"So," Arnav said, pouring himself another beer, "we're saying that Eve's dad and Flemish painters were aware of the illusion of matter before everyone else?"

"Oh, that would probably be the Buddhists," Howard said, pulling his gaze from Eve. "I'm just saying look at what everyone else in Europe was painting around that time and tell me those early Flemish artists weren't all magic. That self-portrait of Jan van Eyck with the red turban? The one at the National Gallery? Now there's a magician. There's an obvious double in that painting, too. The artist's looking-glass twin outside of frame."

"Why this obsession with doubles?" Arnav asked, leaning back in his chair.

Howard shrugged. "Because there's beauty in replication? Beauty in symmetry? We look for it in our work, after all."

Arnav sighed. "Where did this idea come from, I wonder, that equal proportions are automatically beautiful? As my mother likes to say, perfect symmetry isn't art, it's self-plagiarism."

Howard laughed heartily at this, which, for a moment, seemed to soften Arnav.

"It's also the art of fascists," he went on, "all those perfectly uniform flags and parades? Nothing a Nazi hated more than degenerate art, which is to say the chaotic and asymmetrical. And, quite honestly, I don't see why the laws of physics are supposed to adhere to some Nuremberg Rally idea of beauty."

Eve's eyes widened in surprise. Not just because Arnav appeared to be contradicting his earlier assertion of strict, mathematical parameters for beauty, but because she had never heard him speak so passionately. It was as though Howard's presence had both irritated and invigorated him.

"What an odd comparison," Howard said. "I'm not especially fond of supersymmetry myself. Not when there are far more thrilling iterations to be found."

"I can't imagine what you could be referring to."

"No?"

Arnav threw Eve a look of disbelief. "Here's where you tell us you're hunting for, what, a looking-glass dimension? Worlds existing alongside our own?"

Several pigeons had begun venturing toward their table, flapping their wings in a bid for scraps. Howard tossed them some bread from his sandwich.

"Why not?" he said, his eye on the birds. "Parallel worlds are within the realm of theory." While the healthier pigeons fought over the crumbs, Howard aimed several pieces at a bird hobbled by a diseased leg.

"Is that what you're hoping to find with ATLAS?" Arnav asked, incredulous. "You may not want to mention to Chloé that you're trying to prove the many-worlds interpretation of quantum mechanics. Not in your second week."

After making sure the injured bird had gotten more than its share, Howard turned to Arnav. "Is the idea so ludicrous?"

"At this stage, yes."

Eve didn't think Arnav was being fair. Some physicists believed that the only way to reconcile probabilities at the quantum level was to presume that all versions of reality existed somewhere. Not just doubles, but infinitely replicating worlds. For every decision you made, there was a version of you who had made the opposite choice—or rather, numberless choices, splitting off into endless variations of your life. It wasn't a leading theory in their field exactly, but it wasn't entirely baseless.

Howard leaned back in his chair, regarding Arnav with a combination of interest and amusement. "What do you want, then? Why did you come to CERN?"

"Er, to tidy up the Standard Model. To reconcile the quantum world with general relativity. To witness dark matter and dark energy at some point before I die. You know, your basic to-do list."

"Noble goals."

"But not yours, I take it."

Howard seemed to consider his next words. "Aren't we all looking for something miraculous? A total revolution of our scientific worldview? Why plod along writing uninspired papers so we can get yet another post-doc, or secure tenure at some tedious school? I didn't come here to pick low-hanging Standard Model fruit."

A single note of derision issued from Arnav's throat.

Eve wondered if writing physics papers and teaching physics classes were, in fact, puny ambitions. Sure, they all wanted to find something amazing while they were in Switzerland. But to say they were here to foment a scientific uprising, or to find other worlds lying beside their own, particularly in a time of austere budgets, seemed tantamount to confessing a belief in woodland fairies. And yet, something about the way Howard spoke, maybe it was his searching restlessness, moved her in a way she hadn't felt for some time. It wasn't simply the familiar stirrings of career ambition or scientific curiosity. It was something far deeper: *wonder*.

"If this is all a pitch for us to join your private revolution," Arnav said, turning to flag down the waiter, "you can count me out . . . *L'addition, s'il vous plaît?*"

After navigating another series of cobbled streets, the three arrived at the lakeshore, shielding their eyes from the sun glancing off the water. Howard announced he was going to keep walking to the History of Science Museum on the opposite bank.

"A boat's faster, mate," Arnav said, nodding toward the ferry dock. "The bridge will take you ages."

Howard squinted toward the Mont-Blanc Bridge. "I prefer a stroll. It's such a pleasant day. Either of you care to tag along?"

Arnav began to step away. "I need to head to the lab, actually."

Eve hesitated, sensing some kind of crucial friendship test. "I should probably get back, too." There was a flash of something on Howard's face that Eve couldn't identify. She wanted to believe it was disappointment.

Arnav started off in the direction of the tram station, a hand raised in farewell.

"Oh," she said, turning back to Howard. "Maybe another day?"

"That would be nice. Although another day doesn't always come."

He said this with such sincerity, she felt at a loss to respond. She was vaguely aware of a self-destructive resistance within her, some old instinct to push away things she truly wanted. Months later, she would wish she had accepted his invitation, if only to have added another scene to her memories of him. She would later imagine an alternate sequence of events that might have unfolded had she walked with him across that bridge. Would it have changed what happened later? Did these small choices, like the proverbial flapping of an insect's wings, generate monumental outcomes? Potential disaster? At that moment, of course, she couldn't know what was coming. Despite their talk at lunch about the many-worlds interpretation of quantum mechanics, she wasn't thinking about limitless versions of her life branching out from a single point, like the rivulets of a tributary.

"Another day, then," Howard said.

"See you Monday?"

"Monday, yes."

Eve gave him a wave and turned to catch up with Arnav, who looked unsurprised by her reappearance. They were quiet on their walk to the station. It was only when they were seated on the tram that Arnav spoke: "I imagine he's looking at one of those old-timey telescopes right about now, pontificating endlessly to no one. *You know the fascinating thing about the refracting lens is . . .*" Arnav mimed falling asleep. When Eve didn't crack a smile, he said, "I realize you have the impression that I hate everyone—"

"You do."

"Okay, maybe. But that has got to be one of the most insufferable, pretentious twits I've ever met in my life."

A smile formed at the corners of her mouth. "At least we caught a possible glimpse into his area of research."

Arnav rolled his eyes. "He can't be serious. If Howard wants to sit around making conjectures not based in reality, he should go join the Theory Group."

"I think you kind of like him."

"You're telling me that he didn't annoy the hell out of you for the past hour and a half?"

The truth was that she had liked Howard immediately upon meeting him, while also realizing he most definitely would read to the vast majority of the planet as a pretentious twit. Maybe he was arrogant; he was intellectually ambitious, certainly. But pretentiousness is a mask worn by the insecure, and she believed Howard to be an authentic person with simply a great depth of feeling about a variety of subjects.

CERN, naturally, was filled with passionate people, passionate about science and method, real capital-*I* intellectuals. But had she ever met someone who wore his intellect on his sleeve so obviously? That quality of meeting the world with one's brain—and not just trotting out an assortment of news items and pop culture references, as was most people's habit—was rare these days. And then, of course, there had been his attentiveness to that lame pigeon, which had gone straight to her heart as if she had been run through with a lance.

"No," she said finally. "He did not annoy the hell out of me."

As the tram whined along a curve onto the Route de Meyrin in the direction of their scientific home, they fell into a silence that lasted the rest of their journey.

CHAPTER 11

December 1

Now

Sabine had been on the Anderby case for nearly three days and still hadn't found anything useful on the lab's security footage. Granted, it had taken some time for the security office to compile data downloaded from twenty-five cameras, containing hundreds of hours of surveillance from the week leading up to Howard's death. And so Sabine found herself up past her bedtime, scrubbing through recordings at her dining room table. Of course, since she'd gotten the call from Yvonne telling her a body had been found in the tunnel, her circadian rhythms had been nonexistent.

Scrubbing was a daunting task, only slightly mitigated by the fact that James Spencer—the Caltech grad student and computer whiz whom Yvonne had sent her—had taken half the footage off her hands and was presumably at that moment also huddled over a laptop. She'd given him the far more boring scenery (parking lots, streets, warehouses), whereas she'd kept the larger swaths of the CERN campus and building entrances to herself, with the idea that these were more likely to be the stage for any drama.

But as she'd been warned by the security office, much of the footage, regardless of its location, was dodgy. For one thing, the lab's dated surveillance system yielded video that was either frustratingly grainy or uselessly high contrast. Second, the entire area had been blanketed in a dense fog in the days leading up to Howard's demise. And to top it all off, on the night of November 27, one of Geneva's biblical storms had descended. When a figure did appear on camera, more often than not, it was obscured in the downpour or blocked entirely by an umbrella.

The image she was currently examining, taken from a well-placed camera near the LHC Control Room, was particularly fruitless given that the hood above the camera was either nonexistent or broken. On the night in question, all that was visible of the control room's exterior were raindrops battering the lens and the occasional shadow that may or may not have been human. So acute was Sabine's frustration that she considered calling Anna Segre at her home and demanding an explanation for the security office's spectacular failure to secure anything. She could almost hear Segre's clipped reply: *You know, there's a coffee maker in our break room that dates to the eighties and tastes like it. Yet we accelerate matter underground to 99.9999 percent the speed of light. So.*

Yes, so.

Sabine looked up for a moment, her eyes adjusting to the darkness outside her dining room windows. There wasn't a day that went by that she didn't feel grateful to have a little plot all to herself on Lake Geneva's left bank, an inheritance from her maternal grandparents who had bought real estate in Cologny village back when it had still been attainable for the middle class. Her modest cottage sat on a hill overlooking the western end of the lake, and during the day, if she peered through a spyglass, she could inspect the leafy tangles of the botanical gardens, and beyond them the Parc de l'Ariana and the austere classicism of the Palais des Nations. Farther still, there was the dark swell of the Jura Mountains at the French border.

Her eyes adjusting now, Sabine could just make out lights dotting the lake: evening boats escorting tourists and lovers from the far bank to the intimate streets of Old Town. Unlike residents of Zurich or Bern or Basel, who might have accused Geneva of being dull, Sabine couldn't believe how beautiful her city was. It was only dull if you didn't observe; it was, perhaps, the fortunate few who could truly see Geneva in its full complexity. The English Romantics had seen it. Lord Byron and the newlyweds Percy and Mary Shelley had set up house in a Cologny mansion—a mere fifteen-minute walk from Sabine's house—to make merry, make love, and make art. One night, Mary Shelley had looked out on a view not unlike this one and conceived of a terrible monster named Dr. Frankenstein. Because, of course, the real monster of that story was not a revivified corpse but a scientist stripped of all humanity. Sometimes Sabine wondered that if Shelley was to be credited with the invention of science fiction, might she be equally to blame for the insidious stereotype of the heartless scientist?

She forced her attention back to the rain-pummeled image in front of her, which had barely changed for the past twenty minutes, even though she had doubled its speed. She hit Pause and massaged her temples. A cup of coffee might buy her another hour or two.

She put on a moka pot to boil and pulled two mugs from the cupboard. Music issued softly from the living room, where Chloé had been working her languorous way through Schumann's *Kreisleriana* on the baby grand. Sabine had bought the vintage Bösendorfer many years ago, part incentive to take up the piano herself, part bribe for Chloé's company. Mostly the latter. While the two had never dated—Chloé was married and sex had never entered into their dynamic—Sabine would have to admit there'd been an undeniable romance to their relations going back to their school days. The spark was still there, even if Sabine could never be sure it wasn't one-sided.

The piano had recently sat unused, but now after months apart from it—and with her husband out of town at a conference—Chloé had craved its discolored keys and church-like resonance. Sabine partly had Chloé's husband to thank for the recital she was now enjoying. On top of Jurgen's fabled lack of enthusiasm for anything to do with physics—a source of initial amusement for Chloé, though now less so—he wouldn't abide a piano in their small town house. He claimed the place was already too crammed with his vast academic library, which Chloé conceded. But Sabine always wondered if Jurgen was one of those rare people who couldn't appreciate music and felt threatened by those who could. Whatever his reasons, his piano embargo left his wife with limited options for playing.

Chloé loved music as much as she loved science, perhaps more. Sabine recalled one night during their first year at university, when she, Chloé, and Yvonne had been cramming for a physics exam. The recording of a Beethoven piano sonata had floated in from one of the neighboring dorms, and Chloé, suddenly reduced to sobs over her *Introduction to Classical Mechanics*, confessed to feeling torn between two suitors: high-energy physics and the piano.

One evening soon after, in the throes of indecision, Chloé scored three cheap tickets to see the Orchestre de Paris perform Rachmaninoff's Piano Concerto no. 2. After the show, Sabine and Yvonne watched her approach the pianist on his way to the Metro station. The weary musician, cigarette dangling from one hand, disabused Chloé of any romantic notions. *If you work very, very hard, you might cobble together some sort of career. But if you are not one of the chosen recording soloists, your fate is uncertain, a guest cog in the symphonic machine. Besides that, there's the loneliness of touring, the tendonitis, the bursitis, the same repetitive movements day upon day. It can get to the point where you don't even hear the music anymore; it's just rote motions of your fingers over the keys. Beethoven and Mozart played to the brink of tedium, if not madness.*

Sabine advised Chloé not to heed embittered artists, or those merely having a bad day, but Chloé had made her choice. *What if, in the end, every vocation is labor? At least I can play music in my off-hours. One can't be a freelance physicist.*

As the kettle began to rumble, Sabine's phone pinged, displaying the name of the grad student James Spencer. His text read: *Check the Bldg 40 footage from that night. 23:22:00.*

Sabine frowned. She hadn't given James the Building 40 footage. She texted back as much. Her phone pinged almost instantly: *I have skills.*

She stared at his response. Evidently, James had used his "quite terrifying" computer acumen to purloin footage from the lab's system. CERN may have invented the internet, but that didn't mean it was safe from an inside hack job. Leave it to an American to simply take what he wanted. *You might have asked me first,* she wrote.

His reply: *Don't worry about it.*

Sabine shut off the range and returned to the dining room. She pulled up the footage James had suggested: a high-angle shot of the grass outside Building 40, the Shiva statue dancing in its ring of fire near the center of frame. Calling up the indicated time stamp, nearly eleven thirty on the night of Howard's death, she pressed Play.

Behind the blur of that night's downpour, a dark shape appeared from the screen's bottom right, flashed across the grass, and disappeared just as quickly. Realizing she had left the player on double speed, she played it back in real time. The shape revealed itself to be a black umbrella, the person beneath pausing for a moment at the base of the statue before dashing out of sight. Viewing it at a slower frame rate, she was able to make out a dark coat just visible beneath the umbrella. From the gait, it looked to be a man. There was something erratic about his movements, panicked even. Sabine's heart pounded in response.

She sped up the video. Twenty time-coded minutes later, a second person entered the scene. Again, there was an umbrella, this one half-broken, under which looked to be a smaller figure. A woman? Sabine watched as the figure paused by the statue before dashing off in the direction of the first. Peering closely, Sabine could discern a striped scarf, dark pants, and a pair of Adidas sneakers.

Chloé's piano abruptly switched from Schumann to a Chopin nocturne, and the melancholy tune lent a strange, discordant mood to the action on-screen.

Sabine rewound the footage and contemplated a single frame of the initial figure, a man frozen in flight. Suddenly the nocturne stopped, and she looked up as Chloé appeared, mug in hand. The weight of recent events bearing down on her friend was obvious. Upon Chloé's arrival at her house that night, Sabine had registered in her eyes and in the lines etched into her regal forehead the compounding stress of Howard's death. A largely remote and unsupportive husband didn't appear to be helping matters.

Chloé glanced past her to the computer screen. "My god, is this what our security footage looks like?"

"Don't get me started." Sabine played back the scene. "Does this look like Howard to you?"

"Could be, but then, it could be anyone."

She ran the footage ahead to the second figure. "How about this one?"

Chloé leaned in. "Hard to tell. Not much to go on."

Sabine reversed the video to a still image of the first figure as it neared the statue, feet floating above the grass. "Is Shiva a good luck charm for physicists or something?"

"We aren't typically a superstitious bunch," Chloé said, frowning as she considered the image. "This is from that night?"

Sabine nodded. "Almost eleven thirty."

"I realize you don't know when or how he entered the tunnel," Chloé said, "but the entrance isn't anywhere around here. It's on the other side of the lab, near the ATLAS warehouse."

"But there's more than one tunnel entrance, right?"

"Sure, but you'd have to cross the French border for the others. And I understand that's not where his body was found."

"You mind taking a look at something else? A shot from the tunnel?" When Chloé appeared to flinch, she added, "Not the body. Just a close-up."

She had no desire to upset her friend more than she already was. Chloé had, after all, brought Howard to CERN, and Sabine knew her to be grappling with feelings of responsibility and guilt. *Could it be that I missed something?* she had confided to Sabine after the body was discovered. *Something that might have saved him had I seen it early enough?*

Switching from the surveillance footage, Sabine produced a still image of the mystery object from the tunnel. "This is a long shot, but do you remember Howard carrying around a notebook, leather maybe?"

Chloé stared at the blurry shape. "He always had a book or notebook on him, or both. But then many of us do. What was in it?"

Sabine grimaced. "That's the thing: whatever it is has disappeared. I think the engineer who discovered the body may have some kind of compulsion."

"You think he stole something from the scene?" Chloé asked in bewilderment. "Can't you get it back from him?"

"Unfortunately, he's in Malta for the next ten days. A mental health cleanse, ordered by his supervisor. Security gave me permission to inspect his workstation and locker, but there was no trace of any notebook."

"What about his house?"

"He lives alone, and getting a warrant to search his apartment requires more external involvement than Yvonne is willing to risk."

Sabine remembered how sorry she had felt for Claude the day he'd come to her office. Now regretting her leniency, she wished she had insisted on the return of the missing item that day. Assuming she was right, and it was a notebook, what insights into Howard's death might it contain?

Chloé set down her mug to check her phone. From the extended pause, Sabine guessed it was a message from her husband.

"He's taken a late train back tonight," Chloé said finally.

"Is everything okay?"

Chloé nodded unconvincingly, then inclined her head toward the piano. "I can always come here, can't I?"

She needn't say more. Chloé had complained about Jurgen in the past, but this time Sabine detected something different in her tone: a kind of weary resignation. She wondered if this weariness were to be nurtured, if it might lead Chloé to leaving him at last. At the thought of Chloé being free again, of their romantic friendship being renewed, of long evenings with music and laughter, Sabine's heart began to feel lighter.

"I should probably be home when he arrives," Chloé said, pocketing her phone.

Sabine blinked up at her. "But aren't you smashing particles right about now?"

"During a shutdown?"

"Stay for one more song."

Chloé smiled, though her eyes were wretched. "You know just what to say. It's almost irritating."

When sheet music began to rustle in the next room, Sabine returned to the image of the fuzzy apparition hovering above the grass. On impulse, she grabbed a screenshot and imported it into a photo program. After playing around with the brightness and color balance, she magnified the image. Zooming in to the figure, she was able to discern blue jeans, dark sneakers, and just the hint of a white shirt extending from the sleeve of the coat. These were the exact items of clothing Dr. Anderby had been found wearing.

"Where are you going, Howard?" she whispered. Switching back to the video, she replayed the scene in its entirety, and by the time she had sped forward to the second figure in pursuit, Chloé had resumed her haunting soundtrack.

CHAPTER 12

September 22

Before

E ve took a fresh glass of champagne from a passing waiter as she maneuvered through the crowd. It was not often that one saw nearly the whole lab—the physicists, mathematicians, and engineers, anyway—congregated in one place, heady with drink. Not even the annual holiday party, and its increasingly popular theatrics, drew this kind of turnout. Eve supposed that the last time this much of the lab had gathered together, they had needed an entirely new particle as an excuse.

With some jockeying, Eve was able to find a decent view of the evening's main attraction: a digital projection running along one wall of the ATLAS warehouse. The warehouse—a kind of hangar that serviced CERN's largest detector with maintenance and equipment—was not the typical location for lab celebrations, but the rented party lights and DJ were doing their best to turn the frigid venue into the event of the season. Tonight, the lab would be unveiling to the world a liquid xenon tank, whose construction several kilometers away in a natural cavern beneath the French countryside was now complete and whose live-projected image everyone at the party was now examining.

This particular tank featured a liquid xenon core, surrounded by a much larger volume of water, which was in turn swaddled in layers of insulation and a special foil designed to cut down on stray "noise" pouring in from the universe. Eve didn't think it looked like anything that had been engineered recently, but more like an artifact from a cult sci-fi movie.

"What do you think?" Niels was suddenly standing beside her in a dark cloak. In the dim of the party lights, he looked to be wearing liturgical vestments.

"It's very striking, Niels."

"Isn't she?" He beamed at the projection.

The wide-angle lens had been placed close to the tank's shiny bulk, and through a thick window at the center of frame, one could just make out, through the water, the precious container of xenon within. Given that the actual physics of the experiment—capturing dark matter particles— would be invisible to the eye, this window was a shameless gimmick. But not even CERN was above bowing and scraping to the media. A clock at the bottom of the screen ticked down to the big unveiling: T-minus twenty-two minutes.

Without warning, Niels shouted into his phone: "Eight sharp! It's going live on our app *and* on YouTube. No, the timing is not flexible, Christ almighty." He hung up and shook his head as if to say, *My job, am I right?*

Niels had only recently been recruited to the Large Underground Xenon Tank (or LUXT) team—leaving many to wonder what sort of leverage he had wielded with Simon behind the scenes—but the way Niels talked, you'd think he'd been on the project since its inception. He began to chatter anxiously: "From the public's perspective, it's, like, fifty million euros spent on, what, a giant tank? It's not just a tank, but *they* don't know that. It's my job to communicate that. Otherwise, we don't get more funding. It's not sexy, of course. But you know what? No money, then no big discoveries on the inner workings of the universe. That's the very unsexy math of it."

Eve wondered which word she hated more, *sexy* or *unsexy*.

"That's why we need you, Niels. You keep us all very sexily employed."

"Sorry . . ." Niels pecked at his phone. "Simon's flipping out over something."

As Eve let her eyes wander around the warehouse, she spotted Arnav and Teo making small talk with Chloé and her very large German husband, who had some fairy-tale name like Georg or Gunther. He was an art history professor and deeply uninterested in particle physics, a fact about which Chloé sometimes joked. Eve imagined Arnav and Teo having to fall back on the couple's dogs as a topic of conversation.

"I'll let you in on a little secret," Niels said into her ear. "You get to see this twenty minutes before everyone else." He pressed an app on his phone named LUXT and up popped an image identical to the one projected on the wall. Below it, a counter displayed seven zeroes, like something you'd see in a car that's never been driven.

"A particle odometer?"

"You're quick," Niels said with a grin. "The counter will tick over the instant the tank detects a speck of dark matter. Simon's idea. It will likely never go beyond a few particles, at least not at first, but it's an arresting image all the same. It makes for good marketing, and that's half of what our jobs are now."

He proceeded to go into detail about the exciting properties of xenon, a rare element whose mass and sensitivity made it an ideal snare for capturing theoretical dark matter. To be the first to bag evidence of this great "dark whale of particles physics," as Simon De Vries liked to say, would be history-making. To be on the team to discover this whale would all but guarantee an invitation from the king of Sweden.

Though Eve wouldn't have called herself an expert in dark matter science, she was hardly starved for a lecture on the topic. She discreetly scanned the room, hoping to spot Howard. She had seen him at that week's Monday meeting, but as had become typical in the month since his arrival, she and Arnav had exchanged only a few pleasantries with Howard on their walks back to their respective offices. They never saw him at R1 for meal breaks or even coffee. Eve had started to wonder if their lunch in Geneva last month had actually happened. Remarkably, he did make appearances at the lab's traditional Friday happy hour—and though Eve had occasionally chatted with him in the company of a larger group, she hadn't been able to get him alone. She'd seen him several times in deep discussion with one of the theorists, evidently preferring their company to that of his own team. In group meetings, Howard was still cagey about his own work but felt free to comment on the research of his colleagues. In fact, his insights into their analyses were always cogent and persuasive, sometimes frighteningly so—including her own. Chloé didn't pressure him on his own progress and, in fact, seemed to encourage him to take his time. Thirty days in, Howard Anderby was still as mysterious as the day of his arrival.

Eve was now wondering what it would be like to have a private conversation with him without Arnav around. She hadn't imagined it to be on a crowded dance floor. Not that anyone was dancing exactly, but a pounding bass, combined with multicolored lights gyrating above, seemed to demand it.

There was something about scientists and academics attempting to cut loose that sent a pang of embarrassment through her, not unlike a childhood memory of watching her parents get drunk at a neighbor's party. But maybe she was merely embarrassed for herself, standing there in an asymmetrical blue chiffon dress, her default attire whenever she was invited to a wedding. Her exposed right shoulder peeked out brazenly from one strap. She had felt silly putting it on earlier, as though she were trying to convince the world that women scientists, too, can be enticing. But in truth, she felt genuinely attractive tonight.

"It's quite thrilling to believe dark matter history could be made in our lifetimes, let alone this year," Niels was saying. "You know, if it hadn't been for Simon . . ." Eve tuned out the rest. There was something about the way Niels spoke about Simon that felt put-on. She wondered if he didn't in fact loathe the Dutch physicist and simply wished to inhale the secondhand fumes of his reputation.

A passing waiter handed Eve a second glass of champagne. As she was bringing it to her lips, she spied Howard across the room, back half-turned as he considered a life-size mural of the ATLAS detector on the opposite wall. He was wearing a dark tweedy jacket and adopting a contemplative pose similar to the one he'd had at the museum that day. But instead of regarding a Flemish canvas, he was considering the lab's biggest celebrity, an enormous mechanical flower that absorbed millions of subatomic explosions per second, which then dispersed from its central pistil ever outward into complex petals for processing. The real ATLAS, of course, sat one hundred meters beneath their feet, which Eve always thought made the mural redundant—but then, many who worked here would never venture underground.

Niels followed her gaze. "Isn't that the China guy?"

She nodded. "Howard Anderby." Saying his name out loud felt very nice.

With a sudden jerk of his head toward the stage, Niels said, "It's nearly showtime. Wish me luck."

In the vacuum left by Niels, Arnav materialized at her side, a highball in hand. He took a swallow and stared after Niels with poorly disguised distaste.

"Nice timing," she said.

"What did the bartender say when a neutrino walked in and ordered a—"

"'For you, no charge'?"

He raised his glass to her grudgingly.

She noticed that, beneath a smart blazer, he was wearing one of his gag T-shirts: a spiky-haired David Bowie from the movie *Labyrinth*, standing in a mazelike version of the LHC tunnel, with the words EVERYTHING

I'VE DONE, I'VE DONE FOR YOU. Eve found Arnav's weakness for physics memes weirdly comforting.

"If only the CERN labyrinth were real," she said, eyeing his shirt. "Sometimes I think there must be some truth to the rumors."

"If it were real," he said with a nod toward the projection, "the twat who built this would be our Goblin King."

Eve took a large gulp of champagne. "You're just afraid Simon's tank is going to find dark matter before ATLAS does."

"Maybe," he admitted. "But it's passive science. Do you know how many years it will take before a single flyspeck of dark matter passes through that cave? We'll both be in a home for the infirm before that thing lights up with a mote of anything. Give me aggressive collisions any day, thank you very much." He knocked back the rest of his drink. "Anyway, hardly matters. The Chinese will beat us to it."

"Tell me you're not buying into the China paranoia."

"Eve, we're talking about the same country that built a twenty-one-thousand-kilometer wall as a massive fuck-you to their enemies. Their tunnel is going to kick our tunnel's ass."

"If it gets built."

He was about to respond, but his eyes locked on something across the dance floor. Turning, she saw that he was looking directly at Howard, who appeared to be not so much observing the party as considering a space beyond it.

"Someone should tell him that the barmy-genius routine fell out of favor half a century ago," Arnav said.

"Why don't you surprise yourself for once and like somebody?"

"If he solves quantum gravity while he's standing there, I'll consider it."

But Eve barely heard him. She was thinking of that oft-repeated, though probably apocryphal, story about Einstein visiting the California Institute of Technology in the 1930s. As Einstein was being fêted one night at the Pasadena campus's dining club, a group of distinguished guests, including astronomer Edwin Hubble, had glanced over to find the middle-aged physicist, in his tweeds and bow tie, sitting by himself picking at his dinner plate. He bent over his meal with great concentration, as though the most pressing task for his remarkable brain were deboning a piece of fish. Hubble and his friends just stared, and after what seemed like an age, the great man finished his last bite, set down his napkin, and wandered off to the men's room. What the scene illustrated depended on who was recounting it. On the one hand, you could say that, however playful and fun-loving Einstein had been, however brilliant and admired, that didn't inoculate him from the very human reality of contemplating one's dinner plate alone. The second interpretation was that Einstein's contemporaries had been so intimidated by the man that no one had dared engage him. At that moment, he was not unlike the most beautiful girl at the dance.

Howard didn't quite have this reputation, but there was something about him, a certain inaccessibility, that Eve sensed intimidated everyone in their group, and perhaps everyone at this party.

"I think I'll go say hello," she said.

She started across the room, but just as she approached, Bella appeared at Howard's side and handed him a dark cocktail. She was undeniably stunning that night, her hair falling in waves down her bare back and her bias-cut silhouette echoing the curves of her champagne flute. It was as if she were a hologram accidentally projected from a film noir. For what else could Bella be among this crowd but some sort of technological error?

Eve swerved to avoid them, lifting her head confidently as she strode to the drinks table. She waited a few seconds before glancing back at the pair, who were now chatting amiably.

Her buzz starting to flag, she ordered another glass of champagne and swiftly downed half of it. When she turned to the room again, Bella had vanished and Howard was now facing the tank projection, which read T-minus thirteen minutes. Seizing the moment, she stepped toward him. "Do you think they'll find anything?"

Howard gave her a rapid, almost imperceptible appraisal, eyes flitting to her bare shoulder. "Oh, probably," he said. "People with that much swagger and influence often get what they want."

"Do you really think so?"

He tilted his head, considering. "I guess we should cross dark matter off the list at some point. It's not what I would look for given the funds, but why not?"

Eve recalled what he had said in Geneva about wanting a scientific revolution, and wondered what, if anything, he planned to do about it. She also remembered the doubles in the John the Baptist painting. *Like two worlds lying side by side.* Had he been serious about the many-worlds interpretation of quantum mechanics?

Howard continued, "Maybe the more important question is, Why are we watching live footage of an unmoving object?"

It was true, there wasn't much to look at apart from the general sci-fi vibe of the thing. Although, upon closer inspection, she could see a slice of darkness beyond the tank, including a few stalactites just visible at the edge of frame.

"Niels thought it would be more dramatic, I guess, if you could visualize dark matter penetrating the cave."

"Right, I saw you two talking earlier."

Eve tried not to look pleased that he'd noticed her, but she could feel her cheeks flushing. "There's a LUXT app, too," she continued, "where you can follow the tank's dark matter count in real time. It's a secret, so try to act surprised when he announces it."

"Seriously?" He laughed before turning to study her face.

She broke eye contact and took a sip of her drink. "Wouldn't it be fun if we suddenly appeared in that cave? I'd like to see the look on Simon's face."

"It can be done." He sounded strangely earnest. "If you want to badly enough, you can get anywhere."

"Oh?"

She blinked at Howard inquisitively, waiting for him to reveal how he proposed to breach a 1,500-meter subterranean cave guarded by cameras and accessible only by a freight elevator. But before he could answer, Arnav brushed past.

"Oh, hello," he said, pouring on the happenstance. "Just headed to the punch table. You two plotting the next revolution?"

Ignoring the comment, Eve indicated her empty glass. "I'll take another of these, if you don't mind. I'll need it to get through this announcement."

"Nothing for me, thanks," Howard said, raising his cocktail. "But I recommend the evening's signature drink, the Dark & Stormy Matter. It's got rum and charcoal or something, which sounds awful but is actually pretty good."

Arnav rolled his eyes, as if he'd suddenly lost his taste for puns. "Thanks, mate. I'll consider it."

Howard watched him fold into the crowd. "He doesn't like me, does he?"

"Oh, Arnav's like that with everyone. My first week here, he was totally obnoxious to me."

This was partly true. Arnav had been memorably prickly with her on her first day at CERN. Though Eve quickly realized it was because he was loath to share what had been his private office for the previous year. After he'd gotten over another person occupying the other side of the partition, they'd become rapid friends, and his prickliness soon found other targets.

But she could see from Howard's face that he'd already mentally moved on. He glanced at his watch and then toward the exit. "Are you sure you want to stay for this?"

"I don't think we have a choice."

"You think our boss is going to stick around?" he asked, nodding in Chloé's direction. "Watch, the second the lights dim, she and her husband disappear."

Evidently, Howard had already picked up on their group leader's disdain for the tank and pretty much anything associated with Simon. Yet across the room, Chloé looked the very image of a supportive colleague, confronting the projection with something resembling professional interest. She wasn't fooling anyone.

When Eve turned back to Howard, he was already striding purposefully toward the door and to who knows where. He looked back briefly and held up a hand. Was he waving goodbye? Or beckoning her to follow?

At that moment, Niels appeared onstage, tapped the mic, and launched into a spiel about the great historical and scientific significance of that evening. He spoke of what a rare project the LUXT was and how lucky CERN had been—how lucky Niels himself was—to count Dr. Simon De Vries among their number.

"But before I introduce the man of the night," Niels continued, "a little about dark matter for you folks watching our live stream, because not everyone out there is familiar with this mysterious substance. The shocking truth is that, smart as we are, we physicists can only observe about five percent of the universe's component matter. You could say that makes us ninety-five percent idiots." He paused for laughter. "Because, you see, the other ninety-five percent of reality is completely invisible to us, and dark matter is twenty-seven of those percents. That's what this tank behind me is about, located just kilometers away from where we stand now, housed deep underground so as to protect it from the cosmic rays battering our planet . . ."

Eve watched Howard disappear through one of the exits. Her pulse quickened at the notion that she could follow him to wherever he was going, that she didn't have to remain and listen to Niels and Simon drone on for the next hour about their contributions to scientific exploration.

Her decision made, she turned from the stage, slipped through the crowd, and escaped into the night.

CHAPTER 13

December 2

Now

Four days into Sabine's investigation, news of neither Howard's death nor the LHC shutdown had yet leaked to the press. During a brief meeting that morning, however, Yvonne had prepared her for the inevitable: "At a lab this size, it's only a matter of time before somebody calls one of the papers. Doesn't even have to be a physicist. All it takes is someone in the cafeteria to catch wind of it, and the next day, the dogs are sniffing at our front gate. If we don't have answers by that point, it's a pretty grim forecast for particle physics." Sabine could see the suppressed apprehension on Yvonne's face, though she didn't know what to say other than she was putting in sixteen-hour days and hoped to make some headway that morning with members of Howard's work group.

Most everyone at CERN not directly associated with ATLAS or the New Particles Group had declined to be interviewed on the grounds that they simply had not known Dr. Anderby well enough. As Sabine set a Nespresso machine brewing in a corner of her office and arranged various snacks on a tray, she mentally surveyed the areas of Howard's life she hoped to illuminate. But as she was about to discover, even those in his work group would have similar claims about his inscrutability.

The first at her door that morning was Kennet Olstad, a slim, fair-haired Norwegian nearing the end of his postdoc and currently applying for an extension. From the moment he entered, Olstad's agitation was palpable. Refusing both refreshment and chair, he paced the floor and explained his research in staggering detail, as if it were Sabine, and not the University of Oslo, who might extend his fellowship. After she had learned more than she'd thought possible to know about the behavior of muons, she steered the subject toward Howard.

Olstad hesitated. "I don't mean to sound unkind, but since the day he arrived in our group, Howard struck me as somewhat impatient with our methods. I can't say that I understood his particular course of research, other than he was always looking for energy deficits, but he gave off a vibe of being sort of above it all."

"Can you tell me what you mean by energy deficits?"

He went quiet for a moment, as if translating to layman's terms in his head. "He wanted some of the energy in our collisions to be missing. And I don't just mean *apparently* missing in a way that might point to a new discovery, as is pretty standard in our work. I mean *totally vanished*."

Sabine frowned. "I'm not a physicist, but I'm pretty sure one of your laws is that energy doesn't just disappear."

"Yes, that is what we learn, isn't it?" Olstad squinted toward the windows. "But another law of physics, one you don't necessarily learn in school, is that any physical phenomenon not strictly forbidden is inevitable. Even if the chances are infinitesimal, energy could potentially disappear from our universe and leap to another next to our own. That would mean energy conservation laws apply to not just our universe, but the entire theoretical multiverse."

"Is this what Dr. Anderby believed?"

Olstad heaved a sigh and took a step toward the door. "Honestly, I can't be bothered with what other people believe. I have my hands full trying to convince my program that my work here needs to continue."

"What will you do if you don't get your extension?"

He gave her a pained smile. "Well, that's the big question, isn't it? You can't be a postdoc forever. People think being a musician or movie star is competitive." He laughed. "Try being a scientist."

At that bon mot, Olstad wished her luck and left.

The Taiwanese physicist Weiming Wu had similar things to say about Howard, impatience being a recurring theme. As Wu stirred cream into his espresso and munched a cookie, he confessed, "I can't say that I understood why Chloé selected him, other than that his work was supposedly inspired. That may not be fair given he wasn't here for very long, and I will say that he was extremely quick at finding the weakness in a colleague's research. In very few words, he could get to the heart of why someone's analysis was faulty. Howard had little tolerance if a member of our group kept on a track he found pointless. He didn't speak often in meetings, yet when he did, he could be intimidating. We were all waiting for his own research to be brilliant, but he was pretty secretive about his work." Wu smiled nervously, adding, "I hope you understand, I had nothing against him. Of course, I have no idea how or why he was in the tunnel that night."

When Sabine asked him what he thought about Howard having worked on the Chinese accelerator project, emotion clouded his face. Whether it was anxiety or anger, or both, she couldn't be sure.

After a long pause, he said, "I would never work on the Chinese collider myself—and believe me, they've been quite aggressive in their recruiting efforts, to the point where I sometimes wonder if someone is following me. But physics is a worldwide endeavor. No one should have a monopoly on the truth."

"Do you have real reason to believe you're being followed?" she asked. "Here in Switzerland?"

He shrugged, but the casual gesture was unconvincing. "Let's just say coming from the part of the world I do, one stays watchful."

Sabine nodded, weighing whether she should pursue this line of questioning or let it go. The day after she'd been brought on the case, Yvonne had apprised her of potential Chinese infiltration at CERN. Though Yvonne had initially thought word of Chinese spies to be nothing more than lab gossip, that was before Howard sat her down privately soon after his hiring. He outlined specific dates and times of ATLAS information dumps, data he claimed to have found in possession of the Chinese lab where he had worked.

"It wasn't hard evidence, of course," Yvonne told her. "And I did wonder if Howard was mistaken about what he thought he saw at the Qinhuangdao facility. But when I had a team of ATLAS computer engineers conduct a full data audit, significant information was found to have been rerouted from the detector to an unknown location. Someone had been cleverly siphoning from the ATLAS dumps for years, hoping no one would notice misplaced 'junk' data. I was very close to shutting down the LHC this year—not just for scheduled recalibrations, but completely, until we identified the source of the thefts. By that point, of course, more than one person in the security office had questioned Howard's integrity and wondered if he might be a Chinese operative himself. And then, November twenty-seventh happened."

When Sabine asked if Howard's disclosure of the information didn't, in fact, prove his innocence, Yvonne hedged. What if he had been working with a CERN mole the entire time he was overseas and had intended to become one himself? What if Howard's revelation of an ATLAS leak was, in fact, a classic espionage maneuver to forever remove suspicion from himself? Yet after his death, the security office uncovered zero evidence of suspicious activity on his computer, in his office, or in his apartment.

"For that reason," she concluded, "we need to explore all facets of this case. As sensational as the China angle may be, we can't assume the missing data is necessarily connected with Howard's death."

Sabine agreed. After all, when she tried to picture a scenario in which Howard had been killed because he knew too much about data thieves— or, having outlived his usefulness as a Chinese operative, he'd been swiftly executed—she couldn't make the piece about the tunnel fit. His dying alone while sitting in a tripped particle accelerator just didn't make any sense. There was a vital portion of the story missing, and one that might well have nothing to do with a rival laboratory.

Then again, across her desk, Dr. Wu's distress at the mere mention of China was obvious. Pearls of sweat had condensed at his temples and he shifted uneasily in his chair.

"I hope you know that what you say in here is confidential," Sabine assured him.

Dr. Wu's agitation appeared only to increase. "I don't doubt it," he said. "But that's really all I can offer about Howard."

He wiped his brow with a napkin, thanked her for the coffee, and left.

The American from Stanford, Bella Yoshimura, spoke more kindly of Howard than her colleagues. Her eyes quickly became glassy. "He was actually a very sweet guy. It upsets me that everyone thought he was full of himself. I think he carried around a lot of pain he didn't like to talk about."

"Do you feel you knew him better than others in your group?"

Dr. Yoshimura stared down at a mug of aromatic tea she had brought in. "I mean, we chatted at coffee breaks and at Beer O'Clock. But Arnav and Eve knew him best. Toward the end, it seemed they were always together."

"When you did chat, what would you talk about?"

"Oh, shop mostly, like everyone." She took a tentative sip of tea. "Although he was really into the philosophy of science. Most of us are so focused on the day-to-day work, often at the expense of the bigger picture. But Howard wanted to know the *what* and *why* of it all. Why are we here? What's it all for? That sort of thing."

Sabine leaned forward. "I understand he admired Schopenhauer."

This seemed to pique Yoshimura's interest. She set down her mug. "I haven't studied much philosophy myself, but yes. Howard was fascinated by Schopenhauer's idea of a kind of force—or no, he specifically said it *wasn't* a force, more of an *essence* underlying everything we experience. The *Will*, it's called. Schopenhauer said the forces of nature, like gravity and electromagnetism, arise from this Will. In fact, everything we see, objects, humans, all of it—" She gestured around the room and toward the windows. "It's all a projection of the Will. Howard wondered if maybe physicists, philosophers, and even religious leaders aren't all, in their own way, talking about the same underlying *thing* behind everything—which isn't a thing at all, but more the invisible framework from which things emerge? Or a vast universal consciousness from which things emerge? When I told him it all sounded a bit Buddhist, he said, 'Well, where do you think Schopenhauer got his ideas? Not to mention every other philosopher and guru running around these days?' Though he did suggest that the Will was much closer to the Hindu idea of Brahman. He once said that our lab's Shiva statue has a deeper meaning than the whole cosmic dance of creation and destruction. Shiva is actually one manifestation of Brahman, the ultimate reality underlying our world."

She laughed. "I'm sure it all sounds a bit woo-woo for a scientist. My point is, he was more open-minded than a lot of people around here—almost in a way that the old, dead quantum physicists used to be, like Bohr, Schrödinger, or even Oppenheimer. I caught Howard reading a Wolfgang Shreft book once, if you can believe it."

Given Howard's philosophical appetite, and having caught a glimpse of a Shreft volume or two in his apartment, Sabine could. When she turned the topic to Yoshimura's own work, her guest just shrugged and began to gather her things. "There are so many false alarms, it never pays to go shooting your mouth off. The first year I presented at a conference, Simon De Vries said my plots were garbage. Maybe he's right."

Sabine hadn't meant to hit a nerve.

"It's fine," Yoshimura continued. "This whole thing has been so destabilizing. Death is like that, but not in the way they say. It can actually make you bizarrely selfish, to the point where you question your whole life." She stood. "I don't know what I'm saying. I should really get back to my office."

"Dr. Yoshimura?"

The young woman hesitated at the door.

"Did Howard ever give any indication that he had a personal life, inside or outside the lab?"

Yoshimura just laughed.

"Sorry, is it a funny question?"

"It's just that the real romance is with the LHC," she said as she opened the door. "Every other relationship is trivial."

The Italian postdoc from the University of Milan, Pietro Moretti, stopped by on his way to lunch. With his bike helmet still on and a guitar strapped to his back, it was clear he didn't intend to stay long. On the subject of his late colleague, Moretti had little to say at first, other than that Howard had seemed "like a totally cool guy," and though he didn't know much about his work, he seemed "freakishly smart, like he had a lot going on inside, you know? The guy went deep, you could just tell."

Hovering near the door, Moretti continued, "Some say Howard was arrogant, but it seemed pretty obvious to me that he struggled with some sort of anxiety. We had a couple of group outings on the lake, and he always backed out."

"Maybe he wasn't the water-sport type?"

He shrugged. "The only time I saw him outside of group meetings was at lab events, like the xenon tank party this past fall. Sometimes at Beer O'Clock."

Sabine knew from Yvonne that Beer O'Clock was a Friday happy hour held on the R1 patio, weather permitting. It had been around so long that no one knew who had started it or when, but it had grown in popularity over the years. Apart from drinking, there were lawn games and Ping-

Pong. It was the one night a week when CERN physicists allowed themselves to forget their research.

"Drinking loosened him up a bit, I think," Moretti went on. "Though he didn't tend to stay long, and when he did, he was usually off interrogating one of the theorists about their work."

This confirmed what Sabine had already learned from the few members of the Theory Group she'd spoken to. But apart from having fielded Howard's abundant curiosity, the theorists could offer no useful information about Howard himself. The interactions had been entirely one way. The Argentinian theorist Teo Rico had confided to her: *I mean, there's nothing I love more than discussing string theory mathematics. But one night I had to excuse myself because Howard's probing was kind of relentless. I often felt he was hunting for something behind what I was telling him, if that makes any sense.*

"Do you know if Dr. Anderby had a social life outside the lab?" Sabine asked Moretti.

He laughed at the question, similar to the way Yoshimura had. Though Sabine wasn't entirely buying the idea that the LHC was stopping physicists from having love lives.

"Eve and Arnav were the closest to him of anyone," Moretti said finally. "You should talk to them."

Sabine would have liked to, but their appointment slots came and went, two o'clock, then two thirty, with no appearance from Dr. Bose or Dr. Marsh.

After looking up the location of their shared office, Sabine grabbed her coat and scarf. She was grateful for the cool blast of air that hit her face as she exited onto Higgs Field and headed east across campus. A few minutes later, she was confronted with the concrete brick of Building 33. Two stories of venetian blinds shielded the south-facing offices from the low sun. Several window ledges displayed scientific tchotchkes: an Einstein bobblehead, one of those mystifying bobbing birds, and, propped against the glass, a Ping-Pong racket decorated with German physicist Werner Heisenberg's bespectacled face. Sabine recalled how among the items found at the scene of Dr. Anderby's death—dosimeter, thermos of coffee, wind-up wristwatch (still ticking), cell phone, wire earbuds, key ring, a pill case for his medication—there had also been a Ping-Pong ball discovered in one of his coat pockets. *Up Quark* had been written in black ink across its surface, one of six varieties of quarks (up, down, charm, strange, top, bottom). She had thought this curious until she'd been informed by the security office that the entire lab was mad for a particle-themed version of table tennis, and that a postdoc filching one of the balls was maybe not so unusual.

When she had finished cataloging the window detritus, Sabine noticed a young woman standing to the side of the walkway on a patch of dying grass. She appeared to be regarding a pair of office chairs that sat facing each other. She had a pale, thin face and dark, disordered hair. Beneath her coat, she was wearing a drab outfit that looked to have been pulled from a laundry hamper. Sabine recognized her from her digital file: Dr. Eve Marsh.

"Excuse me, hello," she said, stepping toward her. "I'm Sabine Leroux."

Marsh looked up, revealing a bandaged left cheek. Sabine immediately regretted her earlier stereotyping of scientists as emotionally reticent, because good god, this woman's face was the portrait of pain. Sabine had a strange impulse to swaddle her in a blanket. Or mercifully smother her with one.

"Dr. Marsh, is it?"

"Oh, did I miss our appointment?" Her voice was clipped and strained.

"Not to worry. We can do it now if you're up to it." Sabine held out her hand. "How are you feeling? I hear you took a pretty nasty fall in the auditorium."

Marsh absently shook her hand. "I'm fine. A colleague sort of caught me, but not before my head met one of the seats."

"Was that Dr. Bose who caught you?"

Marsh nodded.

"Have you seen him today by chance?" She peered at the building.

"We don't always work in our offices," Marsh answered vaguely. "Sometimes our best work is done on walks."

Sabine let the matter drop. "If you don't mind, perhaps we can head back to my office in the security building?"

"Actually, a walk might be better. I could use the fresh air."

"Yes, good," Sabine agreed. "I've been cooped up all morning."

Without another word, Dr. Marsh started off, leaving Sabine to follow.

CHAPTER 14

December 2

Now

E ve didn't know why she had told the detective she needed some air. She could have simply confessed that Howard's office window in Building 36 was visible from her own office and that she couldn't bear the sight of it. Had Eve agreed to go with Sabine to the security building, she'd have had to confront the Gargamelle bubble chamber sculpture at the edge of Higgs Field—which would only elicit memories of an evening spent with Howard reclining on the grass. Even the two abandoned office chairs outside her building upset her, evoking one night when she, Howard, and Arnav had held an impromptu tea party. But why get into all this with a stranger?

She had been avoiding reflective surfaces all week for fear of catching a glimpse of her wretched face. Her appearance had gotten far beyond her control, betraying feelings in bold subtitles for the world to read. Though more troubling than actual mirrors were the emotional ones now infesting the lab, positioned as if in a carnival attraction, duplicating once happy times spent with Howard in an infinite recursion of horror. What was worse was that Eve didn't know how to express her current state to anyone, not even to Arnav. If Howard had officially been her boyfriend—or even if their feelings for each other had been public knowledge—it might be easier. When someone dies before you, or the world, can truly define your relationship to that person, how do you properly grieve?

As they headed toward the abundant evergreens at the edge of campus, Eve struggled to concentrate on what the detective was saying, which was some sort of introduction. Sabine Leroux was not tall exactly, but something about her lean, athletic proportions lent her the illusion of height. She probably had only an inch on Eve, and yet it seemed she was looking down at her as they walked.

Word had already gotten around about Sabine's long-standing friendship with Yvonne and Chloé, but Eve listened as she spoke of CERN needing an investigative consultant to keep Howard's death out of the press. In addition to the lab having long ago been granted a certain degree of legal autonomy, Sabine had used her sway with the Swiss Police to keep law enforcement at bay. For now. She assured Eve that these initial interviews were voluntary and free from pressure, simply a way to get a sense of Dr. Anderby as a person, particularly from those who knew him well.

"I understand you worked closely with Dr. Anderby in the ATLAS New Particles Group," Sabine said, stating it as a fact to be verified rather than a question.

Eve wondered vaguely if their conversation was being recorded. Not that it mattered. She wasn't bothered about anything at the moment, apart from Howard being abruptly gone from the planet. This cold, bare fact stood at the summit of all earthly things she had ever cared about. Far below that sat other items: alarm about rising sea levels; a vague worry about her aborted presentation at the conference and the soundness of her research; and far below that, the question of whether or not Sabine had pressed Record on her phone. It hardly mattered anyway; Eve didn't intend to reveal the contents of her mind or heart. She was typically good at concealing things—thoughts, feelings, exhaustion after long days spent coding at her desk, *hide it away, stuff it down.*

"Yes, Howard and I worked together," she heard herself saying in faint imitation of a normal, functioning person. "But *closely* is a relative term. It can take a while to grasp a colleague's research. Sometimes you have to wait for someone to publish before fully understanding their work."

"But you and Arnav were friends with Howard outside of work." When Eve didn't respond immediately, she added, "Correct me if I'm wrong."

"We were friends, though much of our social life takes place at the lab."

"Right," Sabine said. "I understand he enjoyed Beer O'Clock?"

A sudden image came to Eve, and with it a kind of exquisite pain: Howard on the R1 patio, eyes merry after a pint or two. For those couple of hours during the week, she and her colleagues might let their eyes linger on each other for a beat longer than was professionally appropriate. She could observe Howard—who was usually off grilling someone from the Theory Group—and not worry about the admiration that must have been writ large on her face. Sometimes, when he wore a specific T-shirt or oxford, she could detect just below the hem a small swell of stomach, a flaw she'd found deeply endearing. Why classically handsome men—Rodrigo Peregrue on CMS, for example, or even Pietro Moretti, whose curly hair and talent for strumming folk tunes on the lawn drew the female gaze—why guys like them made her want to pass out cold was a mystery. Whereas just the mere glimpse of one man's belly would make her skin burn.

The detective's voice intruded into her daydream. "Might Howard's social life have strayed outside the lab?"

"He was pretty focused on his work," Eve found herself saying, almost irritably. "Don't know if you've picked up on it, but we don't have tons of time for extracurriculars. We're all low-grade sleep-deprived."

She wasn't sure what to think of Sabine's next question: "If Howard had a girlfriend or romantic interest of some kind, I assume that's something you'd be aware of?"

Eve wondered if the detective was being coy. Did she know more than she was letting on? Or was she simply fishing?

Sabine went on: "The way I figure it, the men outnumber the women here. There are only so many possible romantic candidates. Unless he preferred men, of course. In the summer and fall, there's an influx of interns and grad students. I hear there can be quite a bit of fun. Like an Olympic Village for brains?"

"It's not as thrilling as all that."

"All young people need romance, no?" Sabine pressed.

This line of questioning was making Eve's head hurt. "Most of us have the ability to put that on pause during our postdocs. Out of sheer necessity. Arnav has a girlfriend in England, a fiancée actually, but most of our work group is happily single."

"And you?"

Eve wasn't about to divulge anything to the detective about her romantic life, not that she'd know what to say exactly even if she wanted to. *After a string of on-again, off-again boyfriends in college and grad school, I arrived at CERN contentedly alone? Until the day I met Howard?* Instead, she said, "I'm not sure how our love lives, or lack of one, is relevant."

That's when she noticed the detective had stopped and was staring into the trees. Without thinking, Eve had steered them deeper into the woods, right past the Chateau. Here was another emotional land mine.

Sabine contemplated the proud stone bulk of the house. "I didn't realize this was back here."

To Eve's surprise, she marched over to the two-story building, mounted the steps, and tried the front door. Finding it locked, she returned.

"Who has access?"

"Maintenance? I'm not really the person to ask."

As they walked on, the detective continued to examine the house. "Have you been inside?"

"It's reserved as a bed-and-breakfast for visiting theorists," Eve said, by way of an answer. "It's shut up most of the year."

She pushed away an image of following Howard through these woods toward the Chateau one evening. Another of him sitting on the front stoop, waiting for her. And yet another image from that night when she might have done something to stop him from coming here at all—when she could have made a different choice, thereby selecting a different timeline of her life. Instead, she had chosen the version in which she currently found herself trapped.

Through a part in the trees, the bronze Shiva statue came into view. For a bizarre instant, it looked as if Shiva had sprouted yet more arms, each pointing in a different direction, as though the god were CERN's signpost. *These are all the ways you did not go, the paths you did not take, and now it is too late.*

The detective was still looking back at the Chateau. "Do you know if Howard had ever been inside?"

"I don't," she lied.

Part of her desperately wanted this interview to end, but an equal part craved an excuse to talk about Howard: about his mannerisms, his odd behaviors, the art he had liked. She would have gladly discussed his musical tastes: Bach, Beethoven, Brahms, mixed with a penchant for the holy minimalism of Tavener, Górecki, Pärt. It had been rare to catch him around the lab without earbuds stuffed in his ears. If you managed to get close enough, you might hear the sweet strains of a symphony orchestra as he rushed past.

Eve became aware that Sabine was asking her something. "Sorry?"

"I just wondered if you might tell me how you came to CERN? And a bit about your role here?"

Eve couldn't understand how this was relevant, but she launched into the automatic response she gave anyone who inquired about her job. When she'd been in grad school, she said, it had seemed like a dream to work with the protons that collided a billion times per second belowground. After her dissertation on the behavior of collision-produced particle jets had caught the attention of Chloé Grimaud, her dream had miraculously turned real. She sometimes liked to compare her job to art criticism, the ATLAS detector being a massive canvas of collisions, whose wild gestures of color and texture she and her group were left to interpret. But her mood being what it was, she gave Sabine a more desolate analogy. She spoke of the physicist as crash investigator—each proton collision a horrific plane or car wreck, after which she and her colleagues must sort through the resulting devastation for clues. For months alone, she might work on a single scrap of metal or stray body part in the debris. Far more exhilarating, of course (the whole point of the endeavor, really), was to stumble upon a rare shape or substance one couldn't identify, a completely alien *thing*. A thing, in fact, that had been formed out of the crash itself. What might this newfound object say about not just the collision but the makeup of our universe?

She usually found it satisfying to hear herself so clearly illustrate her life's mission. To articulate why CERN saw fit to spend billions upon billions of euros on peering at nature through an oversized microscope while the physical world crumbled around them—well, it could be counterintuitively soothing. But Eve felt none of this today. When she concluded by saying there was no better vocation than to stare the universe in the face and demand that it confess its secrets, she wasn't sure if she still believed it. She felt only exhausted and empty.

Sabine listened attentively, asking a few polite follow-ups, but as they headed back through the woods in the direction they had come, the detective fell silent. It was the start of coffee break, and Eve's colleagues were making their way toward R1: another emotional hot spot.

The detective slowed her pace as they neared Eve's building. "Is there any reason you know of that someone might have wished Howard harm?"

Eve frowned. "I understand that Howard died of radiation exposure, likely because of a collider malfunction."

"Right. But we still don't know how a man with no tunnel clearance got down there in the first place. Whatever happened, there may have been a second party involved. To put it bluntly, did he have any enemies? Somebody who would gain by his being gone from the lab?"

Eve stared at her. "You're asking me if there is research valuable enough at CERN for someone to irradiate a rival in the very tunnel that generates that research?"

"I realize this is a world-class laboratory, not a Victorian drawing room," Sabine said dryly. "But we need to explore all options."

"I can't be the first person to tell you this," Eve said, "but physicists by nature are a pretty cooperative group. There are some assholes among us, but they tend to be the exception. We're not all trying to murder each other on our way to collect a Nobel Prize."

"Well, gosh, Dr. Marsh. You make me feel foolish for even bringing it up."

The detective gave her a gentle smile, which left Eve feeling slightly shamed. She didn't know why she was being so combative with a woman who was simply doing her job.

Sabine thanked her and said she'd be in touch, but just as she turned in the direction of the security offices, she checked herself.

"Before I go, would you indulge me by watching a brief clip?" She drew a computer tablet from her bag. "I'm showing it to everyone."

Something told Éve this was a lie, but she obliged.

Sabine pulled up what looked like nighttime security footage of the lawn in front of Building 40. The scene was blurred by rain, but she could just make out a figure with a broken umbrella dashing across the grass to the Shiva statue. Her stomach immediately tightened. It was all she could do to stare at the screen with an impassive expression.

Sabine paused the image. "Does this person look familiar to you?"

Eve swallowed. "Could be anyone."

"You swiped your badge at the gate that night. Minutes before this was captured."

Eve's head was pounding hard now. "Many of us work late. That's the culture here."

"How about the shoes?" The detective cast a pointed look at Eve's sneakers, which looked to be similar to the ones in the video.

"They're Adidas," she said flatly, not bothering to point out that Sabine was wearing the same brand. Of course, in typical European fashion, the detective wore hers with a kind of chic indifference that Eve had never been able to replicate.

"And the scarf?"

"Not mine." This much was true. What she didn't say was that the dark pants in the video were actually a pair of pajama bottoms.

Sabine stared at her for a long unblinking moment. Eve could see that the detective knew she was being lied to. But what was the alternative? What would happen if she told this woman everything she remembered about that night? It certainly wouldn't change anything, other than potentially making everyone believe that Howard Anderby had been quite insane. Perhaps he had been. But she didn't see how it was her job to tarnish his memory for those who remained, for those who had loved him.

"I'm sorry I couldn't be of more use to you," Eve said.

"Howard is seen twenty minutes earlier in this footage, pausing at the same statue. Do you have any idea where your friend might have been going that night?"

Eve shook her head. "There are a lot of things I evidently didn't know about Howard." At this, she took a step away. "I have a rescheduled group meeting to get to. Chloé gets cranky when we're late."

As though on cue, the sound of an electronic piano traveled across the grass—a Chopin nocturne. It was Chloé at her office keyboard in Building 40, Eve knew, the melody carrying crisply from her open window through the chill air.

Sabine cocked her head. "Sounds like your boss is otherwise occupied. All the same, I thank you for your time, Dr. Marsh."

When the detective had gone, Eve was left with the unsettling feeling that Sabine hadn't really wanted to question her, but to observe her. She felt deeply seen all of a sudden, and not in a way she liked.

Back at her office, a single envelope was waiting in her mailbox. Opening it at her desk, she found a postcard inside, featuring a photograph of a snowcapped mountain she didn't recognize. When she turned the card over, there was nothing to specify the location, only a handwritten note:

Dear Dr. Marsh,

I am sorry to reach out during this terrible time, but I was referred to you by a colleague and hoped we might meet at your convenience. It is a sensitive matter, so I cannot get into it here. If you would contact me—preferably from a private email account—I would be very much indebted to you.

Regards, E. Giovanni

A Gmail address was written below. Eve didn't know an E. Giovanni, nor could she imagine why one would want to reach out to her in a private exchange. But then, Yvonne had warned everyone that journalists were going to catch wind of Howard's death at some point and find inventive ways to extract information from his closest colleagues. "We must be vigilant about our communications outside the lab," she had written in an email to her work group. Looking at the note, Eve wondered if this was what she'd meant.

She turned to her desk, where the twenty-nine physicists of the 1927 Solvay Conference stared back at her. Though she'd had the diorama for nearly two decades now, it was Howard who had forever changed her feelings about it. He had not stopped by her and Arnav's office more than a couple of times after group meetings—but when he had visited one evening that fall, for what would be the final time, he had spied the diorama from its place behind the photograph of her parents. Howard had picked it up and brought it to his face for inspection, smiling at the tiny figures. He, too, noted Einstein's childlike pose in the front row. But Howard noticed something she hadn't: Einstein's left hand, the thumb and forefinger held together in a circle. It was the vitarka mudra, he said, a ritualistic gesture in Hinduism and Buddhism, signifying the transmission of profound wisdom. This would have made sense, he explained, as Einstein had been a longtime admirer of Hindu philosophy. Eve had immediately scoffed, pointing out that this was just the casual way Einstein had rested his hand on his knee. *Maybe,* Howard conceded. *Or was it Einstein's mystical signal that there is, in fact, a realm beyond the comprehension of even our finest scientists? A world outside the clutches of this prestigious assembly?* At which point, he replicated the mudra with his own hand. This kind of talk always made Eve nervous, and she'd let the matter drop. But later, when she idly searched for images of Einstein—including the earlier 1911 and 1913 Solvay Conference photos, and another photograph from the 1940s—there it was, that exact gesture. Right hand loose at his side, left hand lifted in the vitarka mudra. After that, whenever she looked at the little inch-high Einstein on her desk, she couldn't unsee it. She couldn't unsee Howard's hand raised in the same gesture.

Now, propping the mountain postcard against the Solvay Conference's front row, she blocked out Einstein, the vitarka mudra, and half the conference. Then she pushed the diorama to the back of her desk and promptly forgot all about it.

CHAPTER 15

December 3

Now

I t was not often in the course of an investigation that Sabine found an excuse to use her old blue Cilo, a racing bicycle once manufactured on the shores of Lake Geneva. But it was an unusually balmy day, and feeling her muscles in danger of atrophy, she left her Volkswagen in the drive, rode to the nearest station, and, bike in tow, hopped a tram west. The lab was not her destination today. Instead, she would pedal a route partly traversing the span of the LHC tunnel, a cycling trail designed for sightseers to explore the aboveground wonders of the famous collider. With signs posted at various points of interest, the trail allowed tourists to ogle the buildings that stood sentinel above the subterranean detectors; and if cyclists were lucky, they might catch a glimpse of a physicist or two roaming the grounds.

Once upon a time, Sabine had made this very trip with Chloé. With a picnic lunch in tow, they had laughed at how mightily CERN struggled to make visible to the public a largely invisible science. Most amusing were the carnival-style displays stationed along the route, faceless physicists sporting hard hats in front of ALICE or CMS. An entire biking family might stick their heads in the face-sized cutouts in lieu of that trip to Disneyland Paris the kids had begged for. In truth, children were quite receptive to the idea of throwing particles together at high speed. Sabine remembered having visited Chloé long ago at the lab and spotting a pre-teen girl at the CERN gift shop, carefully inspecting through thick glasses a collection of snow globes, each with a different detector inside. The earnestness with which the girl turned over the globes and watched the snow swirl over the miniatures had made Sabine want to weep. For joy, but also for something else: for that sad unnameable thing that always accompanied memories surrounding Chloé.

But today's journey was not about re-creating a long-ago platonic romance. Sabine was headed to Howard's apartment for a thorough examination of his belongings, which, in the confusion following his death, had not been possible the first trip. Her visit was none too soon, as much of his flat would be packed up in the coming week, its contents shipped to Howard's aunt across the lake. Frances Schoenberg, though still officially a CERN consultant, was proving evasive. Sabine had tasked her new assistant with pinning her down for an interview. Once James had gotten past his surprise that Howard was related to *the* Frances Schoenberg, he eagerly took to the task.

"The woman is kind of a legend around here, you know," James had said in their last phone conversation, only their second interaction not by text.

"Is she? Someone suggested she was a crazy bat."

James sighed heavily. "Sounds like Simon De Vries."

"How'd you know?"

"Because Simon can't comprehend a person who is good at their job but doesn't go grabbing all the credit. Crazy or not, Schoenberg is an engineering genius. If you look at the original blueprints for the LHC, her initials are on everything."

"One of those quietly excellent people who only cares about the work?" Sabine replied. "I like her already."

Route de Prévessin was wide-open, with few cars on the road, and Sabine sped all the way along Voltaire's estate. Beyond an expansive lawn stood the so-called castle, though it was less a castle than your standard eighteenth-century French chateau. With its limestone facade, mansard roofs of dark slate, and a neoclassical entrance bordered by decorative columns and a carved pediment, it seemed a grander version of CERN's woodland chateau. During her interview with Eve Marsh, she couldn't help but notice that the stone house sat in the direction in which Howard had fled that night. When she mentioned this to Yvonne, her friend said there would have been no reason for his accessing the house at all, other than to lounge in dusty, picturesque rooms before his premature death.

Speeding past Voltaire's gates and veering right onto the Rue de Genève, Sabine watched an oxidized bronze of Voltaire come into view at the roundabout, the town's founder regarding the intersection with a kind of batty benevolence. She turned onto a quiet residential street of motley architecture and braked in front of what looked to be the oldest building on the block, made of stone and peeling plaster. After leaning her bike against a tree, she mounted the outdoor steps to the second floor and inserted the key given to her by CERN security into a hefty wooden door. From the dark entryway, she proceeded to the living room, its bright windows overlooking a small park. Two young women sat on the faded grass, playing fetch with a terrier.

Sabine wondered if Howard's aunt intended to rent out the place soon, as the contents of Howard's bookshelves had been already emptied into boxes and stacked against one wall, evidently at her request. Sabine found this disappointing, but then, she'd already gotten a pretty good idea of the man's reading habits. Squatting briefly, she inspected a low cabinet that held a vintage record player. It didn't surprise her that Howard had been one of those *analog just sounds better* people. She had been struck over the past week by his love of music. After reviewing more of the surveillance footage, some with less inclement weather, she had caught glimpses of Howard on the way to his office in the morning and away again in the late evening, always with wires leading to his ears. He had a way of moving that seemed propelled by an unheard melody. She opened the cabinet below the player and flipped through his collection: the usual classical giants, along with more recent composers Sabine had not heard of. She noted Mozart's Requiem in a shabby sleeve: Herbert von Karajan conducting the Vienna Philharmonic. She wondered for a moment if there might be a connection with the Requiem that had been cued up for the first beam run in the LHC Control Room. But then, this was a different recording. Besides, what proper classical music collection didn't have some version of the piece?

Turning down the hallway and into a bedroom that might have been the quarters of a Trappist monk, she found the room as she'd seen it on her brief first visit: a single chair and an unfussy queen-sized bed, left unmade, with rumpled linens and two flattened pillows. If he had been entertaining a lover, as the extra pillow and bathroom toothbrush might indicate, his guest hadn't particularly cared for comfort. Recalling her walk yesterday with Eve Marsh and the clear agony on her face, she now pictured the young woman lying on one side of this bed. She imagined her waking up in the night, finding Howard gone, and following him to the lab. But why? What did she know?

The room's only decoration was a framed William Blake print hanging on the wall above the headboard, a watercolor of a man giving up the ghost, the feminine rendering of his soul hovering above his corpse. It seemed an awfully spiritual choice of artwork for an apparent atheist. But then, so was Mozart's Requiem. What, she wondered, would constitute scientific art? An abstract painting of the double helix? An aria singing the praises of Sir Isaac Newton?

As she stood there, wondering if she'd ever been moved by a fact-based work of art, a metallic squeak came from somewhere down the hall, followed by the sound of footsteps. She acted quickly, but just as she rushed into the living room, she heard the back door slam. Hurrying to the kitchen, she dodged an overturned plant on the tile and threw open the back door in time to see a hooded figure, a dark bag slung over its shoulder, rounding the stone staircase and disappearing into the courtyard below. She grabbed the wooden railing and flew down the steps two at a time, ignoring the splinters that dug into her palm. She made a chaotic dash through the courtyard, and its bizarre maze of low hedges, toward the entrance of the building.

Glancing wildly up and down the street, she saw no one. There were only the two women from the park, who were chasing their dog. They shouted after the little terrier, whose name was, preposterously, Candide. But then, Sabine once had a schnauzer named Karl Barx, so she was hardly one to judge.

"Candide! Candide!" they cried.

"Excuse me," Sabine called to the women. "Did you see someone run out of this building just now? In a hooded sweatshirt?"

They shook their heads and continued after their dog.

Sabine didn't understand how the man—had it been a man?—could so quickly disappear. Then again, he might be very close still, catching his breath around a corner or watching her from behind a shrub. She made a cursory search of nearby bushes and alleys but, finding nothing, returned to the apartment.

How had the person gotten in? As far as she knew there were only two keys to the flat: the one in her pocket, which had been found on Howard's body, and the second with Howard's aunt. That's when she noticed the window on the back door had been forced partly open, allowing access to the interior door handle.

After cursing aloud to herself, she surveyed the apartment afresh, with an eye toward disturbed or missing items. The living room appeared as it had when she arrived, but upon returning to the hallway where the noise had come from, she realized something felt peculiar. A door led to the bathroom on one side, and on the wall opposite hung a woven rug, American Southwest in style. The wall was situated in such a way that would appear to accommodate a closet, yet there was no closet door. When she pulled back the rug and knocked on the wall, an echo from within told her there was, indeed, a cavity. Her phone's flashlight revealed a hairline crack running vertical to the rug. She pressed on one side of it, and something gave way: a panel opened, as if on a spring. Its hinge made a metallic squeak.

She stepped into a windowless space and felt around for a switch. After she flicked on an overhead bulb, a small, bare room appeared, furnished with a desk and chair. If this had been somebody's office, it was the most depressing workspace she'd ever seen. On the desk were fresh stencils of dust where papers or books had been. Turning to the opposite wall, she could make out the large, rectangular artifact of something that had once hung there, and what appeared to be fresh tack marks in the corners. Clearly, someone had just beaten her to the room's contents. She swore to herself again.

As she stood there, wondering at the motives of the person she had just chased and why Howard had been using a concealed study, the possibility of his perishing in that tunnel by suicidal intent—or by some sort of freak collider failure—dropped further on her list of plausible explanations. She was aware of a familiar rush of excitement, the kind that always followed an unexpected shift in a case.

In one corner of the room, a built-in cabinet stood half-open, a lock dangling from its metal clasp. Fresh scratch marks suggested someone had recently broken into it, but when she opened the cabinet and shone her light inside, she saw that the space wasn't entirely empty. Far in the back, a few Moleskine notebooks had been left behind.

She took them into the living room and spread them out on a threadbare Turkish rug. Turning pages, it began to dawn on her: this was Howard's interior life, or part of it. Here was a man who did not share much of himself with others. Little of his true nature could be found online, beyond academic accolades and appointments. He'd had no social media accounts of any kind. But here, among the pages of several notebooks, she felt as if she were moving closer to his inner self.

A few of the volumes, unsurprisingly, contained his thoughts on his philosophy studies. There was another notebook jumbled with mementos, photographs, and drawings, accompanied by what looked to be spontaneous thoughts on life and science. Family photos, both 35mm and Polaroid, included Howard at various ages posing with the couple from the refrigerator snapshots. His parents, clearly. Plus another woman, similar in appearance to his mother, who Sabine guessed was the aunt. But the majority appeared to have been taken at his college. MIT? Princeton? A handsome brown-skinned young man appeared in many of the snaps, his arms often thrown around Howard. The pair were pictured in quads of ivied brick, in wood-paneled bars gripping pints of beer, and most frequently, paddling on a lake. It was in these images that Howard looked at his most relaxed and happy.

Starting at a noise behind her, she realized it was only the furnace kicking on. She gathered the notebooks, loaded them into a tote, and locked up the flat. But when she returned downstairs to the tree where she had left her bicycle, she saw that her cherished Cilo was gone.

CHAPTER 16

September 23

Before

Eve rushed toward Building 40 with a cup of coffee sloshing in one hand. Having slept little the night before, she'd been spacy all morning, and now she was late for the group meeting. She could have easily blamed last night's LUXT party for her current state, but the truth was that after following Howard out of the warehouse, she hadn't returned to the party at all. Now, in the sober light of the next day, the impulse to ditch a work function because the colleague you have a crush on extended some vague invitation to flee with him into the night struck her as a bit demented.

Having left the ATLAS warehouse in the middle of Niels's speech, she had entered the cool, clear evening with cautious expectation. Spotting Howard some distance off, she started after him toward the Route de Meyrin. Given that the ATLAS project sat on the north side of the lab, her pursuit required skirting the luminous wooden Globe of Science & Innovation before crossing the road back to the lab's main entrance. Once inside the gate, she trailed Howard over walkways and through grass in the general direction of Building 40, her pace hobbled by heels. She waited for some sign that he was aware of her presence, but he hadn't glanced back once, which made her question whether she had misinterpreted his implied invitation. When he reached the Shiva statue, he stopped and touched the god's foot before dashing into the woods. Approaching Shiva, she used her phone's flashlight to study the bronze figure dancing in his ring of fire, balanced atop what looked like a baby but was actually a demon. She couldn't fathom what Howard had been doing. It seemed to her that he had touched Shiva's foot almost reverently.

She eventually tracked Howard to the Chateau—or thought she had, because where else could he have gone? But when she tried the door, it was locked. If he was inside, he had clearly not wanted company. Peering through the windows, she was able to make out the faintest light between gaps in the curtains. Or did maintenance always keep a light on? After trying a back entrance and waiting for what felt like half an hour, she'd eventually given up. By then, she was slightly embarrassed and very cold, and the thought of returning to the warehouse celebration depressed her. On the tram ride home, she tried to summon reasons that Howard would leave the most important CERN function of the year to disappear into an empty house alone. But none she could invent seemed remotely plausible.

A nightmare had kept her up for most of the remaining night. This particular one featured Eve underground with her father, helping him to lay cable. And when the ceiling above them buckled, her father shoved Eve out of the way of the falling debris. But this meant she was alive to witness the soil and broken asphalt collapsing around him, and her own arms useless in attempting to dig him out of his early grave.

Upon her acceptance to CERN, she'd been offered the rare chance to visit the LHC tunnel when the collider was offline. It was an opportunity few physicists were given—partly because one couldn't visit the collider when it was operational, which was most of the time, but also because the tunnel was the realm of engineers. While delighted at the prospect of glimpsing the Machine, she'd given some excuse about being claustrophobic. It wasn't a lie, but it also wasn't the whole story.

She downed the rest of her coffee, stuffed her reusable cup in her bag, and began to run. Her fear of being late for the meeting was likely overblown, yet she ran all the way to Building 40 and up the steps to the third floor. The door to their conference room was closed, which was odd; it typically stood open until all were present. She resisted the urge to knock, and stepped inside. The first thing she noticed was that Howard was absent, also Bella. The second was that Arnav, Kennet, Weiming, and Pietro were eerily silent, not even bothering to look up when she entered. But most alarming was that, at the head of the table, Chloé looked as if she'd been sitting there all night, without sleep or food. Beneath a slouchy sweater, the collar of her blouse protruded rumpled and crooked. Eve wondered how she had appeared so calm the night before when she now resembled a woman in a mental tailspin. Chloé stared at the empty chairs, her hands folded on the table in mock imitation of normalcy.

Eve slid into a seat.

"Good of you to join us, Eve," Chloé said, appraising her with vacant eyes. "Did you happen to encounter our two absentees on your way here?"

"I didn't," she answered warily.

Chloé looked around the table. "How about the rest of you?"

After a round of replies in the negative, Chloé studied the upper edges of the room, as if expecting the pair to emerge from the ventilation.

Turning back to scan their faces, she referenced the previous night in an attempt at humor. "Was there a party I don't know about?"

Eve could feel Arnav scrutinizing her from across the table, but she refused to look at him. She hadn't seen him since he'd gone to fetch more champagne for her, and she somehow didn't have the strength to explain or apologize.

"I was hoping," Chloé continued, "to have the full team today, if for no other reason than that we've got a problem that needs discussing."

Kennet gave a sharp bark of laughter, which seemed oddly out of character.

Chloé turned to him. "Seems you know something about it already, Ken?"

He shifted uncomfortably. "I'm not going to pretend I haven't heard the rumors."

"And what have you heard?"

He sighed, as though this were all beneath him. "That data has gone missing."

Chloé went to the door, opened it, and peered into the hall before closing it again. She took her seat and folded her hands primly. "Something like that, Ken. Yvonne has just confirmed with me this morning that for a month, at the very least, data has been siphoned from the ATLAS dumps by an unknown party."

The ATLAS dump, as everyone knew, was the runoff data from the detector that the computers had deemed either useless or less likely to provide quality physics. With trillions of collisions occurring daily at the LHC, its four main detectors could process only so much information. Some of it—indeed, much of it—simply had to be thrown out.

"But if it's from the dump," Arnav ventured, "that's garbage data, right?"

"Right," said Chloé. "So you wouldn't care if you caught someone rifling through your trash at home? Mining your bins for your dirty laundry?"

Weiming spoke up. "That's an interesting analogy, but this is garbage data that we've all agreed to throw out, isn't it?"

Chloé frowned at him. "Given that someone has been dipping into this supposed garbage repeatedly, I think the question should be, Is it garbage at all? What if, as Yvonne suspects, somebody has written code specifically to dump valuable data—to keep our lab from using it and make it easy to pilfer without anyone noticing?" Chloé looked around the room again before her gaze came to rest on Eve.

Feeling put on the spot, Eve asked, "But who would do that?"

"The Chinese," Weiming offered. "You know that's what everyone's thinking. Why don't we just say it?"

"I would prefer," Chloé said as evenly as she could manage, "not to go tripping down Conspiracy Lane. Still, our boss is concerned. In an effort to stay ahead of this, she asks that you turn in your laptops today to be scanned for viruses, strange code, or anything that may appear suspicious. We can't rule anything or anyone out."

At the thought of surrendering her laptop immediately, Eve felt a stab of panic.

Arnav stared at Chloé. "Who's the conspiracy theorist now?" When she shot him a look of displeasure, he went on, "I'm not trying to antagonize, just to understand."

"No antagonism taken, Arnav. We'll all understand much better when we get to the bottom of where the data is being funneled, which, through all the firewalls, is difficult to detect. All Yvonne is asking for is everyone's cooperation in tidying up lab security."

Eve ran through a mental catalog of her computer, wondering if there might be anything vaguely incriminating on it. There were, of course, her illicit climate models, the ones she was using to replicate the movement of greenhouse gases and possible methods physicists might use to elegantly recapture these gases. It was all very speculative, but she had spent significant work hours toiling over them. Of course, attempting to delete or transfer data from her laptop might inadvertently draw attention to the thing she wished to conceal. It wouldn't take much for someone to make the connection with the article she'd written for the upcoming issue of *Courier*. Better to do nothing.

Chloé stood. "I'm ending the meeting early so that you can put your computers on Niels's desk within the half hour. I'll have to track down Howard and Bella. But should they materialize, please send them to Niels."

Pietro, who had been sitting quietly at the end of the table, asked, "Why is it always Niels?"

"Because he's assisting Yvonne in the matter," Chloé replied curtly. "And no gabbing to anyone about this, please. Certainly not to the CMS people."

"Niels," Arnav muttered. "The servant with two masters. How do you know he hasn't already informed Simon of the breach?"

Eve realized she had been anxiously gripping the arms of her chair for the entire meeting. She cast a warning look at Arnav. He was really pushing his luck with Chloé's mood.

"Because contrary to popular opinion," Chloé responded, "Niels's allegiance to the xenon tank does not translate to one for Simon."

"How are we supposed to work in the meantime?" Kennet objected.

"Gosh, Ken, try having some fun? I believe Beer O'Clock is later today?"

Chloé gathered her things. As she made her way to the door, she looked over Kennet's shoulder at his phone, which sat face up on the table. It was open to a live image of the xenon tank, its particle counter displaying seven zeroes.

She picked up the phone and stared at it with unconcealed disdain.

"The LUXT app," Kennet needlessly explained.

"I know what it is," she said. "Are we supposed to stare at it and wait for the counter to tick over?"

He shrugged. "Maybe it's silly, but—"

"It's not silly, it's downright offensive. Everyone last night was gaping at that idiotic thing when we all know full well it's a PR stunt. That counter is never going to budge while we're alive, and frankly, it's irresponsible science to go around telling people it will."

Chloé slapped Kennet's phone face down on the table and gave the group a feeble smile. "Niels is waiting in his office," she said, before throwing open the door and hurrying from the room.

CHAPTER 17

December 7

Now

On an overcast Wednesday morning, Sabine met James Spencer at the western tip of the lake. This was only the second time they had met in person, the first being the previous evening when she had invited him to her house to peruse the Moleskine notebooks gathered from Howard's apartment. After that, the next step had been obvious: pay a visit to the mysterious aunt who had perhaps known Howard better than anyone.

When Sabine arrived at the ferry just before ten, James was already on the top deck, leaning against the rail, face tilted toward a heron whirling overhead. He was hard to miss: a lanky Black American sporting round wire-rimmed glasses and an outfit that looked to have been entirely purchased from the CERN gift shop: a CERN-branded ski hat, an ATLAS scarf, and a sweatshirt with an atomic symbol on the chest.

"Did you get the CERN socks as well?" she asked, claiming a nearby bench seat.

He turned from the heron. "What can I say, Sabine? I like my work."

She eyed his hat. "Do you also like to ski?"

He shook his head. "The only skis we had in Florida were jet."

"Well, you've come to the right place. After we put this case to rest, we'll head for the mountains."

He made a face and laughed, as if she'd just suggested they go skinny-dipping. "I'll consider it."

Minutes later, they were cutting through choppy waters toward the French village of Thonon-les-Bains, which lay just inside the curl of the croissant-shaped lake. The small blue-and-white ferryboats that traversed the water were largely crammed with tourists in the warmer months, but nearing winter now, it was mostly local commuters. As the ferry picked up speed, Sabine turned her face into the wind and toward the expanse of whitecapped water ahead.

Her call with Yvonne that morning had confirmed what James had already told her: that Frances Schoenberg was not just any CERN consultant, but had been integral to the team that had designed and built the LHC. The lab's engineers still relied on her expertise, as did the control room. "Howard was her only nephew and closest living relative. He died within the very structure she in part created. You can imagine her pain." Before hanging up, Yvonne added dismally, "The inevitable has happened, I'm afraid. I received multiple calls yesterday from journalists asking why the LHC is shut down. I can deflect for only so long. By Monday, this will be international news. At that point, I'll have to give them something." Sabine could sense the stifled panic in her voice, and its subtext: *Work faster, my friend.*

Upon docking at the village, Sabine and James headed along the water, past the sailboats and yachts that clogged this stretch of Lake Geneva. As her companion retreated into his own thoughts, she mentally reviewed the previous evening's research. At her dining room table, over several refills of coffee, the two had combed through Howard's bulky Moleskines well into the night.

During a break from reading, Sabine had been pleased to discover from the spilled contents of James's backpack the dog-eared pages of a Georges Simenon and a Patricia Highsmith hiding among a handful of physics journals. Perhaps his taste for the crime genre shouldn't have surprised her given his recent plunder of CERN's security system.

While James pored over Howard's journal entries, Sabine studied the doodles in the margins of another volume, if doodles were what you would call almost mathematically precise illustrations. Most looked to be scientists perishing in grimly apt ways: an entomologist consumed by ants, an astronaut floating in space with a cracked helmet, an astronomer burned up by a telescope pointed at the sun. It brought to Sabine's mind a morbid nursery rhyme she had learned long ago.

A is for Alice who fell down a well
B is for Bertie trapped under a bell
C is for Charles who held his own breath
D is for Dora who giggled to death

Was that how it went?

H is for Howard, irradiated in a large hadron collider

Many of the pages were stuffed with mathematics and what looked to be phases of the moon, indicating its perigee and apogee to Earth. When she showed them to James, he just sighed.

"Looks like he's tracking the moon's gravitational pull on the planet? God knows why." Gesturing to the notebook before him, he continued, "His thoughts on science and philosophy are extensive, to put it mildly. He has plenty to say on just about everything. Here I thought I had opinions about things, but this guy is brimming with *opinions* about *ideas* about *ideas* and *opinions*." He shook his head. "Just looking at these makes me want to nap."

Sabine suppressed a laugh and continued to sift through the notebooks. James produced several images of Mr. and Mrs. Anderby, some of them

Polaroids, evidently snapped by Howard in yet another retaliation against the digital. "They were professors, you said?"

She nodded. "Dad, art history. Mom, comparative literature."

"They're both dead?"

"Quite dead. Car accident."

He frowned, then pushed over several shots of Howard and his handsome friend from school. "And I'd like to know who this guy is. He's everywhere."

Sabine selected one of the pair on a small boat. On the back, it read: *Lake Carnegie*. "Maybe the aunt can identify him? I'll let you do the honors with that one tomorrow."

Sabine knew the French village where Frances Schoenberg lived well enough not to consult the GPS on her phone, and after twenty minutes of winding past expensive lakeview estates, they found themselves in a neighborhood of grand stone houses. Against a gloomy sky, the knobby skeletons of pollarded plane trees seemed to transform their surroundings into a haunted storybook. Sabine stopped in front of one especially large tree, behind which stood a hedge and a three-story mansion that had been converted into flats.

"Top floor," Sabine said, nodding toward the uppermost apartment.

James whistled. "I'm amazed a career in physics gets you the top floor of anything these days, let alone this place."

"Well, it's not lakefront. But family money helped, I should think."

After climbing two flights of hefty timber steps, they rang a bell and waited as footfalls echoed within. The door opened and a white puff of a cat slunk out. A second later, a woman appeared, the same one they had seen in a few of Howard's photographs, now with silver hair. She stooped to sweep up the cat.

"Good morning," she said from behind a pair of chunky spectacles.

Clearly, Simon's reports of Howard's aunt being some kind of mad recluse had been exaggerated. The woman in front of her looked to be in full possession of her wits, although Sabine would never have guessed her to be an engineer. With her long hair and flowing garments, she would have bet on a yoga teacher, meditation guru, or any of the vaguely spiritual jobs there were to be had nowadays. She had the kind of skin that suggested it had never seen the sun or civilization. Sabine wanted to ask what sort of moisturizer she used.

"Dr. Schoenberg? Sabine Leroux. And my colleague James Spencer."

"Come in. Call me Frances."

She threw open the large oak door and retreated into the house.

Following her into the main room, they were confronted by generous, multipaned windows overlooking the lake. The clouds must have just parted, for a beam of sunlight fell on the stone floor. The walls, which soared up to a vaulted ceiling of exposed beams, were covered in either open shelving or bare architectural sketches hanging from clips. Half the shelves were laden with oversized books, while the other half were occupied by peculiar, mechanical-looking sculptures.

"Help yourself," Frances said, waving them toward a raw wood coffee table in the center of the room, topped with a kettle and three teacups.

Sabine and James barely registered her hospitality, as each had been magnetized toward the strange sculptures, which looked like a cross between robots and windup toys. Most were no taller than a foot, made of some kind of plastic fashioned into multijoint limbs, each revolving around a fulcrum.

"*Sanftebesties*, I call them," Frances said. "Gentle beasts."

James brought his nose close to a millipede-like figure with small sails protruding from its head. "They're stunning."

"That's Frank." Frances gingerly lifted it from the shelf.

She set Frank on the floor and hit a button on the wall, prompting air to jet from a nearby vent. The air caught the sails and the millipede's legs began to churn, pulling the delicate creature across the floor.

Sabine stared, fascinated. "They're wind powered? Incredible."

"I'm thinking of making one to incorporate Howard's ashes. Sounds morbid maybe, but I think he'd like it." She set the creature back on its shelf and shut off the air. "Is tea okay? Or would you prefer coffee?"

Sabine was still staring at the creature, wondering how it could hold the ashes of a person. "Tea's fine, thank you."

Frances gestured to a sofa, then poured hot water into teacups and opened a small coffin-shaped box to reveal every variety of tea one could wish. As she settled into a pod chair opposite, an orange cat curled into her lap and began to purr.

Sabine had learned from Yvonne that Frances had not wanted to see her nephew's body. *I'm not a coroner*, she had said tersely, *so what would be the point?* This had made Sabine wonder at the woman's capacity for emotion. But now she saw Frances blink back tears and discreetly wipe at her eyes with a napkin.

"I'm very sorry about your nephew, Dr. Schoenberg. We're grateful you could meet with us."

Their host cleared her throat and said, "Still being a scientist of a kind myself, I do understand the importance of gathering evidence while the tracks are still fresh. Which is what Howard did, of course. Follow particle footprints like a bloodhound."

Sabine couldn't resist the comparison. "I've always thought of science as not so far from detective work."

Frances nodded sadly and settled back with her cat. "Physicists are the universe's sleuths, after all. What exactly would you like to know?"

James removed his hat and sat on the sofa's edge, notebook at hand.

Sabine selected a mint tea. "To start, we'd just like to get a sense of your relationship with your nephew. How close were you?"

Angling her face toward the light, as if it were the source of her recollections, Frances began, "I'm surprised as anyone about all this, of course. Howard and I were close, before we even knew each other, if that makes any sense. His mother and I were estranged for many years—I won't get into the reasons, other than to say it's your standard tale of siblings squabbling over the family estate. And so, Howard grew up without knowing me. It was only when he began to express a deep interest in science—particle physics in particular—that his mother thought it best he know me. Maybe because physics runs in our genes somehow? As some kind of passion or memory that is passed along? How else to explain his wish to work at CERN as a young child, not knowing that his own aunt would have a hand in the LHC's design? It almost makes one believe in things one cannot see or measure . . ."

She trailed off dreamily, taking a moment to sip her tea.

"So you were reunited with your sister before the car accident?"

Frances appeared unfazed that Sabine knew about the crash. "Not exactly," she said. "Felicia told me she'd meant to reach out, but it was only when she was in the hospital that I got the call. The accident was terrible luck, of course, one of those *wrong intersection, wrong time* sorts of things." She paused, as though considering an alternate chronology of events in which her sister was still alive. "She and David hung on for a week at Boston Medical in a completely grisly state. But at some point, my sister was alert enough to reach out and put Howard on the phone. He was taking time off from MIT to sit at his parents' bedsides round the clock, so he wasn't much in the mood for catching up with an estranged aunt. I said goodbye to Felicia over the phone, and two days later, she was dead, followed quickly by David. He apparently left some sort of love message for her, passed to the nurse, not knowing his wife had already died." She smiled. "Must be something to love a person that much."

Though Frances had relayed the story almost dispassionately, Sabine could sense more complicated feelings about her sister's death concealed behind her words.

As Frances topped off her guests' cups, Sabine took a moment to further examine the room. The light had been so bright upon entering that she had missed a large map hung on a wall near the windows. It was of

CERN and the surrounding area, with the rings of the LHC and its feeder tunnels superimposed upon it.

"I still dream about that machine," Frances said, following her gaze. "I was one of many engineers, of course. Yet there are elements of the design that are distinctly mine."

James leaned forward with sudden interest. "You really dream about the LHC?"

She laughed softly. "More like nightmares, mostly about my having to work through some intractable problem. It's a bit like having a dead loved one appear in a dream, only for them to pick a fight with you. Grappling with mathematics in one's REM cycles does not make for a restful slumber."

"Do you ever solve the problems?" he asked.

"If I do, I don't remember them long enough to write them down. It hardly matters anymore."

"Yvonne tells me they still very much rely on you," Sabine said, hoping to lead the conversation toward Frances's current CERN involvement.

Frances waved a dismissive hand. "Oh, I still drop in occasionally. I'm one of the few consultants with a secure line into the LHC." She nodded toward a half-open door behind them, through which a computer station was just visible. "Nikolay calls from the control room now and then with some emergency or other." She added pointedly, "Not, as it turns out, for emergencies that actually matter."

"I take it you weren't logged in that night?" Sabine asked with an eye toward the office.

Frances's response was brusque, almost hurt. "To the control room? On the night my nephew was killed?"

She couldn't help but notice that Frances hadn't answered the question. In fact, it seemed to Sabine there was something slightly guarded about her answers so far—as if she were being quite deliberate about the information she was divulging.

"Of course," Sabine continued. "We understand no one was in the control room that evening."

"So everyone says. The energy plot suggests otherwise. Nikolay suspects a malfunction, but if things like that can happen to my Machine, maybe it's time for me to bow out. My career, I'd say, is finished."

"I understand CERN is considering a new collider?"

Frances scoffed. "Four times the size. I doubt I'll be around to see it."

"Or the Chinese will beat us to it?"

She shrugged. "Well, that's the worry, and not an entirely paranoid one. Getting Western countries to wrangle the untold billions needed for the next one will be a feat. There's a growing chorus that says all funds should be directed toward saving the planet. Just funnel the cash somewhere else, right? Of course, people who suggest such things tend to think of science as a kind of monolith. As if we all hang out at the same parties." She gave a slight snort and shifted in her seat. "For the public's sake, physicists say things like 'We wouldn't have all our gadgets and current way of life were it not for particle physics, blah blah.' This may be true, but it isn't the reason scientists get up in the morning. We do what we do simply to know how the universe operates. CERN can dress that up in all the fancy language they want, but the real reason that lab over there exists is because of selfish curiosity, the aching desire to *know*. Nothing more." She sighed wistfully. "No one wanted to *know* more than Howard did."

Sabine pressed on. "Could you tell us about the last time you spoke with your nephew?"

Frances stirred some honey into her tea. "We hadn't talked for a couple of weeks, which I regret. I come from the school of giving children their space, letting them come to you. But that final time, I actually called him. It was evening and he was his usual self, excited about some project. He said he couldn't get into the particulars just yet, and I didn't press him. The call was brief, as I sensed he had plans."

"The project he couldn't get into," Sabine asked, watching her closely for a reaction, "is it one he may have been working on in the room off the hallway?"

Frances looked up, openly surprised. "Ah, you found it. I see. Well, I've been asked to stay away until the investigation is over. You'd have to tell me."

"The room was mostly empty," Sabine answered, hesitant to reveal her encounter with the intruder. "Though I was curious what the space was for."

Frances frowned, as if momentarily puzzled. "I'd always meant to fix it up as a proper study but never got around to it. The wall was open when I bought the place and I thought it would be fun to install a hidden door. I guess I've never gotten over girlhood fantasies of secret chambers. Had there been space for it, I probably would have installed a rotating bookcase." Her eyes shone with distant amusement.

"He did leave behind a few notebooks," Sabine said. "Notes on philosophy, but also quite a few photos."

Frances's eyes flitted to a stack of photographs that James had produced from his own notebook.

He slid them across the table. "We were hoping you might help us identify some of these."

Selecting a Polaroid of her nephew on a grassy quad, she smiled. "His love of everything analog. If there had been a totally impractical way to perform high-energy physics without all that computing, I imagine he'd have tried it." She chuckled to herself. "Of course, Howard was also technically brilliant. His dissertation turned out to be quite something, though not everyone recognized it."

James pushed up his glasses and consulted his notes: "'On the Investigation of Energy Loss in Proton Collisions as Evidence of Adjacent Worlds Within Our Multiverse'?"

Frances nodded proudly. "Yes. Howard's hunt for the numberless universes that exist alongside our own. It's all theory, of course, and some of his professors found his approach a bit of a stretch. But his paper grabbed the attention of Chloé Grimaud and earned him his postdoc position."

Frances sifted through the remaining images, most from Howard's MIT and Princeton days. "I won't be able to identify many of these. Friends and professors, I'm guessing. But this one . . ." She reached for the Lake Carnegie photograph, regarding it fondly. "Stuart Greenwood. Closer friends I've never seen."

"How close?" Sabine asked.

"Oh, it wasn't romantic, if that's what you're suggesting. Howard typically didn't confide in me about that sort of thing. Still, I'm fairly sure he preferred women."

"Would you know if he had been seeing anyone?"

She appeared to consider this, then shook her head. "I'm afraid our closeness revolved around other things."

"Do you know how we might get in touch with Stuart Greenwood?"

"I'm not a medium," she answered. "Stu is dead."

Sabine stared, taken aback by her bluntness. "Stuart died? When?"

"A few years ago now." She indicated the photo in her hand. "On this very lake, in fact. Howard and Stu had completed their coursework at Princeton and were just starting their dissertations. Neither of them was particularly sporty, but they both got into rowing for fun. One night, they took the boat out to celebrate, and only one of them returned."

She handed back the photo. "He didn't like talking about it. Since that night, he'd developed an intense fear of water. If he was in the city, he wouldn't even get on a ferry to come see me, but would insist on taking a complicated series of buses and trains. There are several news items about the accident online, I'm sure, though it's not the first thing you'll find in a Howard Anderby internet search."

Sabine examined the image of the pair on the lake with renewed interest. "Forgive me if this is a sensitive question, but could his friend's death be why Howard was in therapy? His health records indicate he took both antidepressant and antianxiety medications."

Frances removed her glasses and pushed at her eyes. "Howard was in therapy long before his friend died. The loss of his parents was incredibly debilitating for him. He was very different from Felicia and David, of course. They were not science people. They much preferred the slippery realms of literature and art, and yet there was a deep understanding there. Howard needed that friction, I think, between science and the arts. His parents provided that for him." She frowned, recollecting Sabine's question. "I don't mean to minimize mental illness, but it would be an abnormal talent to be as smart as Howard was and also be consistently happy. He had moments, naturally. But just look around you. Our world is an absolute nightmare and only gets worse with each passing year. It amazes me that anyone manages to do anything, let alone bother looking for elusive subatomic particles on a daily basis."

Sabine was surprised to hear this confession from a woman who so clearly relished being alive. But then, maybe it was only by creating this artistic haven in her apartment that Frances Schoenberg could bear the horror that lay outside it.

Their host stood abruptly and started in the direction of the foyer. Sabine rose to follow but hesitated in front of what looked to be an unfinished blueprint on one wall, though not of the LHC tunnel or any of its injector tunnels: These weren't circular at all, but a kind of twisting, ghostly maze.

"Is this a map?" she called out.

When Frances turned around, Sabine caught an expression that passed over her face. It was almost imperceptible, but it looked something like fear.

"It's a fanciful blueprint," she answered tepidly. "Nothing of interest."

When Frances had turned away again, Sabine swiftly took out her phone and snapped a photo. James threw her an approving grin.

On the way to the foyer, she and James lingered at a framed photograph of a much younger Frances standing in Moscow's Red Square. Judging from her puffy jacket and Dorothy Hamill hairdo, it must have been taken in the '80s.

"A happy memory," Frances said. "My career was just beginning and I found myself, much to my surprise, in demand."

"By the Russians?"

Frances gave her a coy smile. "I'd just done a stint at the Jet Propulsion Laboratory in California, and before I started at CERN, Russia tried to recruit me for their space program. They flew me over, gave me the grand tour, and not just of their scientific sites—there were museums, restaurants, tickets to the ballet every night. I told them I wasn't ultimately interested in rocket science, but they were extremely persistent. It began to feel like if they couldn't have me, then no one could. To this day, I wonder if I won't find a nerve agent at the center of my morning pain au chocolat." She laughed, but there was an edge to her laughter that said it wasn't entirely a joke.

"These days, of course, it's China you have to worry about?" Sabine asked.

Her face darkened. "I advised Howard against going there. Of course, that boy's inquisitive nature never kept him from anything."

"Just curious," Sabine ventured, keenly aware of their host's waning patience. "Did he ever discuss with you his experiences there?"

Frances tilted her head. "He rarely spoke of their collider project, only to say that he wanted to know how other countries did things. And quite honestly, how could I blame him? I may have tried the same thing at his age. I nearly did with the Russians. Of course, the maternal side of me wanted to protect him from the judgment I knew would greet him upon his return."

Sabine glanced again at the photo of bowl-haired Frances. "Do you think China might have been after him to stay there? Like the Russians were with you?"

At this, Frances's entire body seemed to sag. "Sometimes, as a scientist, you have to admit you just don't know. His memorial is this weekend. I suppose then, this will all be real."

"We'll be there," said Sabine gently.

"As part of your investigation?"

"Well, yes. Also, we feel we've come to know your nephew."

Frances regarded her doubtfully. "Really? Because no one truly knew him. Not even me."

CHAPTER 18

December 10

Now

On a crisp evening, nearly two weeks after his death, the colleagues of Dr. Howard Anderby bent into a strong headwind to make the twenty-minute walk from CERN's illuminated Globe, down the Route de Meyrin, and into the town proper. At one time, Meyrin had been little more than a village abutting the ample sheep pastures and vineyards of the region. But after CERN's construction in the 1950s, it would be forever associated with the high-tech lab dominating 550 hectares of former pastureland. Despite this, Meyrin was not a science town, and a legion of physicists on its streets would ordinarily have been an event. Tonight, however, the locals were otherwise occupied with the annual Fête de l'Escalade—a regional festival commemorating the 1602 Genevan victory over the invading Duchy of Savoy—and in their revelry, those gathered outside the cafés of the main square barely registered a disturbance. They sang, danced, and toasted each other in flamboyant seventeenth-century fashion, while their neighbors to the north somberly made their way to the town church.

Sabine arrived by rail from Geneva—having fought festival traffic all the way from her house—and as she exited the tardy tram, she scanned the landscape for a telltale spire. The Église Saint-Julien stood on the near side of the town square, next to one of those ubiquitous animated fountains devoid of both statuary and charm. The church itself was of a familiar plaster-and-stone build, as common as gas stations throughout Europe, and its medieval flavor replicated itself in the surrounding houses and shops.

Dodging a plume-hatted band playing fifes and drums, she mounted the church steps and entered the vestibule, the draft sending candles flickering. She was confronted with a general hush and the beatific smile of Howard's aunt, who stood at the glass door to the chapel greeting mourners. In her flowy black garments and a high-collared overcoat nearly cocooning her head, she looked like some kind of New Age priest.

As Sabine made her way toward Frances, she studied the art lining the vestibule, mostly Christian action figures painted in the arresting colors of medieval iconography. The fact that a not especially religious scientist—despite his apparent weakness for Wolfgang Shreft—was being honored at a Catholic church seemed to her an odd choice. Then again, maybe he had been one of those God-as-metaphor sorts of physicists. As if in answer to this, she heard Frances murmur to Weiming Wu: "What can I say? Howard was full of contradictions. He was a pushover for beauty, and he just loved churches. This is not the most beautiful church in Switzerland, true, but its proximity to the place Howard loved is what matters. The icons are quite charming, no?"

After exchanging polite greetings with Frances, Sabine passed through the door and into a warm bath of votive candles and the pulse of an organ fugue. In the glittering apse, Chloé bent over an ancient keyboard console, a martyred Christ hovering above her. It wasn't a grand organ but Sabine felt the vibration in her bones, and smiled as she recalled the music that had filled her home during Chloé's visit. Scanning the pews, she spotted James sitting apart from the crowd, in the equivalent of house-left orchestra, a hand lifted in her direction.

Sabine stopped at a basin of holy water and, out of a long-ago habit, genuflected toward the faraway crucifix. As she made her way down a side aisle, she noted the fourteen stations of the cross above, rendered in gold bas-relief along the perimeter of the nave. So taken was she with a depiction of Christ stumbling with his burden, she nearly tripped on a flagstone before claiming the aisle seat next to James.

She was pleased to see him. It was a convention of detective novels, of course, that the hero needed someone to talk to in order to give voice to his theories. But actual detectives needed a sounding board as much as any fictional invention.

He leaned in conspiratorially, extracting a manila folder from his bag. "I dug a little deeper on the friend's death," he whispered.

After their meeting with Howard's aunt, Sabine had combed the internet for articles on the fatal boating accident. As she well knew, the top results for Howard himself were mostly academic pages. Only when she searched "Stuart Greenwood," "Lake Carnegie," and "drowning" had the bleak headlines appeared, mostly from small New Jersey papers: "Lake Carnegie Boat Excursion Ends in Death of Student," "Lake Carnegie Outing Turns Deadly for PhD Candidate," and, more to the point, "Princeton Student Drowns in Lake."

As the articles reported, the two friends were out late one night after having gotten the green light on their dissertations. A celebration in the Herrontown Woods arboretum led to a spontaneous adventure on the lake, which resulted in a man overboard. Stuart's body was pulled out the next morning. Bizarrely, Howard's name never appeared in any of the articles apart from repeated references to "Greenwood's classmate." The incident was widely believed to be nothing more than a freak accident. Perhaps most remarkable was that nearly all of the lake was shallow enough to walk in, barely seven feet at its most extreme depths.

"See," James said, "I kept wondering, how does a man drown in a lake with an average depth of five feet?"

Flipping open the folder, James revealed an official report from the Mercer County medical examiner. Sabine knew that this was not public record.

"How did you get this?"

"Let's just say I have a friend back home whose digital gifts surpass mine. Official cause of death is drowning, not surprisingly, but check this out." He turned to the second page where, at the bottom, Stuart's blood content was listed. His finger drifted down the list of amphetamines, barbiturates, opiates, and alcohol, all of which were negative. He stopped on *PSILOCIN: positive.*

Sabine frowned. *"Champignons magiques?"*

He nodded. "Maybe not such a big deal, given they were celebrating. Heck, I've tried mushrooms myself and didn't end up at the bottom of a shallow lake. But then, if you pair it with this . . ."

He pointed farther down the list, where the result for MDMA read *Inconclusive.*

She clicked her tongue. "They may have been mixing, then?"

"Even if it was a small amount, the guy might've reacted poorly. I thought it was worth flagging in case either showed up on Howard's autopsy."

She shook her head. "His blood was clean. They probably would've found antidepressants had they looked, but otherwise, nothing. Psychedelic overdoses are not such a good look for Princeton. Maybe it's not so shocking the university had this buried."

James considered this. "Howard doesn't strike me as the drug-experimenting type, let alone poison-your-best-friend type. But then, nerds are capable of anything, aren't they?"

"I shall have to remember that," she said with a tight smile.

The organ fugue suddenly rose in volume and pitch as latecomers filled the pews.

Sabine tucked the folder into her bag and, turning in her seat, began to mentally check off those in attendance. Beneath the gold image of Jesus being condemned sat Yvonne and her husband, who worked as a senior official at the UN and whom Sabine had met only a few times, including at their wedding. On the far side of Yvonne were various physicists from CERN's smaller research projects, whom Sabine recognized from the contentious conference room meeting.

Beneath Christ stumbling for a second time, Pietro Moretti from the New Particles Group sat with Bella Yoshimura, rubbing her upper arm in an attempt to comfort as she pressed her eyes with a tissue. On the far side of the pair, Teo Rico and several of his theorist colleagues huddled together in discussion. Something about their expressions told Sabine that the topic was mathematics, not the deceased.

She was astonished to find, sitting below the depiction of Christ disrobing, the engineer Claude Touschard, evidently back from his mental health vacation. Except for some color in his cheeks, he showed no signs of having enjoyed an island recuperation. He sat slightly apart from the mourners, his piteous eyes repeatedly glancing at the exit. When he caught sight of Sabine, his eyes grew wide and he turned away. She had left a message with his supervisor the previous week, asking that Claude contact her immediately upon his return. In addition, she had slipped a handwritten note into the locker of his workstation: *Dear Claude, will you please come see me when you are back? The future of the LHC may depend on your generosity.* —*Sabine Leroux.* It was shamelessly manipulative, but the only leverage she had with the man was his evident love for his job. Now confronted again with his skittishness, she knew she would need to be firmer with him.

At the wall of votive candles, Eve Marsh held a lighting taper in one hand and a wad of Swiss francs in the other. She bent over the donation box, awkwardly stuffing bills inside, as if looking for any distraction from the moment at hand.

On an aisle near the back, where Christ was being affixed to the cross, Simon De Vries sat with two young colleagues from his group, looking as though he'd been led here at gunpoint. Though she was hardly pleased to see Simon, Sabine was impressed that so many of Howard's colleagues, even those who did not know him well, were in attendance.

She spotted Nikolay Levkin of the control room a couple of rows back, seated with Anna Segre of the security office. They both gave Sabine somber nods, which she returned. Niels Thorne had to be here somewhere, though she had no wish to make eye contact for fear he'd be at her side for the rest of the evening. Niels was accompanying her tomorrow to the precise location of Howard's death, security just having granted her clearance. Despite the fact that an LHC engineer would be there to escort her, Niels had managed to insinuate himself. Maybe she'd better start warming to him if she was to be stuck underground with him for half the morning.

There were several in attendance who, judging by their period dress and painted faces, looked to be Meyrin townspeople. Just as Sabine was wondering if this was a PR risk, she noticed Ms. Segre jumping up to escort them to the door. Near the back sat a handful of Swiss and French employees who worked in food and janitorial capacities at the lab. Sabine had gathered over the past twelve days that however much of a snob Howard might have been, he had always been friendly with CERN's nonphysicist staff. Besides, memorials have a way of elevating one's connection to the departed.

The organ ceased and a kind of holy silence followed. Only the distant thrum of the town's celebrations could be heard. A small balding man whom Sabine vaguely recognized shuffled down the aisle and took a seat near the front. When the lights of the apse lifted to reveal a solemn Yvonne at the pulpit, the memorial service for Howard Anderby began.

––––

Eve had never felt so queasy in her life, not even on that terrible morning when Anna Segre had interrupted the conference with her announcement. The festival drums in Meyrin's square alone had amplified her anxiety, making her want to run from the church and back to the quiet of the lab.

Earlier that evening, Chloé had slipped her a small pill and instructed her to put it under her tongue—*No need to torture yourself tonight, Eve, please*—but so far, she felt only nauseated. The nausea was her fault, as she'd been too upset to eat anything all day. Upon her arrival at the church, she had headed straight for a bank of votives and had begun setting as many dark candles as she could aflame, as if it were a birthday cake. At some point, Arnav had gently taken the lighting stick from her and steered her to a seat.

When she was very young, Eve had liked churches. She had found the Catholic ones in her city to be quiet and beautiful. That is, until she was thirteen and her view of them abruptly changed. Without explanation, Eve had been sent to stay with one of her mother's friends for several days. Were her parents splitting? Was somebody sick? It was only the day before the funeral that her mother found the strength to fetch Eve and tell her the worst thing she would ever hear in her life: that her father would not be coming home. The church service had played out before her like a horror show, one in which her own mother had been incapable of offering comfort. Now it seemed that Howard's memorial was simply a modern-day reworking of that ghoulish spectacle.

When Chloé disappeared from the organ and the eulogies began, Eve felt her pill finally kick in. A wave of numbness washed over her, which she both welcomed and resented.

She watched Yvonne rise from her seat next to her husband and proceed to the pulpit. Eve didn't process much of what Yvonne said, other than that Howard had been not only greatly admired, but loved. And that even though he hadn't been with them for long, their little plot of land would forever feel barren without him. Yvonne ended with an anecdote about Srinivasa Ramanujan, the Indian mathematician who had died before his talents had come to full flower.

High as a kite at this point, Eve said to Arnav, "She's comparing Howard to a self-taught mathematician who lived most of his life in poverty and obscurity?"

Arnav bent close to her ear. "It's a bit more nuanced than that. Also, you might want to keep your voice down."

Eve sank into the pew and waited for the next tribute.

There was a pause between speakers during which Chloé reappeared at the keyboards. Eve wondered if their group leader was going to say anything about Howard and the now empty seat in their group, or if the organ was her preferred instrument of mourning.

The music must have lulled Eve to sleep, because the next thing she knew, her head was on Arnav's shoulder, and an ethereal-looking woman whom Eve remembered having seen in the church lobby was at the front. She was describing how the physicist Richard Feynman had dealt with the death of his beloved wife while he was working at Los Alamos on the Manhattan Project.

"Richard Feynman was a brilliant scientist, no one disputes that, but as a man, he could be insufferable." A few laughs followed, mostly from the women in the room. "Yet these words from Feynman about his wife Arline ring truer for me than anything else he wrote: *You, dead, are so much better than anyone else alive.* I don't know if anyone here tonight feels that way about Howard. But I certainly do. He was my favorite person, and now he's gone. The presence of unspeakable evil is often easier to take than the absence of a loved one. Because someone *not being there* when they should be is one of the hardest things to bear." The woman's voice cracked on her final words: "And you, my dear Howard, should be here."

Suddenly realizing who the woman was, Eve straightened, hoping to get a better look, but Howard's aunt was already returning to her seat. Eve wished she hadn't fallen asleep.

Sensing her distress, Arnav whispered, "We'll find her after."

She nodded, but wondered if she was capable of having a coherent conversation with anyone.

The next speaker made Eve and Arnav turn to each other in disbelief. A little balding man climbed the steps and, after adjusting the mic to his height, grasped the podium. A murmur made its way through the church as the assembly registered a celebrity in their midst, and the pews groaned faintly as everyone sat up a little straighter or leaned forward. Teo appeared to be the only one leaning back in his seat, as if to create as much distance between himself and the contagion that was Wolfgang Shreft.

"I did not know Howard long," Shreft began, in the kind of soft voice that was confident it had everyone's attention. "But what I did know of Howard Anderby made an impression on me, and I'd like to share this impression with you." He cleared his throat and further lowered the mic. "I met him only recently, after I'd made several visits to CERN for a documentary film. I consider myself fortunate to have access to such a wonderful place. Dr. Niels Thorne, for instance, has been particularly accommodating of my whims to visit your incredible lab." Shreft peered out, as if to locate Niels, but a pigeon began flapping in the rafters above, causing him to chuckle at the interruption.

"Howard was on a quest to understand the perceived phenomena of the universe, as are all of you. But I've never met someone so devoted to the investigation, so willing to surrender his ego, and to ask difficult, perhaps even unacceptable, questions. In this way, Howard and I formed a deep friendship in a short period of time. You may be surprised to hear that it is also my quest to unlock the mysteries of life in our universe, and this stuff we perceive as matter. You and I have very different approaches, but I would ask: Is the goal not the same?" The pigeon flapped again, punctuating the question.

"Some of those closest to him know that Howard was a great admirer of Eastern religious and philosophical texts, which he hoped might shine a sliver of light onto the darker corners of your discipline. Of course, he would not be the first physicist to dip his toe into the vast pool of philosophical thought that lay outside the bounds of modern science. Many of your best twentieth-century physicists were admirers of Buddhist and Vedic concepts, if indirectly. Albert Einstein, for one, read widely of Western thinkers who borrowed from the East. Einstein is said to have been inspired by the notion of a single substance or set of rules governing the whole of reality, which may have led to his radical ideas on space-time and the nature of light. He even admitted that he might not have created the special theory of relativity without his philosophical studies. Howard, I sensed, endeavored to do the same: to arrive at a new and daring discovery of the physical world by unorthodox means. Would he have succeeded had he lived?" Shreft let the question hover in the air for a moment. "We can never know that. However . . ."

As he paused, the incongruous melody of a fife drifted in from the square.

"However, I hope we might take some comfort," he continued, "in one of your physical laws that says energy can be neither created nor destroyed. If we extend this to everything, it means that in a way we, too, are neither created nor destroyed. It means that our essential selves—the beings at our core that cannot be broken into smaller pieces—are eternal. You, me, Howard, all of us are indestructible."

There was something in Eve that rebelled against the very idea of Wolfgang Shreft being here. But there was another part of her, the smaller, tender animal part—and not the part that was under the strong influence of a benzodiazepine—that found the idea of Howard existing somewhere, even if it was in a state of "raw energy," or whatever the so-called soul was made up of, comforting. She resisted the temptation to look at Teo, who by now had likely worked himself into a lather.

Shreft let out a small sigh before concluding, "I know I am an unlikely person to be delivering this message to an assembled group of empiricists, but I hope that whatever your beliefs, this idea might be of some solace to those of you who knew and loved him." He gave an almost imperceptible bow, and as he started back toward his seat, something strange happened. A man in the back pews suddenly yelped in surprise.

The entire congregation turned at once toward the back of the church, their attention narrowing to a young man seated next to Simon De Vries, whom Eve recognized as one of his grad students. The man stared dumb-struck at his phone, eyes round. With a trembling hand, he passed the phone to Simon, who in turn gaped at the screen and immediately rushed down the aisle out of the church. The student hurried after him. And then, like the ripple of a tossed stone on the surface of a pond, the disruption moved steadily outward, increasing as it went.

Eve suddenly wished she were not high, for she desperately wanted to make sense of what was happening. She turned to Arnav, whose face had registered some kind of understanding. He took out his phone and sifted through the apps until he found the one labeled LUXT, and opened it.

He held the screen inches from his face before clasping his mouth.

Eve could think of only one thing it could be: the particle odometer. She never imagined they'd find dark matter in her lifetime. Being alive for the Higgs had almost been enough. Her heart began to pound with the thrill of impending discovery, even if it was not her own.

"They found it?" she whispered.

Arnav just looked at her in a kind of distant amazement. No, horror. He turned the screen around so she could see the live image of the tank. The counter read *9,999,999*. She blinked at the number, wondering if it was even possible to detect that many dark matter particles.

She then brought her attention to the camera feed itself. Somewhere in the thousands of gallons of water, backlit by high-pressure bulbs, she could make out something alien. It wasn't the smaller tank of xenon, but something nearly as substantial suspended in the water just to the left of it: a large, bloated, irregular mass. Even on the small screen, the shape was unmistakable. It was the static hulk of a floating body.

PART 2

Neither from itself nor from another, nor from both, nor without a cause, does anything whatever, anywhere arise.

—Nāgārjuna,
The Fundamental Wisdom of the Middle Way

CHAPTER 19

December 11

Now

The cave was an ungodly temperature. Though she was outfitted in gear suitable for a polar expedition, Sabine had never been so cold in all her life. But then, apart from it being the middle of the night, she had never felt so far from the sun: 1,500 meters below the Earth's surface to be exact, deeper than the LHC tunnel, and far more of an endurance test than she was prepared for. Subterranean heaters had been installed to allow for technicians to comfortably service the tank—but these, she was told, were partly inoperable. In addition, the overhead lamps in the concrete passage were out, which meant they had to bring their own light.

Heading up their party of six was Simon De Vries, who, as director of the LUXT project, insisted he be on the scene. He held a lantern out before him like a scout in an adventure story, though his considerable size, bulked up with winter clothing, nearly blotted out the light. Behind him, three CERN security officers—strong Frenchmen knowledgeable in the peculiarities of scientific equipment—hauled knapsacks equipped with the various tools needed for the task ahead. Last, walking in front of Sabine, was an agent from Interpol, a compact Swiss German in his midthirties named Ulrich Brod, who said little and whose watchfulness made Sabine's jaw clench. His smart black GORE-TEX snowsuit, with IN-TERPOL emblazoned across the back, seemed to positively sneer at Sabine's puffy ski costume, which, with its bright colors and fur trim, made her feel as if she were on a mountain holiday in the 1980s.

Given that CERN was largely a self-governing territory on the border of two countries, she had thought it possible to keep law enforcement, or the Swiss Police, anyway, out of the Anderby investigation for a while longer. Or, at least, until the news hit the press about an American's death and the US got involved. Of course, the live and very public feed of the LUXT tank had guaranteed that the International Police would arrive at the lab, though she hadn't imagined it would be so swiftly.

She trudged on through the murk, aware of a growing impulse within her to run back up the corridor and into the freight elevator that had ferried them down into this cold hell. Having flipped through one of Howard's many Moleskines the previous evening, Sabine now tried to recall some Schopenhauerian morsel that might put her current discomfort into perspective. Through the lens of Howard's mind, she had found the metaphysics of the dour German strangely pacifying. Naturally, Schopenhauer had much to say in the "all life is suffering" vein, ideas he'd borrowed heavily from the East. But among Howard's scribblings were echoes of what Bella Yoshimura had expressed about Schopenhauer's theoretical *Will*, a vast foundational underpinning to everything we experience in the world. Howard's many cross-references to the philosopher Immanuel Kant suggested that Schopenhauer had taken the Enlightenment thinker's ideas on the nature of reality and had run with them, concluding that there is only one *true thing* in existence—the Will—and that human beings had access to it through contemplation. After Sabine had perused a few essays from Howard's *The World as Will* paperback, what struck her most was Schopenhauer's strangely familiar assertion that the spatial-temporal world we live in—and everything supposedly solid that populates it—is not real in the way we think of as reality. Our world is instead a convincing illusion projected by the Will and made apparently dimensional by our mental processes. Hadn't quantum physicists been circling a similar idea for the past century? The notion that life, the universe, all of it, was one giant magic show? One that needed an audience in order to exist at all?

And yet the claustrophobia bearing down on Sabine felt not at all illusory. Just when she was certain she couldn't take the frigid confinement any longer, or the popping in her ears from the change in air pressure, a bright light appeared before them. After a few more steps, the cave ceiling rose and the tank loomed into view. She had seen the live feed, but nothing prepared her for the thing itself. Her first impression of the LUXT was of a spaceship—one that, instead of rocketing upward, might burrow to the center of the Earth. It was a massive cylindrical monster, its silver exterior illuminated by vertical banks of lights installed on the cavern walls. It soared thirty meters above them, with hydraulic lifts attached to the tank on two sides, providing access to the top and, presumably, to the water. Once the spaceship image had subsided and Sabine considered the sheer pressure of the liquid within, it was difficult not to fear the thing bursting. A nightmare briefly played out before her in which the tank surrendered its contents, sending walls of water into the cave's byways, leaving their party snatching at air pockets. She imagined telling herself just before she lost consciousness: *The water in my lungs is not real; it is merely a representational projection of the Will.*

From his place at a control panel along one wall, Simon shouted, "The top has been left open."

Agent Brod turned to him. "Is this surprising?"

"Not really," Simon admitted. "He wouldn't have exactly closed the tank after himself."

By now, they were all fairly confident it was a man.

Sabine shivered as she watched the three officers climb onto the hydraulic lift platforms and begin their ascent up the sides of the tank. As the lifts whirred above them, Simon explained that the tank was heated, the water inside needing to remain a certain temperature to serve as a buffer to whatever cosmic rays managed to penetrate the cave walls. Sabine inched closer to the tank, imagining she could feel some of its heat. Nearing the side that had been visible on the app, she spotted a mechanical eyeball mounted near the control panel. When she turned to take in the camera's view, she was faced with the same window that had appeared on the app: a large glass cutout with curved edges, almost like a porthole, its bottom edge several meters from the ground. Behind the thick glass, she could make out the water within. As her eyes adjusted, the oblong silhouette of the inner xenon container came into focus—and floating next to it, a human body. It was impossible to see any significant details about the corpse, other than the unmistakable outline of a partly unbuttoned shirt, flying out from the victim like a cape.

She'd seen drowned bodies before, but never from this vantage point, as if she herself were one of the shipwrecked, frantically calculating the distance to the water's surface. She started to back away from the window when she nearly tripped over Agent Brod, who stood behind her snapping photographs with an intimidatingly complex camera. She made an apology and stepped out of his way.

Everyone felt quite certain whose body was in the tank. After the discovery on the app, it didn't take long for Sabine to pinpoint the most likely candidate. Niels Thorne, who had been employed on the xenon project, had been both absent at Howard's memorial and unreachable on his mobile afterward. When she began to make immediate inquiries, none of his colleagues could remember having seen him all day. His mobile provider could locate no signal from his phone, which meant it had been either out of range, deliberately switched off, or no longer operable. That same night, Yvonne had contacted Niels's parents in Canada to ask if they'd heard from him. They hadn't. Evidently Sabine's first impression of Niels as a banker hadn't been too far off the mark, as his entire family were

170

financial muckety-mucks of some kind in Toronto. Given the worldwide visibility of the LUXT app, it didn't take more than a few hours for Interpol to knock on the lab's front door. Now, at three in the morning, here they were on a macabre fishing expedition.

Although the tank was being drained of water via a pipe that fed into the cave wall, the complicated process would take a few days. As the officers reached the top of the tank, they began shouting at one another. One of them called down, "It's quite dangerous up here with the top open. Somebody could easily fall in."

"You'll be careful, then," Simon shouted back before turning to the Interpol agent. "Do you know how idiotically expensive it is to sterilize a tank of this size and refill it with ultrapure water?"

"I don't," Agent Brod answered, continuing to find new angles on the colossal instrument. "You know what I do know? How devastated this man's poor family is going to be."

Sabine looked down to hide a small smile.

"Hey," Simon snapped back, "Niels was a colleague and friend. We certainly don't need Interpol coming in here and doing an empathy dance for us."

The agent held his gaze. "However you felt about your colleague, Dr. De Vries, the fact is, it's going to be some time before your experiment resumes. This is a crime scene now."

Simon just stood there, his face probably flushed with rage, though Sabine couldn't bear to look at it any longer.

Pointing to the window, the agent continued in his thick German accent, "You are sure this body is belonging to Dr. Thorne?"

Sabine couldn't help note the strange construction of his sentence and the supposition that a body belonged to someone outside that body.

When Simon didn't respond, she stepped forward. "Apart from the lack of a signal from his phone, security has confirmed that Dr. Thorne was the last to swipe his badge at the cavern entrance."

"No one is supposed to wander down here without a colleague present," Simon explained. "Niels knew the rules."

She suddenly recalled Niels telling her on their walk to the control room how he liked to come down here just to marvel at the tank. She had thought nothing of his comment at the time but now wondered how often Niels visited the cave alone to simply watch the space where he hoped dark matter would appear. Studying the window now, she couldn't exactly see how this would endanger his life.

She turned to Simon. "Is there only one window?"

He nodded toward the top of the tank. "There's a second on the viewing deck."

"Viewing deck?" She followed his gaze up to where the security officers now stood. "For what purpose? It's not on the app."

He stared at her as if the answer were obvious. "It was for our purposes. To get a visual on the mechanism from above."

"Don't you have a digital representation of what's going on inside without needing actual windows?"

Simon drew himself up a little taller. "One of the windows was for the app, but the one on the viewing deck was purely for our enjoyment. I spent a decade building the thing, and sometimes you want to see its inner workings."

"Did Niels Thorne enjoy seeing the inner workings?" Brod inquired.

Sabine thought of answering this in the affirmative, but Simon did this for her. "After we brought him on, he often came down here to admire the tank."

"Without a colleague present?" Brod pressed.

"Well, obviously," he said, motioning toward the floating body.

"You knew this and didn't speak to him? It's your project, no?"

Simon stared at Brod as if he were an idiot. "Well, I hardly thought he was going to take a dip, did I?"

Agent Brod frowned at the window. "Any reason to think he did this on purpose?"

"Like the guy in the tunnel, you mean?"

By now Interpol knew about Howard. Yvonne had hardly seen a point in hiding it anymore. But Agent Brod appeared only dimly interested in the suicide angle.

"It is highly unlikely, isn't it?" Brod wondered. "Two unrelated suicides in as many weeks?"

There was a look on the agent's face that told Sabine he fully grasped the absurdity of these deaths. As tragic as it all was, this second body had cast the first in an almost comic light, as if they were all staring down a sequence of physics-themed "accidents." Physics as serial killer. *It'd be a real shame if someone were to be found chopped up by a black hole*, the wry fictional detective in her head quipped. *Murder by event horizon. What next? Death by electron gun? Was the victim killed by a particle or a wave? Ha-ha.* And suddenly she had to beat back the part of her that wanted to hand over the entire case to Interpol and go peck away at a cozy mystery series.

Sabine moved away from the window and reached her hand out for the tank's exterior, which was covered in a reflective foil. It was warm to the touch.

One of the officers shouted something in French from the platform above. He had just pulled his gloved hand from one of their nets and was grasping a frighteningly long, stringy object. As the officer began to bring it down on the lift, Simon craned his stiff neck to stare up at the dark, hairlike snarl, as if contemplating an unlikely Rapunzel. When the officer reached the ground, Simon backed away.

"What the hell is that?"

Registering his repulsion, the officer extended the wet thing to Sabine.

She slapped on an antiseptic glove, pulled out a plastic evidence bag, and gingerly accepted the object. It clearly wasn't actual hair or even anything human, but the dripping thing made her want to double over. She knew this was irrational, and yet she recalled a similar physical response from her early days with the Swiss Police, when the torso of an unidentified male had been found in the woods north of Geneva. Apart from that case, which had never been solved, there was something singularly terrifying about a body part found out of context. Without teeth or clothing to identify it as a person, it was just a hunk of anonymous flesh, like meat hanging at the butcher's.

She forced herself to examine the dark mass and noticed what looked to be faded lines running through it. When she held up one stringy end for inspection, she saw the remains of woolen fringe and a partially corroded tag.

"It's a scarf," she called out. "Though it looks bizarrely torn up for having been sitting in water."

Simon strode over but stopped short of touching it. "Ultrapure demineralized water, when exposed to air, is quite corrosive. Acidic, actually. Over time it eats metal and hair."

She cast a worried glance at the officers on the deck. "What about skin?"

"They'll be fine," he assured her. "But let's just say it's good we're fishing the body out now."

Agent Brod approached, slapping on a pair of gloves. "If you don't mind." Sabine handed over the scarf.

He squinted at the barely legible tag. "Wild vicuña?"

"A kind of llama, I think. Softer than cashmere."

He raised a brow and bagged the thing. "Must be nice."

One of the French officers shouted down again. "There is something wrong with the platform."

"What do you mean?" Simon called back.

"Farther in, it looks like one of the grates supporting the platform is broken," the officer said. "More than one bolt is missing."

"Impossible," Simon hollered. "I just built the thing."

The officer gestured emphatically to the tank. "I'm just telling you what I see. It's extremely unsafe. Maybe this was how he fell in?"

Sabine, Simon, and the Interpol agent grew silent as they digested this new piece of information.

N is for Niels who fell into a large underground xenon tank . . .

The three stood there for a long time as the men continued to dredge the water. It was an arduous process; one officer had to lower the net to the bottom while the other two tried to fish the opposite end out with hooked poles. After nearly an hour, the men began to shout.

"We've got him," said the officer who had found the scarf.

"He's heavy," said another. "Might take a while to get him out."

Simon sighed, pulled out his phone, and started to dial. Then, remembering he was standing in a cave with zero reception, he returned it to his pocket and said, "Let's get on with it, then."

CHAPTER 20

September 23

Before

Beer O'Clock was eerily subdued. After the LUXT party the previous night, coupled with news from Chloé that day about a data leak, it seemed the lab didn't know whether it should be hung over or depressed. Observing Simon's group huddled conspiratorially, nursing beers and eschewing the Ping-Pong tables, Eve wondered if news of the data breach had somehow circulated beyond their own work group. Or maybe it was just that everyone had had quite enough of merrymaking.

The only ones present who did not look gloomy were the theorists. At the far end of the R1 patio, Teo Rico and his cohort had begun playing a math-based game on a whiteboard, which may as well have been beer pong for all the ruckus they were making. Eve was surprised to find Niels watching the game from a swivel chair a short distance away, staring pensively at the theorists, yet somehow past them. Given that, not two hours before, he had taken her group's laptops, Eve was amazed he'd shown up at all. When a cluster of grad students suddenly arrived to surround Niels—several of whom Eve recognized from his acting troupe—his face transformed from one of somber reflection to forced mirth.

Meanwhile, the New Particles Group—minus Howard and Chloé—were sitting on the grass in the shade of a fir tree, draining a second round of lagers. For the past hour, Eve, Arnav, Weiming, Bella, Pietro, and Kennet had been struggling to make sense of the rumored data theft and their boss's rather frightening shift in mood, mostly by cracking jokes to defuse the tension.

"Don't look at me," Weiming said. "I'm Taiwanese."

"No one's looking at you, Weiming," Bella said. "And if you go around protesting too much, people will talk."

"At least I show up to our meetings on time," he countered.

Bella shrugged. "The way Chloé was acting, I'm kind of glad I missed it. Anyway, I didn't escape Niels. He was on me like a . . ." She searched the air for an appropriate simile.

Eve offered an image from the night before: "Like reflective foil on a xenon tank?"

Bella raised her glass. "Nice."

Pietro, meanwhile, had taken out his guitar and was gently strumming. He subtly turned to Bella, as though his music was only for her. "Who do you suppose is rifling through our computers anyway?"

Bella nodded toward the far side of the patio. "Don't everyone look over at once, but it can't be Niels himself."

Arnav squinted at Niels and his groupies, as if the scene hurt his eyes. "God, he thinks he's a celebrity." He took a long drink. "Whoever's combing our laptops, I just hope they don't find the nude photos of my fiancée."

Weiming gaped at him. "You left naked photos on your work computer?"

"God no, I'm not a moron."

Weiming began to laugh uncontrollably, the alcohol clearly going to his head. "But you just said you did, you just said—" He stopped to wipe tears from his eyes.

"Arnav always means the opposite of what he says," Bella explained kindly.

"You know," Kennet broke in, "British irony is really just Scandinavian irony, an import from the Norman invasion."

Arnav looked skeptical. "That can't be true."

"Oh, it is. Before 1066, you were all just a bunch of earnest bastards. Couldn't be amusing to save your lives."

Arnav had begun to correct Kennet that his ancestors had actually been in Asia at the time, perfecting a Bengali form of sarcasm, when Eve noticed Howard halfway across the lawn. He had just stepped up to the beer table to help himself, looking intently at the tap as he poured. Turning from the keg, he caught Eve's eye and held up his glass in a mock toast.

Pietro shook his head in Howard's direction.

"What?" asked Eve.

"Just wondering when he's going to feel comfortable hanging out with us, is all. He can't be the new guy forever."

"Howard!" Bella shouted. "Get over here!" But he showed no sign of hearing her.

Pietro turned back to his guitar and began to pick out a Simon & Garfunkel tune, mangling the lyrics in the process: "*I do not care for friendship . . . friendship is not my friend . . .*"

"Stop that," Eve said, not taking her eyes from Howard.

He was now at the Ping-Pong table, selecting a paddle and ball from the basket. No one actually played real table tennis at the lab, but instead a variation dubbed "particle tennis," which really was just Ping-Pong with physics trivia tossed in, the goal being to collect as many "particles," or balls, as possible. Howard waved his paddle at Eve in silent invitation. She turned to make sure he wasn't in fact looking at someone else, like Bella. But Bella had joined Pietro in a duet.

Eve stood and started across the grass, but a hissing in her ear made her whirl around. Arnav was at her elbow.

"Hey, where did you go last night?"

"Who wants to know?"

"I saw you follow the weirdo out of the warehouse, never to return."

She had no intention of telling him about her and Howard's movements the previous night, mostly because there was nothing to tell.

"Anyway, I was worried," he said. "With all this talk of data breaches, odd behavior kind of sticks out."

Eve folded her arms. "You think Howard and I went to siphon data off ATLAS while everyone was getting drunk?"

She could see that he knew how ridiculous this sounded.

"If you want to know the truth," she continued, "I didn't care to hear Simon going on about how important he is. I'm amazed you of all people stuck around."

He blinked at her, incredulous. "You're an awful liar."

"Excuse me," she said, turning away. "I'm going to play particle tennis with the weirdo."

Howard was waiting patiently, paddle in one hand and a ball labeled *Up Quark* in the other. The two smiled shyly at each other.

Eve wondered if she should make reference to last night, but she was somehow unable to find the words. She grabbed a paddle. "You should know, beyond two beers, I'm terrible at this game."

He served the up quark with a question: "Murray Gell-Mann took the name *quark* from which work of literature?" *Thwack.*

"*Finnegans Wake.* James Joyce." *Thwack.* "Now quote the passage in which the word appears."

Howard recited with ease the rhyme involving a few quarks for a certain *Muster Mark*. He continued on to the next verse before stopping himself. "Sorry, am I showing off?"

"Is that your next question?"

She sliced at the air but missed the ball. Turning to pick it up, she found Arnav standing there.

"Save me, please." He jerked his head toward their gathering, which

Niels and his grad student posse had just crashed. Evidently having to be friendly with Niels was worse than tolerating Howard.

"Your hatred for that guy is starting to border on obsession, you know. It's embarrassing."

Arnav looked genuinely flustered. "Oh, *I'm* the obsessive?" he whispered. "What about your monster crush that is bleedingly obvious to everyone?"

She thrust the paddle at him. "Your turn."

Arnav stepped to the table just as Howard readied his serve.

"Which dead physicist would you most like to get pissed with?" Howard asked as he sent a graviton flying.

"That's your question?" *Thwack.*

Howard nodded. *Thwack.*

"Has to be Albert, I guess. Though a pre-relativity Albert." *Thwack.*

"Why pre?" *Thwack.*

"Just so I could scribble $E = mc^2$ on a napkin, slide it across the bar . . ." *Thwack.* ". . . and watch his face."

Howard grinned at this, just managing to return the graviton.

Arnav flicked it back. "Serious question: Did you know our laptops would be taken today, and therefore intentionally skipped the meeting?"

"Niels waylaid me in the middle of Higgs Field and forcibly relieved me of my entire bag. Does that answer your question?"

As the graviton bounced past Arnav, he laughed with what seemed to be genuine amusement.

"Did he really?"

"Lucky for me, there's little of value on my laptop."

Arnav picked up the ball and tossed it to Howard. "What an odd thing to admit. There's your work, surely."

Howard pocketed the graviton and plucked a photon from the basket. "I keep the stuff I actually care about elsewhere. Don't you two have work outside the lab?"

Thwack.

Arnav snorted. "Call me boring, but no. Eve?"

Thwack.

Deciding against outing her side passion for disaster science, she said, "Do I practice freelance physics in my off-hours? Unfortunately, I don't have my own proton collider."

Abashed, Howard let the photon fall to the ground. "I'm not saying it has to be the new relativity papers or anything. Pet projects, is all."

Eve thought about last night, about Howard's escape to the Chateau. Had that been for one of his pet projects?

Arnav put an aggressive spin on his next serve, a muon. "Do you think it's true about the data leak?"

Howard hit back with a forceful backhand. "Yes."

"How can you know?"

"It doesn't go beyond this table, but . . ." Howard popped the muon across the net. "Who do you think alerted CERN to the breach?"

Arnav let the ball bounce to the ground and, with Eve, stood staring at him.

Howard smiled. "I'm not saying I approve of how Yvonne and Chloé are handling it, which is apparently to make everyone panic."

Arnav groaned. "What did I tell you about China, Eve?"

"Is it really China?"

Howard selected a gluon. "What do you think I was doing over there that whole time? Did you imagine I'd defected?" *Thwack.*

Arnav lunged at the ball. "You must know that's the rumor."

Howard kept the play going. "All this sneaking around, stealing information, is counterproductive. We should be sharing everything. Humanity is supposed to be in this together."

"That's heartwarming, Howard, truly. But you're saying that while you were in China, you uncovered a mole at CERN?"

"Yes, Howard, is there a mole in the Circus?" Eve echoed.

"That's not what I'm saying. I found evidence of an ATLAS data leak, which is not the same thing. The Chinese lab appears to be in possession of data that they shouldn't have. This is to say nothing of their tactics in trying to recruit me beyond my consultant position—these things combined gave me pause."

"So they did try to flip you as a spy?"

"They're cleverer than that."

Arnav let the gluon sail past him. "Okay, time-out. Who else knows this?"

They both stared at Howard.

"I informed Yvonne, who in turn told Chloé and Niels. And now, there's you two. Is that weird?"

"A little," Eve stuttered. "Why us?"

"Because I trust you."

Arnav retrieved the ball. "Look, mate, we all had lunch in town a while back. That doesn't make us confidants."

Howard's face fell with what looked to be honest dismay. "That may be true, but I don't see why we can't all be friends."

It was the last thing Eve would have expected him to say, something so vulnerable and childlike.

Arnav's face betrayed something equally vulnerable: shame mingled with a kind of emotional thaw. He tossed the gluon back to Howard. "I forfeit. The news of the day calls for another pint, no?"

He left Eve with the paddle and went to the beer table. She picked another ball from the basket, a strange quark, but couldn't concentrate enough to serve.

"Last night—" she blurted out. "I followed you to the Chateau."

"Did you?" Howard looked pleased at this.

"I don't understand how you even have access to that place."

"If we agreed to meet there, maybe I could show you."

She felt her face warm at the invitation. "Did you want me to follow you?"

He smiled. "I wasn't opposed to the idea."

A moment later, Arnav reappeared with the beers. They put down their paddles, toasted each other, and much to the surprise of all three, were inseparable for the rest of the evening. Through an increasing state of inebriation, they played a few more rounds of particle tennis, briefly crashed the theorists' math game, and then, realizing they were quite tipsy, decided to put something solid into their stomachs.

Arnav had the brilliant idea of raiding the top-floor kitchen of Building 40. On Fridays, snacks were restocked and the cupboards filled to bursting with the best Swiss chocolate and biscuits. According to Arnav, this particular kitchen had uncommonly good tea, with a spectrum of builder's and upmarket English brands. When they found an unopened package of Jaffa Cakes, he practically danced for joy.

"This is shaking up to be a proper party."

After arranging snacks and setting tea to steep, they assembled some abandoned office furniture into a makeshift tearoom on the grass behind the Shiva statue, complete with a multitiered cake stand made from letter trays. Then, pinkies in the air, they drank Earl Grey from paper cups and munched through several sleeves of chocolate-covered and jelly-filled treats.

"We're going to get fired, you know," Eve said, laughing.

Arnav tilted back in his creaky chair and looked up at the emerging star cover. "If they fire us, Howard will get us jobs in China. Won't you, Howard?"

Between biscuit crunches, he replied, "It's not as if the Chinese lab doesn't keep tabs on all our published work. I wouldn't be surprised if they recruited you without my help."

"Really? They have headhunters?"

Howard gave him a patient smile. "It's an arms race, Arnav."

Eve and Arnav shot each other a discreet look, as if neither could believe they were getting Howard to divulge quite so much about China.

When Eve leaned toward Howard, she wasn't sure if it was to ask a question or to just be a few inches closer to him. But she found herself saying, "Why did you go there in the first place, again? I missed that part."

Howard took a swallow of tea as he frowned in the direction of Shiva's silhouette against the ever-darkening sky. "Because they invited me. And because I feared that once I came to CERN, I would never leave. I wanted an experience away from the West."

"Oh, is that all?" Arnav said dismissively. "Please tell me they have nicer digs than this at least."

Howard appeared to consider this. "Everything over there is shiny, all glass and light. There's more money for the sciences and less political maneuvering required to get it. In some ways, it's preferable."

"Sounds dreamy," Arnav sighed. "This whole hat-in-hand, *Oh please kind minister sir* routine every time we need repairs is getting old, frankly."

"I don't mind our little plot of land," Eve said, staring toward their motley laboratory. "Old buildings don't bother me."

Arnav pretended to spit out his tea. "Oh, come on, if it were the Cambridge campus plonked down in the middle of Switzerland, you wouldn't hear me complain. But this?"

Howard leaned back to take in the faint stars. "You know, I grew up among old, ivied buildings. It doesn't mean the people in them weren't completely miserable."

"And I, sir, grew up in a London council house. I can guarantee you we were miserable."

Howard laughed.

Hooking into this personal tidbit of Howard's, Eve subtly moved her chair closer. "Were you miserable? In your beautiful ivied buildings?"

They were now so close that his eyes went slightly cross-eyed as he focused on her face. "Oh, not me specifically," he said.

But there was an emotion in his voice that sent a shiver through her, a shiver at the promise of further shared confidences. Arnav, meanwhile, had looked away, as though embarrassed. She suddenly wished he were not there.

Howard opened his mouth to say something else but was interrupted by the distinct crunch of leaves coming from the woods. They all turned, but the crunching stopped, as if someone were trying to avoid detection.

"An animal?" Eve whispered.

Howard tilted his head, listening as the sound started and stopped again. "A pretty big animal."

They strained their eyes toward the trees.

Arnav suddenly bolted upright and checked his phone. "Good lord. How is it nearly midnight? We should call it."

Eve was reluctant to move, but she forced herself to stand as they began to gradually stack the tea things. They were about to head back to Building 40 when the crunching footsteps returned. Without warning, Arnav set down his armful of biscuits and made a bold dash for the woods, the sound of his steps receding among the dark trees.

Peering after him, Eve and Howard laughed at the abruptness of his departure. They stood watchful for a while, but with the lack of moonlight couldn't make out much. When he didn't return, they gathered up the dishes and furniture, and took them inside. Fifteen minutes later, Arnav still had not reappeared. Howard stared, puzzled, in the direction of the woods. "Where would he have gone?"

Eve was about to suggest the Chateau, if only to gauge Howard's reaction. But at that moment, her phone buzzed: *Didn't see any spies, so I went home. Sorry to make you guys clean up.*

She showed the message to Howard, who looked relieved. "I like Arnav," he said, "but, frankly, I've been waiting all night to be rid of him."

Eve was so pleased by this, she didn't know what to say.

The two left the lab together for the tram station. On the ride across the border, they sat close but quiet, suddenly shy now that Arnav was gone. But twenty minutes later, as they emerged from the tram and into the cool night, they began to say everything they had wanted to that evening but had felt they couldn't. It came tumbling out, as if they were running out of time. On the walk from the Prévessin station to Eve's apartment, Howard told her how his parents had died one Boston winter a decade ago. He relayed the story in such a strange, almost impartial way that Eve suspected the feelings behind it to be so overwhelming that, if he gave in to them, he wouldn't be able to tell it at all.

"They were coming home from a chamber music concert, crossing an intersection," he said. "Somebody in a pickup ran a red light. He wasn't drunk or anything, just not paying attention. The guy tried to brake, but the roads were icy and he plowed right into them."

Eve quietly took his hand as he continued.

"Funny thing is, they almost didn't go to the concert. My mother bought the tickets by mistake thinking it was Schubert, when it was really Schumann, which my father didn't care for. But in the end, she talked him into it. *Who doesn't like Schumann?* she said. My parents were so young, barely fifty, and I kept thinking of how both those composers also died horribly young." He laughed sadly. "One of the final things my dad said to me was *I used to think Schumann was so sentimental, but your mother is right—what's wrong with sentiment?*"

When Howard turned the subject to her own parents, Eve hesitated at the thought of emptying her emotional cupboards all at once. She wondered if she should save the story of her father for some other intimate evening, but quite suddenly tears were spilling down her face and it all came out. It was as if she were telling it for the first time.

"He was more supportive of my interest in science than anyone," she said, "but if I could give up my position here . . . if it meant he hadn't died that day, I would throw it all away in an instant."

He clutched her hand. "I know you would. I would work in a coal pit for the rest of my life if only they had arrived at that intersection seconds later."

When they reached her apartment, they stopped outside the door to her building and looked at each other for a long moment, as if both making future calculations.

"What if . . . ," he said, hesitating. "What if we could bring them back? What if there were a way?"

She looked at him quizzically but saw only sincerity in his face.

"I mean, what if there were a way you could have your dad back and I could have my parents?"

At a loss how to respond, she opted for nervous laughter. "Well, this is the land of Frankenstein."

"That's not what I meant."

"Oh, good. Because I don't know if I have the stomach for reanimation."

When a pained expression came over him, she regretted her crassness. "Do you mean like that painting at the museum?" she asked, the image suddenly coming to her. "Where there were doubles of everything, but each slightly different. A version where John the Baptist was beheaded, and one where he wasn't. *Like two worlds lying side by side.*"

His eyes crinkled in amusement at the phrase. "Something like that."

"So how do we get to the other world?"

"Well, that's the question, isn't it?" He smiled, but no longer seemed to be in the mood for speculation. "Good night, Eve."

He turned, and just as he took his hand out of his pocket to give her a final wave, one of the Ping-Pong balls fell to the ground.

She laughed. "Do you steal all the particles you've won?"

In a single movement he picked it up and tossed it to her. "Just this one. I'm sentimental."

She caught it. It was the up quark. She slipped it into her pocket.

As Eve watched Howard head down the block toward the station, she closed her hand around the ball. It was still warm from the heat of his coat.

CHAPTER 21

December 13

Now

Sabine followed a cluster of exposed ceiling pipes through a warren of hallways until she reached Yvonne's unassuming office door. With its wide-angle shot of the LHC tunnel tacked to the wood and various science-themed cartoons pasted around it, she might have been rapping on a geeky college student's dormitory.

After a clipped *"Entrez,"* she stepped inside to find Yvonne at her desk computer, reading glasses perched on her nose. In one of two free chairs on the near side of the desk sat Chloé. When they both turned to Sabine, gently beaming, she was hit by a sense of familiarity so profound, she was convinced for several seconds that she'd already been here. Except Sabine had never seen Yvonne's office. All their meetings thus far had taken place in the security building.

Settling into the empty chair, Sabine looked back at her friends for a speechless moment. They both had that dazed, war-weary look about them—excavated eyes, drooping mouths—which had progressively worsened over the past two weeks. Yet Sabine was pervaded with a companionable warmth that made her temporarily forget that this was a serious meeting about the case. She couldn't remember the last time the three of them had been alone. Yvonne and Chloé were always making promises to Sabine to *meet up* and *do something fun, just the three of us*—and in the day-to-day turmoil of their lives, these promises mostly went unmet. She envied her friends' continued closeness, even if it was mostly professional proximity. But here they were, not rushing to squeeze in a quick coffee date, with one of them inevitably canceling, but just sitting together in a room. For three women with no children, how extraordinarily difficult they managed to make the simple task of being together. But now, they might well have been back in the Paris dorms, drinking cheap wine and attempting to vent cigarette smoke out of louvered windows.

Chloé whispered conspiratorially, "I think time just collapsed."

Sabine laughed. "Or ate its own tail."

"Seriously," Yvonne sighed. "Who has the cigarettes?"

"Classy joint, by the way," Sabine said, glancing around, which drew an amused snort from Yvonne.

Sabine thought Yvonne's office resembled more the workplace of a struggling travel agent than a physicist of renown. Behind Yvonne hovered an array of framed mountain photography: Mont Blanc, the Eiger, and the Matterhorn, faded in a pattern consistent with the light streaming in from a single window. The images were mostly Alpine, but there was one majestic snow-covered rock that Sabine knew to be in the Apennines. It was the Italian Gran Sasso, beneath which lay the second most famous underground physics laboratory in Europe.

Yvonne followed her gaze. "Maybe we should get jobs there and be done with this place, eh?"

"Only if Sabi can come," said Chloé.

The desk phone rang and Yvonne made no move to answer it. She removed her glasses and, with eyes ringed red, exhaled wearily.

"Journalists?" Sabine asked.

"If you can call them that. I already made a statement to the press about withholding judgment until Interpol does its investigation, but some of these rags have the collective IQ of an oyster bed. Can you imagine a world where the tabloids care as much about scientific research as they do gruesome deaths? I'll have to make another statement, of course, if only to correct the headlines."

On the tram ride in, Sabine had caught the bizarre header emblazoned across a British tabloid: "Is Scientist's Death in €50M Tank the Poshest Drowning Ever?"

"Have you seen today's *Le Monde*?" Yvonne swiveled her monitor to reveal the headline: "Search for Dark Matter Cancelled After Grisly Death."

"The London *Times* may be the worst." She opened another tab: "Shut Down CERN Now, Demands MP."

"Listen to this guy," Yvonne said, plucking a choice quote. "*Yvonne Faye has single-handedly let the place go to seed. She and her entire lab can take their God particle to the devil for all I care.*" Below the headline, the minister—pink and jowly—was practically spitting at the camera. "Do you suppose that if CERN's director-general looked more like himself, he might not be having convulsions? Look at him, he can't even believe they let me past the gates." She did her best impression of the irate Englishman, which consisted mostly of sputtering, blinking, and collar tugging.

Sabine couldn't help but grin, and as Yvonne continued her imitation, she doubled over, laughing harder than she had in some time. Chloé tried to resist but was soon holding her side in the combined pain of laughter and misery. In an instant, Sabine was brought back to those dizzy college evenings, when the three of them would chatter late into the night, occasionally making fun of an obnoxious professor or classmate. Because they didn't own televisions and the internet had not yet arrived, they relied on books, music, and each other for entertainment. Would they ever be that enchanting and lively again? Would they ever be as close to anyone? What would have happened had Sabine followed the example of her friends instead of answering the call of law enforcement?

As much as she loved her job, physics was an alternate-life fantasy she couldn't help but occasionally indulge. And yet, for this one moment, it felt as if Sabine were back in the fold, in on the joke, a part of their rarefied world.

Yvonne tried to contain herself. "Oh god, what is wrong with me? None of this is remotely funny. Two people are dead and I'm responsible."

"Don't put this on yourself," Chloé said, all signs of mirth banished from her face.

Yvonne gestured at the headlines. "Why not? The world is. It's only because of our spectacular tank disaster that the press hasn't yet fixated on Howard's death. On top of everything, Simon has been hounding me all day about securing even more funds for the LUXT. That man's sense of timing is rich. His colleague has been dead, what, all of three days? It's not as if dark matter is going anywhere, and yet he wants the tank up and running again by the first of the year."

Sabine frowned. "Is that realistic?"

"Simon has a way of getting what he wants, even from me," she answered, shrugging. "You wouldn't know it to look at him, but he's been incredibly savvy at bringing funds to our lab. And despite the fact that dark matter has eluded him his entire career, he also happens to be a very good physicist."

Chloé visibly soured. "Please. If Simon had focused less on his hypothetical Nobel Prize and more on the integrity of his tank, Niels might still be alive."

Taking this as a cue, Yvonne selected a folder from her desk and slid it to Sabine. "The autopsy on Niels Thorne."

"Interpol hasn't taken over?"

"Officially, yes. Unofficially . . ." Yvonne threw her hands up. "If this place is deemed unsafe, our funding goes. Scientists as a group already get so little leeway. You think Agent Brod gives a good goddamn for CERN's future?"

It was true, Sabine thought, that for all its gifts to mankind, for all its enrichment of our culture, science as a whole was still cast as the villain. All one had to do was look at popular movies in which a deranged PhD is plotting some horrible experiment. Audiences loved sneering at the well degreed: *Where did all that book learning get you, huh? It didn't teach you the wisdom of the heart. It didn't teach you how to be human.* The perpetual lesson, it seemed, was that logic was bad, feelings were good. One had to choose.

Yvonne leaned forward. "Sabi, listen. We need to have this wrapped up before the Global Physics Conference next month. It's basically where we argue for more funding from our member states. If we don't resolve this fast, the conference will transform into a trial, with me defending to the entire CERN council an outdated security system that evidently allowed two men to die."

Sabine was about to respond when the door was flung open, and Simon stepped into the room.

"You appear to have a working telephone, Yvonne."

"As you can see, I'm in a meeting."

"Looks more like a coven," he said, taking in the women yet simultaneously avoiding eye contact. "I don't suppose there's an extra chair?"

"Take mine, please," Chloé said, rising. "I was just leaving."

"If you insist."

"Try not to break it like you did your xenon tank," she said sweetly before breezing out of the door.

"Try not to fall off your broom on the way back to your office," he shouted at her retreating back. Regaining his composure, he turned to Yvonne. "You know I get anxious when I don't hear from you."

She regarded him with her usual forbearance, but Sabine detected a strain in her jaw muscles. "We were about to discuss Thorne's autopsy," she said, "which has no immediate bearing on the finances of your project. But you're welcome to hear it. After which, you may as well answer to the horrendous security blind spots on your tank. Not to mention a faulty viewing platform that likely contributed to Niels's fall."

Sabine didn't think Yvonne was being forceful enough on this point. She was quite certain that the unsound platform, combined with the tank having been left open, was the reason for Niels's death. After his swollen, puckered body had been lifted from the water, she and Agent Brod had inspected the upper viewing deck, one section of which had been missing two support bolts. Both were found lying at the bottom of the tank. It would have been more than easy for Niels to step from the hydraulic lift, perhaps just long enough to register the exposed water, and promptly lose his footing. It was a wonder that one of the officers dredging the tank hadn't done the same.

Simon leaned back, chin in the air. "The loose bolts were unfortunate. I blame myself." The women appeared surprised by this admission, but he immediately undercut any sincerity by adding, "However, I won't be blamed for our lab's long-standing tradition of valuing science over costly surveillance."

Not taking the bait, Yvonne returned to the postmortem. "Apart from that, there is evidence that he was alive for some time, that he struggled inside the tank. It's unspeakably horrible. I can't imagine what it must have been like for him—" She stopped, emotion breaching her cool surface. She reached for a few tissues to dab her eyes. Despite her quavering voice, she went on: "The water level in the tank not being high enough to reach the rim, there were abrasions to his hands, and some of his fingernails were almost gone, as if he tried to claw his way out. If the LUXT had been working properly, the system should have signaled an alarm the instant his body went in, isn't that right? But it wasn't until hours later—during Howard's memorial—that the particle counter on the app registered anything amiss, and his body floated into view of the window." Yvonne looked to Simon for a response. "How is it that your tank could theoretically perceive a fleck of dark matter, but not the presence of a floating human being?"

Simon shifted uncomfortably, the chair creaking beneath him. "I've admitted there were flaws with the project. We were still in beta testing. Besides, the particle counter was designed for one task. Frankly, I'm amazed that several hours later, it registered his body at all."

She confronted him with barely disguised contempt. "What I'd like to know is why he was down there alone in the first place. Were you aware of this?"

He stared back. "Of course I was aware. I asked him not to, but he was more than a little obsessed with that tank—a project he had no hand in, I might add. He made a habit of sitting up there on the platform and staring through the glass. Clearly, that night for some unfathomable reason, he hit the lever to open the top, took a hydraulic lift to the platform, and fell in. I mean, what else could it be?"

Yvonne continued, "There's footage of Niels letting himself inside the cavern entrance on the late morning of December tenth. From there, he disappears from view. One interior camera was down due to an electrical short from the last thunderstorm, and the second camera has a range limited to the high-pressure window. Niels was presumably in the tank for seven hours before his body drifted into very public view."

To this, Simon had nothing to say.

She turned back to Sabine. "There were two items found on his body. His phone, and this, tucked in a hidden inseam pocket of his trousers." She pulled up a photo on her laptop of a small object, what looked like a sushi-shaped eraser, encased in an evidence bag.

"Flash drive?" Sabine asked.

"Yes, quite corroded by water. Can't pull a single byte from it."

"Interpol tried?"

Yvonne nodded. "Agent Brod found similarly sized pockets sewn into other items of clothing in Niels's closet. Seems he carried this with him everywhere. But why would he feel the need to wear it at all times?"

Simon gave a derisive laugh. "I can think of a reason or two."

"I have no idea what you're talking about."

"Don't think I haven't heard of the ATLAS data breach. I hope Interpol is conducting a thorough search of his home and work computer."

"They have, and do you know what they found? Work, Simon. Most of it for you." She gave him an icy look before turning back to Sabine. "Niels's family has some political clout, which means they're putting intense pressure on Interpol. I'd advise you to stay clear of that investigation for now and continue to look into Howard's death. With an eye toward both, of course."

"You're assuming they're related?" Simon broke in.

Yvonne blinked at him, as if he'd lost his mind.

"Don't give me that look, Yvonne. Scientists can't assume anything."

"There are only so many coincidences one can stomach in one's life. I think I've about reached my limit."

Sabine took the autopsy report and slipped it into her bag.

Simon looked at his watch. "This reunion of school chums is very sweet, but can we wrap this up?"

"I'll check in later, Sabi."

Sabine nodded and stood. As she walked to the door, Simon roughly shoved her chair aside and moved his closer to the desk. The childishness of this grown man made her want to laugh, but she was also aware of a deep pity for him.

When the door shut behind her, she overheard Simon begin to speak in a hushed tone, which Sabine took as her cue to press her ear to the door.

"That woman," he muttered, "doesn't have enough sense to solve one murder, let alone two."

"Murder?" Yvonne asked with feigned surprise. "Are you suggesting that Howard and Niels did not, in fact, do themselves in?"

"It's just an expression," he responded vaguely.

"*Murder* is an awfully funny expression."

"We're all murdered in the end, Yvonne. By time if nothing else."

CHAPTER 22

October 27

Before

The thick fog that rolled over the lab near the end of October seemed to fit Eve's mood, or perhaps, more accurately, her hazy mental state. Making the walk from the tram stop to her office felt like moving through an airy sludge. Anonymous colleagues passed by cloaked in mist, and buildings appeared suddenly before her as if flown in by stagehands.

On one particularly opaque Thursday morning, she ran headlong into Arnav at the doors of Building 33 as he was lurching toward the stairs. Even the soupy atmosphere could not mask his red eyes and generally grim appearance. He was squinting miserably, as though it were a bright, sunny day; and the rings around his eyes were so dark, he might have been wearing makeup. It was true that the demanding routine of their profession could sneak up on a person, to the point where it seemed to hasten the aging process. But in Eve's experience, she didn't notice this sort of physical deterioration in overworked physicists before the age of thirty-five. Arnav appeared to have matured ten years overnight.

Besides this, he had on the same T-shirt he'd been wearing for two days, which featured Samuel L. Jackson from *Pulp Fiction* aiming his gun, with the phrase SAY GOD PARTICLE ONE MORE GODDAMN TIME. She remembered Howard once wondering aloud if these joke T-shirts of his—plus all the scientific kitsch that geeks so loved to collect—were not a kind of substitute for religious paraphernalia. Arnav had countered that his love of science was not a replacement for religion on the grounds that one does not need a substitution for nonsense.

Eve reached out to steady him. "You okay?"

"I just need to lie flat for about sixteen hours."

"You went all night again?"

By way of responding, he held up his laptop. "To be honest, I'm not sure what day it is."

"Maybe you should eat first. Come on, let's get breakfast."

She looped an arm through his and the two headed in the direction of R1. Arnav stared at the ground, putting one foot in front of the other, fugue-like.

"How is an overworked postdoc like an electron wave function?" she asked.

"I don't know, how is an overworked postdoc like an electron wave function?"

"Because when you so much as look at them, they collapse."

Arnav frowned. "In my current condition, I barely know what that means."

As they approached the cafeteria, Howard appeared on the Route Marie Curie just ahead of them, head down, emerging as if from a cloud. Either he was too preoccupied with his thoughts to notice them, or he pretended not to.

Suddenly alert, Arnav called, "Hey, Anderby!" But the fog had already reclaimed him.

"What a fruit bat," he said. "He's either giving us a lecture or acts like he doesn't know us."

Eve was silent. After the three of them had bonded at Beer O'Clock, they had begun hanging out regularly. Her romance with Howard, however, sparked by that night of hand-holding and shared histories, was put on pause. It was as if, in the company of Arnav, neither knew quite what to do next. After all, their relationship was supposed to be professional.

Lunches had become a near-daily occurrence, the three friends chatting without pause, as though they were merely picking up the threads of a long-ago conversation. It seemed to Eve to be one of those effortless friendships, the kind that comes so easily to children, with topics spun from the air. One especially heady afternoon at coffee break, they had gotten to talking about the peculiarities of their discipline, and by the end of their conversation, Eve had felt strangely light-headed, as if buzzed on terrible moonshine when all she'd had was an espresso.

Arnav had started it with an impersonation of her: "*What are we even doing here, Arnav? We're all just flirting with a giant subterranean robot, trying to get it to tell us its secrets. But we're never going to get to the thing at the end. It's Russian dolls all the way down, don't you see?*"

"You're exaggerating," Eve protested.

But seeing that she was smiling, he continued: "Seriously, I'm constantly reminding you: *Just speak to the Machine. Do the code. That's what we're here for.*"

Embarrassed that Arnav was revealing her neurotic tendencies, she gave Howard a sidelong glance. "I get in a state sometimes."

"Come to think of it," Arnav said, turning to Howard, "she wasn't this bad before you arrived."

"Really?" Howard looked to her for confirmation.

She hid her discomfort with a smile. "I don't know. Maybe I should read some of your philosophy, because our jobs are starting to feel increasingly absurd lately."

Howard glanced out the window, and as he did, the wind picked up and a picturesque corkscrew of autumn leaves floated to the patio. Eve saw it, too, and they glanced at each other in silent appreciation of this small moment.

"Sometimes I'm convinced," he said, "that the closer humans get to discovering what's behind the veil of matter, the more quickly an unseen hand moves just out of reach, continually creating a new particle for us to find, simply because we were looking for it."

She was still staring at the fallen leaves. "I'm pretty sure the universe is the most tedious magician of all time. We're all just stuck in our seats, watching it pull an unending scarf out of its sleeve."

Arnav, usually impatient with this sort of talk, indulged them: "Or are *we* the magicians? We keep sawing the lady in half, and halves again, and on and on until there's nothing left?"

Now, with their friendship having inexplicably cooled over the past week, Eve wondered if these conversations—the kind one has when one is young—were behind her. She had the strong sense that Howard was avoiding them, or rather, avoiding her. During their group meetings, he would barely meet her eyes. Was Wolfgang Shreft's appearance at the lab to blame? Or was Howard's fascination with the man merely a symptom of something else? She wondered, too, if she would ever find out what Howard had meant by his cryptic comment to her—the one about their parents—as he escorted her home all those weeks ago: *What if we could bring them back?*

In an effort to remind him of that night, she had mischievously returned the up quark to him, discreetly slipping it into the pocket of his coat when he wasn't looking. Surely, he had discovered it by now. She half expected it to reappear in her own pocket, but maybe he wasn't in the mood for a playful repartee between their respective coats.

As she and Arnav entered R1 and made for the breakfast buffet, he said, "Oh, don't pretend you don't care."

"About what?"

He nodded in the direction Howard had gone. "About our weirdo acting distant. It bothers you."

"If you must know," Eve said, "I was thinking about the data theft."

This was a cover, of course, but it was true that she still wondered about the leak and why nothing had apparently come of any of it. Chloé had seen to it that everyone's laptops had been returned within twenty-four hours, after which she had not spoken of it again. It seemed to Eve that the entire laptop episode had been trotted out for show, only for the whole thing to be hushed up. Chloé's mood in the ensuing weeks had leveled out somewhat, though her strung-out appearance never entirely went away. Eve couldn't help but notice that a new tension had embedded itself in their work group. During meetings, she could sense that her colleagues were still deeply on edge about the incident. Besides this, Eve felt newly paranoid when preparing her presentation for the upcoming conference—not to mention working on her forbidden atmospheric models—that her computer was watching her. Had spyware been installed to root out the spy?

But Arnav appeared in no mood to speculate about the laptop episode or the ATLAS leaks. With single-minded focus, he grabbed a tray and heaped an assortment of eggs, toast, and fruit onto his plate. Eve did the same. As they moved along the buffet, the crunching of fake autumn leaves came from underfoot. Looking up, they found plastic jack-o'-lanterns suspended from the ceiling.

"Oh god, is it nearly Halloween?" Arnav muttered sourly.

"Who doesn't like Halloween?"

"I don't like Halloween because it means it's practically Christmas, which means they're already preparing this year's holiday comedy," he explained, plonking butter pats onto his tray. "I hate when we try to be funny."

The holiday party, hosted by the lab's Spooky Action Players, of which Niels was president, had over the years turned into a kind of roast. Amid much drinking and gaiety, the theater troupe would lampoon that year's events in physics, which involved painful caricatures of CERN's prominent personalities. Last year's performance was possibly the most cringe-making event Eve had ever witnessed. Yvonne Faye had been turned into a ridiculous Renaissance woman who had a secret life as a champion downhill skier and Olympic gold medalist. The crowning joke was that in her spare time, she was also the street artist known as Banksy, revealed when a passerby unmasked her while she was stenciling onto the Palais des Nations. The caricature of Chloé was less kind: an evil genius plotting world domination from her hidden lair within the LHC tunnel. The least charitable spoof—and the evening's single highlight for Arnav—had been the work of an anonymous actor, who, dressed as one of the horses from Simon De Vries's property, accepted the Nobel Prize and gave a whinnying speech to great applause. The suggestion that Simon got all his good ideas from his animals did not go down well with the target of the skit, who had been memorably dour throughout the performance. But the American playing the horse had been identified at some point—it was unclear how—and in the new year was sent packing back to his grad program in the Midwest.

"Given last year's moronic pantomime," Arnav said, "I hope we all just get drunk this time and be done with it."

They ate their breakfast in silence, and when Arnav had cleared half his plate, he stood. "I'll be in the library with my muons."

"Hey, wait a second—" But he was already halfway across the cafeteria.

Sometimes Arnav worked so hard that Eve felt guilty about her own work ethic. Should she be staring at collisions until her eyes hollowed out? Until she was close to collapse? She made a note to check on him later.

After picking up a second coffee, Eve headed back along the Route Curie toward her office, the fog appearing to lift with each step. Propelled by Arnav's increasing devotion to his research, she resolved to spend the next few hours fine-tuning event displays for her upcoming presentation. But when her eyes fell on the spot of grass where the three of them had held their late-night tea party, she veered toward Howard's office instead. It suddenly seemed urgent that she end what felt like unbearable, suspended animation. *What am I to you? A friend? A colleague? And what did you mean that night about bringing them back?* There was an indescribable pull between them, yet she sensed he was tugging backwards with equal force.

Approaching the door to Howard's building, she sensed someone on the steps behind her. She whirled around and nearly fell back with surprise. Hovering in the evaporating mist was a giant papier-mâché face. With its mustache and mass of white hair, it was like an Einstein bobblehead come to life. She clasped her chest, realizing who was underneath it.

"Christ, Niels. What the hell?"

Niels lifted Einstein's head to reveal his own. "Sorry. We're having old Albert here emcee the holiday party. I figure when you're ribbing your colleagues, it doesn't hurt to be anonymous."

"That didn't seem to help the poor guy in the horse costume last year," she said, still annoyed by the shock.

His expression soured, as if he had taken the student's removal personally. "We'll just have to be more careful this time. Besides, it's all in the spirit of fun."

"Someone might want to tell Simon that."

Niels stepped back, appearing to study her. "We're looking for more players, you know."

"You're asking me?"

"It'd be hilarious if you were Chloé. And Arnav was Simon?" He grinned at the thought, but grew serious again. "This year is going to be something special, actually. I have a feeling some uncomfortable truths may be revealed."

Eve raised her brows. "I'll leave the excitement to the grad students. Besides, Arnav and I have actual work." The instant she said this, she regretted it. She could see that she'd wounded him. "I didn't mean it like that, Niels. It's just, you have boundless energy. I don't know how you do it all."

"Neither do I." He started to turn away but stopped. "You're not looking for Howard, are you?" It sounded like an accusation.

"I was."

He nodded into the distance. "Just saw him, headed for the woods. Probably looking Byronic under a tree by now."

She hurried past him down the steps. If Howard was at the Chateau, she intended to catch him this time.

But feeling a twinge of remorse for her earlier comment, she turned back. "Did I ever tell you how much I loved your *Much Ado*?"

He stared at her for a moment before his face broke into a genuine smile. "My favorite of his comedies."

"Mine, too. Plus, I'm a sucker for a gay Benedick and Beatrice."

"You're very kind, Eve."

With a nod, Niels tucked Einstein's head under his arm and headed back into the lifting fog.

Choosing an indirect route to the woods, Eve circled past Building 40. Recalling Howard's movements the night she'd followed him, she approached Shiva, who looked away from her indifferently. She made sure no one was watching her and, on instinct, reached up and ran her fingers along Shiva's balancing foot. Beneath its arch, her fingers found a round groove: a button. Smiling to herself, she pressed it, and moments later was running through crackling leaves toward the Chateau.

The stone house, as usual, was shuttered and by all appearances unoccupied. There had been talk from the Theory Group of having several Canadian physicists stay that autumn to expand on one of the leading alternatives to string theory, but their guests had canceled at the last minute. Teo said it was because they'd gotten a better offer to stay at a charming island dacha off the coast of Vladivostok, the prospect of long seaside rambles presumably the stronger draw. *Fine by me*, Teo had said. *Let those loop quantum gravity nuts go pretend they're in a Russian play.* And yet squinting toward the Chateau now, Eve could just imagine the house and surrounding woods as an ideal setting for Chekhov.

As she approached the front door, a feeling of déjà vu descended from the night of the party. Just as she had the first time, she tried the knob. But now the knob turned and the door cracked open, the sound of rust and old wood potentially announcing her arrival to whoever may be inside. She detected faint music coming from within—*piano?*—which further excited her thudding heart.

For a moment, she nearly retreated back across the threshold. But instead, Eve swung the door wide and stepped into the house.

CHAPTER 23

December 14

Now

Sabine was just draining the pasta when the doorbell rang. Peering at her home security app, she found a bundled James blinking up at the camera. Even fish-eye distortion couldn't mask his fatigue. In addition to the demands of this case, James was simultaneously writing a PhD dissertation. If he was going to spend his evening poring over surveillance footage with her, she had better feed him. She buzzed him in.

James sauntered into the kitchen and unshouldered his backpack, though he kept on his jacket and CERN ski cap.

"There's a coatrack in the hall, you know," she said.

He shook his head. "This entire country is freezing. No one believes in heaters."

"How else are we to toughen you up for the slopes?"

He cast her a doubtful look. "What is everyone's pathological obsession here with skiing?"

Not bothering to wait for an answer, he began to take in his surroundings. It was the second time she'd had James over, and he still seemed to be making judgments about her decor. He frowned at a series of animal watercolors framed along one wall.

"You like Albrecht Dürer?" she asked as he examined the print of a red squirrel.

"Not really my taste." Spying a motion sensor in one corner, he added, "But it's some security you've got here. Had a few of your exterior cameras been in that tunnel, this case would be over."

James pulled his laptop out of his pack, settled at the table, and sniffed the air. "I hope it's vegetarian."

"Veggie Bolognese." Sabine had been unable to stomach meat for years; she suspected it had something to do with her time on the police force and having seen one too many human remains. She held up a wineglass. "Red or white?"

The question appeared to amuse him. "Brown, please. As in coffee."

"Your generation is so boring," she said, grabbing a can of grounds.

"Hey, I'm not trying to write my dissertation drunk."

"You know, I've never even asked about your research."

He distractedly tapped at his computer. "I'm looking into the initial properties of the quark-gluon plasma in the fraction of a second after the Big Bang, and how those properties evolved over time to create our Standard Model of particles."

"Oh, is that all?"

"I've sat in on some CMS and ATLAS meetings out of curiosity, but I much prefer the soupy origins-of-the-universe stuff you get with the ALICE detector. It was Niels actually who first sold me on it. The way he spoke about the lab, ALICE in particular, I couldn't resist."

She turned from her place at the stove. "You knew Niels before?"

James looked up, surprised by the question. "Niels championed my coming here. He gave a remote talk at my college several years ago. Some people didn't care for him, I guess. But he was one of the most decent physicists I've ever met."

Sabine felt a pang of shame as she remembered having immediately disliked Niels, probably for no good reason.

James looked out at the lake. "You know what I think? I think the problem with Niels was his failure to choose. He tried to do everything. On top of joining the LUXT team, he had his educational and outreach duties, all his extracurriculars, plus being on call for Yvonne. I'm all for passion, but my god, living your life like that will drive you insane."

She set the coffeepot to boil. "So, being excited about life is where you think he went wrong?"

He ignored the sarcasm. "I'm not saying he drowned in a tank of water because he was a show-off. But you have to find balance. If you deliver your entire life up to the lab, you can lose everything. It makes me wonder what else he got up to, is all."

An hour later, pasta in their stomachs and Sabine with a glass of Bordeaux, they sat on her sofa reviewing tank surveillance footage. James had rigged her laptop with a nifty attachment to project the LUXT like a home movie. But first, they watched the video taken from a camera posted at the cavern entrance. Niels arrived late morning, bundled in his dark coat and plaid vicuña scarf. At the door, he touched his ID to the reader and let himself inside. From there, the only other camera underground was the one on the tank itself.

James started the tank footage from the moment of Niels's arrival in the cavern. But the camera had been set up for the benefit of the LUXT app, not for security, and the view on the tank was limited to the window, the far side of the tank, and only a narrow slice of the cave. Niels could have ridden the nearer of the two hydraulic lifts to the platform without ever showing up on camera. James scanned ahead to 15:00 hours, roughly ninety minutes before Niels's projected time of death, and hours yet before his lifeless body floated into view of the window.

After half an hour of watching nothing more riveting than a dripping stalactite at the edge of frame, James pulled off his glasses and collapsed against the sofa. "I'm beginning to think this is some kind of art house film neither of us understands."

"Why don't you catch up on more lab footage," Sabine suggested. "I'll watch the tank."

He agreed, pulling out his own laptop to review yet more laboratory surveillance.

Sabine continued where they had left off with the tank, wondering if sitting here waiting for something to happen, when most likely nothing would happen, wasn't perhaps a metaphor for the life of a dark matter physicist. Still, she was alert for anything: a flicker, a sudden movement.

Drip drip . . . drip drip . . . drip . . .

It got to the point where Sabine knew when the stalactite drips were going to come. *Drip.*

Then she saw it: a flash in the water.

She rewound. There it was, unmistakable: the blurred image of a hand diving into view of the window, briefly grasping for the glass, before disappearing again. Thinking back on the handsome man who had escorted her to the control room that day, she imagined how he must have treaded water in his very nice winter ensemble; how he must have peeled away the heavy layers to improve his chances of survival. She shuddered.

"James, I found him."

Sabine replayed the crucial few seconds, slower this time. The desperate groping hand, and then nothing.

James stared, sick with amazement. "If someone had only been looking at the app."

She nodded grimly, scrolling ahead to see if there was another attempt. But between the wraithlike hand and Niels's body drifting into view, there was only water.

"That window is pretty deep," she said, "twenty meters from the top of the tank. If he fell through the broken platform and struggled for a while to get out, he might not have had the energy to keep diving." Sabine sat back. "I requested a list from Simon of everyone who has access to the cavern. Anyone who could have tampered with the platform. It's a long list."

"There's something else," James said, turning back to his laptop, where he had pulled up footage of the control room from the night of November 27. "Watch."

Toggling through, he found the eyes of the mouse darting across the screen, the same one Sabine had spotted during her control room visit. He scrolled ahead. Twenty time-coded minutes later, the creature appeared again, scurrying for the wires before vanishing.

"*Merde*. That mouse is not disappearing into the wall, is it?"

He shook his head. "It's disappearing because the clip ended and started over. It's a goddamn loop."

They looked at each other, registering all this could mean.

"So if someone put these on a loop to get rid of evidence," James reasoned, "why not get rid of the tunnel stills as well? Why not wipe everything?"

"That likely would have been too obvious," she said. "You have skills. Can't you resurrect the original footage of the control room somehow?"

James snapped his laptop shut and stood. "If somebody wants it gone from the system badly enough, it's gone."

"Where are you going?"

"There's an early ALICE meeting tomorrow."

"You're leaving just when things are getting interesting?"

"I prefer to think of it as catching the last tram back to France."

He gave her a wave and headed to the door.

Sabine just sat there, digesting all they had seen. The control room loop, of course, cast everything in a new light. If someone at the lab had the ability to alter security surveillance, what other footage had been tampered with? Could she and James trust any digital evidence at all? This also solidified for Sabine what she had already known: that the LHC had not malfunctioned the night of Howard's death, and that Niels was not merely the victim of a faulty viewing platform. Someone at CERN was sweeping up after themselves. A terrible exhilaration pulsed through her; she could now be certain what sort of case this was.

Realizing she had never heard her front door shut, she stood. Rounding the corner, she found James lingering near the door, regarding the watercolor print of a hare with interest.

"I've made a Dürer fan out of you after all."

"No, it's just . . ." He took a step back from the frame. "You know how they're always finding new layers behind old master paintings? I always thought that would be a pretty great job, art radiography. You know, get inside the head of the artist? See all that mess layered beneath the polished facade?"

Sabine knew what he meant. She'd once seen an infrared image of a Dürer self-portrait, impressions of the artist's thumb made visible in the paint five centuries later. But she wasn't sure what James was getting at.

He turned to her. "Remember that weird blueprint in Schoenberg's apartment?"

"What about it?" In the wake of Niels's death, she had put it to the far back of her mind.

"Can you find the photo you took? I have a mildly insane idea."

Sabine brought her laptop to the dining room table and scrolled through her photo library until she found the curious blueprint. Surrendering her laptop to James, she left him to play with the image for the next ten minutes. He would most definitely miss his tram.

"Holy hell . . ." He leaned back and shook his head. "I thought this was just talk. Grad student gossip. What if it's actually true?"

"What if what is true?"

He moved aside to reveal his work.

On the screen was a map of CERN.

She stepped closer. "I don't understand."

That's when she noticed, hovering behind the entire map like a phantom, the spectral image from Frances Schoenberg's apartment. Its maze-like network spidered out from the center of the lab, just skirting the edges of the LHC and its feeder tunnels, as if they had been snapped into place. She stepped back to gain perspective. While the collider and its injectors were uniform and circular, the pathways of the blueprint varied wildly, like catacombs following their own bizarre logic.

He looked at her sideways, a mischievous smile spreading across his face.

"Spell it out, James. I have no idea what I'm looking at."

Using a keyboard shortcut, he zoomed in to one of the strange shapes as it intersected with a feeder tunnel. Then, turning to her, he said, "You're telling me you've never heard tales of CERN's mythical underground labyrinth?"

CHAPTER 24

The Chateau's interior was darker than Eve had imagined, despite several lights having been turned on, including the chandelier overhead. But then, most of the windows were shuttered, and the abundant dark wood of the walls, floors, staircase, and ceiling beams sponged up the available light.

There was a living room to her right, with a motley of faded furniture, art, and rugs, assembled in the peculiar attitude of haphazard accumulation. In front of the fireplace, a massive blackboard stared vacantly like a flat-screen television. Eve imagined that beneath all the chalk dust, artifacts of Stephen Hawking's black hole mathematics still remained. She spied a nub of chalk in the tray and wondered if it was the piece no one was allowed to touch because it had once been used by Hawking's group. She couldn't help but feel a little rush of excitement at the thought of all the bright lights of theoretical physics who had reportedly stayed here, wrestling with the most perplexing puzzles of their time.

The music she'd heard upon entering sounded farther away now, though she couldn't tell from which direction it was coming. Taking another step into the foyer, she shut her eyes to better isolate the sound. It was the counterpoint of a piano, issuing from somewhere below and to the left of where she stood. She noticed a door ajar at the far end of the hall, warm light seeping through the cracks. The music grew louder as she approached. Pulling open the door, she found a set of stairs leading to a basement.

The sensible thing to do would have been to announce her arrival, to call out Howard's name, or utter a simple *Hello?* But the undeniable thrill of covert discovery was coursing through her. Besides, she didn't want to be fed answers. She wanted to see whatever it was for herself.

The light coming from the basement was enough to illuminate her way down the stone steps. Turning a corner at the bottom, she braced herself to confront Howard. But what she found instead was what looked to be the secret estate sale of a recently deceased antique dealer. The unoccupied, windowless room was one of such unexpected expanse and splendor, she almost gasped. Reproduction and vintage chairs, chaises, occasional tables, and ottomans sprawled out before her, the timeline of French history no doubt well represented.

Ornate wall sconces encircled the room, punctuating stretches of library shelving built into the walls. Glancing at the gold-embossed spines of leather-bound volumes, she spotted all variety of titans from science and philosophy: Newton, Kepler, Galileo, Laplace, Berkeley, Spinoza, Hume, Kant. A comforting woody scent practically demanded she select a book from the surrounding shelves, prop her feet on a pouf, and make herself at home.

The soft baroque keyboard she had detected earlier seemed to issue from unseen speakers, contributing to an overall lulling effect. But despite the beauty of the room, there was something distinctly off about the place, as if she were standing on the stage set of a French farce. The unsettling nature of the decor recalled to Eve's mind the conversation with

Howard about the universe being the ultimate magician. She couldn't help but see the space as designed to deceive, and her skin pricked with fear.

She became aware of a chill in the air, as if there were a window somewhere that had been left partly open. But it being a basement, this was impossible. She was feeling suddenly very closed in. And yet, despite the creeping claustrophobia, she stepped closer to the source of the imagined draft. As she approached the opposite wall, it seemed to her that the room was lopsided. But no, it was only that part of the wall was jutting into the room as if it were on a hinge. She drew closer to the dark wood panel and saw that it was, in fact, a door. Cold, stale air poured from the crack like icy breath.

Eve edged the door open and peered beyond it into an inky blackness. Opening it wider to let light from the room spill in, she could make out a kind of concrete passageway. It was impossible to tell how far it went, but something in her bones told her it went farther than the length of the Chateau, burrowing deep into the ground below the lab.

For a moment, it seemed she'd stopped breathing because when she next inhaled, and took in the scent of earth and mildewed concrete, her entire body recoiled with nauseated dread. She wasn't even standing in the passage, yet she could almost feel its walls closing in, the structure buckling. She squeezed her eyes shut. An image of her father played on the screen behind her lids, his beautiful, long-fingered hands—artistic hands, oddly delicate for a working-class man—scratching frantically at the crumbled earth and collapsed road that had deprived him of air.

She thought she heard something calling from the dark of the tunnel, a kind of summons, but she couldn't be sure if it was real or that peculiar illusion made by hollow spaces. Whatever it was, she didn't care to find out. She stumbled across the room, dodging furniture as she made for the stairs. Even to her own ears, she sounded like a frightened animal. She rounded the corner and scrabbled her way back up to the first floor.

She burst into the foyer, yanked open the front door, and ran for a cluster of oak trees ahead. All she wanted was to huddle in a ball, safe aboveground, in the open air. But as she crunched across the forest floor, she heard someone calling her.

"Eve! Eve, wait!"

When she reached the oaks, she threw her entire body at the nearest tree, pressing herself against it. She turned to find Howard rushing from the Chateau, concern and panic on his face.

"Eve. Are you okay?"

Her head was pinwheeling and her heart beat strangely in her chest.

Howard stepped closer. "Tell me what happened."

Her hand went to her mouth, but she pulled back the sobs. She really didn't want to have an ugly, emotional episode right now.

"I'm fine," she managed to choke out. "A bit claustrophobic, apparently."

His kind eyes regarded her with skepticism. "You don't look fine."

This was true, but she didn't want to think about the horror of that underground burrow or her body's alarming reaction to it. Right now, she just wanted to understand.

"So they're real?" she managed to say through hitched breaths. "The tunnels?"

He frowned, still watching her with concern.

"I thought it was just a lab fairy tale," she continued. "The stuff of memes and dumb T-shirts."

He shook his head. "Yeah, I mean, no. They exist. I would have warned you had I known you were coming. You should have told me you were coming."

Maybe she should have, but she didn't see how that mattered. "What are you doing down there?"

Howard's frown deepened. "Look, it's hard to explain all at once. And now is not the time to dump this on you."

"Why not? It seems like the perfect time, actually." She laughed in frustration. Not just because he was avoiding her question, but because of all his recent chilliness. "I really don't understand you."

She pushed herself from the tree and began to walk away, but he reached out for her. "Eve, I know I've been weird."

With his hand on her arm, she stopped and looked at him, waiting.

He offered nothing, but there was a change in his face that kept her rooted to the spot. He reached into his coat pocket and produced the up quark. Then he took another step and slipped it into her coat. As he did so, he pulled her toward him and put his lips to hers. It was a tentative gesture, asking for permission—and she granted it, though at first with hesitation. After all, she knew he was using the kiss as a kind of feint. But there was something else in it that said it was far more than that. And so, for the moment, she forgot everything.

CHAPTER 25

December 15

Now

The day after James revealed the possibility of secret tunnels running beneath the lab, Sabine resolved to either confirm this bizarre theory or put it to rest. But when she arrived at the security building that morning, fresh distractions awaited her. Two items had been slipped under her office door. The first was a sealed envelope bearing her name in a small, precise script. Opening it, she found a handwritten message:

Detective Leroux,
*   Would you please meet me at Café Honegger tonight at eight? I have information valuable to your investigation, but would prefer to keep our meeting private. Thank you for your discretion.*

She was familiar with the café. But given the manner in which the note had been delivered, and its lack of signature, she found it odd that the sender was asking to rendezvous in such a public place. Café Honegger stood at Place de Neuve, a square at the busy intersection of Geneva's opera house, music conservatory, and the grand Musée Rath. If this had been Paris, it wouldn't have been unlike requesting a furtive meetup at a coffee shop across from the Louvre. Setting the note aside, she picked up the second item, which had been hastily covered in brown paper fastened with what looked like electrical wire. Unwrapping it, she found a black leather-bound notebook with an elastic closure. It was similar to one of Howard's Moleskines, but of a different brand, both smaller and thicker. A sticky note on the cover read: *Pardonnez-moi. –C. Touschard.*

Sabine heaved a sigh. "Oh, Claude. Thank you."

After all this time, she wasn't sure what to expect from the missing notebook, other than content similar to Howard's many Moleskine scribblings. But when she settled at her desk and cracked the volume open, she knew she hadn't been anticipating what stared back at her: page after page of numbers, strings of them. They were written in black ink, and in a generic block hand one might use to obliterate the author's identity. Preceding each entry was a date and a cryptic word or name.

15/7 Fox: 46.22208596219957 6.15198356806512
29/7 Balcony 32-19: 46.2017854124818 6.142669268504853
5/8 Vallotton: 46.19880352665775 6.13766243292251

Sabine stared hard at the words and digits in front of her, struggling to locate a pattern. If she was at all uncertain why she'd never become a physicist, it was obvious to her now. Strings of numbers instantly bored her.

And yet, as she turned the pages, she noted that each series began with the same digits: *46* and *6*. She looked away from the book for a moment to rest her eyes, her gaze falling on the antique globe she hadn't touched since her first days at the lab. With sudden purpose she rolled her chair across the room and spun the globe to Europe. When she had located Geneva, she smiled in triumph. She may have been bad with numbers, but she was pretty decent at knowing where her city was located on the planet.

After spending several more minutes online verifying that her instincts were correct, she double-checked the tunnel images to confirm that the notebook on her desk did, in fact, resemble the missing object from the scene, blurry though the likeness might be.

Within the hour, Sabine was walking into Yvonne's office, quaking with the excitement of her discovery.

Yvonne regarded her with round eyes. "The vanished item has returned?"

Sabine threw open the pages on the desk in answer. "Filled with geographic coordinates," she said. "Each is preceded by a date, going back more than two years. The entries pinpoint a location in the city, all of them public: museums, theaters, parks, restaurants."

"What about these words?" Yvonne asked, running her finger down a margin.

Sabine tapped the final entries. "Fox—the History of Science Museum has a taxidermy exhibit featuring a red fox. Balcony 32-19 is an assigned seat at the Grand Théâtre. Vallotton is a Swiss painter on view at the Museum of Art and History. It's page after page of this."

Yvonne looked up with grim understanding. "They're drop-offs."

"Wouldn't be so hard to hide something in these exhibits, would it? Underneath a seat or bench. My guess is, these dates will correspond roughly to your data leaks."

Yvonne quietly swiveled to her computer, and after several minutes of comparing her records with the notebook, she appeared to sink in her chair. "Each entry is a day or two after the recorded ATLAS thefts." She removed her glasses and pressed at her eyes, as if struggling to process this new information. "If Claude took this from the scene, it doesn't look good for Howard, does it?"

"You wouldn't think so," Sabine said, opening her laptop, "except I found this just before I came over . . ." She pulled up the LHC stills from that night and selected an image of Howard slumped against the tunnel wall. "See, the notebook not only vanishes after Claude's arrival, but was also absent when Howard appeared on the scene and immediately following his death." She clicked back to the first shots of Howard sitting upright and very much alive, eyes closed, and by all appearances, listening to music. "Notice the notebook isn't here. It only appears in a much later frame, twenty minutes later, after he's already dead."

Yvonne clicked through the progression herself, staring hard as the edge of the notebook seemed to materialize out of nowhere. "But how? There are no frames of anyone else entering the tunnel before Claude arrives."

"And yet," Sabine said, toggling between the images, "with each still taken sixty seconds apart, who knows what might have happened between frames? Strange thing is, I don't know that I would have spotted the notebook's earlier absence had Claude not later taken it from the scene. The discrepancy is already so subtle."

"But if the notebook didn't belong to Howard," Yvonne reasoned, "who put it there?"

"I think we were meant to believe it belonged to him."

"Even if the drop-off dates don't align with his employment at our lab?"

Sabine shrugged. "All moles need accomplices, don't they? Especially while posted in China?"

The two women let this idea fully register: that Howard was to have been framed for playing a role in the data thefts, and that Claude Touschard's kleptomania may have saved him from a wrongful, if posthumous, accusation.

Yvonne continued to study the screen. "If someone planted the notebook on his body, they would need to wait for the radiation to dissipate. Even if they got down there without detection, they would have had less than a minute to avoid the cameras."

After a few more clicks of the laptop, Sabine produced James's image from the previous night: a winding series of passageways overlaid on a map of the lab.

"I snapped a photo of these passages from a blueprint in Frances Schoenberg's apartment. If this is accurate, it would have allowed Howard—not to mention a second person—to completely bypass the elevators."

Yvonne looked up, regarding her with an almost comical disbelief. "Don't you think if there was a full-blown rabbit warren underneath my lab, I'd know about it, Sabi? It's a fairy story."

"You know what else is a fairy story?" Sabine said. "Two people appearing in an underground tunnel by magic."

Peering at the strange map again, more closely this time, Yvonne seemed to reconsider. "It does make me wonder about the lab's construction during the Cold War," she said, squinting at the image. "A CERN architect was supposed to have drafted plans for underground bunkers in case of a nuclear fallout. Tunnels were to connect them—which is how, I imagine, these rumors got started in the first place. Except that as far as anyone knows, the bunkers never got built. Anyway, if they were, where's the entrance?"

Sabine leaned back in her chair. "I was hoping you'd know."

Yvonne shook her head at the map, looking only slightly less skeptical than a moment before. "The thing that surprises many people about CERN physicists—and despite my position, I still include myself among them—is that we rarely venture belowground. Our underworld is the realm of engineers. As long as they keep the Machine humming, the rest of us are happy. Did you ask Frances about it?"

"She claimed that the maze was a fanciful blueprint."

"Well, she would be the one to know. Back in the day, she and her team rooted around this place quite thoroughly."

Yvonne closed the notebook and handed it back to her. "But before you go digging up the lab, we need to know who was making these drop-offs." She gave Sabine a stoic smile. "Though I'm not entirely sure I want to know the answer."

That evening, after a day of what felt like misdirects, dead ends, and a failure to secure the remaining interviews on her list, Sabine arrived at Café Honegger well before the appointed time. Settling in at a courtyard table beneath a heating lamp, she flagged down a waiter and ordered a café au lait and a generous slice of cheesecake. Whether or not this lead panned out, she'd at least have a nice buzz to power her through the rest of the night.

Sabine angled her chair so as to have a better look at the café's entrance, over which loomed a stern plaster bust of the composer Arthur Honegger. It seemed fitting that this Parisian-style café bore the Swiss composer's name, given that he had preferred the excitement of 1920s Montparnasse to his home country. Switzerland was no place for an artist craving a scene. Yet she could almost hear Chloé objecting, *Are we physicists not artists of a kind?*

Her order arrived, the cheesecake topped with a chocolate treble clef. She was just savoring the first bite when her phone buzzed with a text from an unknown number: *Take it to go.*

She hesitated. Another buzz.

The dessert will wait.

Glancing around the courtyard, she studied the café's patrons. Nearby, three bored tourists stabbed at their phones. At a table in the corner, a couple on their soup course mooned over each other. Close to the entrance a large group of young people, students probably, still dressed in the costumes of the previous weekend's festival, argued amid several bottles of wine. Near them, a sulky young man in a large scarf and hoodie obscuring half his face was studying a menu.

Another buzz: *Change of plan. Avenue du Mail 155. More privacy.*

When she looked up, the man in the hoodie had disappeared. She downed half her café au lait, raised her hand for the waiter, and asked for the bill and a to-go container. He grudgingly supplied the latter.

A few minutes later, bundled up against a bitter wind blowing off the lake, she headed west toward the busier section of town, where sidewalk cafés gave way to the less historic commercial district. After several blocks, she became aware of the sensation of being shadowed. She stopped to linger at the window of a corner restaurant, pretending to inspect the menu, but when she glanced back, her imagined shadow was nowhere. Sabine continued across the intersection toward a congestion of businesses and shops. Consulting the given address, she arrived at a run-down mall that consumed the better part of a city block. In its courtyard, she paused in front of a suite of tinted glass and no signage. The distinct heartbeat of bass issued from within. Cupping her hands to the window, she tried to peer inside. At the same moment, a glass door swung open, and a large man in uniform appeared.

"I think you've got the wrong place, madame," he said in French.

She shrugged. "Maybe I like to dance."

He gave her puffy winter ensemble a contemptuous once-over, then stepped aside.

Inside the door, she winced at the barrage of pulsating lights. The music was electronic and abysmal, the kind that young people supposed promoted intimacy. Or perhaps its very lack of intimacy was the point.

The man in the hoodie and scarf from the café appeared before her, his compact frame outlined by strobes. He shouted something she couldn't make out, then headed deeper into the club, pulling the hood and scarf from his face as he went. She followed, and when she didn't notice any other women in the place, the penny dropped. If her clothes hadn't told the bouncer she was in the wrong place, her gender had.

After exchanging a few words with a bartender, Mr. Hoodie headed to a booth in the back room. It was more private but provided little buffer to the electronica hammering her eardrums. Near a disco ball showering the walls in cheerful prisms, Sabine slid into the booth and took in the young man seated across from her. Up close, she saw that his hair was heavily gelled and his eyes were rimmed in smoky makeup. An instant later, she realized this was the physicist she'd been trying to chase down for more than a week.

"Arnav Bose, isn't it?"

She must have had an amused look on her face because he said, "Am I not allowed to have a life outside the lab?"

"Is this where all the geniuses come to let loose?" she asked, glancing around.

"On occasion. Don't tell Chloé."

"I didn't know there was a gay club tucked away in this part of town. Geneva continues to surprise."

"What gave you the impression it was gay?"

She turned to consider the vast sea of glistening male bodies in the next room.

"Observing human behavior is my profession," she said, matching his wry tone.

His gaze flitted past her to the crowd. As the bass dropped, Sabine detected a wistfulness in his eyes, as if he were recalling a moment to which he could never return. She wondered if his makeup was, in fact, an attempt to cover whatever emotions he might be battling. Still, Sabine was irritated by the manner in which he had arranged their meeting.

"Tell me," she said. "How does this offer more privacy than the café where I was enjoying my cheesecake?"

"More decibels always equals more privacy," he explained. "Why do you think they play this sort of music in clubs?"

She gave him a wary appraisal. "How do you know I haven't brought anyone else with me?"

He motioned toward a far corner, and Sabine turned to find a man in a jacket, skin reddened with cold. Her shadow. "He told me you didn't."

She nodded, not without some professional embarrassment. "You have stealthy friends. Don't you have a fiancée back in England? A woman, I mean?"

He blinked at her. "And?"

"Just curious."

"You're not going to make me explain how human sexuality is a spectrum, are you?" He tilted his head, considering her. "Something tells me you're not squarely at one end of it yourself."

At that moment, the bartender appeared, bearing a tray with two cocktail glasses and several bottles of spirits. He set them down before handing Sabine a rolled napkin with a set of flatware.

"For the food you brought in," he said with faint condescension.

But Sabine no longer felt like eating dessert. She was too focused on the man sitting across from her, in his curious combination of hoodie, oversized plaid scarf, and makeup.

"I didn't know what you'd like to drink," said Arnav, arranging the liquor bottles. "We can improvise."

"I don't generally accept drinks from strangers."

He arched a brow. "We're at a gay nightclub. In Geneva."

"I'll take anything with gin, then," she said. "And while you're pouring, you can tell me why making me do a merry dance across town was more sensible than just scheduling an appointment. Or why you're the only one in your work group who's managed to avoid me."

Arnav began to mix a gin cocktail with expertise; it was clear he must have been a bartender at some point. "I had nothing to contribute about Howard."

"You were friends, no?"

"Anything I could have told you, Eve would have said, and said better. Besides, I have information that is more valuable than anything I could have revealed about Howard. And for all I know, it might have bearing on both cases." Stirring her drink, he continued, "I have an item in my possession, and I hoped you might be able to do something with it."

He leaned forward, sliding the cocktail to her. As he did so, she could feel his hand beneath the table, pressing something small and plastic into her palm: a flash drive.

"Put it away, if you would."

Without so much as looking at it, she tucked it into an inner pocket of her coat.

"Am I to know what's on it?"

"It was given to me by a friend." Arnav poured himself a neat whiskey and drank half of it, as if to brace himself for what he said next: "By Niels Thorne."

Sabine felt her eyes widen involuntarily in response. Whatever she might have expected from a meeting with Arnav Bose, it was not this.

"Are you aware," she asked, "that a water-damaged flash drive was found on Thorne's body?"

He nodded before knocking back the rest of his glass. "He told me he always carried a copy on him. This one you should be able to open. With a little effort, anyway."

She regarded him skeptically. "You and Niels were friends?"

"Does that surprise you?" he asked, almost defensively.

"It's just that while I was trying to track you down this week, your other friend, Eve Marsh, led me to believe you wouldn't know a thing about Niels—that you, along with many of your colleagues, didn't particularly care for him."

Arnav shifted uncomfortably. "Eve has become one of my dearest friends, but in many ways, she doesn't know me."

"So you let people think you disliked Niels? Including Dr. Marsh?"

He sighed, appearing to consider his next words. As he did so, Sabine's gaze wandered again to his plaid scarf. She realized that something about it had been nagging at her since they'd sat down. Not only did its obvious quality seem a mismatch with his modest hooded sweatshirt, but there was something familiar about it. It was almost as if this were an intact version of the scarf that had been pulled half-disintegrated from the bottom of the xenon tank. The same one Niels had been wearing when he'd entered the cavern for the last time.

"Your scarf," she said, taking a chance, "it's not vicuña, is it?"

He glanced at her sharply, clearly thrown by this. Then he looked down and worked at the scarf's fringe with anxious fingers.

"I believe a similar one belonged to Niels Thorne," she added.

Arnav appeared to internally crumple, as if no longer finding a point in resisting. He said distantly, "Niels liked nice things. I complimented him on his scarf once, so he bought me an identical one. Couldn't wear it at work, obviously." He laughed miserably. "Sometimes I hated him and sometimes that feeling needed an outlet. I could be vocal about it, it's true, and obnoxious. But then, Niels could be incredibly infuriating, playing hot and cold with me, batting my emotions about. It was the kind of relationship you hope you're done with by the time you're out of university. I guess I never found that sort of drama when I was younger, but I found it here." He exhaled heavily. "I did love him. We loved each other."

Sabine absorbed this confession. It may have been the first time she was meeting Arnav, but she found herself genuinely astonished by his disclosure. "I'm not trying to judge you, just to understand. Why did you and Niels feel that you had to hide from your colleagues?"

Arnav poured himself more whiskey. "Every good Indian boy has a fiancée waiting back home. When you grow up in the West, you have to play games with yourself to fit in. It's gotten to the point where I'm not sure which version of me is me anymore. But the version that doesn't want to disappoint my family is genuine, that much I know." He swirled his drink vigorously, as if trying to dispel self-pity. "As far as your investigation goes, the nature of my relationship with Niels or anyone else is trivial. The thing in your pocket is what matters. It's encrypted all to hell, of course, but at least it hasn't been marinating in a xenon tank. You'll have to find somebody to crack it. I had no luck."

"How long have you been carrying this with you?"

He paused. "It must have been a couple days after Howard was found in the tunnel. Niels and I weren't speaking at the time, but he texted me about meeting up, and then practically begged me to take a copy of the drive and hide it somewhere. When I asked if it had something to do with Howard, he told me not to make him talk about it. He seemed pretty freaked out, so I agreed. Niels was normally very good at putting on an act, though I could see quite plainly he was terrified."

"If he was that terrified, why didn't he go to the police, or at least lab security?"

The question clearly stung Arnav, and he looked away. "God, I wish I had convinced him that day to go to the police. But Niels would only say that he was afraid of the consequences of doing so, of what it might mean for his position at the lab." He continued to stare off, hypnotized by regret. "I think the real reason for his not going to the authorities—and this is going to sound completely asinine to a nonphysicist, I realize—but more than anything, Niels was in love with dark matter. He cryptically said something about how the worst has already happened, and that he may as well 'hold on for a little while longer.' He truly believed that Simon and their team were close to finding evidence of the most elusive substance in our universe. Niels told me more than once that he would rather die than not be there when it was found. His dissertation on dark matter didn't exactly set the world of physics on fire, and he'd struggled for so long to be something more than a glorified tour guide or Yvonne's postdoc charity case—but with the xenon tank, he had a real shot at having his name associated with a history-making discovery. He wasn't about to do anything to jeopardize that. But then . . ." He didn't finish the sentence. *But then it was too late.*

"Why give the flash drive to me and not Interpol?"

"Because Yvonne trusts you," he said simply.

In the next room, a remixed version of the 1980s pop song "Enola Gay" began. Arnav inclined his head toward the music. "Did you know that this catchy tune is about the bombing of Hiroshima? I never know whether to dance or be sick."

Sabine took his non sequitur as a chance to make her own. "Have you heard anything about secret tunnels under the lab? Passages built during the Cold War?"

He eyed her curiously. "Sure. I've also heard that Yvonne keeps a slice of Einstein's brain in her office mini fridge." He stood, flinging his scarf onto the bench seat. "You'll let me know what you find on the drive? Discreetly, of course."

Sabine nodded.

"Now, if you'll excuse me, I'm going to try to forget all of this for the next half hour."

She watched Dr. Bose saunter into the next room and melt into the crowd. When water misted onto the dance floor from overhead nozzles, the crowd screamed in delight.

Sabine looked down at her cocktail. The song about Hiroshima told her that the time was eight fifteen and that was the time it had always been. She picked up the glass, drained it, and exited the club out the back door, taking the remains of her cheesecake with her.

CHAPTER 26

October 27

Before

A fter their kiss outside the Chateau that day, in the shade of the oaks, Eve's relationship with Howard dramatically altered course. Given that embracing in the middle of the day was not an option, the two agreed to meet back at the Chateau after work. When Eve returned at sunset, she found Howard waiting on the stoop of the house, his dark coat buttoned up against the encroaching chill. His cheeks were pink and his eyes shining.

"I'd build us a fire," he said, making a move toward the door, "but the smoke will give us away. No central heating is the one downside of this place. Though I did smuggle in the space heater from my office."

Eve hesitated, weighing the warmth of the Chateau against its dark confines and the possibility of another freak-out. "Maybe we could just walk for a bit?"

"Of course."

Howard locked the door from the inside—the same lock, Eve assumed, that could be triggered by Shiva's foot—and they set off through the woods. Emerging from the trees into the open space of the lab, she was grateful to find it mostly empty; she feared the changed energy between herself and Howard would somehow be immediately visible to their colleagues. In silent agreement, they made their way toward Higgs Field, the orange light of the sky rapidly transitioning to dark blue.

At the far end of the field, they paused to stare up at the Gargamelle bubble chamber. Against a faint glimmer of star cover, the chamber's alien bulk resembled more a retro-futuristic space capsule than a particle detector. Years before either of them had been born, Gargamelle and its liquid Freon core had been critical to CERN's discovery of the neutral Z boson, a particle involved in radioactive decay. Eve wondered what it must have been like, in the middle of the last century, when it seemed a new particle was found every week and the dream of drilling down to the final building blocks of matter appeared a pursuit within reach—or one without end, depending how you looked at it.

"You know," Howard said as he sat back on the grass, "you've never told me why you came here. Why you chose physics."

Joining him on the cold ground, she felt warmed by his mere proximity. "I don't know. There was never anything else? It felt wildly impractical?"

As they both stared up at Gargamelle, she told him about her high school physics teacher, Ms. Gomez. "She said that, like astronauts, particle physicists explore the infinities of space, but in the other direction." She paused, retrieving a memory of her father. "One Halloween, my dad helped me dress up as a Russian cosmonaut, using some insulating material he'd brought home from work. But I told everyone that I was a very tiny cosmonaut, visiting the minuscule planets that orbited the nucleus of an atom." She laughed, a little self-consciously. "I guess I still like that idea—that we're all topsy-turvy space explorers."

Howard studied her, as if vividly picturing the costume. "A tiny cosmonaut Eve, ransacking the stars."

"Except now I wonder," she said, "if I shouldn't be doing something more worthwhile with my time than poking around at the invisible."

This seemed to confuse him. "Like what, saving humanity?"

He meant it as a joke, but she just stared back at him.

"Really?"

At that moment, Eve considered outing her authorship of the anonymous climate article in that month's issue of *Courier*, but so far she hadn't revealed it to anyone. She was now wondering if the entire piece had been a bad idea.

"It's not as if I have it all figured out," she said, deflecting. "One thing at a time."

He appeared to briefly consider whether to let her off the hook.

"Come on," she said. "Your turn."

"Why am I here?" Howard sighed and said into the air: "*One of the strongest motives that lead men to art and science is escape from everyday life with its painful crudity and hopeless dreariness, from the fetters of one's own ever shifting desires.*" He smiled. "Sorry. Einstein."

"Is that really why you picked particle physics?"

He gave her an almost apologetic shrug. "Life is either tedium or catastrophe, isn't it? Physics was the most beautiful distraction I could think of."

His eyes strayed from hers down to her mouth. Given that they were sitting on the very conspicuous Higgs Field, a romantic shift in mood was maybe not a good idea.

She sat up straighter. "Are you going to tell me about our labyrinth?"

He frowned, glancing off in the direction of the Chateau. "Well, everyone already knows about the secret tunnels, don't they? They just don't know that the myth is real."

"So, there's more than one."

"Many." A kind of wonder came into his eyes. "I mentioned my aunt Frances was a CERN engineer back in the day? They were breaking ground for the LHC, testing the integrity of the surrounding land. Initially, she discovered one tunnel and thought it was a fluke. But then this entire network of abandoned passageways kept spilling out beneath the lab. She and her team suspected they were built back in the fifties, as a kind of escape route or nuclear bunker, in case things with the Russians went south. Except they were only partially finished. Bizarrely, she noticed that one of the passages connected to our woodland chateau."

Eve realized she had been staring down at the grass, as if conjuring a maze directly below them. "Why'd she keep it a secret?"

"She was worried, quite rightly, that it would halt construction of CERN's prize tunnel—which was also *her* tunnel. Her job, after all, was to get the thing built. They'd already had significant delays when unearthing Roman ruins during excavation on the French side. You get a bunch of archaeologists or political groups who want to shut it down, they can keep things in limbo for years. If the tunnel went the way of that failed Texas supercollider in the nineties, she'd never forgive herself. And so, seeing that the passages posed no danger to the collider tunnel, my aunt and her team kept it quiet."

"Yet she told you."

He nodded. "Knowing I was obsessed with this place, she gave me a map of the lab as a graduation present, which included the so-called labyrinth. I'll show you sometime."

"But none of the guests staying in the Chateau ever happened upon it?"

"Frances hid the entrance very cleverly, as you saw. She fashioned that panel in the basement—not to mention all the decor—as a sort of misdirect. Plus, you have to twist a sconce a certain way, pull out a particular book just so. It's a puzzle just to trigger the latch."

She smiled, remembering that cunning basement room, and tried to imagine the kind of woman who had created it. "Does anyone else know? About the tunnels?"

He tilted his head uncertainly. "As far as I can tell, everyone thinks it's a joke."

"And so, you're doing what down there, exploring?"

He reached out, his hand grazing hers. "Would you like to explore with me?"

Turning from him to take in the pale constellations, she said, "I think I much prefer aboveground research."

When she looked back at him, he leaned in and kissed her, and all at once her body felt flooded with light, more intensely than the kiss earlier. It was as if the stars above them had all gone supernova, turning inside out to empty their contents. But then, that's what love felt like, she supposed: all the poetic metaphors made real. Perhaps that's what truth itself was: a platitude understood for the first time. If only the answer to the universe's ultimate riddle of matter was a truth that had been staring everyone in the face all along—like the final act of a play that was both surprising and inevitable—so that the whole of their lab could turn to it and say, *Ah, yes, we might have known!*

"Should we head back to the Chateau?" he murmured.

She hesitated, but realized her claustrophobic anxiety, at least in Howard's presence, was gone.

A gibbous moon was just rising through the trees as they walked back in the direction they'd come. When they arrived at the Shiva statue, Eve surprised Howard by reaching up and pressing beneath the deity's foot.

"How did you—?"

"I followed you, remember? Don't tell me your aunt made the button, too."

He laughed. "Given her talents, you think a secret latch to unlock a door a hundred-odd meters away is so hard?"

Howard grabbed Eve's hand and made a run for the tree line, quickly surveying the woods before hurrying inside the house. Eve stood in the light of the chandelier, relieved to see that the basement door was shut, and watched as Howard dashed into the living room to retrieve a space heater.

He gestured toward the floor above. "Care to join me in the Hawking suite?"

"Is there really a Hawking suite?"

He nodded. "You should see his bathroom. The graffiti is *obscene*."

She laughed, then took Howard's hand and let him pull her up the stairs.

CHAPTER 27

December 17

Now

From her seat in a third-row pew of Meyrin's town church, Sabine observed a pair of men tuning the pipe organ: one seated at the console, the other applying a tuning knife to the pipes. Since the evening of Howard's memorial, she had been haunted by thoughts of the Église Saint-Julien, intending to return to the church when it was not packed with mourning physicists. Now alone, she found herself the audience for an impromptu concert of chromatic scales. She had never grasped how bizarre an organ really was—not just the multiple tiers of keyboards and sinister pipes, but the pedals themselves forming their own instrument, a kind of keyboard for the feet.

When the candles sputtered, Sabine turned to find the door swinging and James headed down the aisle. He appeared to barely register the tuners as he slid in next to her, breathless.

"Sorry I'm late."

"Did you open it?"

"I was able to pull a file from the flash drive," he said, producing his phone, "but it's just an energy plot. The graphs we use for LHC collisions. You've seen them?"

She nodded. "Nikolay Levkin showed me one in the control room. Not that I could make much sense of it."

With a weary shake of his head, James clicked a link on the screen. "Well, this one is the longest plot I've ever seen. It's endless. I had to convert it to a video file."

He pressed Play. At first, it was just a black screen, but then the graph began to unspool across it, a series of points climbing up and up, before falling again.

"Settle in," James said. "It goes on like this for twenty minutes."

She frowned. "Could it be evidence of a new particle? A discovery no one else knew about?"

He made a face. "If it is, the energies are completely bizarre. It'd be an unreal number of electronvolts with each collision, a million Higgs bosons. It doesn't look like any physics I've ever seen. It's almost like someone's idea of a joke." He pocketed his phone. "I'll send you a secure link to the file."

He stood and mumbled something about getting work done before that evening's holiday party.

Sabine remembered having seen an invitation for the party appear in her office mailbox earlier that week. In error, she'd assumed. Surely, no one at the lab wanted a detective standing around making chitchat with the people she'd just had into her office for questioning.

"I'm surprised it wasn't canceled."

He shrugged. "Yvonne thought having no holiday party would be worse, I guess. It's not as if they're doing the traditional roast."

"You'll let me know if anything interesting happens?"

"I can tell you right now it'll be depressing as hell."

After James left, Sabine continued to observe the tuners, one of them gently tapping his knife along the rising pipes. She could see that he was talking to himself, though she couldn't make out any words beneath the pulses of the instrument. But even if she could hear him, would she understand his private conversation with an intensely complex machine?

———————

When she got home, Sabine used the link James had sent her to pull up the plot on her computer monitor. As she hit Play on the file and let it unfurl at a larger scale, she wondered if James could be right. Was this graph, with its endless series of rising and falling dots, a kind of joke? If it wasn't real physics, what was it?

Over a glass of burgundy, she watched the patterns oscillate in a hypnotic wave. The longer she stared at it, the more it reminded her of the times she had attempted to teach herself piano with software that would scroll across the screen. One could adjust the speed depending on one's level of proficiency. Sabine always had it on the slowest tempo, but no matter how brilliantly coaxed, her brain was not meant to translate the shapes on a staff to movements of her fingers across eighty-eight keys.

Even so, she counted the lines running across the y-axis, wondering if she could turn the points on the graph into notes on a scale. She printed out pieces of it until she had a series of pages. Then, lining up the sheets on her Bösendorfer, she sat down and tried to make the dots correspond to notes on the piano. It was a painful exercise. Even if she were to find some kind of musical component to the graph, would it be anything more than ascending and descending scales? Maybe she should show this to Chloé.

She was about to go pour herself more wine when something about the pages before her seemed to click into place. After practically kicking the piano bench out from beneath herself, she went back to her computer and began to manipulate the graph as best she could. Sensing she wasn't getting anywhere on her own, she picked up her phone and dialed.

When James answered, she said, "Can I persuade you to ditch that party?"

CHAPTER 28

October 28–November 26

Before

Eve's first night with Howard, spent in an upstairs room of the Château, felt both startling and predetermined. It seemed to her that she'd never felt more in the right place in all her life, yet she marveled at the fact that she got to touch him at all, let alone lie with him in an extremely lavish eighteenth-century bedroom.

The next evening, he invited her to his Ferney-Voltaire apartment to eat takeout on his living room rug. Over noodles, he explained how his aunt Frances, who now lived in a French village outside Geneva, had bought the place during her tenure at CERN. The apartment's layout was awkward, having probably been carved out of a larger flat. Before that, the entire building had likely been a manor house for a contemporary of Voltaire; although, for someone from the American West like Eve, where a century-year-old building was something to gawp at, the timescale of Europe wasn't always easy to grasp.

She found Howard's belongings strangely poignant: only two proper bookshelves, but science and philosophy texts stacked in precarious towers along the walls, and in a corner of the living room, LPs stored inside a record player. It was the apartment of someone who didn't have time for decoration. This was not unusual among postdocs, including herself, who didn't expect to stay beyond a few years. Yet Howard clearly couldn't help amassing the things he loved.

In the hallway, she was surprised to find the passage adorned with something from her part of the world: a hanging Navajo rug, one of an intensely complex fractal design. She idly wondered why he chose to hide such a beautiful piece in the hall. Howard explained that it was a gift from a friend, but didn't elaborate beyond this. His bedroom was simple: a queen-sized mattress on a modest frame, topped with plain white bedding. Above it hung a lone piece of art—a framed William Blake print of a soul rising from a man's body. After dinner, when Howard slipped away to brush his teeth, she caught herself staring at the Blake for several minutes. It seemed a blatantly spiritual choice for Howard. But then she realized the piece made perfect sense—for here was another image of a double.

When he returned to the room, she was still staring at the print. "What did you mean that night?"

She hadn't intended to ask this. She had fully meant to flop back onto the bed and embrace him in his T-shirt and checked pajama bottoms. But instead, the question insisted itself. She could see that he understood.

"About bringing them back?"

She nodded. "Did you really mean it?"

"I think so."

"How would you do it? Theoretically."

He rubbed his face wearily. "That's what I'm trying to figure out. It's hard to explain."

She collapsed onto the bed. "You're good at explaining."

He sat down next to her and gave her a sidelong glance, as if gauging how much she could take. "It's not so much about bringing my parents back. But what if I could get back to *them*? Travel to them."

"By what means?"

"If I knew, I'd be there right now."

This stung a little. Eve didn't want him thinking about being anywhere but here with her.

He reached for her hand. "I want to show you how, but it's not the right time. We have to wait a little while longer."

Frustrated by this cryptic response, she pulled her hand away. "Just so I understand, you'd like to, what, Schrödinger's cat your loved ones back to life? Close the box and open it again, in the hopes that your parents are all snuggled up in there, alive?"

She knew this sounded glib. She hadn't meant it to. When Austrian physicist Erwin Schrödinger had concocted his cat-in-a-box thought experiment back in the 1930s—positing a fifty-fifty chance of a bottle of poison breaking open, therefore leaving the cat in a superposition of both alive and dead until an observer opened the box—he was illustrating what he considered to be an absurd misinterpretation of quantum mechanics. Though Schrödinger had devised the mental exercise to poke fun at the notion of a cat existing in multiple states, or "worlds," at the same time, there were contemporary physicists who considered the idea of many worlds—a multiverse even—to be more than compelling. Eve did not count herself among them, if only for lack of experimental evidence.

Noting her wry tone, Howard said seriously, "That cat has become a crude illustration of an entirely plausible theory."

"What does Wolfgang Shreft think of all this?"

Eve had brought up his fascination with the guru only once after the man's appearance at the lab. She was now expecting Howard to deflect again, but instead he said, "Shreft believes in the limitless nature of the universe and of our souls. He says that if the universe is infinite, why shouldn't all possibilities exist somewhere? In this, he and the many-worlds theorists seem to agree."

Eve leaned back, peering up at him. "Are you a many-worlds theorist?"

He turned to the window, nodding almost imperceptibly. "Sometimes I wonder what the point of all this discovery is—all this *finding* of particles—if we don't have the option to hold on to the things we've lost."

"But maybe that's just what life is," she said. "One long timeline of loss." He smiled down at her sadly.

"We've both lost parents," she continued. "Too early maybe, but everyone loses their parents eventually."

He turned to the window again. "I've been very lucky, Eve. I was born into an enviable life in many ways. But in others, it feels like too many tragedies to bear. Just one loss too many."

His faraway look of old had returned. She hadn't meant to depress him, but she couldn't see how loss wasn't an inescapable part of being alive. Howard lay back with her, and for the rest of the night he was physically affectionate, but his mind seemed to be elsewhere. As if a piece of him had traveled somewhere far away.

The next day, it felt as if Howard had returned to her. They lay in each other's arms that morning, and the next and the next, until the days turned into weeks. She much preferred his place to her charmless box of an apartment the next town over, and Howard never objected. Each morning, they had their ritual eggs and coffee, putting off the moment when they would have to emerge from the apartment and catch a tram for the lab, staggering their arrivals at the front gate and at group meetings to avoid suspicion.

And yet, amid all this bliss, Eve was aware that Howard was concealing more than he let on. More even than his vague allusions to research he couldn't yet share with her. Increasingly bizarre was that she woke up more than once in the night to find Howard gone from the bed and apparently nowhere in the apartment. When he would suddenly reappear beside her, and she would ask where he'd gone, he would just whisper not to worry and to go back to sleep. One night, after he'd returned from such an absence, she pressed up against him to check the temperature of his skin, but he was far too warm to have been outside. So if he wasn't venturing out of the apartment, where was he disappearing to?

CHAPTER 29

December 17

Now

The CERN holiday party, judging by its subdued decor and generally listless energy, promised to be a less than thrilling evening. Those early to arrive seemed determined to get drunk as quickly as possible, as if it were the only compelling reason for showing up. Upon entering the auditorium shortly after seven, Eve instantly knew it had been a mistake for her and Arnav to come. Though this was not the same auditorium in which they had learned of Howard's death, it may as well have been for all its superficial similarities. Besides this, the entire space seemed to mock happier scenes from the past, of laboratory gatherings not infested with memories of the dead. How Yvonne thought this ill-timed event could possibly boost anyone's spirits was mystifying.

Eve was about to pull Arnav right back out of the room, but he was already pushing through the crush at the drinks table.

"Must we stay?" she said into his ear.

He shot her a look of shared torment. "We're in holiday hell. Queue up and drink."

Holding on to Arnav's arm, as if for safety, she glanced around the small theater. Its perimeter was decked out in sagging fairy lights while cheerful jazz insisted itself over the speaker system. Those colleagues not eyeing the spirits and wine were either arranged across the raked seating, as if awaiting a show, or chatting in work group cliques. The ATLAS and CMS people seemed to have scattered to opposite ends of the room, as had Chloé and Simon.

"Our boss scrubs up well," Arnav noted of Chloé's cocktail dress. But as his eyes wandered around the auditorium, he looked increasingly wretched. "With any luck, I'll be passed out in a couple of hours."

As they took their place in line, an American grad student whom Eve vaguely recognized turned and introduced herself. She had on a garish sweater and a pair of reindeer antlers.

"I'm Mary, with the CMS Novel Particles Group," she said eagerly. "I hear they canceled the roast? Is that true?"

Eve was not surprised that this young woman worked in Simon's group. She looked a combination of manic and woefully underslept.

When Arnav confirmed that the roast had, indeed, been canceled, Mary stuck out her bottom lip. "This is my first CERN holiday party. I was so looking forward to it."

"It's been a bit of a year, you may have heard," Arnav said pointedly.

Mary responded by sticking out her chest. "I even wore my best sweater."

Her sweater was bright green with circles of lights interlocking across the torso. Mary pushed a button on the hem, sending red lights flashing along the rings to collide at an embroidered point on her chest marked CMS. The collision produced a bright flash before starting over.

"Wow," Arnav said. "I think your jumper just confirmed the Higgs."

Mary cackled, her voice ringing through the theater. This was clearly not the first drink she had queued up for.

With a comical shaking of her fist, Mary said, "Argh, where was this sweater in 2011?"

"On the back of a sheep, I expect," said Arnav.

Mary laughed again, more loudly than before. When she took her turn at the punch bowl, Arnav whispered to Eve, "What I wouldn't give to never see a gag holiday jumper again in my life."

"Too bad. You'll have to throw out half your closet."

Arnav had worn one of the better sweaters at last year's party, featuring an image of the bespectacled German physicist and Soviet spy Klaus Fuchs, sporting a red stocking cap, over the name SANTA KLAUS.

"I think I'm done with jokes forever," he muttered.

Eve was about to compliment him on his very normal Fair Isle sweater, when she detected a darkness around his eyes that was not due to lack of sleep. "Wait, are you wearing eyeliner?"

"If I were, it'd be my business."

She hesitated. "It's just that—" She snuck a look at him again, detecting mascara as well. Had she been mistaking the remnants of makeup for extreme fatigue this whole time? No. The physical and mental strain bearing down on Arnav was obvious. It occurred to her that she'd been so wrapped up in her own grief, she hadn't bothered to notice what her friend had been going through: the odd hours he'd been keeping, even more than usual, and his sudden disappearances from their office. She found it both touching and perplexing to imagine Arnav had really cared for Howard. Or even Niels, as preposterous as that seemed.

"Sorry," she said. "I'll stop."

"Stop everything," Arnav said morosely. "Stop the LHC. Stop the searches: for dark matter, for quantum gravity. Forget Paul Dirac and Niels Bohr, for none of it matters anymore."

Eve supposed he was riffing on some poem or other, but didn't want to ruin the moment by asking which. Without warning, her eyes began to water. Maybe it was the drink line, or the remembrance of drink lines past, but sorrow rapidly descended. Somebody at the opposite end of the auditorium had begun laughing, and at that moment, it seemed like the most grotesque sound she had ever heard.

Watching her, Arnav reached for her hand and squeezed it. He had known, of course, about her and Howard. He'd figured it out early on, despite her pains to keep their relationship discreet. *You two aren't as clever as you think, you know,* Arnav had said to her after one of their group meetings. When she had stared back at him with astonishment, he'd just laughed. *You both stopped stealing glances at each other during meetings. Dead giveaway. Don't worry, the others haven't caught on.* Romantic entanglements happened at the lab—it was unavoidable—but sleeping with someone in your work group was deeply frowned upon.

Lacking all appetite to mingle, Eve and Arnav parked themselves with their cups of spiked punch on the house-left stairs, which afforded a view of the entire space. Despite the awkward lack of room to stand, Eve much preferred the intimacy of the auditorium over the warehouse for seasonal parties. The stage was superfluous, of course, for as the party committee had said in an email, "given the tragic events of recent weeks," there was to be no show that year.

Taking in the mostly empty stage, Eve recalled the clownish farce from twelve months ago, in which Niels and his troupe had made merciless fun of Simon De Vries. Even with the student in the horse costume banished, she wondered how Niels had made it up to Simon afterward, and how he had gone from Simon's apparent enemy to working so closely with him on the xenon tank. But then, she would probably never know.

Arnav nudged her. "What did Einstein say to Isaac Newton when their plane ran out of fuel?"

She nudged him back, pleased he wasn't entirely done with jokes. "I don't know, what did Einstein say to Isaac Newton when their plane ran out of fuel?"

"Sir, I don't think you quite understand the gravity of our situation."

Just as Eve was summoning her best unsmiling expression, the house lights dimmed and the stage lights lifted. Something inside her instantly rebelled. Whatever was happening, she wanted no part of it. She began to stand, but Arnav tugged her back down.

A figure materialized in the center of the stage, holding a mic. Not just any figure, but a man in a rumpled brown suit wearing the giant papier-mâché head that Eve had seen Niels wearing that day back in October. A small opening between the stiff paper lips allowed the actor inside— presumably a member of the drama troupe—to speak.

Eve snuck an incredulous look at Arnav just as this terrifying bobble-head, with its mustache and shock of white hair, began his terrible imitation of a German accent: "*Guten abend*, allow me to introduce myself. I am Herr Doktor Albert Einstein."

Awkward laughter followed, including an "Oh god no" from Yvonne, who, in the light of an open door, could be seen entering the theater.

"What the hell?" someone whispered nearby. "I thought they weren't performing this year."

"I hope you don't mind the interruption," Einstein continued, his giant head scanning the darkness before him. "The party committee deemed it necessary to keep the gathering subdued this year, but I hope you will appreciate that the founder of the Spooky Action Players would have wanted the show to go on. It seems to me we should respect the wishes of our dead, no? In fact, Dr. Niels Thorne had an entire script prepared for this evening. If you'll allow me, I'll read to you the note he scribbled on the title page . . ."

Einstein pulled out a folded note and began to read: "My fellow Spooky Action Players," he said, "if you are reading this, I have gone to that undiscovered country from which no traveler returns. Whatever happens, I urge you to perform the following piece at this year's party. I hope the show will be in the spirit of the season, but also illuminating for everyone concerned. When the performance is over, and only when it is over, I ask that you deliver this script to Sabine Leroux, if she has not already accepted our invitation. My apologies to law enforcement for the roundabout delivery of key evidence. With much appreciation, Dr. Niels Thorne."

Einstein gave a bow and exited the stage. From the darkened seats, there was a confusion of dissenting voices arguing whether a performance like this should be allowed. Finally, Yvonne's voice rose above the others: "Quiet. If this is what Niels wanted, let them continue. Anyone is free to leave, but I'd like to know what Niels has to say."

The authority of Yvonne's voice had the effect of hushing the theater and pinning everyone to their seats. No one, it seemed, dared move. Eve turned to find Arnav hugging his knees and rocking slightly, like an anxious child.

"Arnav, let's go," she whispered. "I think I'm going to be sick."

When he appeared not to have heard her, she stood.

He looked up. "Don't leave me to watch this alone. Please."

"I'm sorry. I can't."

With a rising mix of queasiness and dread, she mounted the steps toward the exit. But at the last moment, she couldn't make herself push open the doors. The anticipation arresting the entire room was simply too overwhelming. She turned around, leaned against the back wall, and with her colleagues, waited in the darkness for the performance to begin.

CHAPTER 30

November 27

Before

Eve awoke late Sunday night to find Howard missing again, and after calling out to him and receiving no reply, a new kind of fear coursed through her, one amplified by that evening's events. They had spent the day in Geneva, wandering the city and visiting both the art and history of science museums. It had been cloudy and cold, with an icy wind blowing off the lake, but Eve could not have invented a more perfect day. Toward evening, however, Howard's mood drastically shifted.

He'd had the sudden idea of surprising his aunt, who lived in a village halfway down the lake. Howard had told his aunt Frances nothing about Eve. "I guess we've never had that sort of dynamic. But maybe it's time you meet each other." It struck her as an oddly impulsive idea so late in the day. Besides this, he seemed on edge about it, as if he were worried that if they didn't do it now, the visit would never happen. Eve wondered aloud if they should warn his aunt that they were coming.

He waved this off. "We'll call her when we're close. She's a hermit anyway. She never leaves the apartment."

Finding themselves on Geneva's right bank, he suggested a series of buses and trams to get to the French village of Thonon-les-Bains on the opposite side of the lake. But given that they had just wandered down the bank from the History of Science Museum, well within sight of a ferry terminal, Eve suggested hopping a boat.

Howard glanced toward the road. "Or how about a taxi?"

"Too expensive," she said, pulling him toward a ferry that was just boarding. "Come on. We can catch this one."

But Howard wouldn't move, and when Eve looked back at him, she understood from his face that he would not be stepping onto the dock. She was reminded of that summer day months ago, and of his reluctance to take a ferry despite Arnav's urging. In fact, now that she thought about it, it seemed to her that he had been artfully avoiding ferries all day.

"You don't like boats?" she asked, trying to keep her tone light.

Howard was not smiling. "You know, you're right," he conceded. "It's all too rushed. Let's just visit her another day when we have more time?"

He began to walk in the opposite direction toward the bridge, leaving Eve to follow. On the tram ride home, Howard was quiet. Reflecting on the scene at the dock, she realized it was more than aversion she had seen on his face. It was terror.

She reached for his hand. "You know the way I ran from the Chateau that day? That fear only developed after my dad's accident, a kind of secondhand phobia."

Howard didn't take this as a cue, but only nodded distantly. "I'm sorry about the boat," he said. "We'll visit my aunt another time."

In bed that night, after they'd turned out the lights, Howard's hand found hers, as if in apology. Then in a soft voice, he began, "In school, I had a friend named Stuart."

It was then that Howard revealed to Eve the tragedy of his life—the one she realized eclipsed even the deaths of his parents. He and Stuart Greenwood had befriended each other while at MIT and, despite having come from very different backgrounds, had felt an immediate connection that went beyond their shared discipline. When Howard's parents died, Stuart had been there for him. Stuart had lost his own mother, a Diné woman, at a young age. Though raised by a white father, Stuart tried to hold on to his Diné history, including learning the Navajo language and participating in a sweat lodge ceremony. A few years into their grad studies at Princeton, facing down their dissertations, the friends had begun to acquire an insatiable appetite for knowledge and experience beyond the 3D world. Fascinated by the mind-expanding euphoria Stuart had reported experiencing during his sweat lodge, Howard suggested they experiment with psychedelics. What if, for one night, in celebration of starting their dissertations, they were to turn off their hyper, overworked brains?

"Mushrooms seemed the least risky," Howard explained. "After I managed to get us some from an undergrad dealer, we went out into the arboretum past hours and pitched a tent. It wasn't an actual sweat lodge, of course, just a nod to the idea. We lit a fire, brewed some coffee, laid out our sleeping bags . . . But when it came to it, Stu became extremely agitated and wanted to go home. His whole life had been a struggle, he said, and finally he was achieving something. He wasn't about to risk getting arrested because he was 'a brown man on drugs.'"

Howard sighed, searching for how to continue.

"Stu said that even with my parents dead, the world would always take care of me because of my name and my money. I could afford to make mistakes. He was right, of course. But we argued, and he ended up dumping the bag of mushrooms into the lake. I shook it off and agreed that we could celebrate in other ways. What I didn't tell him was that I'd already added half the powder to my coffee."

From the faint light coming through the windows, Eve saw Howard close his eyes. "When Stu reached for his coffee, he picked up mine by mistake. I didn't stop him." Howard laughed. It was bitter and self-mocking. "I watched him knock back the entire cup before I could get a word out. It was the biggest blunder of my life, and I will never stop loathing myself for it."

"It was an accident—" she began.

But Howard wouldn't hear it. "I should have slapped the cup out of his hand. Before long, he realized what had happened, but the euphoria had taken away his ability to care." His voice turned hard as he continued. "We had the brilliant idea to take a boat out onto the water, as we often did. Carnegie's a shallow lake, so I was hardly thinking about safety. I remember how the light of the full moon was reflected on the surface, and Stuart kept saying it was calling to him. Then, without any warning, he just sort of flung himself off the side of the boat. It was the deeper end of the lake, though probably only six feet. He never resurfaced. I went in after him, but the water was so dark and cold. It was so fucking cold.

"The next morning, they found him. The murky water meant they had to trawl the lake with nets to find his body. After that, there was an investigation. No mushrooms were left, but the police suspected there had been something added to the powder that caused Stuart's adverse reaction. Though the toxicology was inconclusive." He shook his head. "Maybe if I had been punished in some way, it would have been easier. Instead, everyone pitied me."

Eve moved in closer, but Howard turned his head away. "Stu's dream was to work at CERN. He deserved to be here."

After it was clear he was finished with the story, she said, "Thank you for telling me." What she didn't say, because it seemed too horrible to say aloud, was that if Stuart hadn't drunk the coffee, Howard might have. Then again, would his system have reacted the same way?

"Jesus, Eve," he said. "I didn't want to chase you off with yet more catastrophe. It's all a bit much, isn't it? Poor rich boy who's lost everyone who ever meant anything to him? I think I would hate me."

She gripped his hand beneath the blankets in answer. *I don't.*

Now she truly understood what he had meant about his life having been *one loss too many*. Could he be faulted, then, for being consumed by the idea of traveling to a better version of it?

Soon afterward, she heard the deep breaths of his falling asleep beside her. Later, she would think back on this and wonder if he hadn't faked his breathing. If he hadn't instead been lying awake the entire time, choosing his moment to leave.

She awoke sometime after eleven to rain tapping at the bedroom window and sweat pooling uncomfortably on her skin. Once again, the space beside her was empty. She wrapped herself in a blanket and stepped into the hall. This time she would find him, and force him to tell her what he'd been doing.

The apartment was still and dark.

"Howard?"

She turned on the bathroom switch, and as a beam of light sliced into the hallway, it illuminated the Navajo rug. She stood staring at the rug, whose unremarkable location in the hall had always puzzled her. Remembering Howard saying it was a gift from a friend, she now wondered if this friend was Stuart. Stepping closer, she ran her finger along a single crimson thread that looked out of place. It was a signature of Navajo weavers that they left their rugs intentionally flawed—a *spirit line* that allowed the energy of the weaver to pass through the rug upon its completion. As she followed the vertical thread, she noticed that it lined up with a subtle crack in the wall, extending beyond the weave. She pulled the rug back from its hooks and ran her fingernails along the crack, searching for some kind of catch. Failing that, she knocked, pushed, and finally heaved herself against the wall. With a *snap* a panel gave way, springing forward and back. She pulled it open to find a hollow darkness beyond. It was slightly cooler than the rest of the apartment, and she wrapped the blanket more tightly around her.

Eve turned on her phone's flashlight and stepped into the void. Finding a switch, she flipped it. An overhead bulb came on, revealing what looked like a shabby office. Along one wall was a blueprint map of CERN with what appeared to be a chaotic system of underground tunnels overlaying it. This must be the map Howard had spoken of that night in Higgs Field. Along the opposite wall hung some kind of timeline of events, complete with phases of the moon drawn along the top.

She went back into the hall. "Howard?"

In the bedroom, she noticed something she hadn't before: a small note lying at the foot of the bed. Her heart plummeted. Sitting beside it was the up quark. They had passed it back and forth so many times, she'd forgotten who'd last had it.

With shaky hands, she unfolded the paper. It read in hasty ink:

Dearest Eve, I can't explain where I am tonight, but please try not to worry. Whatever happens, I hope to see you tomorrow at the conference. Love Always, Howard

She stared at it, attempting to make sense of the message—*Love Always?*—which sounded to her like a goodbye. Her confused heart began to pound.

Pushing both the ball and note into a pocket of her pajamas, she returned to the timeline in the hidden room. With a finger, she traced various CERN activities she recognized—the LUXT party, scheduled LHC recalibrations—until she arrived at the present day, which was where the timeline ended beneath the symbol of a full moon.

Directly below the moon, Howard had written *CROSS OVER*. These two words were accompanied by a strange symbol, a kind of arched arrow, jumping from one looped line to another. The loop, she realized, joined by three smaller loops, was supposed to be the LHC.

Had Howard's obsession with alternate realities been leading to this? Did he really plan, as he had hinted, to cross over to a different universe, one in which his parents were alive and his friend hadn't drowned? But why tonight?

Taking a cue from Howard's moon symbols, she pulled up a lunar calendar. That night, it was a perigee-syzygy moon—commonly known as a supermoon—the closest to Earth it would be for years, and therefore its gravitational pull on the planet strongest. If the LHC had been operational, the control room would have had to account for the unusual gravitational effect on the Machine, correcting the proton beams to counteract lunar influence. But with the collider down for maintenance, she didn't see how the moon phase affected anything apart from the tides and astrological tables. So what was Howard's fixation with it? Because right now, looking at this timeline, it looked to be the work of a deeply disturbed man. She thought of the early quantum physicists who had been driven nearly mad by the relentlessly confounding behavior of quanta and wondered if Howard wasn't continuing in this tradition. Was the man she loved actually insane?

If he was planning some trip to the *other side*, and it involved the LHC tunnel, this was bad. And not just from a safety perspective. If he trespassed belowground, he might get himself kicked out of CERN entirely, ending his career for good. She needed to stop him.

Eve slipped on her sneakers, threw a coat and scarf over her pajamas, and ran out of the apartment to flag down the nearest taxi.

CHAPTER 31

December 17

Now

Wh
hen the stage lights lifted again, Einstein was gone, and a young man and woman—whom Eve recognized as grad students—appeared stage left in a grove of cardboard trees. Eve felt an immediate sense of familiarity, for hadn't she witnessed a scene quite like this? The woman was clearly meant to be Chloé, with her bobbed wig, black jeans, and chunky knit sweater. Opposite her stood a likeness of Niels with his abundant yellow hair and wool blazer. The two clutched script pages and spoke in the slightly stilted manner of actors who were not entirely off book.

"How can I help you, Chloé?" the Niels character began. "Unfortunately, I do have a tour to get to."

"Of course," the Chloé look-alike replied. "If there were more physicists like you, maybe we wouldn't have an idiot populace hostile to scientific advancement."

Eve could hear nervous giggles from the seats, but the auditorium fell quiet as Chloé continued.

"I won't waste your time. You've no doubt heard from Yvonne that data has been pilfered from the ATLAS dumps? I'd like your help in identifying the thief or thieves quietly, without causing alarm. As you know, Yvonne has become extremely agitated about the whole business. The last thing this lab needs is its leader going on a spy-hunting mission, turning desks upside down, or shutting down the LHC entirely. It's bad for physics."

Niels leaned against an oak. "Why do you need me?"

"Because Yvonne trusts you. Once you have hard evidence of our spy, you'll present it to her."

His eyes widened. "Oh? Who did you have in mind?"

"Well, let's ask ourselves: Who is our most plausible suspect? Who has very recently been working for China?" She paused to let this sink in. "If this person happens to be in my work group, so be it."

Niels took a moment to absorb this new information, as did the audience, who exchanged confused whispers. Eve, once again, fought the instinct to run from the room.

"I'm not sure that makes much sense," he finally responded. "Isn't your Dr. Anderby the one who sounded the alarm on the leaks?"

"Yes, but with rumors already swirling about a mole, we can't know that it wasn't a calculated move on his part."

He considered her skeptically. "Why shouldn't I go to Yvonne right now and tell her about this conversation?"

"Be my guest. But first, answer me one thing," Chloé said, sweeping an arm at their surroundings. "What is the dream of every physicist here?"

He shrugged. "The next big discovery?"

"Wrong. It is to remain on this rarefied plot of land for as long as we can, to avoid expulsion to a classroom or the private sector. Only the rare bird among us is allowed tenure here forever."

Amid this peculiar drama unfolding before her, Eve thought these words uttered by an amateur actor sounded like the truest ever spoken.

"Your postdoc expires next year," Chloé continued. "Unless you secure an unlikely extension, you'll be forced to leave. Yvonne can't keep you here indefinitely."

He took a cautious step forward. "What are you proposing?"

"Only a prominent role on the LUXT tank. And when the tank does its job, you'll appear as a coauthor on the paper."

Niels regarded her warily. "The tank is Simon's project. I'm not sure he likes me. He certainly doesn't like you."

"So everyone says." A laugh escaped from her lips. "Do you want the position or not?"

He was quiet for a moment. "Everyone knows I do. But what do you have against Howard? You're the one who brought him here."

She stepped closer. "Deliver evidence of his guilt to Yvonne and all your dark matter ambitions become a reality. It's pretty straightforward."

As Niels paused to consider everything that was being thrown at him, speculative murmurs issued from the theater seats.

"Why not just do it yourself?" he asked.

Chloé shook her head. "The evidence needs to be delivered from a neutral party."

"I don't know what you mean by delivering evidence."

"Do I really have to spell it out for you?"

The two stared at each other for a long beat before the stage went dark. When the lights returned, Niels stood alone among the trees. The actor still occasionally referred to his script, but he was now slipping comfortably into his role.

"As it happens, Chloé did have to spell it out," he said. "In exchange for my new career on the LUXT tank, I was to steal Howard's laptop and plant evidence of purloined ATLAS data. Which, by the way, Chloé would arrange to give me. We would then convince Yvonne to round up laptops in the name of lab security and—voilà!—smoking gun. Howard would be ejected from the lab, possibly arrested, and all this talk of Chinese moles would evaporate."

Niels smiled. "My only condition was that I be installed on the LUXT tank before its grand unveiling. Only then would I deliver. I don't have to tell you that she convinced Simon to bring me on for a trial period. I didn't ask how. When you're working on the greatest dark matter project in history, you don't ask questions."

Eve's stomach tightened as a very tall actor appeared from stage left: black-and-orange Princeton shirt and dark hair pushed back in an unkempt wave.

As Niels watched this imitation of Howard cross the stage, he continued: "You're no doubt wondering how I justified this unholy arrangement to myself. Blame it on my lifelong obsession with dark matter or blame it on my fear of getting older and my career passing me by. I also reasoned that a man who would work for the Chinese competition—whether innocent of espionage or not—was really asking for it. Of course, getting my hands on his laptop was a different matter. I watched Howard for some time, trying to devise a way to take it without his immediately noticing. And as I watched him, I discovered that we had something in common. We both were fans of this odd little man."

Another actor entered, from stage right—oversized cardigan, shabby pants, slip-on sneakers—his movements more of a shuffle than a walk. The imitation drew whispers of recognition from the room.

"While visiting the lab on several occasions with his film crew," Niels went on, "Wolfgang Shreft often slipped away to explore the grounds alone. As I discovered, it was to meet with Howard to discuss various topics at the intersection of science and spirituality."

Howard and Shreft mimed conversation on a bench downstage as Niels stole behind to eavesdrop.

"Howard spoke of various philosophers," Niels continued, "like Arthur Schopenhauer, who had envisioned a kind of source from which the forces of our universe spring. Howard wondered, What if this source was a kind of vast field of consciousness? What if we could travel through this field to other worlds within our multiverse?"

The guru laughed from his place on the bench. "I am intrigued by this idea, my friend. But if I knew how to travel through our field of consciousness to hop around the multiverse, I would not have bought an airplane ticket to get here."

"As I continued to keep tabs on Howard's movements, I began to actually like the man. He had a peculiar yearning for the truth that went beyond that of a typical physicist. He stayed at the lab late every night and would often disappear into the Chateau—for reasons I won't get into just yet. The more I got to know Howard, the less I had a stomach for planting evidence on him, no matter the reward. So instead, I chose to discover what Chloé was up to, and why she was so intent on framing one of her own."

In a pool of light, a door appeared downstage. "I paid her a visit late one night, hoping to stall her on our agreement while discreetly ferreting out her motives. When I arrived at her office, I found another visitor. Given how Chloé had landed me the LUXT position, it shouldn't have surprised me who it was. But what did surprise me were the sounds I heard from the other side of the door—sounds of affection, sounds of *intimacy*."

The door opened, and a cartoonish likeness of Simon, with padded clothing and rouge on his cheeks, appeared. He continued across the stage, oblivious to Niels.

"I kept this secret to myself at first," Niels said in a low voice, "wondering how I might use it to my advantage. Then one day, tired of waiting for me to act, Chloé arranged for the laptops of her entire group to be collected. At first, I led her to believe I would cooperate, but only if she would have Simon secure my permanent role on the LUXT project, including paper coauthorship. When she refused, I threatened to out her relationship with Simon and what I now believed to be her collusion with him. We were locked in a bizarre standoff for weeks, neither of us yielding our positions."

Chloé's office door disappeared in darkness, and previously unseen string lights on the perimeter appeared in a variety of shifting colors.

Niels stepped back into the shadows. "And then, the worst happened."

As the lights spun around the auditorium, Eve realized the room itself was supposed to represent the LHC tunnel.

"Let's consider the night of November twenty-seventh," Niels said. "How was it exactly that a physicist found himself irradiated by the very protons he was supposed to be studying?"

Just then, there was a scuffling in the audience. Niels looked up, holding a hand to his forehead as he zeroed in on movement at the far end of the theater.

Eve could just make out in the dim two people, having risen from their seats, slipping past colleagues and heading quickly up the stairs.

Niels called out, "Now, who would that be, fleeing the scene?"

Eve wondered if the same person controlling the stage lights might throw a spotlight on the pair. But it was then that she noticed her own shoulder practically grazing the light panel. Almost without willing it— as if she were watching herself do it—she reached over and flipped one switch, then another, until all the house lights were on. The bright LED wash came just in time to reveal on the stairs Chloé, head down, stumbling up the steps in her cocktail dress and heels before pushing through the double-door exit. Directly behind her was a beet-faced Simon. The two fled in the kind of way you would if you never intended to come back.

As the doors swung shut behind them, Niels turned back to the audience. "The play's really the thing, isn't it?" He laughed and, when no one joined him, said, "Come on, that's a basic *Hamlet* reference."

It was then that the actor playing Niels looked over at Eve and gave her a nod of acknowledgment. She looked away, suddenly quite sick at all she'd just seen—and what she assumed was only a fraction of the entire story. Her gaze briefly alighted on Yvonne, who had stood from her seat near the center of the theater and was staring at the exit through which Simon and Chloé had disappeared. Her expression was one of utter stupefaction, as if she'd just been clocked in the face. Eve glanced down the stairs at Arnav, who looked back at her, his face a very strange color.

Before she knew what she was doing, she shoved the doors open, rushed for the nearest trash can, and threw up the punch-colored contents of her stomach into the bin liner.

CHAPTER 32

November 27

Before

That terrible Sunday night, the clouds had seen fit to unleash one of the most biblical storms Eve had ever witnessed. Having spent most of her life in the desert, the fact that such amounts of water could fall out of the sky still seemed to her a kind of sorcery. After running from the taxi for the lab entrance, she found a discarded CERN umbrella propped under the eaves of the reception building. It looked in sorry shape, and when she opened it, half its ribs stuck out. But it was better than nothing, and she held it out before her like a shield as she ran in the direction of Building 40.

After slushing through the grass toward Shiva, whose dance of destruction seemed more apt than ever, and triggering the button, she dashed for the woods. But even the trees couldn't block the downpour or the wind. When the umbrella gave up completely, she tossed it aside and ran the rest of the way to the Chateau. The lights were off, and she had to tread carefully so as not to trip on the rough stones leading to the entrance. Throwing open the door, she called out, "Howard!" just as a clap boomed from the sky, like a thunder sheet on cue. "Howard!" But there were no sounds aside from the pummeling of her heart and of the storm slamming sideways into the building.

She groped her way along the wall and flipped the switch for the chandelier. Nothing. Resorting to her phone's flashlight, she rushed across the foyer to the basement door. Halfway down the stairs, the lights below began to flicker, and by the time she rounded the corner into the basement, the sconces came on. But their voltage wobbled in a sick-making pattern, as if the power grid had collapsed and everything was running on batteries.

The wall panel was closed this time. She threw herself against it as she had the one in Howard's apartment, but it didn't move. "Howard! Howard, are you in there?"

The only answer was the storm rattling above.

Glancing around, she remembered Howard having said something about his aunt devising a kind of puzzle to open the door. Something about moving a sconce and a book? She backed away from the wall and considered the ornate brass lights that hung on either side of the panel, casting filigreed shadows on the surrounding wall. She grabbed one and tried to move it, but it wouldn't budge. Trying the other, she felt something give and the sconce click as she rotated it counterclockwise. When it stopped turning, she stepped back to study the bookshelves. How, among the hundreds of volumes, would she know which to trigger? If she were Howard's aunt, which book would she choose?

She scanned all the giants of science and philosophy, hunting for a name or title that didn't belong. But there were too many. Turning her attention to the actual shelves, she saw that they were covered in a thick layer of dust. She stood on an upholstered footstool and ran her eyes along the overhang until she came upon a disturbance in the dust on the fifth shelf up, where a volume had been recently moved: *A Gardener's Guide to Classic Labyrinths*. She pulled the book out to where the dust trail ended. Simultaneously, there was the click of a latch and the wall panel snapped outward.

Stepping from the stool, she felt the cold tunnel air hit her rain-soaked skin and a familiar nausea threatening to surface. She closed her eyes, took a deep breath, and summoned an image of Howard's face.

Pulling back the panel and stepping into the space beyond, she willed away mounting terror. With her phone light held out before her, she barreled down the passage, breathing through her mouth to avoid the dank smell of earth that seeped from the concrete. She tried not to think about how old the tunnel must be, or whether anyone had tested its integrity recently.

"Howard!" Her voice came out halting and choked. She forced the sound waves from her throat. "Howard!"

She slowed as she sensed an obstacle ahead and, as she held out the light, found a corroded metal door. She rattled the rusted handle, but it was locked. Slamming the door with her fists and feet, she made as much noise as possible. The door clanged and creaked, straining its hinges. Exhausted, she stopped to listen. All she could hear was the rush of blood in her own ears.

Eve slid down the wall of the tunnel until she was slumped on the concrete, in what felt like a pose of submission. But submission to what? What exactly was happening here? She tried to imagine where Howard was right now in the tunnel system. For all she knew, he had worked his way to the LHC via a network of concealed passages and doorways. But if he intended to *cross over*, as he'd written on that timeline, how did he know *where* and *how* to do it? What was the mechanism by which Howard imagined this happened? These were inane questions, of course. Such things were not real.

She was wondering how she was going to ever get up again when she heard him, gently scolding: "You weren't supposed to follow me." Was his voice coming from her head or from the tunnel? She hadn't heard the door open, but when she looked up, she found Howard standing there, illuminated by the reflected light from her phone. He was shivering slightly in his black winter coat, hands stuffed deep into the pockets. But otherwise, he looked as he normally did, as if he hadn't broken into an illicit passageway in the middle of the night, but was just arriving for another day of work.

He stepped forward and pulled her to standing. "But I'm happy you're here."

His manner seemed so relaxed that her own conflicting emotions felt overwrought. She was immensely relieved at his reappearance, but still stinging from having been abandoned without explanation. "I found your secret room."

"What did you make of it?"

She fought to steady her voice. "It looked like the cell of a lunatic. A physicist who's lost his way."

He nodded, as if this were a fair assessment. "Well, now that you're here, come with me."

She peered into the void behind him. "Down a dark tunnel that leads god knows where?"

"Yes, to god knows where." He reached out his hand. "Or to the place where my parents and Stuart are still alive. And maybe your father. I can't guarantee it, but it's possible."

She looked down at his extended hand. "Say I believe all this. Say I come with you. What happens to the versions of us who are already there? There is such a thing as conservation of energy, Howard. I mean, what, do we swap places?"

He let his hand fall and began to pace, as if searching for the words to convince her. "It's not body swapping that I'm attempting," he said. "For lack of a better word, consciousness swapping might be the best description. It's my consciousness traveling through the universal consciousness, in search of a better place to live."

She stared at him in sheer befuddlement. It was one thing to entertain his wild notions as an intellectual exercise, but quite another when he was seriously contemplating acting upon it. "And by *consciousness*, you mean what, your soul? Did Shreft convince you of this?"

"Call it what you like, but it's just a word for the part of me that is separate from my body. Essentially, we'd be bypassing matter and traveling through the background field that permeates the multiverse."

"Is this the Schopenhauer talking now?"

"Schopenhauer would call it the Will, Shreft would call it universal consciousness. We physicists don't have a good name for it yet, so I'm forced to borrow terms." He saw that she was regarding him with wariness. "Just because I can't prove the science yet doesn't mean it isn't possible. I believe it to be possible."

"You *believe* it to be possible?" she asked. "Is this what Shreft has you thinking? That you can meditate yourself to another version of your life?"

"In a way, that's what it might look like. Once I'm in the main LHC tunnel at the ideal position, crossing over doesn't involve physical travel. I listen to my music for a while, and something happens, something that seems like magic but isn't."

She closed her eyes, imagining that when she opened them they'd be back in his apartment, safe in bed.

"I'm sorry about your parents, Howard. And I'm really sorry about your friend. But this is all supernatural idiocy. Even if it weren't, how can you know you're not messing up another Howard's existence? Pushing him out of the world he was comfortably living in? What happens to *his* soul?"

He briefly shut his eyes, as if the insight anguished him. "I've thought of that. But if there are infinite Howards living an infinite variety of lives, I can't stop other versions of myself from feeling intense pain. What I *can* control is the life *I'm* living."

"How do you know the world you're traveling to isn't completely hellish?"

He took a deep breath. "Because I've done it before."

She blinked at him. "Sorry?"

"The worlds adjacent to ours—which is where these tunnels would take us—are incrementally different," he explained. "It's not as if we're going to a world where the Allies lost the war."

Eve was still trying to grasp his previous statement. "Back up. You've done this before?"

He nodded. "The first time it was by accident. When I first arrived at

CERN, I wanted simply to explore the tunnels on my aunt's map. I hadn't meant to trespass into the LHC itself. Just to be safe, I waited for a maintenance shutdown before slipping down here late one night. Nothing much happened, apart from my groping around in a maze for about an hour. But on my second trip, I found a concealed door leading from the secret passages into an LHC feeder tunnel. On the third trip, I used that door. What surprised me most is how peaceful the collider tunnels are—calming, yet also charged with a kind of energy I can't explain. My aunt had spoken about their mysterious power, but it wasn't until I experienced it myself that I understood what she meant. That third night, I sat against the tunnel wall—it must have been somewhere near the ATLAS detector—and listened to some baroque pieces. I think Pergolesi was playing, the *Stabat Mater*, when it happened."

"When what happened?"

"When I found myself no longer in the tunnel, but awake in my bed. In my apartment."

Eve tried to visualize his being transported across the border to his bedroom. Or no, transported to his bedroom in another world.

"How do you know you weren't dreaming?"

"Because I tried it again the following night, and the same thing happened. In fact, the Howard you met that first day in work group is not the Howard you're looking at now. I mean, my body is, the *matter* of me is, but not the core. Only, this world is too similar to my original—Stuart and my parents are still dead. So until I get it right, I have to keep trying. I won't pretend to know how it's working, only that it's worked twice before under these conditions, with the moon at its perigee to Earth. Tonight the moon is even closer. If I find that identical spot in the tunnel, I can re-create it."

Eve was feeling increasingly dizzy trying to follow his logic. "So you've traveled twice before from similar universes. Other than being teleported to your bed, how can you be so sure that you've gone anywhere?"

He smiled down at her. "I know it's not the same world, Eve. Because in the other worlds, in the other versions of CERN, there was no you." He stepped closer until she could feel his breath. "You appeared at the museum that day with Arnav and said you were in our work group. Of course, I had no memory of you because in the original version of our group, you weren't there."

The way he was looking at her, she found it hard not to believe him—or at least, it seemed that he truly believed what he was saying. But trying to picture a world in which she did not exist, or at least one where she wasn't working at the lab, was almost too much for her. And yet, she thought back to that day at the museum, how he had looked at her as if she were a genuine stranger.

Struggling for a sane explanation, she said, "No, you just forgot meeting me."

"You honestly think I wouldn't have remembered you?"

His question was so full of tenderness that, when she responded, she was almost saddened when the logical Eve, the one who relied on hard proof and scientific method, spoke: "I'm all for open-minded exploration, Howard, but you can't use quantum mechanics to wish people alive."

He found her hand and grasped it. "But what if we can?"

She was now keenly aware of the part of her that wanted to believe him. After all, wasn't the idea of discovering things beyond humanity's immediate perception what attracted her to particle physics in the first place? What if Howard was right, and there was a place where her dad still sat in his favorite armchair, waiting for her, arms outstretched? She could feel tears building behind her eyes.

"Will you trust me?" He took something out of his pocket and pushed it into her palm. "Here, take this."

She looked down at a white pill, identical to the one she had seen Howard drop near the woods that day.

"It's basically Valium," he explained. "For anxiety, but I mostly use them for claustrophobia. The tunnel gets extremely narrow in places."

As Eve looked down at her palm, visions of *Alice in Wonderland* and

Through the Looking-Glass swirled before her. If she took this pill, she might grow small enough to fit down a rabbit hole and emerge into another world. But would that world be better than the one she was already in? If Howard was truly leaving, to be replaced by a similar version of him, why not just stay here? Maybe the other Howard wouldn't be so intent on running away from her.

"Eve?"

She continued to stare at the pill as the seconds ticked by. If she was honest with herself, she loved subatomic exploration, but she didn't crave *actual, real* physical adventure. She didn't want to be an explorer of the limitless multiverse, even if it meant there was a chance of finding her father alive. She realized that what she truly wanted was simple: stability and sameness, and not to lose the things and people she now loved. She wanted Howard here, in this world, in her bed, that was all.

Her throat tightened. "Are you saying that another Howard would replace you? That whatever happens, you will be here tomorrow?"

"It won't be me, not exactly."

She studied his face, wondering what about this particular Howard might be unique in all the numberless universes.

"But in a way, it will be," she said. "After all, that first day when you walked into our meeting, it was still you."

His eyes grew glassy.

Though her brain hurt, she searched for some semblance of reason. "The way I see it, best-case scenario is your plan won't work and I'll see you tomorrow at the conference. Worst-case, I'll see a slightly different version of you. It will still be you. The essence of you." She hesitated. "Won't it?"

"I don't know, Eve." Howard seemed to wilt. "We can never meet our other selves."

She pushed the pill back into his hand. "I've staked my whole life on this place, and I don't know if I can risk gambling it away on science I don't believe—and on a version of our lives we can't see. We're happy here, aren't we?"

On his face, she could see all the things pulling on the opposite end of the scale: his overwhelming guilt about Stuart, his unending grief over his parents.

He nodded. "Yes, we're happy. But what can I say, I'm a greedy man. I want all the people I love in one place."

She turned from him so that he wouldn't see her cry. "You were prepared to go without me tonight, so go." The fact that her presence in this world wasn't enough to make him stay was overwhelming.

He pulled her toward him. "You're right. Tomorrow morning, you'll have a version of Howard, whoever he may be. He might be alarmed to find himself in the LHC tunnel, but he'll be okay."

In spite of herself, she followed his logic: she imagined such a Howard exchanging places with this Howard, freaking out upon his appearance in the tunnel and rushing toward the nearest emergency phone.

"What if the other Howard doesn't want me?" she asked.

He smiled sadly. "What if the other Eve doesn't want me?"

As she pretended to consider this, he kissed her. A long kiss, just in case it was the last.

Blinking through tears, he checked his watch. Then he stepped to the metal doorway. Behind him, the tunnel burrowed into darkness.

"What if you can't replicate it?"

"Then I'll see you tomorrow." With a mischievous smile, he added, "Your presentation had better be good. It'll be embarrassing if I find out you're a shoddy physicist."

She laughed, but it sounded desperate.

He pulled a key from his pocket, one that looked as old as the door. "As my aunt knew when she explored these tunnels, sometimes you need an actual key. I'll have to lock the door behind me. She made me promise to leave everything as I found it."

As he glanced over his shoulder down the tunnel, she rushed forward and pulled him into an embrace. She breathed him in, the scent of his skin mingling with that of rain-dampened wool. Through the bulk of their clothing she could feel his dosimeter hanging from his chest, and what felt like a coffee thermos stuffed into his coat's inner pocket. The Ping-Pong ball in her pajamas pushed into her leg as they held each other. She took it out and slipped it into his coat.

"Now you'll have to return it to me," she said.

He whispered into her hair. "I will. Even if I have to move matter across the multiverse."

Then he turned, walked through the door, and locked it decisively behind him.

"Wait . . . ," she said, but the word faltered in her throat. She pressed her forehead to the cold metal, willing it to open again, but she knew it was too late to change her mind.

As a new and terrible sensation began to invade her chest, Eve turned and made her way back toward the basement room. The wall panel closed automatically behind her, the sconce and book shifting back into place as though nothing had happened. Emerging from the Chateau into a worsening thunderstorm, she uselessly pulled up the hood of her coat and wrapped her scarf more tightly around her. She had grabbed one of Howard's scarves by accident when she'd left the apartment, one he rarely wore, but it still smelled of him.

None of what he had said made any sense. The tunnels weren't some kind of regret machine that could undo the mistakes of one's past. The very thought was madness.

Eve would meet him at the conference, and everything would be okay. She would go back to his apartment now, gather her things, and sleep at her own place tonight. In the morning, she would break into a smile at the sight of him in Auditorium 1, and it would all return to the way it had been before.

CHAPTER 33

December 17

Now

At her dining room table, Sabine watched James closely reexamine the confusion of dots from the decrypted flash drive file. As tempting as it had been for her to imagine these points on the graph as notes on a musical staff, she now saw them as mere interstitial positions within a much larger pattern.

"You know what it reminds me of?" she said. "That experiment where they shoot photons or electrons at a screen."

James nodded. "The double-slit experiment. Proof that subatomic particles behave both as particle and wave."

"So, what if this is a kind of landscape or seascape? You connect all the dots—"

He finished her thought: "And you get waves."

Without another word, James went to work at the keyboard to do what she had failed to: create elegant lines to connect all the points. It took twenty minutes for him to do just a section of the graph, but when he was done, he sat back and admired the topography of rough peaks and valleys.

"What does it remind you of now?"

She frowned at the distinctive pattern, which had completely consumed the dots. "Looks an awful lot like an audio waveform," she said.

They turned to each other with the realization of what this might mean.

"If it is a waveform," she added cautiously, "is there any way to play it?"

He hedged and began to explain the difficulty of converting an image file into audio. Sabine cut him short.

"But can you do it?"

"It's not totally impossible."

Two cups of coffee and a plate of biscuits later, James gave an exclamation of triumph. He presented her with what looked like an ordinary audio file.

Admiring his work, she asked, "Are you sure you don't want a job in law enforcement?"

He laughed. "Maybe in another life."

James pressed Play on the file, and the two prepared to listen to what he warned her was very raw audio. After several seconds, there was some hissing from her speaker system, followed by a voice at what sounded like some distance from the recording device—what they later guessed to be a phone. James was right about the quality; it was like playing an old Victrola. Even so, Sabine listened in quiet astonishment that extracting sound from that mess of dots was even possible.

Despite the distortion, the first voice was clearly Simon's: "Last person I would expect to see here," he said, in a faux-jovial sort of way. "Shouldn't you be on the LUXT observation deck about now? Fantasizing about co-authorship?"

Niels responded calmly, "As I recall, you seemed more than happy to bring me on." His voice was close to the mic, as if his phone were in a shirt or jacket pocket.

Simon turned serious: "We've been looking for you all weekend. I believe you have something that belongs to us."

"I might have," Niels responded. "But first, how about you tell me what you're doing in here?"

This was when a third person spoke and Sabine's heart dropped. Her brain tried desperately to make the voice fit someone other than her friend. But there was no mistaking it.

"We're keeping an eye on our lab's own Kim Philby," Chloé said matter-of-factly. "A task, I believe, you agreed to?"

"Yes, well," Niels answered, "I seem to have lost my taste for all that."

As their voices continued, the scene materialized before Sabine like a movie. Despite her increasingly twisting stomach, her mind did this effortlessly, as though she were there in the room. She didn't know where they were exactly, though judging from the slight echo, it was a large space.

"Now that you've dropped in," said Simon, "why don't you tell us where it is?"

"Where what is?" Niels asked in a sardonic tone.

"You think we wouldn't notice it was missing?"

There was a long silence followed by the sound of clothing brushing against the mic, as if Niels had produced something from his pocket.

"You two were wise to keep most of your espionage analog," he said. "No digital trail of your drop-offs—all of which are listed here quite cleverly. Like a page out of Le Carré. Rendezvous at practically every museum and theater in town, not to mention some pretty choice restaurants. What were you handing off anyway? Flash drives? Microfilm? I guess it doesn't matter."

Sabine paused the recording and reached into a nearby drawer for the leather notebook. She spread it open on the table, letting the frightening possibility sink in that this notebook belonged to Simon and Chloé.

James examined it in disbelief. "How the hell do you have this?"

"Our engineer was remorseful," she said simply, struggling to submerge her own clashing emotions. "Had Claude not swiped it from the scene, we might have assumed it was Howard's. In a bizarre way, by stealing fake evidence, Claude did us a favor." She pressed Play on the recording. "But we get ahead of ourselves."

Chloé was nearer now, a barbed edge to her voice. "How did you find that, Niels?"

"Easy," he said, not without some pleasure. "I had one of the cleaners let me into your office. It's one of the perks of being friendly with the staff. Hiding the notebook in a cavity beneath your piano bench might have *seemed* clever—but if you'd actually read any spy stories, you'd know that concealing intel inside the trappings of a fantasy identity is a classic espionage blunder. I wonder how you managed to communicate the locations with your, what, Chinese handler?"

"You seem quite satisfied with yourself," Simon responded. "I'm not sure you want us as your enemies."

"Can we be honest for one minute?" Niels continued. "You two have been playing me and this entire lab for years. I mean, it's all been an extremely convincing performance. Very Benedick and Beatrice."

Chloé broke in, the sweetness of her voice at odds with her words. "We thought you were happy. Dark matter glory in exchange for, what, keeping an irrelevant secret? Shifting suspicion to a man who, I think you'd agree, only deserves it?"

"I wouldn't say that I've been happy."

"You looked pretty ecstatic at the LUXT party."

"The science makes me happy, the tank makes me happy, but what I've sacrificed for it . . . I don't know that it's worth it anymore."

"We'll take the notebook now," Simon quietly demanded.

"Go ahead. You should know I've photographed the whole thing." There was the distinct smack of a notebook being tossed on a table.

"Now, if there isn't anything else, Niels, we'll say good night."

"I'm not leaving," Niels insisted, "until you tell me what you're doing in here. The Machine is off."

Sabine and James silently turned to each other, realizing at once where the three were: the LHC Control Room.

"Okay," said Chloé. "Turn on the tunnel camera."

"Why should I?" Niels asked. "There's nothing to see."

"Isn't there? There's a passage leading from the Chateau into an LHC feeder tunnel, and someone tonight used it. We have a sensor on the door. Have you really never seen our friend wander down there? The same person who's been ducking into those secret tunnels for weeks, apparently waiting for a Machine shutdown?"

There was a pause, during which Chloé must have turned on the camera. "Believe us now? What could he be doing down there all alone?"

"I have no idea," Niels said, with increased alarm.

"You know what I think?" Simon said coolly. "I think Dr. Anderby has been stealing data for months, and now he plans to sabotage the collider itself, create damage worse than 2008. He and his Chinese employers want to throw a spanner in our Machine so deep, it'll take years for our lab to dig its way out. And in the meantime, China builds its own collider and owns particle physics for the next half century. In fact, I believe this notebook belongs to Howard."

Niels uttered a guttural note of contempt. "If that's your story," he said, "why do the ATLAS leaks predate Howard's arrival at the lab?"

"Because he's been coordinating with a mole from his post in China, obviously," Simon answered. "I wouldn't be shocked if Frances Schoenberg has been grooming her nephew for years."

Niels had evidently moved toward the controls because Simon shouted, "Step back. If you touch that intercom—"

"What if I do?"

"You'll be dismantling your own career."

Niels laughed. "Oh, I've been doing that quite nicely already."

Chloé added, almost gently, "We know about you and Arnav Bose."

Niels snorted. "And?"

"If you don't care about the ruination of your career, you should care about his. How satisfying do you think Arnav will find teaching secondary school physics back home?"

"Let me get this straight," he said. "You want me to help you murder somebody—and frame them for espionage—so you won't ruin my lover's career?"

There was the swift clicking of a keyboard.

"What are you doing, Simon?"

More clicking.

His panic growing, Niels said, "For chrissake, Chloé. Make him stop."

"Howard is trespassing," Chloé said without emotion. "He knows the risks of the tunnel."

"Good god, look at him," Niels implored. "The man looks like he's listening to music or meditating. No one's going to believe he was about to destroy billions of dollars' worth of machinery."

"Maybe they'll believe he was so racked with guilt, he did it to himself," Simon suggested. "Why else would he be mad enough to go down there?"

"Don't do this," Niels pleaded, his voice rising. "For fuck's sake, Simon, don't."

More typing.

An instant later, music flooded the room. It was some sort of pop song, but the distortion made it impossible to identify.

The music stopped.

"What is this garbage?" Simon muttered. "The least they could do is pick better tunes."

"Think about what you're doing for one minute," Niels practically shouted. "It will be obvious who turned the Machine on."

"Or will it appear as a mysterious system glitch?" Simon asked. "An unfortunate failure of the auto shutdown?"

"Stop. PLEASE STOP," Niels cried.

There was a sound of the mic swishing against fabric. Then a series of confusing noises, possibly a scuffle. Sabine tried to picture the two men in a physical confrontation. Niels was young and certainly not small, but Simon was a physically imposing man despite his age. He could likely hold his own in a fight. There was more yelling, but it was distorted and Sabine could no longer make it out. Someone cursed before the voices stopped entirely and there was only the sound of heavy, gasping breaths.

A long pause followed, during which she and James looked from the waveform to each other. The suspense was agony, but they both knew how this scene ended.

Out of the silence, a second piece of music began, very different from the pop song, tentative at first: the plaintive strains of violins, followed by the pulse of bassoons.

Sabine's hand went to her mouth.

"What is it?" James asked.

"The Requiem," she said, as the basset horns made their sweet entrance. "The system plays a track on the first beam run of the day. Simon just changed it to one more of his liking. Mozart's Requiem Mass."

He turned to her in understanding. "So the Machine is on."

She nodded.

"Jesus."

"Chloé . . . ," Sabine whispered to herself, trying to square the friend she had known—the one who had loved melancholy music and leisurely bike rides—with the woman on the other end of this recording, who was allowing her colleague to suffer an unspeakable death. All because, what, she felt some kind of perverted allegiance to this monstrous man named Simon De Vries? Or was it because the size of her ambition was such that she would rather kill the physicist she herself had brought to CERN than risk exposure as a Chinese spy and expulsion from the lab? Or was the very reason Chloé had hired Howard so that she might serve him up as an eventual scapegoat?

The string section grew louder, accompanied by trombones, before giving way to the baritones and tenors.

The sopranos joined in this aching entreaty to God, and Sabine could only imagine the horror that was unfolding belowground.

Requiem aeternam dona eis, Domine

Et lux perpetua, et lux perpetua luceat eis . . .

PART 3

The more complex the object we are attempting to appre-
hend, the more important it is to have different sets of eyes,
so that these rays of light converge and we can see the One
through the many. That is the nature of true vision: it brings
together already known points of view and shows others
hitherto unknown, allowing us to understand that all are, in
actuality, part of the same thing.

—Alexander Grothendieck,
Reaping and Sowing

CHAPTER 34

December 20

Now

O n a Tuesday before Christmas, CERN emptied out of nearly its total
population. After the holiday party, it seemed the entire lab couldn't
flee fast enough. No one had known what else to do. Everyone expected
there would be a flurry of new interviews as Interpol and Sabine tried
to unravel the accusations dramatized at the party. But both were silent.
If Interpol was already questioning suspects in the murders of Howard
Anderby and Niels Thorne, those who had been in Auditorium 2 for the
revelatory performance needn't ask who they were. Even after Simon and
Chloé had fled the theater, the actors continued to perform the terrible
events of the control room on the night of November 27. For those not
present for the denouement, including Eve, who simply couldn't bear to
watch the rest, word had quickly spread.

After spending a couple of days holed up in her drab Prévessin apartment, preparing for a trip back home to visit her mother, Eve returned
to the lab one afternoon to tidy up her desk and retrieve her laptop. She
hadn't heard from Arnav since the party, though not for lack of repeatedly
trying to reach him. When she arrived at their shared office, something

odd met her: his empty desk. His computer and keyboard were gone, as was his beloved weasel. Even his chair and footrest appeared to have been purloined for use elsewhere in the lab.

As she stood contemplating the coffee-stained chipboard of Arnav's desktop, she became aware of rain tapping at the windows. A snowstorm was forecasted for that week, and she suddenly regretted that she would miss seeing the lab blanketed in white. A different sort of tapping startled her: rapping of knuckles on wood. She looked up to find Arnav in the doorway, in a gray coat spotted with rain.

She blinked at him, unable to speak.

"I'm sorry," he said, turning to the desk. "I tried to tell you. I guess I just couldn't bear it."

"Where?" was the only word she could get out.

"Headed back to London for a bit. To spend time with Parvati and look into wedding planning. She's getting anxious, wants to get a head start on things."

"But your postdoc isn't over for another year. You can't just—"

"I can't stay here."

"Why not?"

He stared at her. "Oh, I don't know, Eve. Because our group leader and her apparent lover murdered two of our colleagues? Seems like a good reason."

Swallowing against a tightening in her throat, she said, "Is that really why you're leaving?"

She wanted to ask him about Niels, about his long-standing preoccupation with him, about the raw pain she had seen on his face after Niels's posthumous performance. But all she could say was "Is getting married what you really want?"

Arnav looked at the floor. "It doesn't matter what I want."

"Then why the hell are you doing it?"

"Because there are some universal laws that must be obeyed. This is one."

Eve rolled her eyes. "Please don't use physics to support your flaky reasoning."

He sighed. "It's easy for you."

"How's that?"

"Like you always say, you came from a kind of void, from a mother who doesn't care. A blank slate is a gift. You can invent your life the way you want it. I come from a family in which my choices were already made long ago."

She could see he wasn't going to change his mind. The power that was taking him away from the lab, the power that had forced him to resign and clear his desk, was stronger than anything their friendship could summon.

"You headed back to Arizona?"

She nodded weakly. "Holiday whodunit marathon with Mom. She has this drinking game for trite dialogue. *Things aren't always what they seem.* Drink. *We're not so different, you and I.* Drink. It's kind of sweet, actually. Just wait until I tell her what's been going on here."

Arnav pulled her into a hug. She returned his embrace but refused to cry. She was sick to death of weeping. "First Howard, now you."

He lifted her chin with one hand, tilting her head back, as if they were in a corny romance.

"Hey."

"What."

"Email the Giovanni guy from that postcard." He nodded toward her desk, where the card was still stuck in her Solvay Conference diorama.

She looked back at it, having completely forgotten it was there.

"That mountain. It's the Gran Sasso lab in Italy, you dummy. There's a Dr. Giovanni who's kind of a big deal over there."

"So what if he is?"

"Just reach out, okay? Do it for me."

She shrugged wearily.

"We'll see each other again, kid."

"Will we? It all just seems so impossible."

He embraced her once more and turned to go.

"Wait," she said, grasping for words that might keep him with her for one more moment. Then she remembered something she'd been saving: "What did Einstein say to his clingy girlfriend?"

He paused at the door. "No idea. What did Einstein say to his clingy girlfriend?"

"I just need a little space-time."

Arnav cracked a smile. Then he laughed, for what seemed like the first time in months. Still laughing, he turned and walked out the door, down the hall, and into what was now a downpour.

CHAPTER 35

December 20

Now

S abine got the call when she was in a chairlift halfway up a ski slope. She had been swinging her legs and breathing in the cool Alpine air, trying to focus on her immediate surroundings rather than the news she was antici-pating. She had strategically chosen this day to flee for the mountains, so as to distract herself from the suspense of waiting for the suspects in the murder of Howard Anderby and Niels Thorne to be arrested. With Yvonne's permission she had handed the evidence over to Ulrich Brod, who had thanked her for her "contribution to the case," before informing her that Interpol would take it from there. *Glad to be of help*, she had said with zero malice. Consulting de-tectives, after all, lived for the satisfaction of their clients, not for public glory. If Brod wanted to claim credit for tracking down the killers of two promi-nent CERN physicists, it was just as well. As to whether Chloé Grimaud and Simon De Vries were also to be tried for espionage, this was not her affair.

"Does it even qualify as espionage?" James wondered aloud from his seat beside her as he looked warily at the snowdrift below. "It is scientific data, after all. Doesn't that belong to, like, humanity? It's not the A-bomb we're talking here."

It was true, CERN was not a weapons lab. How selling physics secrets to the Chinese in this case could qualify as international espionage, Sabine didn't know. So what if one country found a new particle or discovered dark matter before another? Did this, in the larger scheme of scientific exploration, really make any difference? It did to some people, she supposed.

Her phone began to buzz insistently from her multicolored jacket. She unzipped a pocket and stared at the screen. It was Yvonne, calling from her office.

"Can you hear me?" Sabine shouted, hoping volume would make up for her one bar of reception.

"You sound far away," Yvonne said.

"Ski lift."

"Right. Good a place as any." There was a distinct note of defeat in her voice. "Interpol's arrest warrant came too late, I'm afraid. This is on them, not you."

Sabine clasped a hand to her other ear as she listened to Yvonne deliver the news she had been half expecting: Interpol had put out a notice to all airports in the area, posting officers at security checks, but the suspects had slipped through on false passports. Police facial recognition software revealed this only after the fact. They were now in the air.

"Already landed, more likely," Yvonne said. "Is it awful that part of me is happy she got out? I know it sounds incredible given that it's my career on the line here—that people will be crying for *my* head on a plate—but I couldn't see her go through a trial. Even after all she did, I just couldn't stand it—"

"No," Sabine said, cutting her short. "Neither could I."

"That way, I can remember her how she was. We can remember."

Sabine glanced at the time. "It's almost seven in Beijing." She imagined Chloé and Simon celebrating their own cleverness over a dinner of roast duck and dumplings.

"Sabi," Yvonne said, almost gently. "It was Aeroflot. They boarded an Aeroflot."

"Aeroflot?" The Russian airline sounded absurd, like a false note.

"To Moscow. And they weren't alone. Nikolay Levkin was with them."

Levkin. Idiotically, Sabine remembered his giant licorice jar in the control room, the one with the greedy cartoon bear on it.

"It was never China, Sabine," Yvonne continued. "The data breach. It wasn't China—"

That's when the call dropped. Sabine looked at her phone, the single bar of reception vanished. She laughed, replacing her image of duck and dumplings with caviar and chicken Kiev.

"Aeroflot?" James asked. "They're in Russia?"

"Being hailed as heroes, I suppose."

"But how?"

"Fake passports," she said, her mind still in free fall, "no doubt provided by their new employers. They must have had a backup plan in place for a while—ever since rumors of a data breach circulated, and in case their scapegoat didn't pan out."

"Jesus Christ. What do we do now?"

She turned to him, taking in his very young, outraged face.

"We do nothing."

"Nothing? We just forget that actual Russian spies not only ransacked our lab, but got away with two murders?"

"Until Switzerland has an extradition treaty with Russia, yes."

James shouted a profanity into the air, causing the couple in the next chairlift to turn around. One of James's ski poles slipped and fell to the snowpack below.

"I'm sorry, James. I find believing in karma helps." She was surprised at how calm she sounded, when she felt anything but.

"So, I'm just supposed to go back to my dissertation? Like none of this happened?"

"Listen." Sabine pointed in the direction of France. "There was once a philosopher who lived just across the way . . ."

"Oh god. You're not about to give me advice, are you?"

"No, the eighteenth-century philosopher who once lived across the border is going to give you advice, if you'll let him. He was very rich, and he lived in a mansion at the center of a town that he owned, which makes it all the more surprising that he had anything to say at all."

James looked at her sideways. "Yeah, I've read *Candide*."

"Good. You'll know what I'm about to say, then. Voltaire, I think, would advise you to tend your own garden. You are young, after all, and have much to cultivate. I, on the other hand, have some pruning to do. We each must care for our own little plots and forget the things that are beyond our control. Like criminals fleeing to Russia."

Like a person you once loved fleeing to Russia, she did not say.

With an immense weight bearing down on her chest, Sabine looked out at the fingers of young evergreens pushing up through the snow.

"What else can we do, James?"

CHAPTER 36

December 20

Now

Sabine returned from her aborted ski trip with James to find a single letter waiting for her on the floor beneath the mail slot. She stared at it for an aching moment before reaching down to examine it. It had been postmarked from Geneva the day before. She turned the small envelope over in her hands, taking in the graceful handwriting she knew well, before breaking the seal. She extracted two sheets of thin waxy paper, which had been folded into thirds, before sitting down in the dining room to read it.

Dearest Sabine,

This letter is in no way a justification, merely an explanation, which I feel I owe you. First, I hope what I have done does not take away from what was real and true in our friendship. Though I lied to you by omission a thousand times, I have never lied about what you've meant to me. It is the thought that I will never see you again—or play piano in your sweet company—that is almost more difficult than anything. It's more difficult than leaving Jurgen, whose indifference to physics, as you know—and to nearly everything outside the bounds of Western painting—I once found charming, until suddenly I didn't. "But Chloé," I can hear you say, "Simon is not exactly a superior man," and you may be right. But he and I understand each other and there is a strange current between us that I have not found with anyone else—a kind of thrill that became increasingly theatrical as we each played our roles in an imaginary battle of the sexes. Part of the reason I'm leaving CERN—aside from the obvious fact I will be indicted as an accomplice to murder if I stay—is that the Russians are offering me a position that will allow me to live the life I've always wanted: with more time for my music, a pursuit that in recent years has become increasingly elusive. But if I'm honest with myself, I am leaving Europe because Simon is leaving Europe. Supporting his children and three exes on the salary of a physicist had become untenable for him—and Russia has promised him funds to build a tank twice the size of the LUXT, which he always thought of as a mere prototype anyway. By now, you'll know that Nikolay Levkin was also on the plane. Apart from his having recruited us, his position in the control room allowed us to cover our tracks for years as the three of us relayed data to his country. Sending intel electronically was too risky, so we conveyed it to a Russian businessman in Geneva. Some would consider this a betrayal, but there is no such thing as scientific espionage. Science belongs to everyone and no one.

You can recover your bicycle at my house. It was me that day in Ferney-Voltaire, sweeping for any evidence Howard may have had on the data leaks, obviously not knowing you would be there. Simon and I were told by the Russians that the Chinese lab was aware of Russian interference at CERN—China has spies of its own embedded in Russia, after all—and we feared that Howard knew more than he was telling. But then, it hardly matters now, does it? I do wonder if Howard truly cared about the data leaks at all. His mind, I suspect, was always on grander things. My conversations with him after group meetings convinced me that he was a bright light in our field, a rare kind that may be mistaken for irrational or insane.

I had brought Howard to CERN for reasons of self-preservation. Given his background in China, Simon and I thought he might serve as a useful misdirect for the data leaks, rumors of which had begun to spring up as early as last year. The source of these initial rumors remains unclear to me, and may well have been nothing more than heightened lab paranoia. Still, Simon and I put our insurance plan into action, hoping we'd never need to use it. Frances Schoenberg figured largely into our strategy to direct blame elsewhere, helped along by Russia's decades-long grudge against her. But as it happens, our designs to protect ourselves backfired. First, how were we to know that Howard had seen evidence of ATLAS leaks at the Chinese lab? His revelations to Yvonne only brought things to a crisis, requiring us to take drastic steps to avoid detection. Second, we couldn't foresee the engineer stealing our planted notebook from the tunnel. If he had left the scene untouched, Howard's death might have been written off as LHC espionage gone wrong. Of course, Simon and I never intended for two people to die. The entire situation got completely out of our control. Now I wonder, what would Howard Anderby and Niels Thorne have been capable of given the chance?

Please communicate my remorse to Yvonne. I tried to write her, but couldn't find the words to explain why I put her in the position of cleaning up our mess. I dare not ask her for forgiveness or understanding. I barely dare ask for yours.

Goodbye, my darling Sabine.

Love,

Chloé

Sabine crumpled the note, sickened by its contents, then immediately smoothed the pages out on the table. It was, after all, a written confession, and whatever her feelings about it, she couldn't bring herself to destroy evidence. She would tuck it away somewhere, or hand it over to Agent Brod, in the unlikely event that one day it would be needed.

Turning to her Bösendorfer, Sabine wondered if the sight of the thing would become too much for her to stand. Or maybe, at last, she would learn to play it. She recalled Chloé sitting at the bench just weeks ago, performing Schumann, for what she couldn't know would be the last time. And now, as storm clouds over the lake began to surrender their contents, drops stippling her windows, Sabine imagined Chloé's fingers falling on the piano keys like a slow, cleansing rain.

CHAPTER 37

January 3

Now

In the new year, Eve found herself in central Italy confronting the possibility of a new life. The morning after her arrival in the small town of Teramo, a taxi arrived at her hotel to escort her to the underground mountain complex of the Gran Sasso physics laboratory. She was then to be transferred to a shuttle that would convey her deeper into the subterranean facilities, where she would interview for a position in the lab's recently created Climate Research Group. Upon reaching out to the contact on the postcard, as Arnav had insisted, Eve discovered that her *Courier* article had not been as anonymous as she'd imagined. Teo Rico had forwarded the piece to his good friend and former colleague Dr. Ennio Giovanni in Italy. Following her climate map blunder at the ATLAS-CMS conference, it hadn't been much of a leap to identify its author.

As Eve waited to board an open-air lab shuttle, she was surprised to find herself surrounded by a large group of tourists, judging by their clothing, cameras, and stupefied expressions. Not that she looked all that different herself; her mouth, too, had fallen open the second she'd entered the cavernous concrete structure, which only hinted at more monumental spaces within.

She slid into an empty seat next to a middle-aged man with a camera slung across his shoulder. The shuttle lurched, and after several minutes, Eve sensed a rapid change in air pressure. An announcement from the shuttle driver soon informed them that they were 1,200 meters beneath the mountainside, the lab's experiments safely protected from the interference of cosmic rays. She wondered with vague alarm whether her body would begin to rebel at the depth—if she, in fact, would need to be medicated in order to work here at all—but to her surprise, she felt oddly calm.

The man next to her cupped his ears in reaction to the pressure. "I don't know that I've ever been this far underground," he shouted in a thick German accent. "Have you?"

She turned to answer, but the man was staring ahead, and Eve couldn't be sure if he had been addressing her or the woman on the other side of him. It was then, studying his profile, that Eve's stomach did a flip of recognition. His stooped shoulders, his almost threadbare coat. She knew this man.

The shuttle stopped and the group disembarked. The man may not have appeared swift, but he was gone in an instant from his seat, his small frame disappearing among the visitors who followed their guide toward a display of maps and diagrams. Suddenly panicked that she would lose him, Eve tossed aside her coat and bag on a nearby bench and pushed her way through the crowd until she spotted him standing on his own, staring up at the concrete that rose majestically above them.

"Mr. Shreft?" she called.

Wolfgang Shreft turned and looked at her. He was even smaller than she had remembered. "Hello," he said, reaching out a hand to touch her arm as though she were an old friend. She supposed this was how he greeted everyone. "Isn't this tour wonderful?"

"Oh, I'm not actually on the tour," she said. "I'm interviewing for a job."

"Ah," he said, glancing up again. "You are very lucky, then."

The tourists continued to move past them, but Eve was so focused on Shreft, it felt as if they were standing alone. "You don't know me, but I'm Eve, a former colleague of Howard Anderby's."

"Eve." He considered her anew, eyes twinkling. "He told me about you, I think. In one of our talks. You must miss him dearly."

She nodded. "Yes."

"You know, of course, there's no need. To miss him quite so much."

Eve's face flamed with emotion as she remembered Howard as she'd last seen him, and how she might have stopped him from stepping into his grave. Instead, she'd let him march off into a supposed parallel world, when in reality he was about to be irradiated to death by a pair of Russian agents.

"You are with him, you know," Shreft said, detecting her distress. "The place he went, you are also there with him."

Eve feared that if she told Shreft he was wrong, she might be on the receiving end of one of his pseudoscientific lectures. When you chase down a guru in the middle of a physics laboratory, you're kind of asking for it. Still, she entertained a scenario in which she had gone with Howard that night, not in whatever way Shreft meant, but quite literally. Would she have inadvertently saved him had she followed him into the tunnel? Or would she, too, be dead?

"I'm not sure what you mean," she said, as calmly as she could manage. "I'm not with him because he was killed. Murdered, actually."

"Yes, I've seen the news. It's a terrible thing." He peered at her curiously. "But maybe he was able to make his journey before that? And it was, in fact, a different Howard who perished in the tunnel?"

Eve felt her chest constrict uncomfortably. She hadn't considered this. "Maybe. But I'm not sure I believe the whole 'journeying' thing is possible."

"But is that not a theory of quantum mechanics? Alternate possibilities? Worlds that lie next to our own?"

"It's a theory. One not all physicists subscribe to."

He appeared to search her face, his brow crinkling in some kind of understanding. "Some people assume I have it all figured out. But the work you physicists do reminds me that I don't have all the answers. And not having the answers is a comfort."

Eve realized she was supposed to be meeting Dr. Giovanni any minute. It wasn't wise to keep him waiting just because she'd happened upon a celebrity.

"Don't you want the answers?" she asked.

"If I'm honest with myself, no. The Heisenberg uncertainty principle, the idea that not everything is to be measured and perceived? That you have to choose which measurement to take and which to leave a mystery?" His cheeks flushed. "Sorry, I didn't mean to define it for you. Bad habit. But I've enjoyed learning about Heisenberg, because his is a principle to live by—uncertainty."

Eve thought briefly of Teo, and how he would cringe at this entire exchange. Yet she felt herself agreeing with Shreft. Even Einstein had written about the importance of the "eternally unattainable" in life, and how without something forever held out of reach, life would paradoxically feel empty. She listened to Shreft go on a bit more in this vein. Maybe it was because she wanted to hold on to the piece of Howard that had admired this man.

"Can I ask what you and Howard talked about? During your visits to the lab?"

"Oh, many things," he said, unfazed by her curiosity. "I had partly selfish reasons for befriending him. I wanted to get his ideas on a book of mine. Would you like to hear it? It's just some thoughts I've been knocking around."

She nodded, knowing that she'd be late for her meeting now.

"I'll keep it short," he began, clearing his throat. "Most people, rational people, think the spiritual world is separate from the scientific one, as if they are antithetical to each other: enemies, in fact. But it used to be that these two things were intertwined. In the Middle Ages, monks were among our best observers of the natural world. It was Christianity's fault perhaps, in the age of Galileo, to see science as a threat to the spiritual. It's unfortunate that this dichotomy was set up. Because, you see, if you could turn your microscope on the so-called supernatural world, you would see it is embedded in the very fabric of the material one. They are the same. What we perceive as the objective world with our senses is merely a reflection of energies beneath. You deal in energies in your work, yes?"

She smiled. "You might say that's all our work is."

"The energies you measure in the 3D world are just reflections of the spirit world. The folly, I would say, is to think that the 'spiritual' is magic or made up. Howard had begun to suspect as much. Perhaps the information is threatening in some way. Which is why people must keep the worlds separate."

"It's an interesting premise for a book." She wanted to sound generous, but the liberal use of the word *energy* outside of its scientific definition always made her uneasy.

"It's not a book you will be reading?" he asked with a chuckle.

"I may not agree with the concept, but I do understand the argument."

"You don't believe what I say about Howard being very much alive in a world next to our own?"

Eve bristled at the fantasy. "The idea of Howard leaving our world because he thought he could live in an alternate one, I find it not just difficult to accept, but sad. And I wonder . . ."

"What do you wonder?"

"I wonder, if Howard hadn't bought into an idea not founded on empirical evidence, if he would still be living. In my experience, science is what keeps us alive."

Shreft looked skeptical. "Perhaps."

Eve found herself growing frustrated by his vagueness. "What do you think is going to keep us alive on this burning ship of a planet, if not science? It won't be thoughts and prayers."

He nodded. "Science may keep us alive, Eve, but is it what makes life worth living?"

"Right now," she answered, "science may be the only thing I'm living for."

The tour group was moving on.

"Are you coming with us?"

She shook her head. "I have my interview."

He waved his arm at the cavern wall. "Our guide was saying earlier that the entire universe might be a hologram. A two-dimensional world projected to appear 3D. Isn't that strange and wonderful?"

She followed his gaze up to the ceiling.

"Do you think that means our 3D separation from others is merely an illusion?" he asked. "And so will be our separation, yours and mine, when we part?"

"It's a nice idea," she said.

He reached for her arm one last time. "It was good to meet you, Eve. Maybe our paths will cross again?"

She looked down at this odd little man and smiled. "Maybe so."

Apart from catching him on television, she wasn't sure she would ever see him again. But she let the idea that endings and separations were just an illusion hang in the air for a moment.

With a wave, Shreft turned, and she watched him shuffle off to learn more about the universe and maybe his place in it.

Eve started for the elevators, fearing she would really be late now. She stopped to retrieve her things from the bench where she'd left them, but when she picked up her coat, something fell out of it and onto the concrete. It rolled a few feet from where she was standing.

She blinked slowly, half expecting it to be gone when she opened her eyes. But there it was: a Ping-Pong ball. She walked over to where it had come to rest and picked it up. In black ink it read *Up Quark*.

As she stared at it, bewildered tears collected in her eyes. Had it really been in her coat pocket this entire time? How could that be when she had slipped it into Howard's coat that night in the tunnel? Or had she, in fact, taken it out of her pajama pants and slipped it into her own pocket by mistake, the dark wool of their coats having merged in that final embrace? There was no other explanation.

Except. The longer she stared at it, the more it seemed that this ball was not quite the same. After all, she had known her and Howard's up quark well. The handwriting of this one was nearly identical, but the shape of the letters was ever-so-slightly off: the loop of the *P* a bit smaller, the tail of the *Q* not as curled. As if it were the same ball, yet not the same ball. An up quark from the other side of the looking glass.

Then she remembered Howard's final words to her about returning it: *I will. Even if I have to move matter across the multiverse.*

Her legs seemed to fail her as she fell back onto the bench. She knew that Dr. Giovanni was somewhere in this complex, waiting for her on the other side of an elevator ride.

Eve closed her damp eyes and imagined Howard opposite her at particle tennis that evening last fall. She could see clearly on the screen of her mind the way he had looked at her as they had volleyed the fundamental particles of reality back and forth. It was a look filled with the promise that this was merely the beginning of their story, and that they had all the time left in the universe. And maybe somewhere, in some faraway place, that was still true.

ACKNOWLEDGMENTS

I couldn't have conjured a better agent than Lisa Bankoff, whose enthusiasm, mad attention to detail, and continually surprising skills deserve multiple rounds of cocktails from the very top shelf. One of the great joys of this book was reuniting with my editor Kaitlin Olson, whose profound insights into story and character surpassed my every expectation all over again. Thank you also to Ifeoma Anyoku, Elizabeth Hitti, publicist Megan Rudloff, Maudee Genao in marketing, and the entire editorial, art, production, publicity, and marketing teams at Atria for their limitless talents. To Jeffrey L. Ward for the beautiful map. And to Chelsea McGuckin for designing a cover I wouldn't mind disappearing into.

I wrote the majority of this book in a state of deep admiration for the people who devote their lives to better understanding the quantum world and the nature of our universe. The dedication is for the generous people of CERN, who one sweltering July allowed me to visit their lab and to turn what they do into fiction. Given that I wrote the bulk of this story during a global pandemic, I am also thinking of the scientists who worked swiftly to bring the world lifesaving vaccines. Thank the ever-expanding heavens for them.

ACKNOWLEDGMENTS

If I could thank every single person at CERN, the list would still begin with Sarah Charley, who was a more welcoming and energetic host than I could have hoped for. She made my visits to the lab feel as if I'd been the wildly lucky recipient of a trip to particle physics camp. I still can't believe my luck. Much appreciation to David Stickland for championing my visit, for talk of luminosity and Higgs events, and for taking me on a windblown convertible ride across the border to the CMS project. Thank you to Roberto Vega-Morales and Tien-Tien Yu for graciously providing a glimpse into CERN's Theory Group during their lunch hour—and to Molly Holland for the introduction. Much gratitude to James Beacham for a fascinating tour of the LEIR accelerator and for letting me pepper him with questions over coffee. Chris Martin proved a knowledgeable guide for the ATLAS control room, not to mention the lab's various office warrens. Claire Lee took time from her ATLAS research to chat with me in R1 about her work and lab culture, for which I am grateful. Andrés Delannoy helpfully steered me in the direction of further readings on CERN culture. Thank you, Mirko Pojer, for cheerfully showing me around "mission control." Much appreciation to Jeremie Flueret and Christian Hunin, who illuminated the peculiar dangers of LHC radiation and put me through a surprisingly action-packed safety training exercise. David Yu was an ideal biking companion for the Passport to the Big Bang ride, the perfect closeout to my trip. Additional physicists and engineers who took time out of their workday to chat over coffee, lunch, or make for formidable trivia night companions are: Juliette Alimena, Kathryn Chapman, Rachel Hyneman, Paul Lujan, Bing Xuan Li, and Rachel Yohay.

I am infinitely grateful to Riju Dasgupta, without whose generosity, good humor, and passion for particle physics, this book would have been, in the words of Pauli, *not even wrong*. What began with my tagging along on a CERN work group meeting, somehow turned into his reading a draft, checking facts, and vetting physics puns. In other words, the reader of my dreams.

Everyone I met at CERN was thoughtful, kind, and made the research portion of this book an absolute delight. All mistakes, exaggerations, or misrepresentations are either for fictional purposes or are oversights on my part. For the latter—and for anyone I may have missed on this list—I apologize.

Thank you to my dear readers, who reviewed drafts in various stages of readiness and disorder: Holland Christie, Kate Kennedy, Elizabeth Liang, John Douglas Sinclair, Jonathan Rabb, and Peter Spiegler. Peter also generously lent his expertise (obsession?) on Arthur Schopenhauer. His copy of *The World as Will and Representation*, vol. 1, is no doubt as annotated and dog-eared as that of my character's.

I am grateful to the scientists, historians, and writers whose work helped me to better illuminate the strange world of the quantum and beyond: Stephon Alexander, Sean Carroll, Pauline Gagnon, Jim Holt, Sabine Hossenfelder, Michio Kaku, Bernardo Kastrup, Alan Lightman, Chanda Prescod-Weinstein, Andri Pol, Tom Roston, Carlo Rovelli, Silvan S. Schweber, Leonard Susskind, and Gary Taubes.

I'm in great debt to colleagues whose support and friendship over the years cannot be measured: Rebecca Agbe-Davies, Heather Blanda, Andrew Cummings, Hannah Elliott, Chris Gray, David Howard, Jeff Meier, and Matt Sugg.

Thank you to my family, the Jacobs, Rabbs, and Eklunds, for their unflinching enthusiasm and support. And to Jeremy, who sat for hours in a decrepit leather chair that we were trying to give away and read a draft as if he were bingeing on a crime series. His eye for detail, ear for dialogue, and deep love of language are why he is one of my very favorite readers.

ABOUT THE AUTHOR

N ova Jacobs has an MFA from the University of Southern California School of Cinematic Arts and is a recipient of the Nicholl Fellowship from the Academy of Motion Picture Arts and Sciences. Her first novel, *The Last Equation of Isaac Severy*, was nominated for an Edgar Award by the Mystery Writers of America. She lives in Los Angeles with her husband, Jeremy.